W9-CFB-897

THE KILLING LAND

THE KILLING LAND

JACQUELINE SEEWALD

FIVE STAR

A part of Gale, Cengage Learning

GALE
CENGAGE Learning®

Farmington Hills, Mich • San Francisco • New York • Waterville, Maine
Meriden, Conn • Mason, Ohio • Chicago

GALE
CENGAGE Learning®

LIBRARY OF CONGRESS CATALOGING-IN-PUBLICATION DATA

Names: Seewald, Jacqueline.
Title: The killing land / Jacqueline Seewald.
Description: First edition. | Waterville, Maine : Five Star, a part of Gale, Cengage Learning, [2016]
Identifiers: LCCN 2015035879 | ISBN 9781432831196 (hardcover) | ISBN 1432831194 (hardcover) | ISBN 9781432831189 (ebook) | ISBN 1432831186 (ebook)
Subjects: LCSH: Man-woman relationships—Fiction. | GSAFD: Western stories. | Romantic suspense fiction.
Classification: LCC PS3619.E358 K55 2016 | DDC 813/.6—dc23
LC record available at http://lccn.loc.gov/2015035879

First Edition. First Printing: January 2016
Find us on Facebook– https://www.facebook.com/FiveStarCengage
Visit our website– http://www.gale.cengage.com/fivestar/
Contact Five Star™ Publishing at FiveStar@cengage.com

Printed in the United States of America
1 2 3 4 5 6 7 20 19 18 17 16

For Monte, with my love always.

ACKNOWLEDGMENTS

A special note of thanks to my amazing editor, Alice Duncan. A true Westerner and fine Western writer, Alice lends support to fellow authors. She is the authentic voice of the American West.

PROLOGUE

"For the right price, we'd kill just about anybody." Russell Harris studied the man sitting across from him in the saloon and tried to determine what effect his words were having.

The rancher met his level gaze with a look of satisfaction. "I like to get my money's worth. You and your brother have big reputations. I want to make certain you can live up to them."

"Long as you pay us," Russell emphasized, rubbing the carrot-colored stubble on his chin.

Russell gazed across the saloon and saw Luke coming toward them. Several cowboys looked at his brother and then got out of his way. Russell smiled to himself. That was the way Luke affected anyone with half a brain. Luke was a solidly built man over six feet tall with light blue eyes that held a look of menace. Fast with his fists and even faster with his guns, Luke just naturally inspired awe as much as fear. Luke joined them at the table and downed several shots of whiskey before he would talk business with the rancher.

"There are people hereabouts that don't belong in Arizona, pushy folks trying to force their ways on us," the rancher told them. "This here's cattle country. No one else has a right to use the land, not mutton punchers, not sodbusters. One way or another, these folks who don't belong got to be removed. That's the job I need you to do. Are you willing?"

"Yes, sir, I do agree them folks ought to be taught the error of their ways." Russell turned to his brother. He knew Luke had to be talked to in just the right way. "I believe this is the Lord's work, brother."

Luke's eyes grew unnaturally bright. "We'll do it then."

After the agreement was struck, the three men walked out of the dark saloon into the glaring desert afternoon, the rancher walking on his way with spurs jangling. Luke's attention was drawn to an altercation in front of the general store. A woman was berating a cowboy as a small girl cried.

"How dare a grown man like you frighten a small child that way! Where is your sense of common decency?"

The girl buried her face in the woman's calico skirts.

"That female's feisty, got steel in her spine," Luke said with approval. "I like the way she stood up to the cowpuncher."

Russell observed the woman. She was a homesteader by the look of her.

"I want that gal," Luke said, surprising his brother.

Rus saw right off the woman was all prim and proper. "Luke, that ain't no bordello whore. You can't pick her out and have her just like that." Rus snapped his fingers.

Luke's eyes took on the unfocused look that always made Rus a tad uneasy. Rus squinted in the direction of the woman again. She was no great beauty. But her features were vivid—big, dark eyes, cheeks bright. "When a stallion wants to mount a mare, it's best to choose a gentle one. You don't want no wild bronc givin' you grief."

Luke smiled as he continued staring at the woman. "Reckon I'd like to ride a buckin' bronc just for the sheer satisfaction of tamin' one." He spat into the dusty street.

Rus knew better then to pursue logic any further with his brother; Luke didn't pay no mind to reason. You just had to influence him into seeing things from the right point of view. "If it's the Lord's wish you have her, He will provide."

"I will have me that female," Luke said in a quiet but determined voice. "Expect I can wait a time."

CHAPTER ONE

"You're a fool."

Mary MacGreggor stared up at the ice-blue eyes of the hand-some cowman in front of her with surprise bordering on shock. She simply did not believe he could be so rude. Surely, even in the West, people must learn manners? The tall rancher looked from Uncle Isaac to her, shook his head, and then dismounted.

"Am I to understand you won't do business with me?" Isaac asked in a calm, quiet voice.

"Didn't say that, Mr. Stafford." The rancher glanced over at Mary, raking her boldly from head to toe with a single look she found embarrassing. Unconsciously, Mary's hand went to her head to straighten her bonnet.

"I never discuss business in front of a lady, not even a pretty one." His tone was arrogant and patronizing. But then, wasn't that just the way with rich people, thinking and acting as if they were so much better than everyone else?

And there was no doubt this cowboy was rich. Uncle Isaac had explained to her that Cal Davis owned Rancho Royo and the Thunderbolt, both of which were large spreads, and taken together, the biggest cattle ranch in Arizona. Cal Davis's property also included much in the way of forested acreage, which was what interested them.

"Mr. Davis, I should introduce you to my niece, Mary MacGreggor. She is also my partner in the farm, since half of the financial investment is hers. You'll also find she has a good head for business."

The rancher looked down at her with what she could only interpret as an amused air of superiority. She felt the blood rising to her face and averted her gaze.

"I was told that you planned to meet me here today to ask about buying some of my lumber," Davis said in a flat voice.

"That's right. We intend to build a permanent dwelling, and therefore, it should be the best structure we can afford."

"Why don't you join me while I pick up some things in the general store and we'll talk this over." Although his voice now sounded polite, his manner was still disdainful.

They followed Cal Davis into a store that bore the sign "Emporium" in the front window. Once inside, Mary looked around, noticing that harnesses hung from the ceiling, along with saddles and bridles. The store seemed to sell a little of everything; big sacks of sugar and flour were piled up in one corner, bolts of calico in another.

Cal Davis walked up to the counter and asked the store owner about checking over some accounts. Then he turned back to them once again. Mary surveyed the man. He seemed just as tall out of the saddle as he had looked in it. He was lean but well-built, with broad, muscular shoulders and narrow hips. The man wore fine black leather boots which extended to his knees. A brown work shirt, jeans, leather vest, and brown Stetson completed his wardrobe. Strapped to his thigh was a holstered revolver, which made him look dangerous.

"There's plenty of good pine and fir trees up in the hills. We've been blessed that way. But the fact is, I don't think you'll be needin' it."

Isaac wrinkled his brow, looking much older than his thirty-seven years. "What makes you say that?"

"Plain truth is the land you've claimed ain't fit for farming."

"I don't understand," Mary said. It was the first time she had spoken and both men looked at her. Mr. Davis, in particular, seemed surprised at having a woman comment during a business discussion.

As he removed his hat in what seemed to be a gesture of deference to her, she could not help but notice how sun-streaked his light brown hair was or how it fell in waves over his long forehead. There were slight creases at the corners of his eyes as if he were accustomed to squinting at the sun.

"Ma'am, we've always used that land for grazing Thunderbolt cattle. It just ain't fit for anything else."

"My uncle thinks it could be."

His mouth smiled, but his eyes were anything but friendly. She met his level gaze directly, looking up into the tanned, weather-beaten face.

"This place ain't nothin' like the East. I think you folks are underestimating the difficulties you'll find out here."

"There's a stream on the property I plan to use to irrigate the crops," her uncle said in a meek voice. "I'm certain we can manage."

The cowboy stood with arrow-straight posture, his erect bearing giving the impression of a man who held himself aloof, while in contrast, her uncle's shoulders were slightly stooped, suggesting a yielding and gentler temperament.

"Suit yourselves," Cal Davis said with a shrug. "But you're wasting time, money, and effort on land that's fit for nothing but cattle ranching. I think you folks would do well to move on." Mary noted he had a soft, controlled voice with just the hint of a Southern accent.

"How can we trust your advice, Mr. Davis, since it seems fairly obvious that you consider the land as rightfully belonging to you." She couldn't seem to help sounding angry and accusing.

"That's true enough, ma'am. As far as I'm concerned, you're

nothin' but squatters." He looked directly into her eyes, his dark blue orbs cold as a lake in winter. "I would like to keep that land for myself. But if you think I'm warning you for selfish reasons, well, you're dead wrong." He spoke through pursed lips.

"That remains to be seen," she countered.

He shot a bolt of blue lightning in her direction. "Have it your way, ma'am, but don't ever say you weren't warned. That land gets hit by drought real regular. When your creek dries up this summer, don't you be surprised."

"Mr. Davis, our family has gone through a lot of trouble to come west and we're not about to give up without a fight." Her eyes locked with his.

"Your niece always speak up like that?" Davis said, turning to her uncle.

Isaac smiled weakly. "She's plainspoken like her father was, Mr. Davis. But she's usually right about things. The fact is when Congress passed the Desert Land Act in 'seventy-seven, I began to think that maybe I could be something more than a tenant farmer in New Jersey for the rest of my life. I always dreamed about owning my own farm, but never could afford it. At first, I thought that we could homestead in Kansas, but so little good land was left unclaimed. Then I thought that we'd venture farther west. I couldn't just go back and admit defeat, not after all we'd gone through to get there." Isaac looked at the cowboy pensively.

"I went into a saloon just to clear my mind. As I drank a beer, an old-timer who looked as if he'd endured a lot of prairie sun and wind came and stood beside me. We got to talking and I mentioned my dilemma to him. He told me he intended traveling west to Arizona. Well, the bartender asked him what they had in Arizona besides Indians and desert. The old-timer said he heard there was gold, copper, even silver. He planned to do some prospecting. Said Arizona was a good place for a man to make his way. I asked him if there was any good farmland. He scratched his head and told me the territory was soon to be open for homesteading, and when it was, a man who settled his six-forty would be able to put in a claim legal and proper."

"And that's what brought you here," Cal Davis said. He shook his head. "Well, can't say the prospector did you any favor. That desert land act you heard about was lobbied through Congress by and for cattle interests." The rancher knifed his fingers restlessly through his hair. "It never was meant as a genuine benefit to farmers, just cattlemen figuring how they could take over more grazing land, but I guess you'll be finding that out for yourself." Davis's voice had a grim and ominous quality to it that caused Mary to stare at him with suspicion. Did his words imply a threat?

Another man came into the store and walked over to Cal Davis. He was not as tall as the rancher but his appearance was just as striking. His hair was smooth and shiny black, worn tied back under his Stetson; he had high cheekbones and bronze skin. Although he was dressed like a cowboy, he looked as if he might be Native American, except for his eyes, which were a startling gray.

"Mr. Stafford, Miss MacGreggor, I'd like to introduce you to my ranch foreman at Thunderbolt, Wolf Raullins."

"Nice to make your acquaintance, Mr. Raullins," Isaac said.

The ranch foreman did not reply but chose to acknowledge Isaac's presence with a quick nod. Then he proceeded to look at Mary, studying her in a devouring manner, the way a hungry man looks at a banquet. His frank and unrelenting gaze made her so uncomfortable that she trained her eyes on the sawdust floor. Back East, at twenty-four years of age, she was already regarded as a spinster. In fact, in her entire life, no man had ever looked at her that way. It made her nervous and yet at the same time she found it exciting.

Cal Davis finally set a price for his timber. Her uncle seemed willing to accept the terms, but to Mary, the amount seemed high, and she told Cal Davis so.

He looked annoyed with her. "It's a fair price, ma'am. Fact is, timber's scarce and those of us who have it won't give it away for free. Take it or leave it."

Her uncle raised his brow, and Mary, with a deep sigh, nodded her head. It was obvious that Mr. Davis was not a man with whom one could negotiate. Her uncle shook hands on the deal, and then they discussed delivery.

Mary watched the two cowboys turn and walk out of the general store. She had never met men such as these before, so bold and intimidating. She could not help disliking Cal Davis; the rancher struck her as being overly proud and full of self-importance.

As they walked back to the hotel, her uncle turned to her. "I know the cost was dear and that you do not approve, but I don't think we made a mistake in our purchase."

"No, I agree," Mary conceded. "Mr. Davis is not an easy man to deal with. He does not strike me as being particularly amenable to the feelings and opinions of others. If you have dealings with him in the future, you'd best do it without me. I'm afraid I was too blunt with the man. Also, my presence as a woman would only have an adverse effect, since he already has developed a dislike for me."

"Mary, I don't believe anyone could ever dislike you."

She smiled at him. "What a good and kind man you are, Uncle. Aunt Elizabeth is very fortunate."

"It is I who am fortunate to have such a fine family." He patted her hand.

Mary surveyed her uncle, noting that in appearance, he was a plain man, dressed in overalls, his hands callused from a lifetime of hard, manual labor. Yet, she contended, he was every bit a gentleman in the true sense of the word—certainly he could give Cal Davis a few lessons in how to treat a lady.

Mary hoped the rancher was wrong about the difficulties they would encounter in the West. It had not been easy for them to make this decision in the first place.

After the death of Mary's father, Isaac had approached her with his plan. "It would make all the difference, Mary, if you came in with us. Your aunt is afraid of leaving her home, and she looks to you for advice and emotional support, just the way she once looked to your mother."

"I could hardly presume to tell Aunt Elizabeth what to do," Mary had protested.

But then Isaac had gone on to tell her that even selling everything they had, there wouldn't be enough money for the trip. "I know your father left you the house and some savings. You don't have much of a life here. I thought you might come with us as a full partner in the farm."

Mary thought about her uncle's offer long and hard. What would her father have wanted her to do? He would probably have preferred her to get married, but marriage was not something she thought much about. Her life had been devoted to caring for her father, acting as housekeeper and nurse since he met with his accident when she was fifteen years old. Her mother had died in childbirth from complications in having a second baby. The baby had died as well.

It had been just herself and her father ever since. She realized how narrow and circumspect her life had become in those years of pious devotion to an invalid parent. It had been difficult for a man as active and lively as Andrew MacGreggor to accept being bedridden. His whole personality changed dramatically; he became demanding, difficult, and irritable. Of course, Mary understood he was suffering and did whatever she could to alleviate the situation; but it was horrible watching him slowly die for so many years.

She and her mother's younger sister had always been close. She loved her aunt and uncle and their children. Somehow, it didn't seem difficult to leave New Jersey behind and make the trip west with her closest relatives. Isaac wanted a better life for his family, and Mary sympathized with that. What she wanted for herself, she couldn't really say, because until now, she'd never considered her own needs or ambitions.

Most of her spare time had been spent in reading literature; she also kept a diary and wrote verse. Mary thought she might find a position as a teacher, if they were needed in the West. In truth, she had no idea what to expect in this land that was totally foreign to her. But at least she was finally doing something with her life, making her own choices, and that seemed significant.

"Don't worry," Isaac said as if reading her thoughts. "It will all work out. We've made it this far. We can do the rest."

A great deal had been sacrificed so that they could come to the West. First, they had to put together the money for the railroad fares, general transportation, farm implements, livestock, seed, feed, and unknown contingencies. Isaac realized they would need enough to keep them going for a year or possibly more, until they could bring in their first good, cash crop. Between them, almost everything they owned was converted into cash so that they could travel light and fast. They planned to buy what they needed once they were out West. Elizabeth even tearfully sold her mother's heirloom silver candlesticks.

Kansas had been a great disappointment to everyone, but they decided not to give up. As the snows of the winter of 1882 began to melt, the family took the railroad as far as they could. Then Isaac bought two horses and a sturdy wagon. He planned to sell or trade the second horse for a yoke of oxen just as soon as they were settled on their own land.

They came to Arizona's Rim country first. Mary liked it because much of it was wooded like the land back home near the Pine Barrens of New Jersey, unlike the Plains, which were flat and treeless. When they found a green, fertile location called Pleasant Valley, the name alone seemed to imply this would be the perfect place to settle. But it was just the opposite.

A feud had started there between the Graham and Tewsbury clans that was on its way to becoming a major range war. Elizabeth was adamant that they not stay in such a violent place. Mary completely agreed with her. And so they pushed on farther into the center of the territory, where they found an area of mountains, forests, and rivers. But all the best land had been taken here as well, and the six hundred and forty acres they finally claimed were little more than desert.

They were located outside of a town called Expectation. It had been a boomtown for a short while, but when the silver ore petered out in the mines, the prospectors left and headed for new claims. Now it consisted of little more than a saloon, a bank, a general store, a livery stable, a hotel that was hardly more than a boardinghouse, and a few rickety domiciles.

Aunt Elizabeth did not directly express disappointment with their new surroundings; still Mary knew how unhappy she was. Although her aunt was twelve years her senior, the two women had developed a close friendship and shared in each other's confidences.

Elizabeth was waiting expectantly when they arrived back at the hotel. She and the children sat in the lobby.

"I've made a commitment to purchase lumber for our cabin. We're going to have a good sturdy house," Isaac said with a reassuring smile.

Jeremy gave an enthusiastic shout. He was nearly fourteen, and as the only boy, he was his mother's favorite and his father's pride. Mary noted that the boy always tried hard to live up to his parents' good opinion of him. Like Elizabeth, he had red-gold hair and a smattering of freckles across the bridge of his nose. Rebecca, the oldest of the three children who survived infancy, said nothing and gave no indication of having followed a word her father had spoken. Rebecca was a pretty, golden-haired girl of sixteen, and if not for her accident, she would have been a lovely woman someday. As it was, a head injury had left the girl permanently confused. The youngest child, Amy, was just eight years old, a bit impish but adorable.

Elizabeth turned to Mary. "What do you think? Has Isaac acted wisely?"

"I believe so," Mary replied. She spoke in a voice that allowed for more confidence than she actually felt.

But her aunt seemed reassured. And that was what mattered.

CHAPTER TWO

They remained at the hotel for only one more night since it was an expense they could ill afford. Besides, Isaac was eager to establish the farm as quickly as possible.

They bought what they needed to get started: farm animals, equipment and supplies, and then they took up residence on their land. The early spring days brought hot, dry weather, but the nights were brisk. Campfires and warm blankets were necessary.

Mary began to see a change in Jeremy and Amy; where both had been homesick before, now they were looking on their new life as an exciting adventure. Some of that same feeling began to take hold of her as well. They were actually living on their own land. Mary began to hope that a new and more fulfilling life was possible for her. For many years, she watched her father deteriorating in spite of her best efforts, and gradually felt as if she were dying right along with him. She never realized until now just how empty and depressing her existence had become.

Isaac and Jeremy set about preparing the earth for their first crop, and everyone helped with the physical labor. Hard work was something to which Mary never objected, since she was well accustomed to it. And Isaac was an experienced farmer who knew about the use of dry farming techniques such as deep plowing and dust mulching, all of which he explained to Mary and Jeremy.

"In truth, these methods require expensive equipment, but

I'm not without resourcefulness," he told them. "I've gotten some ideas from Mormons. I talked with a few of them as we traveled. The main thing is that we conserve water. So we're going to dam our stream and irrigate a field for planting potatoes."

By digging an irrigation canal and connecting ditches, they could water the arid but fertile land. They planted two more fields, one with corn and another with wheat. Mary had never seen her uncle so happy before; he was a man filled with a dream and convinced that they would be successful. His joy was infectious.

"We're going to make the desert bloom like the Garden of Eden," he said, kissing Elizabeth on the cheek.

Her aunt said nothing, but Mary observed the first smile on Elizabeth's face that she had seen in many months.

With the delivery of the lumber, they began working simultaneously on the cabin. Mary's days were far from idle, and there was no time to sit and read. Still, she wanted to visit the local settlers to see if there was enough interest to start a school. She'd not forgotten her plan to teach in the West. It was also nice to meet the people who were their neighbors and find out something about the other farmers and ranchers. As much as she could discover, farmers and ranchers didn't like each other very much and sometimes relations deteriorated into violence, but nothing major as had occurred in the Rim country.

She offered to teach the children at the cabin when it would be completed in the early fall. Thirteen families agreed to send at least one child to her school—but she was told in no uncertain terms by several of the ranchers that she would have to discuss the matter with Cal Davis before anything was definitely set.

"If Cal's for it then we are too," a rancher named Deke Norris told Mary. This infuriated her, since she couldn't see any earthly reason why Mr. Davis's approval had to be sought. It almost seemed as if other people were telling her that nothing could be done in this community without that man's consent, that his power was absolute, as if he were some medieval baron who exerted feudal dominance. She could scarcely believe what she was told! Yet no one would solidly agree to the idea of starting a local school unless it had Cal Davis's backing.

"I cannot bear to ask that man for any kind of favor," Mary told Isaac and Elizabeth.

"I'll ride over to his ranch and ask him to drop by here," Isaac offered in a kindly manner.

"I wish there were some other way." But, of course, there wasn't.

At least, the meeting was held at the farm. That made it easier for Mary to swallow her pride. But when Cal Davis did actually appear, Mary felt much too embarrassed and awkward to ask him directly. Elizabeth offered him a cup of coffee, which he refused. This went far in confirming Mary's initial opinion that Mr. Davis considered himself far superior to them. Asking such a man for a favor proved impossible for her, the words sticking in her throat like a chicken bone. In the end, it was her aunt who brought up the matter.

"I think a school would be a fine idea," the rancher agreed, giving Elizabeth a friendly smile. Then he glanced over at Mary: "That is, if you're up to it."

Mary stiffened her spine and squared her jaw. "I'm not a weak woman," she told him, some of her fierce pride flashing in her eyes. "I think I can deal with teaching children."

"Well, ma'am, educating children hereabouts can be something of a chore. They're independent little cusses and don't take kindly to being told what to do. It's not like working with kids back East."

She ground down on her back teeth. "If I find myself unable

to do the job properly, I will resign, I assure you." She held her head high.

"Fair enough," he said in a smooth voice. "I'll take your word that you're up to the challenge. The others asked you to see me because a salary has to be agreed on, Miss MacGreggor. We need a school and I'm willing to donate the lumber. Some of my men could be spared to put up the building during the summer. There's plenty of room in Expectation for a school-house."

She nodded, although she found it impossible to actually thank the man. She knew her attitude was perhaps unfair, but she couldn't seem to help herself. In spite of everything she still disliked him and she didn't trust him.

As spring turned into early summer, everything seemed to be going very well for the family. Only Elizabeth remained uncertain.

"I don't think I will ever get used to living in such an uncivilized atmosphere," Elizabeth told her.

"It has its charms," Mary said. "I, for one, feel more alive out here."

"Can you actually say you like this savage, arid land full of cactus and mesas, so isolated, stark, and empty?"

Sitting on the ground, Mary brought up her knees and hugged them against her body in the cooling evening air. "When I look up at the sky each night, I say to myself: you can see the stars much clearer here! Everything just seems so much bigger and brighter. I really like the desert, and as for being lonely, well, I've been lonely all my life. Maybe I'm just used to it."

On the Fourth of July, Mary heard rapid, repeated gunfire. Isaac went running, rifle in hand, followed closely by Jeremy. It was only some Thunderbolt cowpunchers letting off steam, shooting off their guns toward the sky. She watched from a distance as Isaac went and talked to Wolf Raullins, who seemed to be leading the group. Isaac returned smiling.

"They say that this is the way Independence Day is celebrated in the territory. Mary, I was asked to give you a message."

"From whom?" she asked in surprise.

"That Raullins fellow. He said I was to make certain to give you his regards."

Elizabeth smiled knowingly and Mary found herself blushing. "Well, dear, it looks like you may well find yourself some beaux out here if you wish, for there is surely no scarcity of menfolk."

Mary wasn't certain how she felt about that. What might have been a normal social life for her had ended when she was just a young girl. There had been no social events of any kind; she'd lived as a semirecluse. There were no gentleman callers to ask her to parties or dances, and she had never expected there would be.

As the summer progressed, the temperatures soared; there was no rain and a paucity of water. In late July, each day was well above a hundred degrees with no relief in sight. It hurt her to recall what Cal Davis had said. However, she had to admit to herself that he might be right. The creek that had so amply provided for their needs in the spring was drying up before their very eyes. They managed water for drinking and cooking but very little else. In the back of Mary's mind was the all-important question: how would the crops survive?

Isaac went to Cal Davis to buy the water they so desperately needed. The precious commodity was not refused them.

"Only trouble is," Isaac explained to the family afterward, "the man wouldn't take any money. Fact is, he flatly refused."

"Is this the same Mr. Davis who gouged us for the lumber?" Mary asked in surprise.

"He said if we were going to live out here for any length of time, we would have to learn that water was a lot more valuable than money." Isaac frowned.

"What's wrong?" Elizabeth asked. "He sounds wise and generous to me."

"Just wish he'd of let me pay him. I don't like to be in another man's debt."

"Really, Isaac!" Elizabeth said. "The man was being kind. We should be grateful."

"I understand just how Isaac feels," Mary said. "Mr. Davis enjoys acting like a king and bestowing his favors. It makes one quite uneasy."

"I believe that you're being unfair," Elizabeth asserted. "He is a very courteous man. And he has good manners. I saw that for myself when he came by here. We should make an effort to get along with our new neighbor and meet him halfway."

Mary surveyed her aunt thoughtfully; Elizabeth, she felt, had a tendency to simply accept people at face value. It seemed to her that Cal Davis was anything but simple.

They'd been told that Arizona was hit by summer monsoons and so they waited expectantly for the turbulent rainstorms to come. Instead, the drought continued. Mr. Jones, who owned the general store, explained it was southern Arizona that got the storms off the Gulf; their particular area was not generally affected.

"I reckon you've begun to discover what the Injuns in this territory knowed all along," Zeb Jones observed cheerfully as he filled their order.

"What's that, Mr. Jones?" Mary asked.

The heavy-set proprietor grinned at her. "Well, it's just that to survive in this harsh land, people have to be strong and enduring like the rocks. They got to adapt to the nature of the land, which means understanding about the scarcity of water. You know them Injuns worship water, regard it as sacred. Ain't that the damnedest thing?"

Wolf Raullins walked into the store, looking as if he had overheard Mr. Jones from the doorway. "My mother's people always realized that water is a gift of the gods. They know how to live in harmony with nature. The white man still has a great deal to learn."

Jones walked away from them, muttering something under his breath about cocky savages.

Isaac trailed after the storekeeper with his list. Mary was about to follow when Wolf Raullins suddenly stopped her by taking her wrist. She looked up at him, shocked by his conduct. His gray eyes were steady but hard to read.

"Are you as prejudiced against half-breeds as most folks around here?"

The bluntness of his question took her totally by surprise. "Are settlers in Arizona really prejudiced against the native population?"

He sneered at her. "Can't you tell? Out here, there's Mex and Anglos, and people don't mix. But there's one thing for sure. Everyone in these parts hates and fears my people."

"I don't think background should make much of a difference. Each of us is a human being after all."

"You really are an Easterner," he said, with something akin to surprise. "Make no mistake, I can be savage when it's called for," he said with an insinuating smile that made her cheeks flush.

"Mr. Raullins, could you please release my wrist. It's beginning to hurt."

He smiled at her again, flashing teeth that were as white and bright as the best china. "Wouldn't want that to happen." Then his eyes looked deeply into hers and she could see he was no

29

longer smiling. The intensity of the moment was shattered when Isaac and Mr. Jones returned to where they were standing and Mary found that she could breathe again.

They had to keep accepting water from the Davis ranch and wait for the unspeakable heat to end, which it did not do until well into September. But by then, they had completed work on the cabin and there was cause for celebration. Isaac shot some game while Elizabeth baked her best biscuits and the children swept the dirt floor clean.

"We're ready to buy furniture," Isaac told them over dinner. They congratulated each other happily.

The schoolhouse was finally becoming a reality as well. Zeb Jones and his wife told Mary how pleased they were to send three of their children to school, and how they didn't mind paying her salary one bit. Zeb, who was the unofficial mayor of the town, carried a lot of weight with other people. Since he was speaking well of the idea of schooling, she was certain that other families would send their children to be educated as well. Mary liked the Jones family. Mrs. Jones was as short and thin as her husband was heavy and tall, but they made a compatible couple all the same.

When the schoolhouse was completed in its entirety, Mary found herself in a log building that was sixteen feet wide by twenty-five feet long with a dirt roof and four windows. There were log pews for seats and the logs had pegs driven through them. She was so pleased with the sight of this rough building that she nearly cried. But she could not forget who was responsible for this miracle, and it rankled her. Without the help of Cal Davis, who had contributed both labor and lumber, there would have been no school. As Isaac had said, it was not an easy thing to be in another person's debt, particularly someone she resented.

Mary began teaching school in the middle of September. There were fewer students than she had anticipated, but that was all right, because she wasn't all that confident of her abilities. Butterflies danced in her stomach. There was no question in her mind that she was educated and intelligent enough to teach; however, could she control the students effectively? She had always been very good with her nieces and nephew—still, they were family. On that first day, she discovered much to her relief that she actually could handle a class of children.

There were only twelve students at first, including her cousin, Amy, whom she brought herself by wagon each day. Mary determined to personally visit each family in the area and find out why so many school-age children were being kept at home.

After a good deal of time and effort, she found that in many of the families, the girls were needed for housekeeping and babysitting while the boys had outdoor chores to do. Then there were the families who simply lived too far from town. But her persistence did pay off; the class enrollment finally rose to seventeen.

Good news came from the farm as well. Isaac and Jeremy succeeded in digging a good, deep well after several false starts. They had found water where prairie grass grew, and everyone felt overjoyed, even Elizabeth. It seemed as if they'd turned a significant corner in their lives. Isaac began talking about what they might do with their money when they sold their first crop. He was thinking in terms of a barn.

"Isaac, your eyes are flecked with rose dew," Elizabeth teased.

"Nothing wrong with being optimistic," her uncle said.

Things were definitely getting better, Mary observed. In fact, she wanted to take Rebecca and Jeremy to see the school and spend the day in town. Isaac reflected that he could spare the boy for one day, so all the children went into Expectation with Mary. It was a special treat for Jeremy and Rebecca, who worked

31

tirelessly and rarely left the farm.

They were both impressed with the schoolhouse and enjoyed meeting the younger children. It was hard to tell what Rebecca might be thinking because she rarely spoke to anyone, but sometimes Mary would see an awareness in the girl's eyes and thought her cousin was not as damaged as everyone assumed.

During the afternoon, Rebecca withdrew again into her own private world. Before Mary dismissed the children, Rebecca removed herself to a corner where she hugged herself, trembling.

On the ride home, Mary turned to the girl. "What's wrong?"

Rebecca didn't answer her. Mary looked into the girl's glazed eyes and brushed a strand of long, straight blond hair back from her face.

"If you could only speak to me as you used to before your accident."

"Home," Rebecca said. There were shadows in her eyes.

"You think something is wrong at the farm?"

Rebecca nodded her head, her eyes still unfocused.

Mary was pensive; she knew fear when she bumped up against it. She wanted to set Rebecca's mind at ease. "We often feel frightened when we're separated from family, from the people we love. You're not accustomed to being away from your parents. Don't worry, dear, everything will be all right."

"No!" the girl cried out, vehemently shaking her head, hair moving like a wheat field in the wind.

Jeremy, driving the wagon, glanced back at them. "Becky, you behave."

"Home!" the girl cried out again more urgently.

"We're going as fast as we can. Mary, my sister sometimes gets strange notions. It's like she knows when something bad's going to happen. Some kind of second sight. Like when she knew that hurricane was going to hit our place back East."

Mary didn't comment. She wasn't certain she believed in the

existence of such abilities; it seemed like foolish superstition.

"Becky'll be okay just as soon as we get back to the farm," Amy said, taking her older sister's hand in her own.

Rebecca had been impaired since she fell from a horse and hit her head against a boulder. Everyone was convinced that she would die. Rebecca eventually returned to consciousness, but her mind was never the same.

Mary was becoming uneasy, wondering if everything was all right at the farm. Rebecca fell silent again and did not speak until they were just approaching the cabin. At that point she began to scream, "Pa! Pa!" over and over again. Mary held the girl in her arms, trying to control her hysteria, but Rebecca was out of control.

"I never seen her this bad," Jeremy said. Frown lines formed in his forehead.

Rebecca started to jump off the wagon even before they came to a complete stop. Mary's efforts to restrain the girl were futile. Rebecca ran into the cabin, totally beside herself. They could hear her continued screams even from outside. The sound was bloodcurdling and sent chills slithering down Mary's spine as she, Amy, and Jeremy went running after her. Mary was convinced Rebecca had taken leave of her senses, and she blamed herself for removing the child from the sheltered environment of the farm for the day.

Rebecca knelt on the dirt floor, crying wildly, her long, golden mane of hair falling into her eyes. As Mary drew closer, she saw what the girl was holding and gasped in horror.

CHAPTER THREE

Mary's eyes opened wide in shock as she stared at her uncle lying in a pool of blood, his unseeing eyes turned upward. There was absolutely no doubt in her mind that he was dead, but she went through the motions of checking for a pulse and heartbeat, only to find that there weren't any. His body felt cold to the touch.

Rebecca and Amy held to each other, weeping hysterically while Jeremy turned to look at Mary.

"Pa's not . . ." The boy choked on the rest of his words. Mary put her arms around him.

"Your father's with God," she said quietly.

Jeremy shook his head as if to deny her words. "No, it can't be!" The boy knelt over his father, staring at gaping wounds; then examining the body, his fingers touched blood in disbelief.

Mary caught sight of Elizabeth. Her aunt was lying in the far corner of the room, dazed and barely conscious. It was startling to see her sprawled out stark naked on the dirt floor. Mary quickly got a blanket and wrapped Elizabeth in it, recalling how modest her aunt had always been. It was important that the children not see their mother this way.

"Elizabeth, what happened?" she asked in as controlled a voice as she could manage.

But her aunt did not reply, and Mary realized that Elizabeth was in deep shock. For the moment, Mary forgot about Isaac and concentrated on her aunt. She made Jeremy take Amy out of the cabin and told him to bring back fresh water. After Jeremy brought the water, Mary insisted that he and the girls stay outside. Then she set about the task of cleaning Elizabeth's lacerations, washing Elizabeth thoroughly and gently as if she were a small child, and finally dressing her in a clean nightgown. Ever so carefully, she put Elizabeth to bed in the main room of the cabin, not in the small bedroom that her aunt and uncle had shared. Mary held Elizabeth's hands in her own until her aunt's eyes finally closed.

Mary would need to know what had happened, but at the moment, her aunt was unable to speak. In reality, she had a fairly good idea of what must have occurred. Elizabeth's pale, delicate body had been badly bruised. Her nose was swollen and there were large welts on her cheeks, arms, and thighs. Some demented, vicious animal had beaten her aunt and raped her; that was the only possible explanation. It was impossible for Mary to conceive of such brutality. And yet Isaac lay before her dead, his life's blood spilled over the dirt floor, his body rent by multiple wounds.

Mary had never felt more helpless in her entire life. Still she knew that for the children's sake, she must be strong and take charge of the situation. After all, this was much worse for them. Mary covered her uncle's body with a blanket, and then told the children to come into the cabin again. She sat them down at the unpainted wooden table and chairs in front of the hearth.

"You've got to get hold of yourselves," she told the girls, who were sobbing uncontrollably.

"Papa's dead!" cried Amy. "What about Mama? Is Mama dead too?"

"No," Mary reassured the child. "She's been hurt, but she's going to recover." She could only pray her words were true. "We've just got to take good care of her." She put her arms around both girls in a gesture of comfort. "Amy, I want you and

Rebecca to make your mother something hot to drink. Brew a pot of strong coffee. It's going to be a long night, and we'll all need some." Mary managed to keep her voice calm and firm although inwardly she was trembling.

Amy took Rebecca by the hand, an incongruous sight since she was much smaller than her older sister. It would be better now that the girls had a task to accomplish, Mary thought.

Suddenly, Elizabeth sat up in bed and screamed with a piercing cry that made the girls start to sob all over again. Mary went to her aunt and held her as Elizabeth began to cry and tremble.

"Isaac! They killed him!"

"We're going to send for the authorities, and they'll catch whoever did this terrible thing to you and Isaac."

"Bury Isaac," Elizabeth said to her. "Put him to rest in the ground." Her eyes cast about wildly. "I want my husband at peace."

"There's plenty of time for a proper burial."

"No!" Elizabeth shouted at her, grabbing Mary's arms. "I want Isaac cared for now!"

"Whatever you say," Mary reassured her.

Elizabeth was shaking, her teeth chattering, and Mary placed another blanket over her aunt.

"Close your eyes and try to rest. Jeremy and I will lay Isaac to rest right now as you wish." She turned to the boy. "Get us each a shovel," she said.

They buried Isaac on a knoll overlooking the fields he had loved so much. The blood-sun was setting over the land he'd worked so hard to farm. Jeremy got Amy and Rebecca to join them in filling in the grave, and they worked in silence because no one knew what to say. Somehow prayers seemed inappropriate.

When they were all done, Jeremy stormed into the house and

looked around. "I guess they even took our old rifle."

"Where do you intend to go?" Mary asked the boy.

"I want to find whoever it was murdered my pa and hurt my mama so bad. I'm gonna kill them!" The boy's normally gentle features were contorted into an expression of anguished rage.

Mary put a restraining hand on his tense arm. "I understand how you feel, and I agree we must take action. But we don't even know who did this terrible thing. Your mother can't tell us anything yet. We'll have to send for help. We're going to need the territorial marshal. When your mother is feeling more like herself, she'll be able to tell him what happened. He'll know what to do, how to handle the situation. I suppose Mr. Davis will know how we can go about making contact, and he is our closest neighbor. Why don't you ride over there now and tell him what's happened? He'll advise us." Mary didn't know if they could trust Mr. Davis, but she felt helpless and confused.

Jeremy nodded his agreement without saying another word. Mary could see how hard he was trying to behave like a man, striving to contain his grief within himself, and her heart went out to the boy. After he had ridden away, Mary turned her attention back to Elizabeth, who seemed to be sleeping. Pressing her hands against the log wall, Mary glanced over at Amy. The child offered her a cup of coffee, which she gratefully accepted.

"Stay by your mother. Keep a vigil by her bedside, and if she wakes, call me." Mary glanced at Rebecca. "You understand that your mother needs both of you?"

Rebecca tearfully nodded her head, walking to the bed where her mother rested, and placed her cheek against Elizabeth's outstretched hand.

Mary stepped out into the chilling air of early evening feeling emotionally and physically exhausted. She walked to the place where they had buried Isaac and sank down on her knees beside the grave. At least her own father had died of natural causes, and he'd been suffering in pain so that his passing could be considered as a relief of mortal agony, a blessing of sorts. God's will, the reverend had said as they laid her father to rest. But how could Isaac's death be God's will? She knew that she should not question it, and yet she could not help herself.

How long she knelt by her uncle's grave, she did not know; she'd lost track of time. The girls had wept openly as they laid their father to rest. Even Jeremy's eyes had filled and his chest heaved with silent sobs, but Mary had not allowed them to see her grief.

Now that no one was here to see or know, grief welled up within her, grief for the loss of a good man like Isaac Stafford, who had never hurt anyone in his entire life, but wanted only to farm his own land and leave some legacy for his family. Her whole body shook with the force of her sorrow for this lost life and the injustice that had been done to him.

She didn't know when it was that she became aware of someone watching her. But then she saw him in the gathering darkness, a man on horseback looking directly at her. She tried to rise to her feet, only to find her legs like rubber. *Oh, God, please, do not let me faint, not in front of some stranger!* But she was dizzy and the world suddenly became lopsided and dark. She heard the man dismount and then felt strong hands reach out to hold her.

"It's all right," he said, cradling her in his arms as one would hold a small child. "You'll be fine." His voice was soft and soothing. His arms were tightly around her, pressing her face against his hard, muscular chest. One hand stroked her hair.

"Y-you can let me go now," she told him in a breathy voice.

"Certainly." But he didn't let her go right away; he just kept holding her against him with his strong hands, and she felt oddly consoled and comforted, as if this were quite natural and she could remain in his arms for eternity.

Yet she realized that was a foolish notion even as she thought it and struggled to free herself from his arms. She looked up into the face of Cal Davis, who stared down at her with concern.

"Really, I'm all right," she told him, straightening. "Where's Jeremy?"

"I made the boy stay at the ranch for tonight. He was all worn out. Plumb tuckered. I decided to come by myself and see what I could do to help you out. I've already sent someone for the marshal, but there's no chance he'll come before tomorrow."

She nodded in solemn acceptance.

"Mind telling me what happened?"

Mary told him everything she knew and he listened attentively. As she finished telling the rancher about how they had buried Isaac, the tears began to flow and she couldn't seem to stop them, much to her own shame.

His arms came around her again and she found herself trembling, as much from his touch as from the grief she was feeling. She needed comforting, and it felt so good to be held by this strong man. She knew she should free herself from him and yet for some unexplainable reason, she was unable. His fingers brushed her tears away as she looked into his face. Maybe it was because of the growing darkness, but his brilliant blue eyes no longer looked cold. They seemed to have darkened with some other emotion.

Cal looked at Mary MacGreggor and thought right at this minute how much he wanted to carry her off to the desert and make love to her under the stars. But he knew he couldn't say any such thing to her, nor could he behave in such a barbaric manner. He could see her vulnerability, her need for strength and reassurance.

He studied her thoughtfully, thinking he couldn't seem to see her the same way now as he had when they first met. She was all sharpness then, prickly as a cactus. She'd made him angry because she made her disapproval of him so clear. He thought women like her were nothing but trouble to a man. And yet, for some reason he didn't understand, he wanted her to think well of him. He realized his true motive in giving the Staffords water and then building the schoolhouse was just to impress her. But none of that had softened her attitude toward him.

He'd been doing his level best to stay away, to forget about her, because he recognized she'd just make him miserable if he ever got involved with her. Then her nephew arrived and told him what happened at the farm. That was when he knew he had to go to her, to offer some help. Finding her crying over her uncle's grave had done something to him. He felt a pain in his own heart. She was a strong woman, but at that moment, she seemed vulnerable and delicate. He wanted to protect her.

"Would you like me to come inside the cabin with you?" he asked her.

She looked up at him and nodded her head. He took her arm and they walked back together side by side in silence.

As they entered the cabin, Cal looked around. The only illumination came from the glowing fire in the hearth. He saw the two girls sleepily holding vigil by their mother's bed and noticed how quiet everything was, like the calm after a terrible, destructive storm.

He watched Mary, observing the worry on her face as she checked on her aunt and cousins; it seemed as if she were shouldering a burden too heavy to be endured by one young woman. He studied Mary's face, admiring the dark, luminous eyes that dominated her other features. They were brown liquid pools, warm as toasted bread. She had a small chin which jutted out determinedly, full, generous lips, and a pert nose that tilted upward ever so slightly. His eyes wandered, noting her small, trim waist and the full womanly swell of her breasts and hips. Her conservative gray dress was austere and plain in contrast to her coppery hair, which curled around her face and cascaded down her back.

"The girls are resting and Elizabeth is still asleep," Mary said. "I'm sorry you came out here tonight. I didn't mean to trouble you."

He smiled at her apology. "It wasn't any trouble. Besides, I don't reckon you women should be alone out here tonight."

She seemed to understand what he was thinking. "You mean you think whoever did this might come back?"

"It's possible. Out here, you never know for sure. I've got a bedroll with me and some blankets. I'm going to sleep outside right nearby. If you need me for any reason, just holler."

She didn't try to dissuade him and actually looked relieved at his suggestion. Out under the stars as he got ready to go to sleep, Cal thought about Mary. He didn't have much faith in women, but he sensed that she was somehow different from most females; she was honest and forthright, a woman with high moral standards and integrity. Of course, it might be that he only wished her to be different. He'd learned many lessons from his father, one of which was that you couldn't trust womenfolk. He'd learned that lesson very well and never allowed himself to care much about any of them. Use them for your pleasure, the old man had said, but never feel anything for them or they'll surely cut your heart out. His father's life was the example. No, Cal hadn't forgotten any of it.

Toward dawn, Elizabeth stirred and Mary came to her aunt's bedside. The girls were sleeping back to back on the floor, and Mary placed an extra blanket over them. Elizabeth began to whimper; Mary put her arms around her aunt in a gesture of comfort. Gradually, Elizabeth became aware of Mary's presence and threw herself against Mary.

"Isaac!" she cried out.

"We buried him as you asked," Mary said in a quiet voice. "We'll go to his grave when you're better."

"It was so terrible, so awful."

"Who would do such a thing?"

Elizabeth shook her head, trembling. "I don't want to talk about it." Elizabeth turned away from Mary and began weeping again.

"I'll fix you some coffee," Mary said and went about reheating the pot that had been brewed the night before. After serving Elizabeth, she went outside to offer a cup to Cal Davis and found he was already up and had cut some kindling for the fire. She immediately invited him into the cabin.

Mary fixed some biscuits and served them to Cal Davis, then sat and drank a cup of coffee with him. He didn't talk at all, but she was aware he watched every move she made intently; his scrutiny served to make her self-conscious.

"Will the marshal come soon?" she finally asked.

"Directly. They'll be a few people coming. Your aunt up to it?"

"I don't know," she answered honestly. "I hope so."

In the light of morning, she could think more clearly. Troubling Cal Davis with their problems disturbed her; it was demeaning and humiliating. She had put herself under his protection and, therefore, in his power. She didn't like that feeling one bit. It was time she took control of her own life again. And yet a part of her wanted to reach out to him, wanted to feel his strong arms around her, making her feel secure.

The men came several hours later. There were three of them, besides her cousin Jeremy, and they were all strangers. She could see by the looks on their faces that they already knew what they would find at the farm. A young cowboy kept his distance, but the other two men came directly to Cal Davis. She could identify the territorial marshal by virtue of the badge he wore pinned to his brown leather vest. The marshal shook the rancher's hand.

Cal turned to her. "Miss MacGreggor, I'd like you to meet our lawman in these parts."

The marshal stepped forward, and Mary noticed that he was not nearly as tall as Cal Davis, but his build was as broad, and like Cal, he looked well-muscled. He wore a black mustache that made him appear fierce, and he didn't look as if he ever smiled.

The marshal tipped his hat to her. "Ma'am, my name's Tim Wade. After the Doc looks at your aunt, I'd like to speak with her."

"I'll see if she's up to talking with you," Mary replied.

"I promise to be real careful with her, right gentle," the marshal said more sympathetically then she had expected.

Cal introduced her to the second man. "This is Doc—he's not a real doctor because we don't have one hereabouts. But Doc's okay—he can remedy men just as good as animals. I figured you'd like someone to have a look at Mrs. Stafford." Cal indicated a grizzled cowboy with a salt-and-pepper beard.

Mary led the way into the cabin. Elizabeth, on seeing these strange men coming toward her, sat up in bed and began to scream. Mary asked the girls to wait outside the cabin and then sought to comfort her aunt.

"It's just Mr. Davis, Elizabeth. You remember him. He's come to help us and brought a doctor and the marshal."

"I don't want any man to touch me, not ever again!" Elizabeth pulled the covers around her.

Mary gently took her aunt's delicate hand in her own. Elizabeth had always looked young to her, but today her aunt looked terribly worn. The tearful hazel eyes were shadowed and held a defeated look, and the red-gold hair hung limp and unkempt.

"I guess you could wait on the doctor if that's what you want, but you've got to tell the marshal what happened here yesterday," Mary said.

Her aunt shook her head vehemently. That was when Cal Davis stepped forward and began talking to Elizabeth.

"It's important for us to know who murdered your husband, Mrs. Stafford. You do want them punished, don't you? The only way that can happen is if you tell us everything. Otherwise, they'll never be brought to justice. We really want to help." He spoke in a calm, quiet manner, but with authority as well.

Elizabeth sighed and turned her face to the wall. She looked like a faded flower, a blasted rose whose petals had begun to fall apart.

"Elizabeth, please, you must try." Mary's tone was kind but insistent.

Jeremy came forward then, pale-faced and shaking. "Ma, don't you let them bastards get away with it!" The boy clenched his teeth, beside himself with grief and rage.

"This is very difficult for your mother," Mary said, trying to calm him, but he pulled away from the hand she reached out to him in a gesture of comfort.

"I hate this!" The boy smashed his fist against the log wall, bruising his knuckles.

Elizabeth sat straight up in response to her son's display of impotent rage. "I'm so ashamed. They did unspeakable things to me. I never dreamt such horrible men existed!"

Mary took her aunt firmly by the shoulders. "Hard as this may be, you've got to describe them and tell what happened. Jeremy is right. We can't let them get away with it. Otherwise, they might come back. And even if they don't, think of all the other people they can still hurt!"

Elizabeth nodded her head, but her gaze was still averted. In a voice that was hardly steady, she began to recount what happened on the previous day.

"I was busy in the house, just finished baking bread, intending to start my mending. It was early afternoon when I heard the sound of horses and went to the window. I could see dust rising and thought from the looks of it whoever it was must be riding very fast. I thought Isaac would probably notice and come back from the field where he was working.

"At first, I just assumed it was cowboys from the Thunderbolt chasing stray cattle the way they do sometimes. But then there was banging on the door as if they would smash it down. They claimed to be thirsty, tired cowboys in need of something to drink. I knew Thunderbolt wranglers would never come to the door, and I didn't like the rude way these men spoke. So I told them there was water in the well and they were welcome to it but to please go away from my door.

"The next thing I knew, they were smashing at the wood. I got frightened and went for the rifle Isaac kept over the hearth. I didn't know how to use it, but I hoped if they broke the bolt, the sight of me holding it would scare them away. Well, they broke through all right, and there were four of them armed to the teeth with rifles, shotguns, and sidearms. I told them to get out or I'd shoot them, but they only laughed at me. One of them said that our old muzzleloader couldn't hurt a fly."

Elizabeth stopped talking and her eyes took on a faraway look as if she were lost in her memory.

"What happened next?" Marshal Wade asked.

"I-I don't want to say."

"Please, go on, Elizabeth," Cal Davis said in a kind voice. "We're all your friends here."

She seemed to respond to that. "They forced me to submit to them. When I tried to fight them, they hit me really hard. Isaac came in and saw what was happening. He did his best to stop

45

them, but they shot him. That man, the worst one, he shot Isaac three times. There wasn't any need. He just seemed to enjoy it. Then he said if I resisted anymore, they'd do the same to me." Elizabeth was trembling.

Mary moved to get her aunt a hot cup of coffee but found her own hands were shaking too much. For several moments, there wasn't a single sound in the cabin.

"Ma'am, can you please describe these men to us. I need as accurate a description as possible," Marshal Wade said.

"The one who did most of the talking had a red mustache, beard and shaggy hair the color of a carrot. He talked smooth and calm, as if what was happening was just an everyday event. The one who killed Isaac and first attacked me had very light blue eyes. They were the strangest eyes I've ever seen. There was a distant look about them, as if his mind weren't really here at all, and he had a scar on the left side of his face. The scar was ugly and purple, extending from his cheek all the way down to the crease in his neck, long as it was narrow. He was the most frightening man I've ever seen, cruel and menacing." She shuddered and stopped talking.

"What about the other two?" the marshal prodded.

"They were both very dark with thick black mustaches and they wore large sombreros."

"Mex," the marshal said with a look to Cal Davis.

"All four of the men were dusty and dirty. I don't think they were really cowboys at all."

"No, ma'am, neither do I," Marshal Wade agreed. "Did you catch any names? Think back real hard."

Elizabeth bit down on her lower lip pensively. "The one with the strange eyes called the red-haired man Rusty. The two dark men spoke only in a foreign language."

The marshal exchanged looks with Cal Davis and Doc, then turned back to Elizabeth.

"Did this Rusty happen to call the other man Luke?"

"I think maybe he did. I sort of lost track of what was happening after a while."

"Mrs. Stafford, you ought to let Doc take a look at your bruises, just to attend to what needs it."

Elizabeth didn't argue any further, and everyone but Doc stepped outside of the cabin to allow her some degree of privacy.

Marshal Wade turned to Cal Davis. "I reckon it must be them again," he said.

"Who?" Mary asked.

"The Harris brothers. They been around these parts lately causing all kinds of trouble. Luke's the older one, the one your sister described as having light blue eyes. He's right loco. A meaner bastard never lived—sorry for the blunt language, ma'am, but there ain't no other way to describe him."

"No one's ever caught them?" she asked in surprise and dismay.

"Nope. Luke Harris is crazy but not stupid."

"I guess I don't understand the ways of the West very well," Mary said, unable to keep a note of bitterness out of her voice.

"Word is the Harrises got friends, important ones."

Cal Davis shot a sharp look in the marshal's direction; the reproving glance was not missed by Mary.

"A lot of things have been attributed to those men, but the fact remains that when the time comes for witnesses to step forward, no one ever does."

"Why not?"

She tried to read the expression on the rancher's face. It was a perfect mask. He looked uncomfortable, but she refused to allow the discussion to drop so easily. She turned a questioning look on Marshal Wade.

"The Harrises don't generally leave any witnesses," the marshal said grimly. "And those who might talk are too damned scared. Mostly, they ride back and forth from Mexico free as birds. Them bastards ought to have their privates cut off!" The marshal flushed. "Sorry, ma'am, guess I got carried away."

"It's quite all right, I'm afraid I tend to agree with your assessment."

"We'll do our best to get them. See if your aunt will agree to be a witness if we can bring them to trial."

Cal Davis turned to her. "You'll need a good man here for protection and also to help bring in those crops of yours. I'm going to lend you one of my hands."

"That won't be necessary," she said with some embarrassment. Was there no end to what they would owe this man?

"I've got to insist. We are neighbors, after all. Billy Travers will help you." Cal Davis pointed to the tall, young man who'd stayed at some distance. "Billy's on the mend from a broken leg. Doc says he shouldn't be doing much riding for a while until it's completely healed. You can trust the boy. He's all right. He'll do whatever he's told and won't be any kind of bother or trouble to you. And if there is any problem, all you'll have to do is tell me."

For some reason she couldn't quite explain, Mary found herself resenting the tone of voice he was taking with her. But before she could say anything, the rancher signaled to the young cowboy to join them.

"Your folks were sodbusters themselves, weren't they, kid?"

"Sure was," the youth agreed cheerfully with an animated smile. "Had a farm just outside of Lawrence, Kansas." His broad grin betrayed a handsome dimple in his left cheek. He was a big, rawboned fellow who looked as if he would be at home on a farm as well as a ranch.

"Thank you, Mr. Davis, but we'll manage on our own somehow."

"No, you won't. Don't be so stiff-necked," he told her. "Can't you see it would pleasure me to be of help to you?"

The way he was looking at her, so intense and caring, confused her mind. There was something terribly appealing about the man when he behaved this way.

Rebecca came up beside her. "Please let him stay, Cousin Mary. Don't send him away." Rebecca was staring at Billy Travers with more interest then she had shown in anything since her accident four years earlier. It was completely unlike Rebecca to speak up this way—in fact, to speak at all.

"Maybe it would be a good idea to have someone around for a while, just in case. All right, Rebecca." She turned back to Cal Davis. "I have been known to be a bit stubborn from time to time. We'll accept your offer of assistance, Mr. Davis. Thank you for your kindness."

The color rose to his face. "It ain't kindness," he responded. "I just want to make certain if you don't make a go of things, it wasn't any fault of mine."

His candor surprised her. "You still want this land, I take it."

"That's right. I still consider it mine."

Their eyes were opposing magnets.

"I should warn you that we're far from ready to give up. Farming this land may have been Uncle Isaac's dream to start with, but it matters to all of us."

"Whatever you say, Miss MacGreggor."

His smile and the tone of his voice were so patronizing, she was infuriated. She felt like slapping the arrogance from his face. How did he manage to raise such powerful and confusing emotions in her?

She watched the rancher mount his horse and then tip the brim of his Stetson, which was easily four inches wide. His eye caught her own and the look was so frank, so stark in its intensity, that she had to turn away so he wouldn't see her face begin to flush. It occurred to her that having so little experience of men and having been so sheltered from the real world, she hardly knew what to make of Cal Davis, nor did she know how to behave toward him. Without question, he was a complicated and dangerous man. The unsettling thought occurred to her that despite his consideration for them, Cal Davis could be responsible for what happened to her aunt and uncle. She shook her head, wanting to make the ugly suspicion leave her mind. But the thought would not disappear.

CHAPTER FOUR

To Mary's astonishment, she found Billy Travers working hard from the first day he was with them. He seemed to know exactly what needed to be done without anyone telling him. In the weeks that followed, he continued to work with the energy and strength of several men. Besides being tireless, he was always cheerful, whistling and singing one tune after another as he worked.

Mary had to admit that Cal Davis had done them yet another kindness by placing Billy on their farm. After the shock and tragedy of what happened, the presence of this affable young man made life much more bearable.

Jeremy began to look up to Billy as if the cowboy was an older brother, and this seemed to make the loss of his father somewhat less wrenching for the boy.

"I been on my own since I was your age," Billy said.

"How old are you now?" Jeremy asked.

"Eighteen years. I been managing all right without family, but still, it's nice to be with one again." He gave them a warm smile.

With Mary and Elizabeth, he was polite and respectful. He joked with Amy quite a bit and made her giggle. Adoration glowed in the child's eyes. But the person who benefited most from Billy's presence was Rebecca. Billy paid her special attention and she thrived on it. She followed him around as he worked and tried to help him as much as she could. He, in turn, spoke to her constantly, never seeming to mind that she rarely answered; he apparently understood that she was listening, intent on his every word. Mary thought if anyone could bring Rebecca out of herself, it would be Billy Travers.

Only one thing bothered Mary about the young man living at their farm: he was doing a great deal for them, and they were doing nothing in return for him. Mary determined that the situation would change. One evening after supper, she brought up the subject.

"Billy, I think we should be doing something to repay your kindness to us."

"Ma'am, Mr. Davis is payin' me wages. Way he figures it, he wouldn't be lettin' me ride even if I was on the ranch right now. Anyway, I really like it here."

"I'm certain they would find work for you to do back at the ranch if you weren't here."

"How did you break your leg?" Jeremy asked with avid curiosity.

"Horse fell on it."

"What?" Mary said with surprise.

"Oh, it's a fact, all right. I was real lucky. Same thing happened to ol' Slick McCoy last year. Only he weren't as good off as me. Damn horse busted up his inners. Wasn't much Doc could do for him. He was a long time dyin'. Doc set my leg right on the trail, and it's been mendin' real good. I hardly even limp no more." He gave them his usual good-natured grin.

"Do you like working for Mr. Davis?" Why she should ask such a question, she couldn't say, but she did find herself thinking about Cal Davis, whether she wanted to or not.

"He's a fine man. I had lots of different jobs, but workin' for him is the best thing ever come my way. Guess there ain't no one hereabouts that don't respect him. Way I see it, he deserves to own all them thousands of acres and beeves."

Mary inclined her head politely, impressed by Billy's praise of the rancher, but feeling it best to reserve judgment regarding Mr. Davis. The fact was, she did not find the man altogether trustworthy, although she had to concede that he had been very generous with them. Still she questioned his motives and sensed he was a very complex individual whose personal ambivalence was not to be easily understood—unlike Billy, who appeared open and candid.

"You still haven't told us what we can do to repay you."

The youth's face took on an expression of embarrassment. "Well, Miss Mary, truth be told, there's only one thing in my life I've always been sorry I didn't have. Hope you folks won't fun me none, but I never did learn how to read or write and wish I had. I know you teach all those children, and I kind of wish there was some way you could teach me too. 'Course I'm old to be startin' school, even if I did have the time."

"Older people often learn more quickly because they're serious about wanting to learn and they appreciate the value of an education. Therefore, they are more apt students. It would be my pleasure to help you. We can have a lesson every night after supper."

Billy's face lit up. "Thank you, ma'am!"

As Mary thought, Billy learned quickly because he was eager and well-motivated. He seemed happier than ever and worked even harder around the farm. Rebecca too was changing. Often when Mary returned from school, she would find Rebecca working in the kitchen humming or singing one of Billy's songs. Rebecca still rarely spoke, but the girl was much improved.

Only Elizabeth was miserable; her depression was as depthless and boundless as the ocean. Mary could not help but worry about her aunt. Mary had taken Jeremy aside and cautioned him to check often on his mother while she was away at school each day. Mary feared her aunt would die—maybe by her own hand. Jeremy understood and shouldered the responsibility manfully.

Elizabeth tended to confine herself to her small bedroom instead of coming out into the main room where the rest of the family gathered and slept. Her aunt took little interest in what was going on around her, leaving the burden of household chores to Rebecca and Amy. Elizabeth's appetite was poor, and her clothes began to hang on her gaunt frame. Once or twice, Mary caught her aunt holding a butcher knife and staring at the sharp edge. Mary couldn't deny it frightened her. She tried talking to Elizabeth, but with little result.

"Do you want to go back to New Jersey?" she eventually asked her aunt.

Elizabeth gave no indication she'd heard the question.

"If going back is what you want, we can leave here any time you choose. Maybe things would be better for you in the East. It might be easier to put this horrible time behind you. You need to take an interest in living again."

"It doesn't matter," Elizabeth responded forlornly. "Without Isaac, what's the difference where I live? Nothing matters. It would have been just as well if those horrible men had killed me too. I feel as though I'm dead anyway."

"You cannot mean that!"

"I certainly do." Elizabeth's hazel eyes filled with an overwhelming sorrow. "Without Isaac, I don't want to go on living. You know better than anyone else how much I loved him. I hardly remember what life without him was like. I'd just turned seventeen when we were married. Without him, I have no life. Stay or go, it's all the same to me. I do not care." Elizabeth spoke in a monotone.

Mary placed her arm around her aunt's shoulder. "This farm was Isaac's dream. Perhaps we should stay and try to make it work, if only so that his tragic death should not be in vain."

"I'm very tired. I just want to lie down and be left alone."

Mary obeyed her aunt's wishes, hoping that maybe time would help to heal Elizabeth's wounds. Mary did her best to encourage her aunt and help with the children in every way she knew how. Elizabeth's physical wounds were healing. Mary wasn't certain the emotional one ever could.

Cal Davis paid a visit to the farm right before the time came for harvesting. At first, she thought he'd come to reclaim Billy. It was a Sunday morning, bright and early, and Mary thought with some embarrassment that she hadn't even had time to brush her hair or pin it up. Amy had gone to the door of the cabin to let the rancher in. He followed her into the cabin, removing his hat as entered. His eyes settled on Mary.

"Hello, Miss MacGreggor. Nice day, isn't it?" His voice was quiet and controlled.

"The Lord has given us a fine Sabbath," she replied, hoping she did not sound as flustered as she felt by his unexpected visit. "Have you come for some special purpose?"

He smiled at her bluntness. "Just to find out how your aunt is doing. Have her bruises healed up all right?"

"The ones on the outside have. Won't you take a chair, Mr. Davis? I'll bring you a cup of coffee and a biscuit."

He shook his head, a lock of light brown hair falling across his forehead. "No, I'm fine. Ate not long ago."

"I don't suppose you've heard anything about those men. Has the marshal been able to find them?"

His eyes in the darkness of the cabin seemed to take on the color of wild blueberries and met her own with jolting directness.

"Not much he can do right now, sorry to say. They probably crossed over the border into Mexico again. They're safe from our laws as long as they stay there. But they'll come back. They always do. And then we'll get 'em. There's a sizable reward. Someone's gonna try to collect it sooner or later."

"Hasn't anyone ever tried to claim it before?"

He frowned. "Not and lived to tell about it."

"And you think they will be brought to justice? Forgive me if I sound skeptical."

"We'll get them. Tell your aunt that for me."

"I wonder." Her voice delivered a challenge, and she saw his complexion turn as red as rare beef roast.

"Don't attempt to stand in judgment," he warned her. "We do get things done."

"I don't think anyone around here really cares about what happened."

"I care." His piercing eyes looked angrily into her own, returning her challenge.

She set her own level gaze into his. "I'm a stranger in the West, Mr. Davis. I don't always know who or what to believe."

"I can understand that," he said, his voice softening. "I've been disillusioned with people in my life too. I don't trust easy either. But I'm not a liar, Miss MacGreggor." He looked away from her. "There's something I came by to tell you. Some folks want to get together to worship on Sundays. They come to me about it. It wouldn't be anything formal. But they were thinking the schoolhouse would be a good place for prayer meetings. Of course, it would have to meet with your approval."

"I think it's a wonderful idea, and you didn't need my approval. After all, you built the school. Do you have someone to conduct the services?"

He brushed his hair back from his long forehead. "There's Peter Jenkins."

"Is he a man of God?"

She studied his face; the rough-hewn features looked as if

they were chiseled out of solid granite. She could see the muscles rippling under his blue chambray shirt. She looked at his brown Stetson and then down at his dusty boots. He was every inch a cowboy. He truly looked as if he belonged to this wild, untamed country. Yet there were qualities of a gentleman about him as well.

"Reckon we're all men of God, Miss MacGreggor, just some of us are more in His image than others. Peter Jenkins studied for the ministry but he never completed. Still, he knows enough. He's a homesteader, like you folks."

"I was used to attending formal services in the church back home, but I'm certain this will do just fine. I'll be glad to help in any way I can," she said.

"Good. I'll let you know when we're ready to get started." He got up to leave, then hesitated and looked at her for a moment as if he had something more to say, but thought better of it.

She walked him outside into the golden sunlight. He ran his hand over his sun-streaked hair and placed his hat back on his head. He was very close to her, so close that she could smell his scent. He actually smelled fresh and clean, not of horses and cows as he had before. She realized with some surprise that he must have taken a bath especially to visit her.

Trying not to look at him, she found herself unable to help a sideways glance. He looked very handsome in his neat blue chambray shirt and leather vest. With his good looks and tall, erect bearing, Cal Davis had an aristocratic air that would have made him stand out anywhere.

Suddenly, he was turning to her and smiling. "I really would like to get to know you better."

Before she could think how to answer him, he was taking her into his arms and kissing her. She really meant to pull away from him. It was in her mind to do that very thing, but her body couldn't seem to move. Her heart started to pound like a hammer. His lips were warm and moist on hers, and then he was releasing her.

"Sorry. I guess I shouldn't have done that." He sounded embarrassed.

She watched him ride away in something of a daze. The men of the West, she decided, were a lot different from Easterners. They lived by a different set of principles and values, she supposed. Maybe it had something to do with the land itself. The vastness and the emptiness of it influenced people. The land gave the people freedom, independence, and a sense of pride. People seemed to make their own rules out here. She stared out as far as she could see. Under the enormous azure sky, the Arizona earth stood old, wrinkled, and thirsty, yet somehow grand.

A thought occurred to her: No one could own the land; it owned them.

Mary did her best not to think of Cal Davis, which proved awfully difficult. Yet she knew that the main thing now was the business of survival. Mary realized she wanted to succeed with the farm for her own sake, as well as for her relatives. Every cent she had in the world had been invested, gambled on this new life. There really wasn't anything for her back in New Jersey. She would have gone back if Elizabeth had wanted it, but her aunt was too despondent to care. Isaac's dream was now her dream. Mary was committed to making crops grow in the desert.

Mary also understood that life in the West was difficult and dangerous and uncertain at best. She was a practical person who realized that if their family were to endure this kind of existence, they would have to adapt to the new way of life. She had already learned one thing: it didn't matter how big or strong a person was if one knew how to shoot a gun effectively. Out here, that served as an equalizer. With that in mind, she reasoned it was time to learn about using weapons. The visit the Harris gang had paid to the farm was never far from her mind. She didn't want her family to ever again be at the mercy of evil outlaws. Her father used to say God helps those who help themselves. She refused to allow her family to be victimized further.

One day after school had ended for the day, Mary visited the general store, bought some needed supplies, and decided to have a talk with Zeb Jones.

"If a woman were to want to purchase a gun, what would be a good choice?"

Mr. Jones looked at her in surprise. "Well, little lady, what kind of weapon did you have in mind."

She felt very much like telling him that she was not a little lady but decided to hold her tongue. "Do you happen to have any repeating rifles?"

"Not many in stock right now. They sell out fast, and what I do have costs dear."

"Just how much?" she asked with unflinching eyes.

"Almost as much as you'll earn from your first crop."

She stared at him in surprise. "Why so much?"

"Lots of reasons," he said, licking his thick lips. "Army takes a big supply. You know we got Injun trouble. Government tries to discourage too many repeating rifles coming into the territory. Afraid of gun runners I reckon."

"Well, what would you suggest then?"

The storekeeper fidgeted and rubbed his mustache. "How about a handgun? I got a real nice thirty-eight here that would suit a lady like yourself just fine." He showed her the weapon.

"What about something bigger?"

"It would be heavier," he warned.

"I'll learn how to use it," she said with determination.

59

"Suit yourself, Miss MacGreggor," the storekeeper said with a disapproving shrug. He brought out a Colt .45 and a box of bullets.

She asked for a second box as well and then promptly paid the bill.

"Want me to wrap this for you?" Mr. Jones asked.

"No, I'll just take it as is." As she turned to leave the store, she almost collided with someone. Strong arms went out to steady her.

She looked up into the face of Wolf Raullins who tipped his hat to her and smiled.

"Sorry, my fault," she said politely.

"Glad you think so. Wouldn't want you shooting me." His voice teased her as if he thought it very amusing that she would be carrying a firearm.

"I don't know how to use this revolver yet, Mr. Raullins, but I have every intention of learning to protect myself and my family."

"Yes, ma'am, I believe you do. I sure do admire a woman with spirit." He continued to smile at her, although she could have sworn it was more like a leer. Yet it was hard to feel anger at his lack of manners, because the man really was attractive in a kind of primeval way, and she realized he meant little more than to express admiration for her. Still her cheeks felt very hot as she reached the street.

In the weeks that followed, Billy taught her as much as she taught him. Billy was competent with a six-shooter. Mary was determined to know as much as he did when they were finished. She also made certain that Jeremy practiced with them. Billy would set up targets for practice. At first, she couldn't hit a single one. But gradually, she improved.

"You just have to keep your eye on the target," Billy explained to her. "Use a two-handed grip to keep steady. Concentrate and let your hands follow your eyes. Now squeeze easy on the trigger."

She followed his instruction and hit the tin can he had set for her.

"Not bad," he responded with a nod of approval.

Billy kept reminding her to fix her eyes, and pretty soon, her aim became accurate. She found she did better using both hands for a firm, steady grip because she wasn't as strong as Billy or Jeremy. But eventually she became more confident, and it was a good, reassuring feeling. She didn't tell Billy or Jeremy how she pretended each target represented a member of the Harris gang, which helped her aim.

Billy was also learning. Although not the most brilliant of students, he worked assiduously, and it wasn't long before he could read, write, and even do sums. Rebecca looked at the young man with loving eyes, and there was no question in Mary's mind that he had become an important part of their family and the center of Rebecca's universe.

Mary gradually began to believe what had happened at the farm would never happen again. Life seemed to being going along peacefully enough. The Harrises had not known the Staffords; what occurred must have been a random occurrence. Surely, they could expect never to be bothered again.

In fact, the most unusual event in some time occurred when Nora Metford, the wife of a large rancher, visited with her briefly before picking up her two daughters from school one afternoon. They had met before, but generally someone from the ranch came in to pick up the girls. Mrs. Metford waited until the other children were gone and Mary's responsibilities were over for the day.

"I wanted to invite you to our ranch for a party come next Saturday evening. We'd like to include your whole family since you are new folks out here."

"A party?" Mary repeated in some surprise.

Mrs. Metford smiled through crooked teeth. "My oldest son got himself a bride, and we're having a party to celebrate and introduce her around. We thought it would be nice to have neighbors coming by. And you are our schoolteacher."

"That would be lovely, and of course I'll accept. It was very nice of you to think of us."

Mrs. Metford flushed and lowered her eyes. "Well, I can't take much of the credit. When my husband invited Mr. Davis, he suggested that your family be included. Of course," she hastened to add, "we thought it was a good idea too."

Cal Davis again! What was the man up to? She really felt like declining the invitation now, but that would be too embarrassing. All the way home, as Amy talked on about how wonderful it would be to go to a party, Mary turned the question over in her mind: why was Cal Davis being so nice to her? He did seem to be attracted to her, just as she was to him, she had to admit. Mary knew she should feel flattered, but instead she felt uneasy and troubled. If only she had more experience with men!

Elizabeth was as unenthusiastic about the party as Mary was, but Amy's excitement was contagious. Soon Jeremy, Billy, and even Rebecca were looking forward to the evening away from the farm.

On Saturday, Elizabeth announced that she wanted to be left at home by herself.

"We can't let you do that," Mary told her. "It wouldn't be safe."

"They can't do much more to me then they've already done," her aunt responded bitterly.

"We'll all stay home then," Mary said.

At that, Amy began to cry, and Elizabeth experienced a change of heart. "All right, we'll all go, but please don't expect me to be in any kind of gay mood."

Amy kissed her mother happily. "Thank you, Mama!"

On Saturday evening, everyone dressed in their best clothing. Elizabeth insisted on wearing her black dress as befitted a widow, but she did allow Mary to fix a cameo brooch at the neck. Mary had one green silk dress that she liked particularly because it accented the copper in her russet curls. The neckline was low and perfect for a party. She had seen the gown at the dressmaker's when she selected her usual plain, drab clothing. On a whim, she had opted for the dress, feeling foolish and frivolous because she knew there was no place she could wear it, and now finally, after three years of admiring it hanging in her wardrobe closet, she would wear this special garment after all. It brought a smile to her lips.

Jeremy waited impatiently for the ladies to get ready. Billy grinned appreciatively when he saw them and whistled softly. "I never seen such beautiful ladies," he said.

"Even me?" Amy asked shyly.

"Especially you," he returned, swinging her around and making the little girl laugh happily.

The party at the Metfords was not in the ranch house, but in a large barn that had been prepared for guests. It was brightly lit with lanterns, and they could hear fiddles playing as Billy pulled the wagon up in front of the place. They were welcomed at the door by several people Mary didn't know, but everyone seemed polite. Billy made an effort to tell them who everyone was, and Mary tried hard to remember. It wasn't very long before she realized that everyone present was involved in cattle ranching.

"Billy," she asked finally, "will the farm families be coming later, do you think?"

He gave her an embarrassed shrug. "Maybe they won't be coming at all. Might not even have been invited. See, Miss

Mary, homesteaders and ranchers don't always get along."

She bit down on her lower lip, feeling that she had made a mistake in having the family come to this party. Well, she would just have to make the best of things and then arrange to leave as early as possible.

She caught sight of Cal Davis dancing with a pretty young girl and thought with a strange pang that they made a very attractive couple.

Billy saw her looking in Cal's direction. "That's Lorette Wheeler," he said. "She's right popular, not just because she's easy on the eyes though. Mr. Wheeler's got almost as big a spread as Mr. Davis. Myself, I don't think she holds a candle to Rebecca."

Billy smiled over at Mary's cousin, whose eyes warmed. "May I have a dance with you?" he asked Rebecca.

The smile faded from Rebecca's face and she shook her head violently.

"If you don't know how, don't worry. I don't dance much better than the steers I generally herd."

"Go on," Mary urged. "I'm sure Billy is a good teacher."

Rebecca accepted shyly, letting Billy lead her out to where the other couples danced. Jeremy invited his mother to dance, but after she refused, he whirled Amy around for a time, much to her delight.

"I'm going to sit down," Elizabeth told Mary, sounding despondent.

"Would you like me to bring you some punch?"

Elizabeth shook her head. "No, I'll just watch the dancing."

Mary was standing by herself, enjoying the sound of the spirited country music when someone took her hand. She turned to see Wolf Raullins smiling at her.

"How are you this evening?"

She replied that she was fine, carefully removing her hand

from his, and waited for him to continue the conversation. But all he did was keep looking at her until she finally averted her gaze in some confusion.

"Has anyone ever told you that's it's rude to stare?"

"It might have been mentioned a time or two."

"Do the ranchers have many parties like this?" she asked.

"Some. I don't usually get invited, so I don't know much about it."

"This is my first party too."

He looked surprised. "A pretty woman like you, I imagine you've had lots of admirers."

"None," she replied. "I hardly left my home from the time I was fifteen. My father was an invalid, and I was the one who took care of him."

"Never would have guessed it. You've got a way about you."

She smiled at his praise. "What about you? Have you had much of a social life?"

He laughed softly. "White men consider me an Injun, while native people know I'm a half-breed and not one of them either. Wasn't so bad when I was little, because I had my mother, and my father taught me everything he knew about cow-punching."

"Your mother was an Indian?"

"Cheyenne. She was a beautiful woman and a good mother besides." His gray eyes sparked with pride.

"Have you decided which world you want to belong to?"

"Guess that's going to depend."

"On what?"

He didn't answer her question, merely flashing an enigmatic smile.

People started to line up for square dancing. "Want to join in?" he asked.

She shook her head. "It looks like a lot of fun, but I really don't know how, and I'm not certain I want to learn in public."

"Can't say that I blame you. Want to take a walk with me—or do you think that might compromise your reputation?"

"I don't see how."

"There's not a woman in this room who would be caught dead talking to me."

"Why would that be?"

"Because I'm a breed," he clarified sharply. "So if you'd be embarrassed or ashamed, I'd understand. You just say, and I'll walk away and leave you be. There's plenty of men in this room itchin' to ask you to dance with them. In case you haven't noticed, there are a lot more men than women in these parts. You can pick and choose."

She looked into his intense face and realized how truly awful prejudice was. "I tend to judge people on their own merits." She placed her hand on his arm, stiffened her posture, and they walked toward the door together. Outside, the night was growing colder, and Mary drew her shawl tightly around her body.

"I admire character."

"You're a very interesting man, Mr. Raullins. I like the way you say exactly what you think."

"You can count on that from me," he said.

"Wolf, could you go inside? Mr. Wheeler is looking for you. He wants to ask about those new harnesses you ordered."

With a sideways look at Mary, the foreman left her with Cal Davis.

There was an awkwardness between them. She glanced at him appraisingly. He looked particularly handsome tonight, well-dressed, his hair trimmed neatly. But no matter how gentlemanly his outward appearance, there was always an edge of danger about the man.

"Didn't know you favored Wolf," he said. His voice was taut and disapproving. "I saw you come out here with him. I don't think that was wise. You'll bring trouble on yourself."

"Why?" She hugged her body, feeling a sudden chill.

"Wolf's a good man, but he's—"

"If he's worthy enough to be your foreman, why should he be unworthy of any woman who will have him?"

She saw him frown and his hands fist at his sides. "I'm no bigot. I'd never have made Wolf foreman at the Thunderbolt if I were. I just hate to see you acting like a fool." His tone was stiff and cold.

She could remember him now as the rude man who had called her uncle a fool on the first day they met. Anger swept over her.

"Why did you want us here anyway? It's obvious we don't belong."

"Maybe I just wanted to see you again on a social occasion," he said, his tone softening. "You look right pretty in that dress."

"I thought you were too busy dancing with Miss Wheeler to notice me."

She saw a wry smile form at the corner of his lips. "Why, ma'am, if I didn't know better, I'd swear you sound jealous."

"I'm not the least bit jealous," she snapped at him. "The fact is, we don't really know each other, and we're not likely to either."

"Well, maybe I should remedy that this evening." With that, his hand took hers and pulled her away from the lights.

"Where exactly do you intend taking me?" she asked in an alarmed voice. With only the moon and stars to light his face, she could not see the expression that was there.

"Maybe a ride in the moonlight, so we can talk a little. Would you object to that?"

It hardly seemed to matter what she thought, Mary noted with some indignation, for the next thing she knew, he was lifting himself into the saddle of his horse and pulling her up in front of him. She felt the muscularity of his chest against her back, his thighs curving around her, one hand pressing against her waist. She couldn't help but catch her breath as he began riding along.

"Where are we going?"

"Just a little ways from here. You'll like it fine."

They didn't speak again until they'd reached the summit of a hill and dismounted. The view even at night was beautiful. She could see a waterfall moving like a veil and emptying into a stream below that shimmered silver in the moonlight.

"It is beautiful," she said in awe.

"Some real nice country out here," he agreed. "Thought you might like to see it."

There was something magical about this view, she thought. But it was chilly up here and the wind cut right through the thin clothing she wore, making her shiver.

"Cold, huh?" He rubbed his hands up and down her arms, making her shiver even more. He pulled her into his arms and held her close.

"You're a mighty fetching woman." He tried to kiss her, but she pulled free of him. She hurried back to his horse. He was there ahead of her, his hand on her arm preventing her movement.

"And you're also a tease, Miss MacGreggor."

She shook her head, trying to shake off a sense of dazed confusion. Cal Davis climbed into the saddle and then pulled her up behind him. He raced back to the party, and she was forced to hold on to him not to fall off.

He didn't say a word when they returned to the Metford barn, leaving Mary standing outside by herself. So much for chivalry. She fixed her gown carefully and tried to smooth the upswept curls of her hair, aware that she must look rather unkempt. There was nothing for it except to return to the party and let people think whatever they wished.

Elizabeth must have been keeping an eye out; her aunt joined her immediately. "Where have you been? I was starting to worry."

"I was outside," she replied, not willing to say more.

Elizabeth furrowed her brow. "You look flushed. Are you running a fever?"

"I just might be," she answered.

"I'm sorry we came," Elizabeth said.

"Have these people been unfriendly?"

Her aunt closed her eyes wearily for a moment. "Not really, but I have nothing in common with them. I feel uncomfortable here. Oh well, at least the children are having a good time." Elizabeth nodded her head in the direction of Jeremy and Rebecca who were dancing together while Amy happily swayed to the music.

Mary glanced in the direction of the ranch families. Deke Norris was talking to another rancher she didn't know. They both glanced in the direction of Elizabeth and her. Their expressions were far from friendly. For a moment, the thought flashed through Mary's mind that one of the ranchers might have encouraged the Harris gang to visit their farm. But no, such an idea was absurd. Why would anyone send vicious murderers to kill a small farmer like her uncle? It made no sense at all. Mary decided she was becoming too suspicious and fearful.

At that moment, an argument erupted between, of all people, Billy and another young man close to his own age. Billy was dancing with Miss Wheeler when the other youth interrupted them.

"Get away from my sister, you lowdown varmint!" The youth had a contemptuous sneer that Mary regarded with disgust. His words slurred as if he were intoxicated.

Billy turned to Miss Wheeler. "Since Ned's one of your brothers, I won't respond, Lorette." He nodded his head politely and started to move away, but Ned Wheeler wasn't having any of it. He let loose with a blow that caught Billy solidly in the chest. Mary could hear the wind knocked out of the boy. Yet before another moment passed, Billy came back with a powerful punch to his antagonist's midsection. Ned Wheeler lay doubled up and moaning on the straw at Billy's feet. Cal Davis and Mr. Metford rushed to get between the two boys and prevent any further trouble.

"That's not the end of this, Travers," Wheeler warned, red-faced and breathing hard.

"I believe it's time we were going," Mary said.

She hurriedly went and gathered up Billy, who looked murderous, ready to exchange further blows. Cal Davis shot a hostile look in her direction that she chose to ignore. Elizabeth helped Mary get the three children, and they settled into the wagon faster than she ever thought possible.

No, Mary reflected on the drive home, it hadn't been the kind of evening she'd anticipated. She thought of the feel of Cal Davis's hands on her body and began to tremble in spite of herself. She vowed never to let herself be alone with the man again, for in spite of his outward manners, he was obviously not a gentleman. The worst part was she wasn't certain she could trust herself to behave like a lady with him. The thought occurred to her that as a homesteader, it would be best to avoid contact with the ranchers as much as possible.

Chapter Five

It was very early in the morning on the day they were to start harvesting when Mary heard the din just outside the cabin and went to see what was going on.

Apparently, Billy had been shaving and Rebecca had slipped behind him to watch. He turned and grabbed her and she began to thrash about, knocking over some of the farm equipment.

"Sorry, you went and gave me a start, Becky. You shouldn't sneak up on a fella that way. No, now don't go running off like a frightened doe!"

Billy caught Rebecca again and Mary wondered if she ought to interfere, but then thought better of it. She hadn't altered her opinion that Billy was good for her young cousin. Yet she watched them cautiously from her vantage near the open door.

"You know I wouldn't ever hurt you," Billy told Rebecca, "so how come you watch me all the time, but you never talk to me?"

Rebecca didn't respond but made a move to leave him; Billy held her wrists tightly.

"You come outside to watch me shave before. Today's not the first time. Either I'm real strange-looking or you like me a little. I want you to talk to me."

Rebecca shook her head.

"It's okay to be shy, but you know I like you a lot."

That brought a smile to Rebecca's lips. "Can't talk. Mama says best I don't."

"Why is that?" Mary could see the puzzlement on Billy's face.

"I'm addled."

"Come again?" Poor Billy didn't have a clue as to what Rebecca was talking about.

"I'm not right in the head. I was touched a long time ago."

"Whoever told you a thing like that?"

"Mama did. Other folks too. That's why it's best if I don't say much. For my own good, so folks won't snicker."

"Shoot! You seem just fine to me. Anyway, who's got the right to say what's normal and what ain't? Don't you go believin' what other folks say. They don't live inside of you. They can't know what's in your head. My ma always claimed that I was dumber than a dog and only fit to slop hogs. Well, she'd surely be surprised now if she could see me learnin' how to read and write and cipher and such. You're a fine person, Becky. You're not like any other girl I've ever known, but that's all right. Fact is, I like you better. You just talk to me any time you feel like it. I'll be pleased to listen, and I won't snicker neither."

Rebecca gave him a warm smile and Billy touched her fine, blond hair, which was the color of husked corn. Then Billy took Rebecca in his arms and kissed her. At that moment, Mary quietly walked away and allowed them a measure of privacy. She thought the feelings these two young people were beginning to share with each other could only benefit both of them. It seemed to Mary that if the relationship grew stronger, Rebecca would have a chance at a normal life.

Everyone was in a good mood over breakfast that morning. Jeremy had already been out surveying the fields.

"We're going to bring in a good first harvest," he told them. "We've got potatoes, corn, wheat, and some alfalfa. Next year, we can diversify more. That's what Pa planned. We can expand our fields to include oats and barley. Bet we could even sell that around here."

"Considering the kind of land you've got to work with," Billy observed, "this harvest is kind of a miracle."

"We can make things grow out here," Jeremy said, sounding to Mary very much the way Isaac had. "You'll see."

Everyone helped with the harvesting and when they were finally done, Mary took Jeremy and Billy with her to see about selling it.

"I feel real good about you including me in the negotiations," Billy told her. "Like you consider me part of your family."

"We all do," Mary told him.

As it turned out, they had to deal with the railroad; there was no other choice. It seemed that the railroad owned all the grain elevators along the sidings. The alternative—that of shipping the crops to market—wasn't really practical. The shipping costs were exorbitant.

Mary met with a Mr. Bridges, a willowy man in a dark suit who was operating through the bank. Apparently, he and Mr. Pemrose orchestrated their business negotiations to benefit each other, and he had an office next to that of the banker.

"I don't understand why the shipping costs should be so high," Mary told the man bluntly.

He gave her a smug smile, his narrow eyes becoming nothing more than slits. "That's just the way it is, ma'am. Everybody knows that freight charges west of Saint Louis are four times what they are in the East."

"That's nothing short of robbery! The railroad is taking advantage of the small farmer."

"Resent it all you like, but it won't change anything. Frankly, there's no one else to whom you can sell."

She turned away and suddenly saw that Cal Davis was standing in the doorway attentively listening to her conversation with the railroad representative.

"Can I do anything to help you?" he asked in a soft, smooth voice, which somehow only served to increase her ire.

"No, Mr. Davis, I am not a dimwit. I can sell my own crop. Just attend to your own business."

"Just as you wish, Miss MacGreggor," he responded coldly, turning away from her.

"I think you railroad people are a bunch of thieves, but I'll sell to you this time because I don't see any other choice."

"At least you've managed to harvest a crop," Bridges said. "That's better than many of the other farmers out here."

"I hope in the future to make other arrangements," she snapped.

The amount of money they would realize from the sale was a terrible disappointment, considering all the hard work that had been involved. She could only hope in the future they would be able to find buyers among those living in the area. Certainly, she reasoned, at the very least, the ranchers would need feed for their horses.

As she walked away from the railroad representative, Mary saw that Cal Davis was talking to Billy and her cousin Jeremy. The rancher was handing Billy some money.

"Just as well that I pay you now," he was telling the young man. "I came in today to pick up the payroll for the men. I guess you want your wages too."

Billy grinned. "Thank you, Mr. Davis." He took the bills that were being handed to him and then turned to Mary.

"Now that the backbreaking work is done for a time, do you mind if I treat myself to a few hours in town? I kind of feel like celebrating. Not that there's much to do in Expectation, but I wouldn't mind having a drink or two in the saloon."

Mary frowned at him, but she knew that she had no right to tell the young man what to do. "Of course. We'll see you back at

74

the farm later. Take care," she said and turned quickly to leave
the bank with Jeremy close behind her.

Cal Davis called after her and she turned to look at him.

"Just a suggestion," he said, "but in the future, you might
want to negotiate along with several other people. You'll get a
better price break that way."

"You think so?"

"I've had my own dealings with the railroad," he replied with
a deep frown.

Their eyes met; the way he looked at her made her blush and
quickly turn away. Why did he have that effect on her?

Cal Davis watched Mary MacGreggor leave the bank. He knew
she was upset about the deal she had just made with Will
Bridges for her crops. The truth was, he could have helped her
do better, but she'd shown such stubborn determination that he
decided to keep out of it. Although he was still angry with her,
he couldn't help but admire her spunk. Cal couldn't bring
himself to give up on her, though why he felt that way, he
couldn't say. But there was something about her, something
that made him want her, even if it didn't make any sense. Who
was he kidding? Every time he was near her, even for a few
minutes, he felt his body react. A man who'd managed to live
thirty years ought to know better. Why not call it what it was? It
was lust, pure and simple; he desired the woman.

Cal met Billy Travers again in the general store as Billy picked
out some ribbons from a selection Zeb Jones displayed for him.

"Got yourself a lady friend?" he asked Billy.

The kid grinned widely and colored. "Well, I'd like her to be.
Think she'll like these ribbons?"

"Girls generally do," Cal told him.

Cal had some other business to attend to at the livery stable
before heading back to the ranch. The last place he visited was

the saloon, deciding to have a quick drink before going back on the trail. That was where he ran into Billy again. The boy was drinking whiskey and obviously it wasn't his first.

"I'd take it easy on the rotgut if I were you," he warned Billy.

"Guess you're right, Mr. Davis," the kid agreed. "I forgot about lunch today and I'm beginning to feel this stuff dancing around in my head."

Cal gave his own order to the bartender and turned back to the boy. "You like working at the farm?"

"Sure do. The Staffords are real nice folks, and Miss Mary's educating me so I won't be ignorant no more."

"I guess I can afford to let you stay out there another month or so if they need you."

The bartender and proprietor, Ike Barnett, handed Cal a shot glass of whiskey and he downed it quickly, even as it burned his throat. He could feel the drink warming his stomach and thought that he might just order another, although he rarely drank at all.

There was a poker game going on, and he ended up watching it with some detachment. A professional gambler was running the show, an elegant figure dressed in a neat, black broadcloth suit and a white linen shirt with a wing collar. Around his neck he wore a black silk cravat and on top of his head was a black felt slouch hat. Cal heard the others at the table refer to him as "the deacon," and he smiled to himself. The deacon muttered a foul curse whenever he lost a hand. Cal felt certain this man was no more of a clergyman than old Ike, who cussed worse than anyone else he knew.

It was early in the day and the saloon was fairly empty. Neither of Ike's girls was around either, probably still in bed after a long night of heavy carousing with paying customers, he thought. He might have liked them being around right at the moment, but it was probably just as well that they weren't. If anything, he wanted to try to forget about women. They only brought a man grief.

There were five men in the poker game, and after a time, one of the cowboys who had been losing steadily left. The gambler looked around for new blood and Cal turned away, ordering his second drink. Apparently, the deacon caught Billy's attention.

"Hey, kid, you play poker?"

"Sometimes."

"If you got the money, you're welcome to join."

Billy shrugged. "I ain't much for gamblin'."

Cal thought the kid's response was a good one but said nothing one way or another.

"Hell, he's nothin' but a dumb cowpoke turned sodbuster. He couldn't play worth a damn if his life depended on it!"

Cal turned to observe Ned Wheeler sneering contemptuously at Billy. He saw the blood rising to Billy's face. Cal didn't have much use for any of the Wheeler men, especially old Sam, and now Ned, the oldest of the Wheeler boys, was turning out even worse than his father.

"You don't have to prove anything to him," Cal said.

But Billy shook his head. "He's insulted me once too often." Walking to the table, Billy sat down in the vacant chair. "I got my wages. I'm in the game."

Ned Wheeler narrowed his eyes, screwing them into bullets. "Boy, you ain't gonna have a cent left when I get finished with you." Wheeler curled his lower lip in a sneer.

"We'll just see about that," Billy said with quiet defiance.

Cal finished his second whiskey, and this time the warmth traveled all the way down to his toes. He felt like leaving the saloon, but he didn't want to desert Billy, who might just need him there. He had a bad feeling about the poker game.

Billy lost the first two hands and was out half of his month's wages.

"Why don't you stop playing now," Cal urged.

"No, sir, I got to play this out," the boy responded.

Cal understood how Billy felt; the Wheeler kid had insulted him in front of other men and even someone with Billy's easygoing disposition wouldn't tolerate that. Even now, Ned was laughing at him.

"You still in, young fella?" the gambler asked.

"Sure. Just deal out the cards, Deacon."

Billy's luck finally changed. He won the next hand and then the hand after that. He and the gambler were both soon well ahead, while Ned Wheeler was the big loser. Wheeler was also drinking heavily and getting meaner by the minute. Finally, after another winning hand for Billy, Ned Wheeler jumped up out of his seat with a face as red as a blood-sun.

"You're cheating, you son of a bitch!"

Billy stood up angrily, gathering his winnings together and putting the money into his pockets. "Time I was leaving," he said, exercising self-control.

"You ain't going nowhere with my money. I'll see you in hell first! You and that tin-horn gambler are in this together, ain't you? I can smell it. Well, nobody gets the best of a Wheeler."

Cal stepped forward. "You're drunk, kid. Go home and sleep it off."

Wheeler gave him a derogatory look but didn't respond. When Cal tried to take his arm, Ned pushed him away.

"He's your man, so you would be on his side."

"I just happened to get lucky," Billy said, trying to sound calm.

"Well, your luck's run out." Wheeler started to reach for his gun, and at that point, the deacon stepped between the two younger men.

"Listen here, fella, no one's cheating you." The deacon opened his black frockcoat, displaying his gun belt.

"That's right," Billy agreed.

"Let's go," Cal said to Billy, and they began to move toward the swinging saloon doors together.

"You make a move to leave and I'll blow your head off!" Wheeler called out.

Cal turned to look at the red-faced youth, and as he did, the gambler put his hand on Wheeler's sleeve in a restraining gesture.

"You played a lousy game, kid. Why don't you just forget it?"

"Deacon, you just run out of aces." Wheeler turned on the gambler and punched him hard in the midsection, sending the slighter man to the floor, doubled over in pain. Then Ned turned back in Billy's direction.

"You and me got something to settle, Travers. I heard that you got a quick draw, but I bet I'm faster."

"Billy's not going to shoot it out with you over a card game, so just forget it," Cal said in a firm voice.

Wheeler curled his lower lip. "This ain't none of your business, Davis. Everybody knows you got him a job working for nesters because he ain't no real kind of man like the rest of us." Wheeler's bloodshot eyes stared viciously at Billy. "You're a stupid, no-account son of a bitch, Travers!"

Billy reached for his gun, pulling out the weapon so fast that Cal couldn't prevent the movement or impede him in any way. The kid shot Ned Wheeler once in the head before Wheeler could even get his gun out of the holster. Cal realized that Wheeler's drunken reflexes had given Billy an edge, but the kid did have a fast draw.

Cal stared down at the young man lying on the floor and there was no doubt in his mind Wheeler was dead, but he made certain just the same. He bent over and felt for a pulse which was nonexistent. Billy just stood there staring at Wheeler in bewilderment.

"I feel sick," Billy said and threw up.

The barroom had fallen into total silence. Cal tried to take Billy's gun, but the youth panicked.

"What are you doing, Mr. Davis?"

"You better hand over that pistol, son, 'cause you're in a heap of trouble," Ike said, moving out from behind the bar.

"What the hell are you talking about! You all saw what happened. It was self-defense. He would have killed me if I didn't shoot him."

Cal could see that Billy was at the breaking point.

"He got you to draw first, so you know there's going to be an inquiry," Cal said. "But there are witnesses. I'll talk for you, kid. You know that." He tried to sound reassuring.

"It don't matter the wrong or right of it," the saloon keeper said. "I don't have to tell you what kind of man Ned's pa is. You better tell the kid the truth, Mr. Davis, for his own protection." Then Ike turned to Billy. "Son, them Wheelers are gonna hang you for sure! You better get your ass out of this territory and never come back. Sam Wheeler's the most vengeful man I ever known. Nobody's gonna kill one of his sons and live to tell about it. You're a dead man if you don't leave pronto!"

Billy's eyes opened wide in terror. "They're gonna lynch me!" he cried out. "Hang me from the nearest cottonwood."

"Billy, listen to me, don't let Ike scare you. It won't be that way. I'll make certain of it."

The kid wasn't listening to him anymore. He was wild-eyed. Billy pushed Cal away from him, holstered his Colt and went running out of the saloon. Cal followed only to see Billy riding as hard as he could out of town, the dust rising high behind him. He could only hope that when Billy calmed down and sobered up, he'd realize the mistake he was making, but Cal entertained no false hopes. Billy Travers was a very frightened young man.

★ ★ ★ ★ ★

Mary knew something was wrong the moment Billy rode up to the farm. Rebecca sensed it too. For one thing, he had been riding very fast; his horse was lathered. For another thing, the color was high in his cheeks. As he came close, she noticed that his breath reeked of alcohol.

Billy reached into a vest pocket and with a shaking hand brought out two ribbons, one yellow and one blue, handing them to Rebecca. "I hope you'll wear these for me."

Rebecca started to cry.

"Don't you like them?" he asked sadly.

"They're beautiful. No one ever gave me ribbons before."

"I got one to match your hair and the other to match your eyes. So you do like them?"

She didn't answer but continued to sob.

"Becky, why are you taking on so?"

"Because you won't be here to see me wear them for you."

Billy pulled the girl into his arms, looking every bit as miserable as she did.

"Is she right?" Mary asked.

By this time, the entire family was gathered around Billy. Even Elizabeth was staring at the young man with concern.

"I shot Ned Wheeler in the saloon today. I killed him. Didn't mean to do it. Never shot anyone before in my entire life. He goaded me though. I don't want to leave you all, but I got to."

Rebecca's face was pale as blanched winter grass. Billy patted her long, golden hair gently with his trembling hands. The girl's eyes were full of pain.

"Don't leave, Billy, please! I'm afraid what could happen to you."

"I don't want to go. You and Mr. Davis think I should stay. He claims he can protect me, but he can't. No one can! Mr.

Wheeler's gonna get his vengeance if I don't go. He'll kill me for sure."

Rebecca's cornflower blue eyes overflowed with sorrow and she shook her head, too choked to speak any further.

"I'll be back. I promise."

"Don't go!" Rebecca cried out.

Billy kissed her lips, then pulled away from her. He went and packed his few belongings, then hurried back to his horse.

"Please take me with you," Rebecca begged.

Elizabeth was about to reprimand her daughter, but Mary shook her head and Elizabeth kept silent.

"You can't come with me. I will come back to you as soon as I can."

"I love you, Billy. Please let me go with you."

"No, I'm a wanted man, and that's no life for you. Truth is, you'd be best off forgetting all about me."

"Never!" she cried as he mounted his horse. "You come back to me, Billy Travers, no matter how long it takes. I'll be waiting."

"I love you too," he called back to her as he rode away, waving a final goodbye.

Mary could not see very well, for there were tears in her eyes too. She could not help but fear what would become of Billy Travers.

CHAPTER SIX

The loss of Billy was yet another blow to the family; perhaps not as devastating as the death of Isaac, but nevertheless, Billy was sorely missed by everyone. Rebecca acted as if her heart had been cut out of her body.

In the short time Billy Travers had been with them, he'd become important to the family. Even Elizabeth missed his cheerful disposition. The atmosphere at the farm became gloomy. No more did Rebecca sing or hum around the kitchen. She ceased to speak. Amy no longer giggled, and Jeremy's shoulders began to stoop. Mary realized that as the only man in the family, Jeremy must feel a heavy weight of obligation and responsibility. Of course, that was a burden she shared. She did whatever she could to make life pleasanter for the others, but it seemed to make very little difference.

October brought life-giving rain, and the creek began to swell again. Mary talked with Jeremy about what they would plant for their next crop and what provisions they would need. She talked to Rebecca as well, trying to draw her out, and urging Amy to do the same. Amy, at least, liked school very much, which helped. It also provided the child with a link to the outside world.

"I always enjoyed school when I was your age," Mary told her cousin. "I liked to read especially. Maybe in the evening, you and I can sit with Rebecca and read to her. It might help her."

Amy readily agreed, and together they began to draw Rebecca out of herself as best they could. Mary knew that no matter what happened, as long as they were alive, they had to make the best of things. Maybe Billy Travers would return one day, but they could not let Rebecca stop living until he did.

Mary was taking to this country better than she thought possible. The immense space, the great expanses of sky and desert, were overwhelming. Occasionally, she wished that she were an artist and could render this unique, rare beauty on canvas. How nice it would be to paint the sunset over the desert. The vivid colors were vibrant, full of fire.

One morning just past daybreak, a band of Indian braves rode up to the cabin. They came quickly, but Mary had time to grab her handgun, which she always kept close by. Jeremy was already out working in the fields, so it was up to her to handle the situation. She felt her heart skip a beat, wondering if they were hostile. Nervously, she bolted the door and waited. Glancing out the window, she saw that the bronze-skinned fellows wore no war paint. She took that as a good sign.

If they had been planning a raid, surely they wouldn't be dismounting as they were doing. Still, she reasoned, it was best to be cautious. She heard one of them trying the door. Then there was a deep masculine voice speaking in English.

"We have hunger. You inside, give us food!"

Normally, she would not hesitate to share food with hungry people. It was the charitable thing to do. But she was not going to open the door if she could help it.

"There's water in the well. Help yourselves to as much as you want. There's game drying on poles and you're welcome to some of that too. But don't try to come into this cabin or we'll shoot you."

She could hear the loud laughter of the one who had done the talking. He obviously didn't respect a woman's words, so she'd just have to back up what she said. Mary stuck her handgun through the window slat and shot a round above the warrior's head.

"That was just a friendly warning," she called out.

When she looked out again, the Indians were moving away from the cabin and walking toward the well. She watched them carefully as they drank deeply, filled their water bags, and then helped themselves to what small game there was. In a matter of minutes, they had jumped on their ponies and were riding swiftly away. She let out a sigh of relief; the Indians were satisfied, she realized, and she had managed not to endanger her life or that of anyone else.

"Mother! Cousin Mary! Are you all right?" Jeremy's breathless voice carried through the cabin door. She unbolted it quickly and let the boy inside. "I just saw Indians riding away. Was there some trouble?"

"We're fine, and no, there wasn't any trouble. They were only looking for food. I hope you don't mind, I let them take those jackrabbits you caught."

Jeremy breathed a sigh of relief. "Cousin Mary, you're becoming more like a pioneer woman every day."

"Not likely," she replied with a wry smile. "I do believe it's time we saw to buying one of those repeating rifles though."

Jeremy nodded his agreement. Elizabeth had just risen from bed and Jeremy told her about their unexpected morning guests. Mary looked from mother to son and thought that Jeremy had his father's eyes but Elizabeth's fair coloring and red gold hair. Somehow he seemed to look more like a man and less like a boy with every day that passed.

Elizabeth was frowning. "Those Indians might have been a raiding party and they could have murdered us all if they wished. It really is impossible out here! The people are so primitive and barbaric. Honestly, Mary, I don't see how you can be so calm about this."

"We'll just have to handle each situation as it comes," she replied.

"I think perhaps it is time we thought about going back East," Elizabeth said.

"We have a commitment here," Jeremy responded, eying his mother sharply.

"We'll see," Elizabeth replied in a tight voice, her lower lip curling.

The following Sunday, church services began in Expectation. Mary, along with her aunt and cousins, put on her best clothes and took the drive into town early that morning after a hasty breakfast. Elizabeth complained a good part of the way about the drive in their open wagon with the sun beating down on their heads.

"I wish we lived closer to town," she said. "I don't know how you do this every day, Mary."

"You get used to it. We'll sew you a better bonnet for protection from the sun."

They crossed the scraggy bush with thickets of mesquite, beds of sand, and thorny cactus, where there was hardly any sign of life. Mary felt strangely at home.

They were right on time for the services, she noticed with some satisfaction. As they seated themselves, Cal Davis came up and looked at Mary.

"That seat taken?" he asked, pointing to the empty place beside her.

She shrugged and looked away from him. But out of the corner of her eye, she could see him watching her with something like amusement. She decided that no more irritating man had ever lived.

"Do I make you uncomfortable?" he asked.

"Not at all," she responded, only realizing after she'd spoken that her voice was too loud.

Elizabeth looked over at her questioningly.

He smiled, a dimple forming in his cheek. "I don't usually have an unsettling effect on women," he said.

Obviously, he was enjoying his little game, she observed with some annoyance. "I'm sure most women just naturally throw themselves at you, Mr. Davis. How could they help themselves?"

Her sarcasm was not wasted on him, she saw with satisfaction.

"It's good to know you appreciate me. Next time we're alone together, should I expect you to throw yourself at me?"

She felt the heat rising to her face; he just had that effect on her and she couldn't manage to control it. Fortunately, the service began and she could look away from him. But several times as Mr. Jenkins spoke of God's love, Cal Davis reached down and took her hand in his. Each time, she quickly extricated her digits and tried to avoid his gaze. She found herself hardly able to concentrate on what was being said. Twice during the hymn singing, she even found herself singing the wrong words, although she knew them perfectly well.

"How did you like the service?" Cal asked, turning to her as it ended.

"I would have liked it a lot better if you hadn't chosen to sit by me."

He gave her a hard look. "You have a very bad effect on me too, but I do my best to fight it."

"Not hard enough." She resented the implication of what he said, as if she were some disease he'd caught and would have to ward off. Was that how he thought of her? But didn't she think of him in a very similar way?

He moved away from her without another word, saying hello politely to Elizabeth and then walking toward some of the ranchers. That was just as well, she decided, because she wanted nothing to do with the man.

The church service had turned out to be something less than inspiring. Still, it did afford them an opportunity to get acquainted with some of their neighbors. Mary thought this was particularly important for Elizabeth, who lived such an isolated existence at the cabin. She believed her aunt's outlook would improve if she had the opportunity to socialize with other people again. Elizabeth had always been very popular back home and had lots of friends with whom she could socialize. Mary knew her aunt could be charming under the right circumstances. After the service, when everyone stood around talking, Elizabeth did become much more relaxed and agreeable.

Mary observed that outside of Cal Davis, most of the people who came were in family units. Cowboys, it seemed, did not attend church on Sunday. But the prayer meeting was an obvious success with the families who had attended.

As they walked out of the school building, Mary noticed that a man was following behind Cal Davis. He put his thick, meaty hand on the rancher's shoulder and tried to spin him around without any success. Davis turned slowly, flashing a look of such hostility that the other man flinched involuntarily as if he'd been punched.

She could see the man was neither a cowboy nor a homesteader simply by the manner in which he dressed, wearing a wide-brimmed sombrero and a brightly colored poncho. Although he dressed in Mexican fashion, his ruddy complexion proclaimed him an Anglo. A large, paunchy stomach protruded over his pants. He was less than medium height and stood in sharp contrast to the tall, lean rancher with his powerful, muscular build.

"Have a word with you, Davis."

Cal Davis gave the man a cold, hard stare. "What exactly do

you want, Phillips?"

"You know damn well!"

The two men faced each other squarely in the dirt street. They were both armed and angry-looking. Mary held her breath, wondering what was going to happen.

"You must know what your boys are doing to my sheep. I don't have to tell you since I expect that you gave the orders." The sheepherder's eyes bulged like those of a bullfrog.

"You're full of your own sheep dip. We don't have any use for your kind, but I never told my men to do anything to your sheep."

"I don't believe you."

"Don't go making accusations unless you first get your facts right." Cal Davis walked quickly away from Phillips, leaving the man standing alone in the dust.

Elizabeth drew Mary's attention back to the group of families clustered together in front of the schoolhouse.

"Mary, do you know Mr. and Mrs. Parker?"

"They've sent me two of their children on occasion."

Mrs. Parker smiled. Her face was round and sun-freckled. "It ain't easy sparing the young'uns from their chores, much as I'd like to send them more for schoolin'. We ought to get better acquainted though. There ain't many farmers out here."

"Why is that, Mrs. Parker?" Mary asked.

"Call me Nancy," the woman said with a warm smile. "It's a hard way to earn a living. Most folks prefer ranching or mining. Our place is near Bill Williams Mountain, not far from the Verde River, in case you want to visit sometime. I reckon our land is more fertile than most. We also got seven big, strapping youngsters to help with the work."

Mary observed that Nancy Parker was no small woman herself. She took a liking to Nancy immediately because of her open, friendly manner.

"The young'uns told me what a fine teacher you are. I'll continue to send them as much as I can."

"They're good children," Mary said, pleased with the compliment Mrs. Parker had given her.

"Well, I meant it when I said I'd like you to come visit us. We don't see folks as much as we'd like."

"Who does?" Elizabeth agreed.

There was so much space and distance between people out here. In some ways, Mary liked it, but she realized that it was not the manner in which Elizabeth had been accustomed to living.

"I thought there would be more farm families here today," Elizabeth remarked.

"Even folks that manage to find good land got other troubles." Nancy cast a furtive glance around. "It's the cattlemen's fault. They don't like us being here, and they do what they can to discourage us. Some folks had their homesteads burned. Farmers were murdered in a couple of places. In one family, a man was shot in the back while bringing a load of supplies back to the farm. Another place, both a man and his wife was lynched. Some blame it on the Injuns. Everyone knows the Apache are vicious. But there's those that don't believe the red men have anything to do with it. A body does well to keep a rifle handy and sleep real light at night, with clothes on."

Mr. Parker, who had little to say up to this point, fidgeted with his mustache and frowned at his wife. "Nancy, you'll be frightening these people unduly."

"Not at all, Drew. We heard what happened to Mrs. Stafford's husband." She turned sympathetically to Elizabeth. "Mrs. Stafford, what happened to you and your husband ain't that unusual around these parts, I'm sorry to say."

Elizabeth shot a look of alarm in Mary's direction.

"Thank you for the warning. We'll be careful," Mary said.

"I didn't realize there were such serious hostilities and tensions existing out here," Elizabeth said. "We were led to believe that what happened to us was an isolated incident."

"That's what they want you to think," Mrs. Parker said.

"Nancy, lower your voice!" her husband said. Mary observed a slight twitch in his right eye.

"Time they found out," Nancy remarked, but lowered her voice to a whisper.

"You think the cattlemen are deliberately setting out to hurt the farmers who try to settle here?" Mary asked.

Nancy shrugged. "Can't rightly say, but it don't really matter. The law's on the side of the cattlemen. Whatever they do to us, they can square it."

Drew Parker put his arm around his wife's heavy body. "Nancy tends to exaggerate a little. Could be a lot tougher than it is. Folks in Wyoming, Colorado, even Montana, they got it much worse than us. Out there, they got cattlemen's associations. They hire themselves killers to get rid of anyone they don't like. Their so-called stock detectives go around accusing innocent people of rustling cattle and then shoot 'em down in cold blood."

Nancy pulled free of her husband. "What makes you think it's going to be any different out here once the army gets rid of all them cursed Injuns?"

"Woman, hold your tongue!" Parker ordered his wife.

"I'll do no such thing! I believe in speaking my mind." Nancy turned back to Mary and her aunt. "Be real careful. Mind what I been telling you. It ain't no foolish talk neither. There's killers out there. A body has to watch out."

These last words were whispered in the face of her husband's scowling countenance. He took his wife's fleshy arm and forcefully pulled her away. There was no mistaking the frightened look on his face.

Before Mary could even comment to Elizabeth about what Nancy Parker had told them, they were approached by Nora Metford and a small, blond woman Mary didn't recognize.

"It's nice to see you again," Nora said to Elizabeth. "We only talked briefly at the party."

"It was a nice party. I'm sorry we had to leave early," Elizabeth said politely.

"Do you know Jesse Wheeler?"

Mary studied the delicate, blond woman momentarily. She was attractive, but there were iridescent circles under her eyes as if she hadn't slept well, and her eyes had a slight puffiness as if she had been crying recently.

"We haven't met formally, but it's nice to make your acquaintance," Mary said.

"I plan to send my youngest son to your school," Jesse Wheeler said. "I would have done it sooner, but my husband didn't approve."

"I've been telling her what a good job you're doing with my children," Nora Metford said.

"That's always nice to hear."

Mr. Wheeler soon came over and joined them. A huge cigar hung from his mouth and he bit down on it impatiently.

"Ain't you ready yet, Jesse?"

"Just another minute, Sam. We're having a word here."

The big, burly man sneered. "You women. Don't have a brain in your heads but you still can chatter on and on about nothing."

Mary took an immediate dislike to Sam Wheeler.

"I just told Miss MacGreggor that I'm going to send Bobby to school. He needs some learnin'."

"You think because she's from the East she knows everything? If the woman had any sense, she wouldn't be a nester."

Mrs. Wheeler looked away in embarrassment as her husband

strode off toward several other men.

"I'm sorry. Sam doesn't mean to be rude. It's just his way."

"I understand perfectly," Mary replied. Obviously, Mr. Wheeler had a very low opinion of farmers as well as women. She thought about what Nancy Parker had said about the cattlemen.

Nora turned to Jesse Wheeler. "I was sorry to hear about your oldest boy. It must be a real tribulation for you."

"For Sam more than me. He's taking it real hard. That boy meant everything to him. He was Sam's favorite. But Ned was wild. He wouldn't listen to anyone, and I often feared his mean tongue and temper would put him into difficulty. It was God's will, I guess," she said with a deep, sad sigh.

As they were getting ready to leave, she overheard Sam Wheeler talking to Mr. Metford, Mr. Norris, and some of the other ranchers. He had a loud, abrasive voice, which carried all too well, and she couldn't help but hear him.

"Did you hear the way that son of a bitch Phillips talked to Cal? Don't know why he tolerates it! A sheep man's lower than a horse thief. Why, it ain't even a fit job for a white man!" Wheeler spat tobacco juice on the ground in disgust, his tone of voice aggressive and assertive. "I don't have to tell you what them sheep do. They eat the grass clear down so that the roots die out. Wherever they graze, they kill off the grass. Then they move on. They destroy everything they touch. Well, this is *our* land. Cattle land. We can't let them no good bastards destroy it for us!"

She heard the mumble of agreement from the other ranchers.

"I set a deadline. If any of them bastard sheepherders violate it, they're in for trouble. My men have orders to shoot them and their sheep dead. Ain't nobody gonna trespass on my land."

"Mary, are you ready?" Elizabeth asked.

"What? Oh, yes, I am."

On the drive home, Mary was in a somber mood. Sam Wheeler's attitude worried her. How could there be any peace with such antagonism going on? Yet at least Mr. Wheeler was out in the open about his feelings. That was hardly the case with Cal Davis. She couldn't tell what the man was thinking. Did he hate homesteaders as much as Sam Wheeler did? Maybe he was just a little bit more refined than Wheeler, a bit more circumspect. But why had he helped them then? Why did he look at her the way he did? No, she had to force herself not to even consider that. He was not to be trusted, and she couldn't let herself be seduced by anything he said or did. There were more ways than one for a man to destroy a woman. She wasn't a fool, and she had to make herself realize that caring about Cal Davis was the very worst thing she could do.

Something Nancy Parker said particularly disturbed her—the possibility that Isaac's death was not merely a random crime, but that the cattlemen might have been responsible. It was a fact that they were living on land Cal Davis considered his. Maybe the cause for Isaac's death was a lot more involved than she had realized. What was more to the point, who had brought the Harrises to their farm? She was beginning to believe that what happened to Isaac and Elizabeth was not accidental. She had tried to deny her suspicions before, but after the conversation with Mrs. Parker, she could no longer do so. A small shiver slithered snake-like down her spine as the wagon rode on through the sagebrush.

CHAPTER SEVEN

With the start of the fall roundup, Cal hoped he would be able to concentrate completely on ranching and forget about Mary MacGreggor. His thoughts had begun to alarm him. It wasn't natural for him to be so preoccupied by a woman. He'd learned a hard lesson about women long ago. Since then, he'd understood the need to avoid any emotional involvement where they were concerned. But with Mary MacGreggor, there seemed to be a problem he wasn't able to handle very well.

It felt good being out on the trail again. He'd hired on a few extra hands at a dollar a day plus food. Now as they sat around the chuck wagon, he was getting to talk with the new men.

Cal dug into his lunch and was disappointed in the food, not that it was worse than most trail grub, but this new cook, a dark-skinned Mex named Ramirez didn't seem to have his heart in his work. He put out the usual beans, bacon, hard biscuits, and bad coffee. Ramirez worked with a large, sharp knife much of the time, so no one dared complain openly about his cooking. Truth was, Cal had hired him more for his ability to drive a team of horses than for his culinary accomplishments. Ramirez would be a valuable asset on the long cattle drives. Right now, all they were doing was a mop-up operation, collecting cows that had been missed on the spring roundup.

The second day out, Cal found too many wolves hanging around the calves, and a few animals had to be helped out of sinkholes in the river, but nothing too surprising or too demanding. They shot what wolves they could; quicksand was a more difficult problem. Cal took several men with him because they had to dig out the cow's feet, double them at the knees, then tie them up. It took a wagon or four men pulling a rope tied to the horns to draw one trapped animal out, and there was always risk.

Cal partnered himself with a new man named Nat Thomas, because he wanted to see if Nat was worth keeping on after the roundup. Nat, a black cowboy who had grown up as a slave in the South, seemed especially competent. Cal liked to watch a man for a while before he decided on him. That wasn't always possible, but right now, he wanted to keep especially busy.

On the third day, he worked with Nat and Tiny Cramer. Tiny stood six-foot-six barefoot, and his nickname was a favorite joke with the men. Cal liked him, because although he rarely spoke, Tiny was the most dependable cowhand on the Thunderbolt and did the work of any two men.

As the three of them sat together sharing coffee and some beef jerky for a lunch break, Cal made conversation with Nat.

"What part of the South did you come from Nat?"

"South Carolina," he said.

"My folks came from Georgia."

"Your folks could have owned mine," Nat remarked.

Cal looked at him appraisingly, his head tilted slightly to one side. "How you feel about that?"

"Not much to feel," he said. "At least I'm free now. I can go where I want and choose to work where I like."

"I suppose freedom is very important when you don't have it," Cal reflected.

Tiny looked at both of them and threw the remains from his coffee cup away. "My ma and pa worked like slaves," he said. "Supposedly, they was free. But both of them worked into an early grave. Killed themselves trying to make their farm pay off.

One time it was grasshoppers that come and eat up the entire crop, the next it was drought. All in all, we owed more than we could pay to the bank and then they finally throwed us off the land. Broke my folks' heart."

That was the most Cal had ever heard Tiny say altogether in the four years he'd known him. Cal was surprised at the big man's bitterness.

"At least they was doing what they wanted," Nat said. "My family didn't have any choice. The owners sold my father off so that my ma and I couldn't even be with him. At least you got to have a family." Nat had intense eyes, and Cal decided that he was an intelligent, thoughtful man. He also decided then and there that he wanted to offer Nat a permanent job.

They worked the rest of the day with bandannas over their mouths and noses to keep the choking dust out of their throats and lungs. Toward dinnertime, it began to rain, a blustery cold storm. He covered himself in his yellow slick, but the dampness seemed to go right through him.

He was grateful to come in for a hot meal. Ramirez had prepared "sonofabitch stew" for supper and everyone dug in.

"What's in this?" Nat asked, wiping up his second plate with a sourdough biscuit.

"Beef, calf heart, sweetbreads, brains, marrow gut, and hot peppers. You like it?" An ugly smile spread across Ramirez's face.

Nat exchanged a pained look with Cal. "I liked it just fine till I learned what went into it."

Cal laughed deeply. It was good to be out here, living under the big sky, with only the company of other men and life at its most basic.

The following day, he worked with Nat and Tiny again. They had chased steers clear to the boundary line they shared with the Wheelers when they rode up on two wranglers from the Bar

W who had their guns drawn on three Mexicans who were branding a calf. There were other mavericks nearby.

"What's wrong?" Cal called out.

"Caught these here Mex rustlin' our cattle. Look, they're tryin' to put their own brand on 'em!"

"Tex is right," said a kid whom Cal recognized as one of Sam Wheeler's sons.

"No, *señor,* these are our cattle. We are taking them to our own *rancho.*"

"They're on Bar W land," Tex asserted angrily.

Cal studied Tex, who he thought must have got his name because he wore a Texas hat with a star on the side of it. He didn't much like the look of the man.

Nat turned to him. "If the cattle don't have your brand or Bar W, then these men should be allowed on their way."

"I say we string them up," Tex bellowed, his gun still drawn and pointed at the Mexicans.

"I am not a rustler," one of the Mexicans protested. "I have my own *rancho.* Please, this is a mistake!"

"Hang 'um!" the Wheeler boy shouted.

Killing didn't sit well with Cal. When he was young and his father was still alive, he had been pretty wild himself, with a reputation for having a quick temper. But all that had changed when he killed a man with his bare hands. They were in a fight, and he had beaten the man to death with his fists. Later, he repented of what he'd done. The man had a wife and a child. He had seen to it that they were taken care of, but the guilt was something he could hardly live with. He had sworn never to lose his temper and act in violence again. He was a changed man from then on, knowing that he couldn't afford to lose control of himself, no matter how furious he got or how hard he was pushed. He hadn't hit a man in anger since that day and vowed he never would if he could help it.

"Let them go," Cal said in a quiet but determined voice.

Both Tex and the Wheeler kid eyed him dubiously. Tex spat on the ground.

"Hell, Mr. Davis, if you got a weak stomach, just ride away."

Cal pulled out his Winchester carbine and readied it. "Don't think you understood me. Be on your way."

The Wheeler boy stared at him, his mouth gaping open in surprise. "You'd turn on your own for one of them?"

"Boy's right," Tex joined in, "these here are nothing but rustlers. They got to be lynched as an example to others like them."

Cal didn't budge. "I don't want to shoot either one of you, so just move on," he said in a calm, controlled voice. "If they're guilty, they'll get justice. If not, I'll be letting them go."

"All right, but you'll hear about this from my father," the kid said, his face red with anger.

"I expect so," Cal replied coolly.

As the Wheeler kid and Tex rode off, Cal turned to look at Nat and Tiny, who had kept very quiet all this time. He smiled to himself as he noticed that both men had their rifles in position as well. It was good to know his men backed him.

Cal got down and looked at the calves that the Mexicans had been getting ready to brand. There were no brand marks on them, but then they were all young calves.

"Got a bill of sale?" he asked them.

With trembling hands, one of the men withdrew a paper from his pocket and Cal saw that it had been signed by James Metford.

"Tiny's going to stay behind to give you a hand," Cal told them. "He'll also see that you get pointed the right way home without any more trouble."

The men thanked him gratefully and he rode off with Nat to finish their own work.

"That was a real nice thing you did back there," Nat observed in his deep, resonant voice. "But won't you be having trouble with your neighbor because of it?"

Cal smiled slightly. "With a man like Wheeler, you can't help but have trouble. Guess I'm a long time past caring about that."

Wolf Raullins came riding toward them.

"Everything going all right?" he asked his foreman.

"Mostly done. Found a few of Wheeler's strays mixed in with our beeves."

"Have Buck run them over to Bar W later. Time we broke for lunch."

They rode in together and he noticed that Wolf seemed fairly pleased with himself. He knew that the roundup was going well, and a lot of the credit had to be given to Wolf, who was getting the job done in record time. Wolf went around letting the men know that it was lunchtime and they all gathered around the chuck wagon.

Old Doc sat down beside Wolf as Ramirez began ladling out beans, beef, spuds, and molasses. They washed the indifferent food down with strong, black coffee.

"Hey, Cookie, don't you know how to cook nothin' besides this hog swill?" Wolf addressed his question to Ramirez, who glared at him.

"Careful, son," Doc cautioned. "Best not get him riled. Man's got a rough sense of humor. I hear tell that he once tied a cowhand's spurs to a log whilst he slept and then roused him with a shout that breakfast was ready. Another fella that criticized his cookin' got pie dough in his beard whilst he slept."

"I can take any man that starts with me," Wolf countered.

"Just meant it don't do to get the cook riled at you. Why, I knew a fella once that got so angry at the cook, he up and shot him. Well, the other men decided that his punishment for killin' Cookie was that he had to replace him. So they ended up tying an apron around his middle. It turned out that he cooked even worse than the man he'd shot."

Cal smiled at the old timer's story; it seemed like Doc had an endless supply of anecdotes that soothed bad tempers.

"How old are you, Doc?" he asked the grizzled cowpoke.

"Near as I can reckon, I've been on this earth forty-seven years."

Wolf stared at him in disbelief. "You look a lot older."

Doc's wrinkled face resembled the cracked, dry Arizona desert. "Listen, sonny, I figure I've earned the right to look this way. Know how many long drives I've been on? Been frying my brains under the hot prairie sun workin' beeves most of my born days. Ain't a bit sorry or ashamed for any of it either." Doc took a plug of chewing tobacco from the deep pocket in his vest. "Care for some Bill Durham?" he asked, offering it around. No one accepted. "Can't say as I blame you none. It's the devil's own habit, but I can't do without it."

Wolf turned to Cal. "What would you say, boss, if I told you I was set on getting married?"

Cal stared at Wolf's earnest young face and smiled. "Better you than me," he remarked.

"Don't you think well of marriage?"

Cal shook his head. "It's all right for some men, I guess, but I saw firsthand how it can destroy a man's life when he cares too much for a woman."

"Well, the woman I want is special. In fact, I don't think there's another like her anywhere. But I don't know that I'm near good enough for her."

Doc started to laugh. "Cal, I think your foreman's gone and fallen in love. Who is this amazing gal? Do I know her?"

Wolf looked embarrassed. "Don't think I want to say anything else until I find out how she might feel."

"Come on, Doc," Cal said. "I got some sick cows for you to

tend. Found a few with screwworm and one that looks like it's got the mange."

"I'll get me the axle grease and the kerosene. We'll fix them up right quick."

Wolf watched Cal ride off with Doc, admiring the way his boss sat in the saddle, tall and erect, and handled his fine ebony stallion, a free-spirited animal that no one else could either ride or tame. He was proud to be working for Cal Davis, and knew that very few other men would have given him the chance to be foreman even if he was a top hand. As Buck played the guitar and sang an old trail song that Wolf recognized as "Little Joe the Wrangler," he thought about Mary MacGreggor and wondered if she really could love a lowly half-breed like himself. But she hadn't looked at him as if he were less of a man because he had Indian blood. He had a feeling about her, a feeling that she was full of passion and just needed the right man to set off those feelings in her. He intended to be that man.

It was late afternoon when Wolf first saw sheep on Thunderbolt land, and they made him angry. They'd just finished branding the last calf when he saw the animals crossing the water over their grazing land. He wasn't going to wait and ask the boss how to handle the situation. He knew what needed to be done. Those damned sheepherders needed a lesson. They'd been told to stay off cattle range. Clearly more than words were needed to put the point across. He rode over to some of his men.

"Whose bleaters are those?" he asked.

"Phillips, I reckon," came the reply from Shorty Talbot, who had just cut loose the last calf.

"Shoot 'em. Kill every last one of them sheep." There were some twenty head and that ought to teach Phillips.

The men started to follow his orders—all except for Nat

Thomas, who just stared at him.

He rode over angrily to the man whose skin reminded him of chocolate. "Why aren't you shooting?"

"Those are good animals. I don't kill just for the sake of it."

"The boss expects it," Wolf shouted at him.

"I don't think so. I saw him in action today. He's not the kind of man who kills easy." With that, the cowhand rode away, and Wolf cursed him under his breath.

Nat Thomas might be right about Cal, but after all, the boss had everything handed to him, didn't he? As for himself, Wolf never had it easy and he couldn't have accomplished as much if he'd behaved like a toothless old squaw. A man had to be strong if he were to be successful. Above all else, he must never show weakness. No, a man could never afford to be too soft-hearted; kindness was generally mistaken for weakness. A real man must not have drunk too deeply of his mother's milk.

Wolf set his jaw squarely, knowing that he was right to be ambitious and just a little ruthless; it was the only way to be successful. Someday, maybe he would own a ranch of his own, one as large as this.

As the sun began to set, he decided to take the time needed to ride over to the Stafford homestead. Ever since he'd seen Mary on that first day, he wanted to get to know her. In his mind's eye, he could still picture her standing in the general store beside her uncle. She was the best-looking woman he'd ever laid eyes on. He had never expected a female that pretty to come out here to live. So few white women braved the territory, and the ones who did generally were already married. There were at least ten men to every woman. And the ones who did come mostly stayed in the towns. He'd known a few white women in his time, mostly prostitutes, whores who paid attention to a man according to how much money he had in his pocket to spend on them.

Mary MacGreggor was completely different, a real lady with character and intelligence as well as beauty. He had singled her out immediately. Marrying a woman like her would satisfy one of his strongest ambitions in life. He would have liked to propose to her on the spot, but he knew she was too good to marry just anyone. He would have to prove to her that he was worthy. She wasn't some young girl who could be swept off her feet either. He could tell she was particular.

He was realistic enough to recognize that he had very little to offer her right now, only his hopes, dreams, and ambitions for the future. But he knew that he could make them all come true. Still, she could have any man she wanted, maybe even Cal Davis. He'd seen the way the boss looked at her. But Cal said he would never marry, so Wolf reasoned that might give him an advantage. One way or another, he was going to get enough money together to start his own ranch and make her his bride.

He arrived at the small cabin at sundown. He hadn't wanted to talk to her in town where that old busybody from the general store would be lurking around like a buzzard and throw disapproving glances in his direction. He was too proud to willingly accept being the object of other people's idle chatter.

As he had hoped, Mary was back at the farm. She had just returned, and her cousin was taking care of the horse and wagon. She looked tired but as pretty as ever. Her warm smile made his heart start to beat more rapidly.

"Why, Mr. Raullins, what brings you out here?"

He dismounted his horse and removed his hat in a show of respect. Suddenly, he felt his stomach muscles tense.

"I came to see you about something," he said vaguely.

Mary looked at Wolf Raullins in surprise, wondering why he had ridden over from the Thunderbolt to visit with her.

"Come in and have a cup of coffee," she said, but he shook his head.

"It's not my intention to disturb your family."

"You won't be disturbing anyone. However, it is truly lovely out here with the sun setting over the land isn't it?" Mary looked up at the sky and smiled.

Wolf studied her but did not speak.

"I love this time of the day. The lilac twilight is so peaceful. It reminds me of a velvet, lavender party dress I wore as a very young girl." For a moment she was lost in her reverie; then she caught herself and looked over at him in embarrassment. "I hope that didn't sound too foolish to you."

"No, it sounded real nice, ma'am."

"Please call me Mary. 'Ma'am' makes me feel awfully old."

"I don't think you're old at all," he said.

She smiled at him and he finally smiled back. He seemed uncomfortable, and she wondered why, because in the past, he'd seemed so bold and untamed. But who could understand men? She certainly didn't!

"Please come in for that cup of coffee. I know you've traveled a long way. And if not for your sake, for mine. I definitely need it."

He followed her inside the cabin, looking around awkwardly.

"You don't spend much time indoors, do you?" she asked.

He smiled and relaxed slightly. "No, I'm mostly outdoors. That's where I've spent my life. Working and living on the land makes me feel close to the things that really matter."

She brought the coffee cups back to the table and he sat down, looking nervous again.

"Is something wrong?" she asked.

He shook his head. But she knew something was bothering him and suspected that it had everything to do with his reason for coming to the cabin today. She heated the coffee in the pot over the hearth as Elizabeth came toward them. Amy stood shyly beside her mother, clinging to her mother's skirt, and stared at Wolf as Elizabeth greeted him politely.

"Has Cousin Mary got a beau?" Amy whispered and then let out a small giggle.

Mary felt her face flushing even as Elizabeth admonished Amy and told her to go to the other room.

"Little girls are sometimes very silly in their behavior," Elizabeth remarked; then she excused herself and joined Amy, firmly closing the wooden door behind them both.

Wolf looked more uncomfortable than ever as Mary poured the coffee into his cup. She avoided looking at him directly, concentrating on serving him some biscuits with the coffee. He gulped the coffee, although she knew that it must still be terribly hot.

"There isn't a man on this earth that I'd be afraid to face, but when I look into your bright, pretty eyes, I just fall apart," he said.

She stared at him in surprise. "I don't usually have that effect on men," she told him.

"Well, you do on me." He looked deeply into her eyes. "There's going to be a dance, Miss Mary, over at the Wheeler ranch on Saturday night and I'd like it if you'd let me take you."

She raised her eyebrows. "Would I be welcome?"

He seemed surprised by her comment. "Why, sure, everyone around these parts is invited."

"Even homesteaders?" She knew her tone sounded sharp.

"Yes, ma'am, I mean, Mary, everyone. Your sister and the children could come too. They'll be tellin' you in town about it at the Sunday church meeting I expect. I just wanted to be the first to ask you."

She thought he would certainly be the only man to invite her, but she didn't say so. Anyway, she liked Wolf and she found him interesting. "On behalf of my whole family, I accept your invitation." She smiled at him warmly.

"To tell you the truth, I hadn't meant to escort your entire family, because I really want to be alone with you. But it's all right."

She thanked him and then walked him outside to his horse. "A beautiful evening, don't you think?"

He looked at her, then pulled her into his arms and kissed her with passion. "Yes, real beautiful," he said.

She was too surprised to speak. As she watched Wolf ride off into the twilight, which had become deep purple, Mary felt an odd mixture of emotions. She liked Wolf, but why, when he kissed her, didn't she feel the same kind of excitement as when Cal Davis had taken her into his arms? Even from her limited experience with men, she knew that her feelings for him were quite different, though she certainly did not understand why.

CHAPTER EIGHT

Mary surveyed her Sunday dress with a critical eye. It was not nearly as appropriate a dress for dancing as her green silk, yet she decided to wear it anyway. When she wore her special dress, Cal Davis had accused her of teasing him. If she dressed primly, he would see that she was in no respect a flirt. Besides, the high-necked collar of the blue muslin dress seemed just right for a respectable schoolteacher.

Elizabeth was standing next to her in the small bedroom. "Mary, you're not wearing your church dress to the dance, are you?"

"Why not?" She stuck out her lower lip.

Elizabeth sighed with annoyance. "Everyone's seen you wear it to church. What about your green dress?"

"No, it's too fancy."

"There must be something else that's appropriate."

Mary examined the few dresses she had brought with her from New Jersey, most of which were rather severe and plain. But there was another dress she'd worn to church some years ago that still looked attractive. She drew it out and looked at it with a critical eye. The bodice was of eggshell lace with an elegant high ruffled collar and matching cuffs, while the full skirt was cream-colored satin. She tried it on and then recalled why she had stopped wearing the dress to church: her breasts had strained against the bodice.

"It's too tight, isn't it?" she asked her aunt.

"I rather like the look. The dress fits you like a second skin and shows your figure to perfection. Most women would die to be able to look like that in a dress. I wish my waist were still as small as yours."

"Thank you for the compliment, but I do not wish to encourage any of the men or give them wrong ideas about me."

"Considering the nature of men," her aunt commented, "I do believe they would harbor such notions as pleased them no matter what you wore."

Elizabeth selected a cameo brooch of hers and fastened it at the neck of Mary's dress. "There, that's perfect. With your hair swept up high, you'll look quite ladylike and proper regardless. And the delicacy of the lace on the gown suggests old-fashioned gentility. So do not fret or be self-conscious of the close fit."

"I suppose you're right," Mary said, though still somewhat dubious.

"Of course, I am. I'm going to make us each a new dress next week, something in a cheerful calico print. Perhaps you'll choose some material for me at the general store."

Mary agreed, recalling how handy Elizabeth was with a needle and thread. How wonderful to have her aunt thinking of practical concerns again! She brushed her hair until it had a brilliant shine, and then pinned it high, displaying a crown of copper curls. That made her look special enough for tonight, she decided.

When she checked on the children, Mary discovered Rebecca sitting and examining the ribbons Billy had bought for her.

"Aren't you going to get ready? Wolf will be here soon."

Rebecca shook her head. "Not going," she said.

"It would make you feel better. You should meet other young men and try to forget about Billy."

Rebecca gave her a mutinous look. "Never!"

Jeremy had been listening and turned to Mary. "If Rebecca

won't go, I'd best stay here. I wouldn't feel right about leaving her alone."

Mary was not about to argue that point. "We'll just take Amy then," she said.

But Amy also refused. "If Rebecca and Jeremy don't go, it won't be any fun. Last time, there wasn't anyone my age. It was all old folks like you and Ma."

Elizabeth actually seemed glad to learn that the children did not want to go to the barn dance.

"Rebecca made a wise decision," Elizabeth said. "Strangers never understand about her, and the young men would most likely be cruel."

"Billy never was," Mary observed.

"Billy Travers wasn't very bright either, or else he never would have gotten himself into such trouble."

Sometimes, Elizabeth disappointed her. Mary realized that her aunt was ashamed of Rebecca. Her attitude toward Billy's predicament also struck Mary as being harsh.

But at least Elizabeth appeared to be coming out of herself after her time of terrible suffering. Going to the dance would be especially good for her spirits. For the first time in months, Elizabeth was taking an interest in her appearance. Watching Elizabeth getting dressed and fussing with her hair, Mary thought her aunt looked years younger again. Mary knew that Elizabeth had been popular when she was young. Her aunt was still an attractive woman.

Jeremy surveyed Mary as she stood by the hearth waiting for Elizabeth to join her.

"You look real nice, Cousin Mary, just like when you go to church."

"Thank you, Jeremy," she said with a small smile.

"I'm sort of glad I don't have to go. Dancing with girls I don't know makes me kind of sweaty."

Mary laughed. "I do believe you'll be looking forward to dancing in a few years."

"Don't think so. But you and Ma have a good time and don't fret, because I'll take good care of the girls." For just a moment, it seemed as if Isaac were talking. Mary gently kissed the boy on the cheek.

"You remind me so much of your father," she said. "You're growing up to be a fine man like he was."

Jeremy inclined his head but didn't speak.

Wolf Raullins arrived early, looking manly and smelling fresh and clean. His black hair was shiny and smooth and his steel gray eyes viewed her with appreciation.

"It's my pleasure to escort the most beautiful lady in the entire Arizona territory," he said.

Elizabeth came out of the other room just then, and she looked lovely. It had been a long time since her aunt had taken such pains with her appearance. She appeared almost regal in a russet taffeta dress that picked up on the color of her curls. The close-fitting bodice was fixed with lace and tiny bows, drawing attention to her ample bosom, while a tightly corseted waist made her look slim. She seemed delicate and frail but with a certain charm and coquettishness.

Wolf stared at Elizabeth in frank admiration. "Guess I better correct myself. It's my pleasure to escort the two most beautiful women in the territory." He extended one arm to each of the ladies.

With a few final instructions to Jeremy, Elizabeth was ready to leave. Of course, Mary knew what was running through her aunt's mind as she saw the look of worry on her face.

"Everything will be fine," Mary said reassuringly, "after all, we're only leaving for a few hours."

They took warm wraps against the chill night air because it was fall, and the nights grew colder, even if the days were still warm. Wolf tied his horse behind their wagon and took the reins. They seated themselves on either side of him and he looked very pleased. It was nice to be going out for a social evening again. Mary felt better about this one, probably because Wolf had invited her. But she was also glad not to be alone with him; she still felt awkward and uncomfortable with men. She hardly knew what to talk about, and it did seem that her strong opinions tended to displease many people. Men especially didn't expect women to think for themselves, and when they discovered she did, many were annoyed. She thought of Cal Davis then and wondered if he disliked her for not being the sort of quiet, gentle woman men obviously preferred. Wolf didn't seem to care that she wasn't meek and mild. But she couldn't help wishing for just a moment that she had her aunt's ability to charm people.

Wolf looked over at her and smiled with admiration; she found herself smiling back. It was nice to be going to a social event with a strong, handsome man like Wolf. She studied him. There was a quality about him, a raw primitiveness that she did find intimidating. She had the feeling he could be very forceful and dominating if he chose. He seemed like the sort of man who lived by his instincts and was ruled by his passions.

She had never allowed herself to be ruled by her emotions, always having been a sensible individual. With her, duty to family came first, her personal desires and needs put aside for the good of others. She never regretted the years she'd devoted to caring for her father; in fact, she had never thought that there was any other choice in life for her. But now, she was confused, not certain what she wanted out of life.

"Tell us something about yourself, Mr. Raullins," Elizabeth said.

He shrugged. "There isn't a whole lot to tell."

"What was your family like? Have you always lived in the West?"

"Yep, I've always lived out here, although I only came to Arizona four years ago. My mother was the daughter of a chief."

"How exciting!" Elizabeth exclaimed.

"My father was a mountain man who came to trade with her tribe, saw her, and fell in love directly. He traded everything he had for her and then some. They lived with her people for a time, but a few years after I was born, they moved on. My mother died when I was small so I don't remember her very well, but my father used to say I looked a lot like her, except for my eyes, which were his." He smiled at both of them as he expertly drove the horse and wagon across the empty land.

Mary thought that Elizabeth had a fine knack of drawing people out. Wolf seemed very comfortable talking to them now.

"Are you finding life out here any better now, Mrs. Stafford?" he asked in return.

"I am not," her aunt responded. "But then I'm not a pioneer at heart. I like living in comfort, and I will never become accustomed to living in a shack with a thatched roof that harbors tarantulas, scorpions, rats, and rattlesnakes."

"Now Aunt Elizabeth, that simply isn't fair. You do tend to exaggerate," Mary protested in a teasing voice. "We may have to endure tarantulas and scorpions from time to time, but you know very well that the snakes do eat the rats."

Mary's remark made Wolf laugh, and even Elizabeth smiled. The evening took on its own special charm even before they reached the Wheeler ranch. They were no longer two women struggling to survive in a harsh and violent land, but rather ladies out for an evening of fun and pleasure, escorted by a romantically handsome man.

The Wheeler's new barn had been transformed for the evening's festivities. Sam Wheeler, anxious to demonstrate his affluence to his neighbors, was intent on showing off.

"No critter's seen the inside of the place yet," he boasted as they joined the neighbors. "Best damn barn in the entire territory—and the biggest!"

Around them, people were dancing to the spirited music. There were two fiddles, a banjo player, and a guitarist. They were cowboys, not professional musicians, but they played with such enthusiasm that Mary doubted anyone could be better.

Wolf got them each a glass of punch, which tasted to Mary as if it had been heavily spiked with spirits. Soon groups were forming for square dancing and they were drawn into it.

"Fiddler's playin' like the devil was chasin' after him," old Doc commented to her with a wink.

Mary was not used to dancing, but she soon understood the calls. Because there were so many more men than women, it seemed someone was always asking her to dance. It was tiring, but a lot of fun.

After a couple of hours of dancing, the Wheelers' cook, a heavyset Mexican woman named Maria, brought out huge trays of delectable tortillas and enchiladas. Everyone was in high spirits and having a good time. Mary noted with satisfaction that Elizabeth seemed to be enjoying herself. She hadn't seen her aunt look so radiant in years. It was the first time she'd observed Elizabeth happy since they'd come west. It seemed that every man present had wanted to take a turn dancing with the attractive young widow. Elizabeth was admired and sought after, and it was doing her a world of good.

"Thank you for bringing us tonight," Mary said to Wolf. "It's been the best thing for my aunt to get out and mingle with other people. Doesn't she look wonderful?"

"I suppose, but you're the best-looking woman here," Wolf said to Mary.

"I doubt that, but thank you for the compliment."

They waltzed together, the slow music a welcome change of pace, as she smiled at his compliment. For a time, she had nearly forgotten about him, so many others had asked her to dance. But they all seemed to understand that Wolf was the man who had brought her and would be taking her home after the dance.

"Are you having a good time?" he asked.

"Of course, I am. Thank you for inviting me."

"I should be thanking you," he replied. Wolf's eyes locked with hers.

Yes, she was right about him; there was a great depth of passion within him, and all of it seemed fixed on her right at this moment. She should have felt pleased, but instead, all she could feel was uneasiness.

She looked over Wolf's shoulder, observing the other dancers. Cal Davis was dancing with Elizabeth. She had seen him dance several times with Jesse Wheeler and her daughter, Lorette, as well. But he seemed to be paying particular attention to her aunt. Watching them smile at each other should have pleased her, but it didn't. In fact, it stirred unwelcome feelings that she did not quite understand. Surely, she did not feel jealous? Why should she care with whom the man danced? The fact that he hadn't as much spoken one word to her the entire evening shouldn't mean anything to her. The truth was, she hardly knew the man at all, and what she did know, she neither liked nor understood. Yet the unpleasant feeling persisted and would not go away.

She tried to concentrate on Wolf, which wasn't difficult since he was monopolizing every minute that wasn't spent dancing. She couldn't be certain, but it did seem as if other men were intimidated by his strong personality. There was a dynamic quality about him, almost a recklessness, that she rarely saw in other people. No doubt, he was by far the most interesting man at the dance. And yet, from time to time, her eyes strayed to Cal Davis. Once or twice, their eyes met, and he smiled as if she were a child whom he had caught doing something naughty.

She also could not help noticing that there was little doubt who the most important and influential man at the social was. Everyone treated Cal Davis with kingly deference, with the possible exception of Sam Wheeler. Cal seemed to take his celebrity in stride, as if it were expected.

She disliked all large landowners and people of established wealth and privilege. She came by this feeling honestly, through her Scots-Irish background. Her own forebears had been fierce, rebellious people who challenged the ruling order. Cal Davis, with his superior manner, infuriated her beyond words. When he finally did approach her for a dance, she felt nothing but hostility for him.

"Miss MacGreggor, may I have the honor of this dance?" His tone of voice implied that she should be grateful for the honor he was seeing fit to bestow upon her.

"Mr. Raullins has already accounted for my time."

"Then the next one," he said with casual ease.

"I think not." With that, she turned and took Wolf's hand, pulling the astonished foreman back to the dance floor.

She thought she heard Cal's final words uttered softly: "Your loss."

She watched with secret satisfaction as he walked stiffly away, his features like a mask, betraying no expression whatsoever.

"Don't think any woman ever turned him down before," Wolf said. "They all kind of fawn over him."

"Well then, it was high time someone did," she replied hotly. "He was in need of a set down."

"You sure do have a lot of pluck," Wolf said with something akin to awe.

"I really don't see why people cater to him as if he were some sort of royal prince."

"Guess it's only natural. You see, whenever anyone needs help, he's right there doing for them. People just naturally go to him with their problems, and he never turns anyone away. He's gathered a lot of respect being generous with his time and money."

She felt a touch of guilt after hearing that. They danced together for a while without words. Mary glanced around the large barn, noticing that again no homesteaders were present except for herself and Elizabeth. But she realized that they were being thought of as available women, not farmers.

Mary noticed how attractive Mrs. Wheeler looked dressed in a pink satin dress of the latest cut and style. Because she was pale and petite, she looked absolutely tiny next to her husband, who was a bear of a man. Her hair was the color of winter wheat and her eyelids fluttered like butterflies. She seemed completely dominated by her husband. As they stopped dancing, Sam Wheeler approached Cal Davis, and the two men began to talk, a rather serious conversation from what she could gather. When Mrs. Wheeler turned to suggest some refreshments, Wheeler glanced at her angrily.

"Go away, woman! Can't you see we're talking business here?"

Mrs. Wheeler didn't say a word, looking as if she were used to being talked to in that manner. Mary shook her head in dismay, feeling sorry for Mrs. Wheeler. To her mind, a woman was better off never marrying at all than having a bully for a husband.

"Mrs. Wheeler," she called out, taking the woman's attention. "I just wanted to thank you for your hospitality. We're having a wonderful night and it's mostly thanks to your efforts."

The delicate blonde smiled at her. "Thank you, but please call me Jesse. I'm glad you could come, and your aunt as well."

Sometime later, Sam Wheeler approached Wolf while he and Mary were standing together talking. If Mary's feelings about Cal Davis were confused, her feelings about Sam Wheeler were clear as window glass. She disliked the man intensely; he represented everything she found abhorrent. She would do nothing to disguise those feelings. But Wheeler did not seem to notice; probably, she thought, because he didn't even care. He was totally self-involved to the point of being oblivious to the sensibilities of other people.

"Raullins, like to have a word with you for a few minutes, in private if you don't mind?"

Wolf turned to her. "Mary, would you please excuse us?"

She really wanted to say she did not excuse them—that in fact, she thought Wolf should never speak to Sam Wheeler at all—but she was realistic enough to know that it would be both a foolish and futile gesture. So she said nothing and walked away.

She was immediately surrounded by unattached cowboys eager to ask her for a dance, but she let them know as kindly as she could that she was becoming rather tired.

Elizabeth came toward Mary, a cheerful smile on her face. "Isn't this fun?" she asked.

"Yes, it is very nice. Are you enjoying yourself?"

"More than I have in quite a long time."

"I'm happy for you. I noticed Mr. Davis has been paying you a great deal of attention. That's quite an honor around here it seems."

Elizabeth flushed slightly. "He's just being kind and neighborly. He really is a considerate and thoughtful man."

Mary frowned. "I'm not certain that I agree."

"I don't see how you can deny it. He's been so kind to us. Do you know what he told me? He said I reminded him of his mother."

"Well, I suppose you are a few years older than he is."

Elizabeth glowered at her. "Why Mary, I'm not so much older than he is!" Elizabeth's voice betrayed righteous indignation, and Mary repented of her comment. "What he meant, I believe, was that I was a gentlewoman like her. When I asked, he told me that his mother had been a beautiful Southern belle before the war, quite genteel and from a wealthy plantation family. When his father married her, he brought her out here to live."

"Is she still alive?"

"I don't know. It seems she couldn't stand the wild, primitive existence or the loneliness, so she finally went back to Georgia."

"Well, if the father was like the son, I can understand why the woman left."

Elizabeth looked at her, head tilted to one side. "Mary, I never would have suspected that you were capable of saying such a cruel thing. I've always thought that you were the most fair-minded person I knew, but when it comes to Mr. Davis, you're quite the opposite."

"I'm sorry. The man just seems to bring out animosity in me. You must admit that he has been intent on our leaving the farm ever since we arrived. I think by comparing you to his mother, he was trying to say that you should leave here just as she did."

"Perhaps, but I do think that you are completely wrong about him." Elizabeth spoke with such conviction that Mary had to wonder.

"Am I? He wants our land, doesn't he? Who knows what lengths he would go to get it back."

Elizabeth smiled indulgently as she would with one of her children. "Mary, dear, Mr. Davis has so much land, I do not believe he would ever be that petty or small-minded."

She was about to say something else, but at that moment, one of the ranchers came up to Elizabeth and asked her to dance. Elizabeth accepted and she was whirled away, her taffeta skirts rustling and her white petticoats billowing. Mary walked toward the outside of the barn, thinking how foolish it was to discuss her feelings about Cal Davis with Elizabeth—or anyone else, for that matter. Besides, the truth was, she hardly knew what she felt about the man and she supposed that troubled her more than anything else.

She was alone now in the chill night air and began to shiver slightly. She realized that she had left her wrap inside and turned to go back but bumped into someone. Looking up, her eyes met those of Cal Davis.

"Good evening," he said woodenly.

"I was just going back in," she said, but he took her arm and did not let her pass.

"I believe this is my dance," he said. "Out here will do just fine since there's no problem hearing the music."

Before she could protest, he had swept her into his arms and pulled her indecently close. His iron grip held her body tight against his own. The slow dances were always shorter, she reasoned; it would be over soon enough and then she would be free of him.

"You've avoided me all night," he said to her.

"I thought it was the other way around," she countered. "Besides, isn't that what you want, what we both want?"

He didn't answer, but his callused hands brought her body closer to his own and she felt as if she could hardly breathe.

"You smell awfully good," he said. "And the way you look could drive any man crazy."

It seemed as if the dance went on forever, and she was aware of every breath and movement he took. There was something about his masculinity that made her heart catch fire. Why didn't she feel that way when Wolf held her? It made no sense at all.

When the music ended, she tried to pull away from him but met with resistance.

"I'd better go back in now," she said.

"Guess you'd better." But he wouldn't release her.

She managed to break free of him and hurriedly returned to the barn, though she could hardly control the way her body was trembling. She glanced around the room and saw Wolf still talking to Sam Wheeler. They were closely engaged in a serious conversation and did not notice her return, their backs to her. The music was loud, but she could hear what they were saying.

"I want you to leave Davis and come work for me. I believe you're the kind of man I need. I'd make you my foreman. Since Ned died, there's been a real need for someone to work with Sam Junior. Boy's still green. I'd give you more money than you're paid now."

"Appreciate it, Mr. Wheeler, but I already have a job."

Wheeler puffed aggressively on his cigar. "Davis ain't really your kind of man. He ain't strong enough. That's why them bastard sheepherders been takin' advantage."

"I don't allow those woolies on Thunderbolt land."

"Hells bells, of course, *you* don't! But sure as God made mules stubborn, Cal ain't gonna take the kind of action that's needed. Now I've heard it said that you know exactly how to handle that kind of problem. I want you workin' for me. I want my sons to learn from you."

Wolf was listening with interest, Mary observed in disgust. He let Wheeler finish before he responded.

"Won't say I'm not flattered by your generous offer, but I do owe a lot to Cal. He's been real good to me, and it wouldn't be right to flat leave him. I owe him my loyalty. Thanks anyway, Mr. Wheeler."

"Well, I ain't acceptin' that as your final answer. You just turn it over in your mind for a while. I'll keep the job open for you."

She walked over to Wolf and slipped her hand through his arm. "Ready for another dance?" she asked.

He looked very pleased. "Anything to oblige a lady," he replied.

Wheeler turned to her, his cigar smoke catching her in the face. "You Eastern women are mighty forward." He smelled sickeningly of a mixture of cologne and strong tobacco and smiled at her through nicotine-stained teeth.

She was about to say something, but thought better of it and held her tongue, turning to concentrate on Wolf.

"I'm glad you turned down his offer," she said as they danced away.

"You heard us then."

"Only part of it."

"You think I'm better off working for Cal?"

"The lesser of two evils I suppose."

He stared at her intently. "You hold strong opinions, don't you?"

"That I do."

He brought her close to him. "Well, I like that about you. Fact is, Miss MacGreggor, there ain't nothin' I don't like about you. You're a mighty fetchin' female."

Before they left the dance that night, Wolf had exacted her promise that she would see him again socially. He had also asked permission to visit her at the farm and she agreed. Once before they left, she caught Cal Davis looking at her; she quickly turned away. Even his look made her quake.

On the ride home, Wolf spoke to her. "What exactly is it about Sam Wheeler that you don't like?"

She answered carefully. "I suppose I believe there are people who are just naturally bad."

Elizabeth laughed. "She's a dour Scot like her father. 'In Adam's fall, we sinned all.' Isn't that right, Mary?"

"I don't believe in original sin."

"Come now, Mary, you know that in your heart you believe

people are born bad."

She thought Elizabeth was baiting her for some reason. "Not quite. I believe that *some* people have a predisposition for evil. Most of us gradually develop a conscience, and that saves us, but some never do—perhaps they are unable. I don't really know."

"I think it has to do with the way children are taught by their folks," Wolf said.

"I agree with you. But there are some individuals who never develop a conscience no matter what their training."

"And you think that Sam's one of those naturally bad people?" Wolf asked.

"Yes, I do," she responded with equal candor. "And that's exactly why I hope you'll stay away from him, no matter what inducements he may offer."

"There was a time when I wouldn't have agreed with Mary," Elizabeth said. "But when I saw those men kill Isaac . . ." Her voice trailed off and she shook her head, plainly overcome with emotion.

"Perhaps we should talk of pleasanter things," Mary said.

The conversation drifted back dreamily to talk of the dance, and the magic of the evening enclosed them again as they returned to the cabin in the moonlit night.

Elizabeth went into the cabin first, allowing Wolf time to be alone with Mary.

"This was a special night," she said.

"It's meant an awful lot to me too."

He helped her down from the wagon, and as he did, Wolf took her into his arms and kissed her soundly. She kissed him back with as much warmth as she could manage, but no strong emotions were ignited within her.

"Thank you for a lovely evening," she said, aware that her words were mere polite courtesy.

She quickly parted from Wolf and went into the cabin, disturbed by her lack of feelings for him. Mary undressed in the darkness. With a small shiver, she crawled into bed, her mind troubled.

CHAPTER NINE

It seemed as if Wolf Raullins had developed an interest in farming. At least that was the opinion Jeremy voiced, because Wolf was visiting the farm a great deal, but curiously, only when Mary was home. He even appeared to become interested in religion and sat through several Sunday services with the family.

Cal Davis, on seeing his foreman's attachment to Mary, kept his distance. Several times, he joined Elizabeth and sat beside her during services, but most other times, he joined Lorette and Jesse Wheeler, both of whom welcomed his company with obvious pleasure, just as her aunt did. Mary refrained from speaking to him; still, every once in a while, their eyes met and she felt the piercing penetration of those startling blue orbs that left her nearly breathless. She hated herself for reacting that way, but she couldn't really help it.

About a month after Wolf had started seeing her regularly, an incident occurred at the end of the school day that changed his behavior toward her. Some drunken cowboys had come out of the saloon and were discharging their six-shooters wildly. Mary had lined up the children to wait for their rides home. She began herding the frightened ones, particularly the younger children, back into the schoolhouse.

One of the rowdy cowboys saw Mary and started coming in her direction, the gun wavering carelessly as he staggered down the street. As he moved, the weapon went off, narrowly missing her head. From out of nowhere, it seemed, Wolf appeared, sliding from his cow pony and pulling her to the ground, then throwing his body on top of hers.

"Are you all right?"

She could barely speak because he had knocked the breath out of her, but she managed to nod.

"Those bastards!"

"Let me up, please."

He apologized for knocking her over and then went after the two drunks, whom he quickly disarmed. Wolf fought them both, punching and kicking each of them, bloodying noses and blackening eyes, forcing them to the ground, one after the other. He swore at them and told them to ride out of town and never come back. The children had gathered around by this time to watch his display of rage.

"Sorry you had to see that," he said to Mary afterward. "But you could have been killed! I thought at first they'd hit you and I can't tell you how I felt." He pulled her into his arms and held her tightly against his chest. "You really are all right?" he asked again, seeming to need reassurance.

"Fine," she answered in a near whisper.

"I'm going to escort you home today."

When all the children had been seen off, Wolf took the reins of her wagon, she and Amy climbing in beside him.

"I'm awful glad you weren't injured, but you could have been," he said. "That's just a matter of luck. Sometimes a person runs out of luck. You never know. It's made me come to a decision about something." He turned and looked at Amy, whose small face was turned up while she listened intently. "Guess maybe I'll tell you about this when we can talk privately."

Amy looked from Wolf to Mary and smiled widely. Mary decided that her youngest cousin was just a bit too precocious, though Wolf wasn't being subtle at all. His concern for her seemed excessive and smothering by her standards, and she wasn't at all certain she liked it. But at least he didn't turn serious again until they got back to the farm. At that time, Amy ran into the cabin and apparently told everyone about how Cousin Mary had nearly been shot by a drunken cowboy. Elizabeth came running out of the cabin followed by Rebecca.

"You are all right?" Elizabeth asked, furrowing her brow.

"Just fine. Nothing really happened."

"But it could have," Wolf emphasized. "Excuse us, ma'am. Mary and I are going for a walk." He took Mary's hand and guided her toward the open land.

"I want to tell you what's on my mind," he said. "I wasn't going to say this now, but today just proved to me that I should. You see, I got feelings for you, deep feelings. Life's got a way of just slipping away from us if we're not careful. Today was proof of that. You could have been lying dead in the street right now. I'm awful glad you're not. Hope you won't think me forward for saying this, but I care about you a whole lot." He stopped walking and turned toward her. His eyes were soft as mist and he was so close that she could feel his warm breath on her cheek. "I want to make you my wife."

Her mouth dropped in surprise. She moved away from him.

"I see you wasn't expecting me to propose. I sort of sprung this on you. I don't expect you to give me an answer now. Just be thinking on it, because I love you, Mary." His face was deeply colored like rich, full-bodied red wine. "I know that right now I got very little to offer a fine lady like you, but it won't always be that way. I got plans for the future. Big plans."

She took a deep breath and then exhaled it very slowly. "Wealth has never been of primary importance to me, Wolf. It's just that this really is unexpected. I do need time to think about it."

"I understand, and I won't press you for an answer. I was going to wait to ask you anyway. It's just nearly seeing you killed today in town, I realized that waiting is dumb."

He moved toward her and his kiss was warm and gentle on her lips. There was something very nice and comforting in that kiss, and she responded to it with equal affection.

Mary watched Wolf ride away and then entered the cabin, collapsing on a chair; she hadn't realized until this moment how tired she was. Wolf's proposal was simply more than she could handle at the moment.

"Mr. Raullins kissed Cousin Mary," Amy said with a giggle, and then hid herself behind her mother's long skirt.

"Quiet!" Elizabeth shushed the child. "He looked very serious," her aunt observed.

"He was," Mary said.

Elizabeth gave her a knowing look. "I told you that there were lots of men out here for you."

"Well, Wolf seems to agree with you, anyway."

Her aunt's face lit up with keen interest. "What did he have to say?"

Mary lowered her eyes. "He asked me to become his wife."

Elizabeth threw her arms around Mary. "And what did you say? Did you accept?"

Mary shook her head. "I couldn't. I'm not certain how I feel about him, how I feel about a lot of things. I need time to sort out my feelings. You see, I've never really given any thought to marriage. I just went along thinking that I would never marry and I accepted that. I'm accustomed to my present way of life, and I don't know if I really want to change it."

"I wonder," Elizabeth responded thoughtfully. "You've always devoted your life to serving the needs of other people. Once your father was gone, you began helping us. And now you've also devoted yourself to educating children. That's all well and good, but you deserve to have a life of your own. Unselfishness is commendable, but there are limits to everything. Don't decide to be a sainted martyr, because it will bring you little satisfaction in the end, and you'll just be taken for granted."

"Aren't you glad that I've been here with you?" Mary said in a hurt voice.

Elizabeth smiled at her, placing a hand on her shoulder. "Of course, I am. We never could have managed without your strength to lean on. But I don't want us taking advantage of you, dear. You're my very best friend in the world, and I want what's best for you. I am a selfish woman, but I do care about your welfare."

Mary smiled affectionately at her aunt. "You know how much I love you all, but that isn't what makes me hesitate to accept Wolf's proposal. I'm just not certain I want to marry him. It would be giving myself over to a stranger."

"Then perhaps he's not the right man for you. If he were, you wouldn't have to think about it. You'd know that you wanted him."

"You don't think I should consider marrying him?"

"I would never presume to tell you what you should or should not do with your life," Elizabeth said. "But even if Wolf Raullins is not the man for you, you ought to realize that there will be a great many other men interested in you if you decide to remain in the West. Teaching school may prove satisfying for a time, but it does not make for a complete or fulfilling life. For that, a woman needs a husband and children of her own."

"Perhaps," Mary said, not entirely convinced that her aunt was correct.

There were questions in her mind. She was afraid to ask them because they were personal in nature, and yet she wanted to know the answers.

"Elizabeth, Mother told me that a lot of young men came around to court you when you were young. How did you know that Isaac was the right one for you?"

Her aunt smiled, her eyes taking on a dreamy look. "It was the way I felt when I was with him. No one else was ever as tender or loving as your uncle. I couldn't help but give him my heart."

"When he kissed you, did it make you feel different than when anyone else kissed you?"

Elizabeth arched one golden brow and stared at her. "Yes, Mary, that's exactly the way it was."

Mary felt her face flush. "I thought it might be," she said.

How could she tell her aunt about how she had felt when Cal Davis had taken her in his arms? Elizabeth suspected something, but Mary couldn't bring herself to confide further, not now while her feelings were so confused.

The following afternoon, Mary came home to find Cal Davis sitting by the hearth with Elizabeth, the two of them chatting pleasantly over coffee and muffins. Her aunt looked up and smiled, her hazel eyes reflecting the golden glow from the fire.

"We've got company," Elizabeth said superfluously.

"So I see," Mary responded in a displeased tone of voice.

"Mr. Davis brought us an entire steer that's been butchered and ready for cooking. Though what we're going to do with it all, I have no idea."

"I suppose some of the meat could be cured," Mary responded. "But why are you bringing us such a gift?" she asked the rancher suspiciously.

"No reason. The steer had a broken leg and had to be slaughtered. I figured you might be able to use the meat, or at least a portion of it."

"I think I could distribute what we don't use to some other farm families who are needy. I know which ones they are from meeting the children's parents at the schoolhouse."

That seemed to please him. "Good idea," he said.

She couldn't help but notice the dimple that formed in his cheek and made his usually hard features look handsome.

Cal turned to Elizabeth. "Thank you. It's always nice spending time with this family," he said. Then he spoke to Mary. "Would you mind walking out with me? There's something I need to talk with you about."

She wanted to refuse but found she couldn't. There was a determined and compelling look in his eyes.

He took the bridle of his horse in one hand and held her arm with the other. "Walk a ways with me. I have to ask you a question."

They were well out of sight of the cabin when he turned to her and spoke again. "Wolf told me this morning that he proposed to you. I had a feeling that he might from what he said before. But he mentioned you hadn't given him an answer as yet. Do you intend to accept him?"

"I don't know," she replied. "I haven't made up my mind. What difference could that possibly make to you?"

Her eyes met his with a level gaze. But she couldn't tell anything from the expression on his face; he was so difficult to comprehend.

"Wolf does work for me, and I care about his well-being."

She realized that he was not telling the whole truth and waited for him to say more.

"I don't want him to make a mistake."

She felt herself become irritated with him. "You think that his marrying me would be a mistake? Why is that?"

"Because I think you have feelings for me."

She felt color rising to her face. "I don't know why you should think that," she responded, hardly able to contain her anger.

"Don't you?" He pulled her into his arms and began kissing her with an almost punishing intensity. She willed herself not to respond to him. Yet as his kiss deepened and his lips molded to

131

hers, she found her resolve weakening.

She tried to free herself from his viselike grip, but he was all hardness and muscle. She punched his back several times, refusing to give in to the feelings he excited in her. She didn't want to kiss him back, she wouldn't! And then, God help her, she did.

Suddenly, he was pulling away from her. "You understand now why I think you shouldn't marry Wolf, don't you?"

She was furious with him. "It amazes me how you can just turn your feelings on and off the way you do! You truly are a cold, calculating man. You play with my emotions the way someone might the strings of a guitar. I don't like you and I don't trust you, Mr. Davis. I'd appreciate it very much if you got off my land!"

"It really is my land, Miss MacGreggor. I think I've been very considerate and patient in that regard."

"Like a chivalrous knight in days of old?" she replied with lethal sarcasm.

"All I was doing was trying to make a point. To let you see the mistake you would be making. I don't want Wolf getting hurt."

"Forgive me, but I must question your motives."

His face had reddened—heated like her own, she noted with some satisfaction.

"Wolf is a man, not a child, and is therefore entitled to make his own decisions. And as for me, I haven't made up my mind as yet."

"Maybe I was wrong thinking you were a lady."

"I doubt you ever thought that anyway, since you've never treated me like one. You'd certainly have taken advantage of me if I let you."

He quickly moved astride his great stallion and rode off looking enraged. She knew she had sorely offended him with her last remark, because whatever else he might be, Cal Davis considered himself a gentleman of the old school. Well, he had been very ungentlemanly toward her, and the accusation was fair. He had no right acting that way toward her, kissing her with such passionate intensity that he set her very soul on fire. She was still shaking inside when she returned to the cabin, but did her best to control it. She reminded herself that lust and love were two very different things. Elizabeth, waiting for Mary, turned to her with a questioning look.

"He told me that he didn't think very much of Wolf and me getting married."

Elizabeth's face registered surprise. "Did he give a reason?"

"Not really," she responded evasively. "I told him it was none of his business."

"Mary, sometimes I've seen your temper get the best of you. I hope you weren't rude to the man."

"I might have been, but he deserved it. Let's not talk about him anymore. I really can't abide it."

Elizabeth gave her a concerned look and then changed the subject to what they might do with all the meat Cal Davis had brought them.

As she helped with the preparations for supper, Mary thought how much simpler life had been when she was back in New Jersey caring for her father. At least there hadn't been this confusion and pain in her heart then.

CHAPTER TEN

It began with a prairie fire that burned out of control for nearly a week. Cal turned the job of putting it out over to Wolf. Under the foreman's supervision, Thunderbolt cowhands slaughtered steers, axing them down the middle and dragging the fresh carcasses across the prairie where the fires were catching new grass. In that way, they were able to smother out the flames. It was a risky business, but it generally worked.

Several of the men received burns in the process, but the fire was finally contained and eventually put out. Cal breathed a sigh of relief, believing that the threat from the fire was finally over. However, what he didn't realize at first was that the fire had taken its toll of the viable grazing land. The sheepherders in particular were desperate. Jack Phillips and some of the others had herded their sheep down from the high country for the winter. A great deal of their grazing land had been destroyed.

It was no accident that Jack Phillips let his men cross Cal's deadline. Buck came riding in to report what was happening. Cal sent Wolf out leading Thunderbolt hands to patrol the boundary with strict instructions as to how the situation was to be handled: no fighting, no killing. Just show the sheepherders that their animals weren't welcome by herding them back across the deadline and giving the sheep men a clear verbal understanding. He knew Phillips wouldn't make a fight of it if they didn't. When the men returned that evening, Cal asked Wolf how things had gone.

"I handled the situation," Wolf replied and said no more on the subject.

Cal was satisfied because he knew Wolf was capable, and trusted that would be the end of the trouble. Except it wasn't.

The following day, a red-faced Jack Phillips rode up to the ranch house with Marshal Wade at his side. Cal invited them into the Spartan adobe dwelling.

"Davis, I told the marshal I want you and that foreman of yours charged with murder!"

Cal stared at the man in shock and amazement. "What the hell are you talking about?"

"You know damn well! Yesterday, your foreman gave the order to shoot my sheep, and when they ran out of ammunition, some of your hands began clubbing and stabbing my animals to death. A couple of your hands rimrocked my sheep, driving them over a cliff. One or two of my herders tried to stop the slaughter, but they're small men and they were on foot, and no match for your well-armed cowboys on horseback. We found two of my Mex herders dead, trampled by horses, and two hundred head of my sheep were killed as well!"

Cal sent for Wolf Raullins and let him hear the accusations. Wolf stood stoically, his arms folded in front of his chest.

"In Texas and Wyoming, they're butchering sheep by the thousands," Wolf said finally.

"That still don't make it right," the marshal pointed out.

"I don't think Wolf intended for anyone to get killed," Cal said in a quiet voice. "It had to be accidental."

Marshal Wade, who was an old friend, readily agreed. "You see, Phillips, no harm was intended." He turned to Wolf. "But if I ever hear of you killing sheepherders or sheep again, you'll be sitting in the territorial jail. Your ass will rot in prison."

"I should have known I wouldn't get justice from you. Your kind always side with the ranchers. I'll have to find my own way!" Phillips was beside himself with anger.

Once the two men rode off, Cal turned to Wolf. "You went against my orders," he said in sharp voice.

"I thought you'd be pleased at the way I handled things, maybe even congratulate me for doing such a good job of getting rid of those pesky sheep."

"I would never reprimand you in front of other people. I know you're a proud man. Still, you have to understand that I don't endorse a policy of cruelty or extermination."

"You make it sound like I did something really bad."

"Didn't you? What if those Mex were your people?"

Wolf stalked away, and Cal did not go after him.

As word got around about what had happened at the Thunderbolt, Cal was paid a visit by several neighbors who voiced differing opinions. Sam Wheeler came by on the following day while Cal was supervising the rebuilding of his barn. He invited his neighbor into the house.

"Well, it was about time you put them bastards in their place! I'm proud of you for showing some gumption." Wheeler smiled through his nicotine-stained teeth, puffing out his chest self-importantly.

Cal felt sick to his stomach. He thought Wheeler never looked meaner or uglier. He often wondered what a fine woman like Jesse had ever seen in him.

"I can't take any credit for it. I only gave orders the sheep were to be kept off Thunderbolt property. My foreman took it upon himself to do the rest."

"That Raullins is one hell of an hombre! Boy really has grit. Must be the Injun warrior in him."

Cal gnashed down on his back teeth and kept silent.

"Anything else you wanted to see me about?"

"Not being very neighborly. How about offering me something to drink while we talk? I rode a far piece."

Cal got out the good sour mash and poured Wheeler a drink. He did not take one for himself and waited while his neighbor finished. He was aware of Wheeler's great size. He himself was six feet two inches tall, but next to the hulking Wheeler, he did not feel very big. Wheeler had the proportions of a giant Kodiak bear.

"I've been thinking it's time we got ourselves organized into a stockman's association—you know, like they got in Colorado, Montana, and Wyoming. If we cooperate, we can rid ourselves of all the cursed sheepherders in the territory, and that goes for the homesteaders as well. You know as well as I do this country's good for only one thing, raising cattle. All them intruders has got to be driven out. Time we got together and acted as a group. Organization, that's the key. Your word carries a lot of weight in these parts. How about it?"

Cal stared at Wheeler.

"Not interested," he replied laconically.

"Hell's bells, Davis, is that all you got to say?"

"That's right."

"Well, I can't believe it! What's wrong with you? Ain't you got no guts? Your old man wouldn't have put up with it. He had iron in his blood. You let them Staffords settle right there on your own land. You should have had them thrown off pronto. You set a bad precedent. Other people have to square things for you."

"Let's face it, Sam. You and I don't see things the same way, and we probably never will."

"I'm not letting the matter drop so easy." Wheeler chewed down viciously on his cigar.

"There's enough land for everyone out here. I got plenty and so do you. No need to be greedy."

"Water's limited, and you know that as well as I do. So is the good land. You're a coward and a damn fool if you're gonna

137

pretend otherwise. Where's your common sense?"

"Wheeler, men like you don't own the land. It owns you."

"To think that my wife wants you for a son-in-law! I'd sooner have my daughter marry the devil."

"Get out of my house!"

"With pleasure. I can't abide a weakling like you."

Cal was in a terrible mood after Wheeler left. There was a time in his life when he would have punched any man in the mouth who insulted him even a fraction as much as Wheeler had done today, but those days were long gone. The practice of self-restraint had become a way of life for him.

The problem was that since he had met Mary MacGreggor, self-control was becoming more and more difficult to maintain. She was the sort of woman who would want a husband and family. He had no intention of marrying anybody. He knew all too well what a woman could do to a man's soul. Mary MacGreggor was a real danger to him. Yet, he couldn't seem to stay away from her, and every time he was with her, he regretted it. All he knew was that he wanted her bad, and the overpowering need scared him as nothing else in his life ever had.

Later that afternoon, Wolf asked to speak with him privately. Cal knew his foreman was still smarting from the dressing down he'd given Wolf about the sheepherding incident.

"I just wanted you to know that what I did the other day, I did out of loyalty to you. I done what I thought was right."

"Appreciate that, Wolf, but it wasn't right. I don't want you killing any more sheep unless the order comes directly from me."

"We couldn't let them cross the deadline."

"You know damned well that there's other ways to handle it. If things got really bad, we could spread saltpeter across the boundary area. It won't hurt our cattle none, but it'll poison the sheep. Granted it's a little subtle for Phillips, but still, he'd get the idea quick enough."

"That just ain't the right way for the Thunderbolt. This ranch taken together with Rancho Royo is the biggest spread in the territory. We got to set an example. Boss, the others look to you. You can't be kind. They'll just take it for weakness."

Cal faced his foreman squarely. "I gave you my orders, and I expect you'll carry them out."

"Can't take them. You're wrong about this. You gotta stand strong or the sheep men will walk all over you."

"I don't resort to violence unless it's the only way left. You ought to know that by now."

"A lot of folks think you're wrong about this." Wolf's fists clenched convulsively.

"Has Wheeler been talking to you again?"

Wolf turned his gaze away. "What if he has? The man's right."

Cal was beside himself with anger. "Go work for him then! I don't need a foreman who questions my authority. You've got wages coming. Take 'em and go."

Wolf squared his angular jaw. "You're wrong about this, Cal, and you'll come to regret it. A man can't straddle a fence for very long without losing one leg or the other."

Cal almost called him back, but found that he couldn't. He knew Wolf meant well. Nevertheless, he couldn't let his foreman make policy decisions. This was his ranch and he had to decide. There was no way he could back down.

Wolf Raullins left the Thunderbolt with a heavy heart. He thought Cal had treated him unfairly. He did not understand his boss's attitude one bit. What he did understand was that he needed another job right away. He knew where to get one and rode directly from the Thunderbolt to the Bar W.

As he had hoped, Sam Wheeler welcomed him with open

arms, especially after Wolf told him about his argument with Cal. If anything, he had grown in Wheeler's estimation because of his handling of the sheepherders. Wheeler wanted to hear every detail and listened to his description of the incident with rapt attention. He even called his three sons in to listen. Wolf related what had happened tersely, not being any kind of braggart. Sam slapped him on the back and offered him a cigar. Wolf realized that at the Bar W, he was getting a hero's reception. He relaxed and began to enjoy it.

"Son, you're a real man. We're proud to have you here. Why, Cal is crazy to let you go. I'll be honored to have you working as my foreman."

Wolf felt vindicated and even allowed himself the luxury of feeling a certain amount of bitterness toward his former employer.

"I just want you to do the same kind of job for me that you did for Cal. That Phillips is stirring up a hell of a lot of trouble. I figure there's only one good way to handle it. We gotta teach him a lesson he won't forget. Are you with me?"

Wolf agreed and waited for Wheeler to continue.

"It's time to kill off his flocks and put him out of business permanently."

Wolf stared at Wheeler uneasily. "I don't follow."

"Smart fella like you, of course you do. I'm even gonna send my own boys along with you. They can learn a lot that way. You'll burn Phillips out. I want those sheep dead, burned in their own corrals. And that goes for anyone who gets in your way. Shoot 'em! You'll be night riding so no one will be able to prove a thing."

Wolf thought about what the marshal had said to him. "I don't know that I'm the man for this particular job."

"I know the problem. You're used to working for a fella who don't have any guts. His daddy give him everything, just handed it all to him. He never had to fight for anything like you or me. It all come too easy to him. Men like you and me, we earn our way." Wheeler put his arm around Wolf's shoulders.

"I don't hold with killing them sheep on their own land. It don't seem right."

Sam Wheeler pulled himself to his full stature. "Seems to me that you're in something of a dilemma. You can walk away from here and hire on as a hand somewhere else. But a foreman's job, that's not easy to come by. My spread is real big, and the way I plan it, it'll get even bigger. Someday, this will all belong to my sons, but right now, they're young and inexperienced. I need a first-class foreman. Ain't had one yet that met my standards. But you'll do just fine. Now you manage this one thing, and I'll know that you're my man. See, I want all them stinkin' sheep out of the territory. We'll start with Phillips. His land is rightfully mine anyhow, and it's a sizeable piece. You know, a man who has a really good foreman would reward him by giving him land and cattle of his own. You'll find I'm much more generous than Cal Davis ever was. I support my people and I do right by those who treat me likewise. But I expect total loyalty and respect in return. Now I want to hear it from your mouth: can I trust you all the way? What do you have to say?" Wheeler puffed vigorously on his cigar.

Wolf thought it through. Wheeler was right, he realized. Finding another foreman's job would not be so easy. And Wheeler was prepared to reward him handsomely for his efforts. It seemed as if Wheeler understood what Wolf wanted and was offering it to him. If he had land of his own and cattle, he could make Mary his wife that much sooner.

He could not expect Mary to wait forever, nor could he expect a fine woman like her to share his life if he had nothing to offer her. He had the fierce pride of his mother's people. If a warrior had nothing to offer, he could not take a squaw. With

Mary, there were a great many men who might try to steal her away from him. There was no question in his mind that she was of great value.

He knew he had to decide quickly. The chances were that he could find another foreman's job, but not around here. The farther away he got from Mary, the less he could see her, and the less likely it would be that she would consent to marry him. She would probably forget all about him if he were gone for any length of time. Scruples, he decided, were for men who already had everything they wanted in life; he was too hungry to afford them. In spite of a nagging feeling that this was somehow a mistake, he decided to accept Wheeler's offer.

The day the raid on Phillips's place was to occur, Wolf rode into town and visited with Mary during the children's lunch recess. His decision weighed heavily on his mind, but he felt better once he saw Mary. Her smile was sunshine. She offered to share her lunch with him but he refused. He was too wound up to eat anything.

"Can we take a walk together?" he asked.

"Certainly, but I'm afraid it will have to be rather short. I have to stay close by to supervise the children."

"I understand. It's just that I have something important to tell you."

They walked away from the children to a quieter, secluded spot.

"First, I just want to tell you how much I love you. I hope you feel the same way about me. Mary, I can hardly wait for us to be married and live together. Have you thought about becoming my wife?" He looked deeply into her dark, bright eyes.

She was smiling at him—that had to be a good sign.

"I've thought a lot about it. But I'm still not sure. I do care about you, Wolf. You're a wonderful man. I'm just not certain that I ever want to be married. I need more time to decide, I suppose."

"You're worth waiting for. I plan to win you. And if you don't love me now, that's all right, because you will in time."

She touched his hand gently and he took her hand and held it tight.

"There's something I've got to tell you. You'll be hearing it soon enough I expect. Cal Davis fired me."

"What? I can't believe it!" Her dark eyes caught fire.

"It's true." He had to look away from her.

"Why would he do a thing like that?"

"Difference of opinion. It don't matter anymore. I took that job Sam Wheeler offered me over at the Bar W outfit."

"You know how I feel about that man," she said.

"Can't help it. Didn't feel I had much of a choice."

"Maybe if I talked to Mr. Davis on your behalf—"

"No!" he interrupted. "Cal made it plain enough. What kind of a man would I be if I had the woman I love go beg for my job? A man's got nothing if he can't hold on to his dignity."

Mary shook her head. "I just don't like this at all."

He didn't like to see Mary looking so upset and worried.

"I'm going to be involved in something. Please don't ask me any questions. I won't be in any trouble over it. It's just that I don't much like what I'm going to have to do. But remember, I'm doing it for us, so we can be together. It's for our future, Mary. And always remember how much I love you."

At that moment, he was overcome by his feeling for her. She was so pretty, so good! He had to win her. He pulled her into his arms and kissed her with all the feeling that was in him. But when she pulled away, he saw the fear in her eyes.

"Whatever Wheeler wants you to do, promise me you'll forget about it! I do care about you and I'm afraid for you. That man has bad instincts."

He took her back into his arms and kissed her gently this time. "I'll be back to see you tomorrow. Everything's going to be fine. You'll see." He mounted his horse and rode off quickly, turning back to look at her only once. She was still watching him with a troubled expression on her pretty face.

That night, Wolf led a group of Sam Wheeler's cowboys to the Phillips sheep ranch. Wheeler sent his two older boys along with him. Wolf felt confident; it was going to be a real easy job, just the way Sam Wheeler had described it to him.

The sheep were in the corrals; Wolf estimated that there were at least six or seven hundred head of the dumb beasts. They had come prepared, carrying kerosene and torches. A grimly determined group, they knew just what had to be done.

Wolf found that he was grinding his back teeth as he began lighting the torches. Suddenly, the dark night was aglow with the fires they were setting all around the corrals. The cry of the trapped animals sounded almost human, like babies sobbing.

The herders came running, alerted by the sound. Some of them had rifles. The sheep men started shooting and Wheeler's men returned the fire. The cry of the trapped animals grew louder as the flames rose upward, consuming hungrily everything in their path. Wolf found himself exchanging gunfire with the herders. As he started to ride away, he felt an overwhelming pain in the center of his back. It knocked the breath right out of him, and he fell from his horse. The last sound he ever heard was the unforgettable moan of dying sheep. He felt his soul soar, riding above the confused commotion, and then the stench of the dead and dying left his nostrils for eternity.

CHAPTER ELEVEN

Mary went into the general store after dismissing the children from school. Elizabeth had given her a small list of items to bring home with her and had also reminded her about looking at material for the new dresses she intended to sew. Mary was disappointed to discover that only Mrs. Jones was in the store and she was busy waiting on Jesse Wheeler.

"Can I play with Bobby for a while?" Amy asked her, noticing the same thing.

"Just don't get your skirt dirty," Mary cautioned the child, recalling that Bobby Wheeler had a tendency to play rather rough games at recess. Amy skipped out of the store and Mary settled back to wait her turn.

She observed that waiting beside Mrs. Wheeler's buggy, two fully armed cowboys sat at alert attention on horseback. Why would Jesse need an armed escort? she wondered.

Mary glanced around the store to see if she could locate the things she needed while the two women were still chatting. She was not impatient by nature, but she disliked wasting time and knew that Mrs. Jones was something of a longwinded gossip.

"We just got in the most delightful material. Would this do for the dress you plan to have made?"

The small, delicately boned blonde studied the bolt of cloth.

"Maybe. I want something that will look well with a bustle. I understand that's the current style in the East."

"You're always so fashionable," Mrs. Jones gushed.

"Actually, this is for Lorette. She's a young lady now and I want her dressed accordingly."

Mrs. Jones pressed her apron against her boney hips. "What a pretty young woman she's turned into. Why I imagine she'll have every single man in the territory casting his eye at her."

"I've got a particular man in mind," Jesse said.

"Might I ask who?" Mrs. Jones questioned, eyes open wide.

Mrs. Walker smiled and shook her head. "We'll just have to see if it's going to work out first."

Their foolish prattle was annoying Mary and she tried to ignore them. But her attention was quickly brought back to their conversation by the next comment made by Mrs. Jones. The woman's voice lowered to the loudest confidential whisper she'd ever heard.

"I was told what happened at the Phillips place last night. Six men dead. How terrible! Wolf Raullins was one of them, I believe."

"I wouldn't know." Jesse Wheeler backed away, knocking over a bolt of calico. "That's Sam's business, not mine," she added abruptly. "I'm in a rush, Emmy. Just wrap up what I've already got. I'll come back and order the fabric another day."

Mary was stunned. Surely, she hadn't heard Mrs. Jones correctly? Wolf dead? Wolf couldn't be dead! It wasn't possible. When Mrs. Wheeler walked out of the store, she approached the storekeeper.

"Can I help you, Miss MacGreggor?" the proprietress inquired.

"I believe you said something about trouble at the Phillips place last night?" She tried to keep her voice even and unemotional.

Mrs. Jones's eyes lit up. Clearly, there was nothing she enjoyed more than relating some choice piece of information.

"Why, yes. I guess I'm the first person that found out about

146

it, on account of Jack Phillips was in here himself trying to order more rifles from my husband, and he was all excited and told us exactly why. Hands from the Wheeler place tried to burn him out last night and kill off his sheep. There might even be a range war! Fancy that. Mr. Phillips was beside himself, absolutely wild with rage. He lost four men and almost a thousand head of sheep. Can you imagine?" Mrs. Jones' eyes opened wide.

"What about Wolf Raullins? I heard you say something?" Mary couldn't keep the tremor out of her voice.

Mrs. Jones puffed up like a peacock preening its feathers. "Yes, I know all about that too. He was leading the men who attacked the Phillips herd. I'm sorry to be the one to tell you. I mean, I know he was sweet on you, but the fact of the matter is, Wolf Raullins was killed last night, shot to death by the herders."

Breath expelled from Mary's lungs as if someone had punched her in the chest.

"You say Mr. Phillips told you that?"

"He did indeed!"

"There's no mistake? You're sure?" she asked.

Mrs. Jones looked offended. "Sure as cactus grows in the desert. I'm telling you, Jack talked to my Zeb this morning. He was ordering shovels and such like to deal with all the damage. The man was fit to be tied and didn't mind who knew what happened. He's so fighting mad, I figure there's going to be blood running hereabouts. It's too bad about Wolf. He was a nice young fella, for a half-breed."

Mary dropped the few items she had intended to purchase and ran out of the store. She was too upset to spend another moment listening to the annoying tongue of Mrs. Jones. She also couldn't bear for the woman to see how upset she was.

She wanted to express her grief in private. Wolf had always

been loving and kind to her, and now she was sorry she hadn't agreed to marry him when he asked her. Maybe she could have stopped him then. But there weren't going to be any tears; she had cried herself out at her uncle's grave and refused to cry again. Tears were a luxury that she could no longer afford.

She found Amy by the wagon, looking dirty.

"I'm sorry, Cousin Mary, but Bobby went and pushed me into a mud puddle."

She didn't bother with a reply, simply helping the little girl into the wagon. It was then she saw Cal Davis riding into Expectation. For some reason she didn't quite comprehend, her entire body began to tremble. Before she even stopped to think what she was doing, Mary walked up to the rancher as he dismounted his spirited stallion.

"It's all your fault!" she shouted at him, shaking with a sense of outrage.

"What are you talking about?" he responded in a vexed tone of voice. His riveting, dark blue eyes were fixed on hers as he tied his horse to the hitching post.

"Don't pretend you don't know. Wolf is dead, and you're to blame."

"Wolf dead? I didn't know. When? How?"

"I know you didn't send him to the Phillips place. Sam Wheeler did that. But you drove him to it! He felt he had no other choice. How could you fire him? Was it because he wanted to marry me? Were you getting even? If so, you are cruel and contemptible!" Her turbulent nature had completely triumphed over her rationality; she was overwhelmed with hostility toward him.

His posture stiffened and his face lost all expression and color. "I do not have to explain or justify myself to you, Miss MacGreggor. There were reasons I let Wolf go, very good reasons, and they had nothing at all to do with you. But you go ahead and think whatever you wish. You probably will anyway."

"You were unfair to him. Of course, that doesn't matter very much to your kind of person, does it? Your wealth and power have made you so arrogant that you set no value on human life."

His eyes darkened visibly, flashing with fury, the way they had the day she overheard his exchange with Jack Phillips.

"Miss MacGreggor, you're so wrong that it's laughable, except that I can find nothing amusing about your insulting behavior and accusations. I have so far succeeded in exercising great restraint with you. I will somehow try to forgive you for the things you just said to me. I realize that you must have cared deeply for Wolf. But that doesn't give you the right to verbally abuse me. It also doesn't change the fact that you are a mule-headed, opinionated female with a completely closed mind. You are also outspoken on matters you know very little about and do not fully understand. The fact is, you very much disappoint me. You are well named, Miss Mary, for you are quite contrary in every respect, and if you were a man, I just might be tempted to go back on a promise I made myself a long time ago!" He stalked off, leaving her still shaking with rage.

On the drive back to the farm, Amy seemed to be fully aware of Mary's black mood; the child uttered not a single word. Mary, for her part, could not bring herself to speak. She was overcome by powerful emotions she didn't understand. When they finally arrived at the cabin, she discovered that an argument had erupted between Elizabeth and Rebecca. Actually, it was Elizabeth who was doing most of the arguing.

"I cannot stand to hear this petty bickering," Mary said to Elizabeth.

Her aunt stared at her in surprise. "Is something wrong?" she asked.

"Must you always be so unkind to Rebecca?" She realized

how irritable she sounded and regretted it, but she felt in no mood to listen to the poor child being berated by her mother today.

"You know very well that Rebecca lives in her own private world and never listens to me. She's full of peculiar notions."

"I cannot cope with this today, of all days." Mary hurried away from the cabin and ran out toward the fields. For the first time in her life, she felt unable to shoulder anyone else's problems.

Jeremy saw her and came toward her. "Are you all right, Cousin Mary?"

"I need to be by myself for a time."

"I'll take care of unhitching the wagon and I'll feed and water the horse. Anything you might want done?" His voice was kind and understanding beyond his years.

"There's nothing anyone can do for me. I'll come back to the cabin later."

When Jeremy was gone, she went to her uncle's grave and sank down on her knees beside the grassy knoll where they had buried Isaac. She stared silently at the sky and the desert and they seemed to stare back at her. The silence suited her mood because there really weren't any words that seemed right.

Rebecca and Jeremy had both stopped attending church on Sunday mornings. Rebecca, in fact, never left the farm at all. She completely retreated back into her own private world, just as Elizabeth had said. Jeremy's reasons for refusing to go were somewhat different. His religious beliefs had been shattered by the nature of his father's death. Mary knew the boy was bitter and confused, but the subject was still so painful for him that Mary had not as yet even tried to discuss it with him.

She and Elizabeth took Amy with them regularly every Sunday morning. This Sunday, after the service had concluded, most of the people who had traveled long distances remained to stand around and chat for a time as they usually did. For many of the women, it was the only form of socializing they would encounter with members of their own sex outside of their families during the week, and they wanted to take full advantage of the opportunity to communicate. Several of the parents of her students wanted to discuss their children's school progress with Mary, and she was quite willing to oblige.

Sam Wheeler approached her just as she was getting ready to leave. His expression was like that of a bull who has seen a red cape.

"I'll have a word with you," he said to her in a commanding manner.

"What is it that you wish to discuss with me?"

"Concerns the way you're teaching my son."

She kept a tight hold on her temper. "Precisely what is it that seems to be disturbing you?"

"You've been filling his head with a lot of bad notions."

"Such as?" She tried very hard not to let her hostility show.

"Dangerous, foolish talk about how all men are equal to each other. I don't like radical notions planted in my young'un's head."

"Sir, we were studying the Declaration of Independence. Perhaps you might have heard of the document."

His face glowered down at hers in a menacing manner. She realized he was trying to use his superior size and weight to intimidate her, but she was not the least bit frightened. If anything, his manner increased her ire.

"You're teaching my boy that some Mex or Injun is just as good as he is. Now what kind of nonsense is that?" He chomped down angrily on his ever-present cigar.

"Sir, your ignorance of American history astounds me."

"I know my history as good or better than you. And I don't

like the way you interpret it. Don't you try to ridicule me in front of my wife and children. I won't stand for it! I don't like your attitude the least little bit. I'm gonna see to it that you lose your job."

"You do as you wish. It has been my experience that some ignorant people dislike anyone seeking a good education, even if it happens to be their own children, because it makes them feel inferior. I believe you are afraid that if your son finds out one group of people has no right to subjugate another, he will lose respect for your opinions. Perhaps it is time you reevaluate your views. People can live together in harmony, even if they are different from each other in many respects. Your prejudices have already taken enough lives." She was thinking of Wolf at that moment. If she had her handgun with her, she might actually have been tempted to shoot Mr. Wheeler.

His face was livid with rage; she observed a vein pulsing at his left temple. "No one dares speak to me that way."

"Maybe they should. High time, I would say." She was five foot seven inches tall, not small for a woman, but certainly small in comparison to the huge, hulking body of Sam Wheeler. Still, she did not feel the least bit frightened or intimidated; her sense of outrage was too great.

"You're just lucky you're not a man or I'd make quick work of you." He pointed his finger in her face as if it were a gun ready to explode and his eyes screwed into bullets.

"I don't doubt you would. However, I am not afraid of you or those like you. My only fear is that your personal greed and selfishness will eventually destroy the very land you covet if you are allowed to continue unchecked."

"That's enough! My son will no longer go to your school, if you have a school after this. You will pay dearly for your insults to me, I swear it. You're going to be very sorry."

Mary held her head high. "Mr. Wheeler, I will never regret

speaking the truth as I see it. Not even when hell freezes over will I be sorry." With that, she turned on her heel and walked toward her wagon, and as she looked back for Elizabeth, she realized with some surprise that everyone had been listening to what had transpired between herself and Sam Wheeler. She exchanged an uneasy look with Cal Davis and then quickly turned away.

Cal Davis watched Mary MacGreggor drive out of Expectation with her aunt and young cousin. He couldn't help thinking that she was a remarkable woman, truly extraordinary. He had never encountered a female like her before. Mary's fierce nature amazed him. Here was a woman of unflinching principles. Even he had never really stood up to Sam Wheeler and told the man what he thought of him. She had done exactly that, and it seemed to him that everything she said was as right as a thunderstorm pouring rain on parched desert land.

He was somewhat in awe of her willingness to take on Wheeler for what she believed was a righteous cause. Mary burned like a fire in the desert. He had never felt more strongly drawn to her. And yet, at the same time, she was everything that he sought to avoid. He had made himself into the calm, cool, conservative, controlled Cal Davis everyone respected. Involving himself with a firebrand radical like her was the worst possible thing for him. Every time he was with her, he lost control in one way or another.

Hadn't being burned once in his life been enough? Hadn't he learned anything from the sheer misery of that experience? And for all her fine qualities, Mary was still a difficult and obstinate person, a prickly cactus. Why should he find her so damned attractive? He had tried many times to put her entirely out of his mind, but it proved impossible. What he ought to do, he supposed, was court some female who was right for him. Jesse kept urging him to see more of Lorette; maybe he ought to consider it. Maybe it would help him to forget about Mary MacGreggor. There could never be anything between them anyway; she hated him too much. She'd disliked him from the first time they met.

What she interpreted as arrogance was just his way of covering up his shyness where women were concerned. He was not a ladies' man. He'd never really learned how to act around women. He'd never acquired the easy charm which women seemed to admire in men. Maybe it was just as well that he aroused Mary MacGreggor's anger; he preferred that to her scorn.

She was such a spirited woman that she tested a man at every turn. It was unfortunate she always thought the worst of him, no matter what he did. Then again, she might have been right about him. Had he dismissed Wolf in part out of jealousy? If he hadn't known that Mary cared about his foreman, would he have given Wolf another chance? He tried to tell himself it wasn't true, but he didn't really know for sure. The thought troubled him. He'd always prided himself on being fair-minded.

No, he had to forget about Mary MacGreggor because his feelings for her were hopeless. Anyway, if he were ever to take a wife at all, she should be a young, innocent girl, someone sweet and gentle—someone like Jesse's Lorette. With Mary, there could only be pain and strife.

His mind turned to pressing, current matters. He was very well aware of the situation growing worse between the cattlemen and sheepherders. It was a serious threat to the well-being of the entire community. He had a personal responsibility to try to head off trouble. Now that there had already been violence, it would be that much harder to stop the trouble from escalating, but he must do his best to see it ended before things got any worse. He saw himself as the only logical person to assume the role of mediator.

There was a rumor that both Jack Phillips and Sam Wheeler intended to hire professional gunmen to settle their dispute, and it really worried him. He hated the thought of senseless destruction and the waste such a move would cause. He remembered when his father had come back from the War between the States and told him about how the entire South was in ruins. He realized even then that warfare really didn't solve any problems.

Since both Wheeler and Phillips attended the church service with their families, Cal reasoned that he might take advantage of the Sabbath to do some negotiating in a peaceful setting. Before either man could leave, he took each by the arm and steered the two of them toward the saloon.

"What's this about, Cal?" Wheeler protested.

"Drinks on me," Cal responded, leading them to a private corner.

"I don't drink with bastards who are out to destroy me," Phillips said.

"And I don't want to be near no one who smells like sheep shit!"

"Your damn cows don't smell no better!" Phillips countered.

"That's enough," Cal said. "I want us to sit down and try to settle our differences."

"Davis, I got nothing to say to the sonofabitch sheepherder." Wheeler said, puffing on his cigar.

"I think it's time you both talked sense to each other. No one will benefit from an all-out range war."

"This ain't your affair!" Wheeler bellowed at him, face reddening.

"Wrong. I lose as much as anybody if there's killing and destruction. The land is as much mine as it is yours. Now sit down." Cal's voice was quiet but forceful.

The two men finally did as he asked.

"I'm going to order drinks, and I want you both to stay and have them. We've got to figure a way out of this mess before it's too late."

They drank in silence. When they had finished, Cal spoke again. "Let's set up some ground rules. No more trading insults. That doesn't accomplish anything. You men got to learn to respect each other's rights. If we start talking decent to each other, maybe we can work out a compromise that will satisfy everybody."

"Don't think so," Wheeler said. "Phillips and I both want the same grazing land."

"Can't we divide it up evenly?" Cal asked.

"You know damn well what sheep do to grazing land! It'll be ruined forever."

Phillips's face turned vermillion. "I don't see no point to this either," the sheep rancher asserted, pulling his colorful poncho around his burly body. "Besides, Davis, you're a rancher too. Why, I got nearly as much trouble with you as with him. Why should I trust you? You'll be sure to give him the best of it."

"I ain't sharing nothing with sheep men. I was here first! His land is rightfully mine anyway. Maybe you can eat roast lamb for dinner, Cal, but it sure as hell would stick in my craw!"

"There's nothing more to talk about," Phillips said, rising to his feet.

"That's right," Wheeler agreed. "We both know there's only one way to settle this."

"See you in hell," Phillips said to Wheeler.

Cal said nothing more, knowing he had failed. Even if he could get them talking again, it seemed hopeless. He did not like what was happening, but he felt powerless to stop it. As far as he was concerned, they were both wrong. He wasn't going to take the side of either one of his neighbors. He'd done his best, and now all he could hope for was to keep himself out of their quarrel if it was possible.

Late that afternoon, an unexpected visitor showed up at the cabin. Nowadays whenever Mary heard riders coming toward her home, she reached for her pistol as a precaution. But when she saw that the rider was Jack Phillips, she holstered her gun and went to the door to greet him.

"Mr. Phillips, why are you here?" she asked.

"I could do with a cup of coffee or even something stronger," he told her.

She invited him into the cabin with little warmth, remembering very well that it was him or one of his men who had killed Wolf.

He seated himself at the table before the hearth as she poured him a cup of coffee.

"Again, I have to ask. What it is you want of me?"

"Well, I'm not exactly here to sell you mutton," he said, trying for an ingratiating smile.

She waited in silence.

He cleared his throat and continued. "I heard the way you talked to Sam Wheeler today and I liked it. Regular folks just don't stand up to the likes of him. They're too afraid. I think it's time we took action against the big ranchers around here and Wheeler in particular, since he's making himself the leader. I'm not a violent man in spite of how it might look, Miss MacGreggor. I just want to be left alone to raise my sheep and take care of my family. I believe that's what the homesteaders want too. Do you agree?"

She offered a nod.

"Good. I've been thinking this thing through real careful. Cal Davis tried to get Wheeler and me to negotiate today, but Wheeler won't have any of it. The man's a menace. Just like you said, he's greedy and nobody's safe from him. It's not just my land he wants. If the cattlemen can do it to me, then they can do it to anybody. Wheeler's men murdered my sheep and my herders in all kinds of vicious ways. I just found another bunch of woolies with their throats slashed today. It's cruel, senseless slaughter. I got no intention of knuckling under to Wheeler, even if it means going into debt to the bank. I'm gambling everything on stopping the Bar W outfit. But my herders aren't gunmen and they're no match for Wheeler's cowboys. So far, he's got the upper hand."

"I am sympathetic, Mr. Phillips, but what can I do to help you?"

His eyes blinked at her thoughtfully. "Ma'am, I like the way you talk. You got good ideas and fine words. I'm planning a secret meeting at my place and inviting everyone that's got cause to fear the cattlemen. I plan to collect enough money to hire some gunmen."

She gasped. "You mean professional killers?"

"Yes, ma'am, that's exactly what I intend to do. One of Wheeler's hands was shooting off his mouth in the saloon the other night about how Wheeler intends to bring in gunmen to kill us off. I think we got to get the jump on him or we'll lose out. I want everyone to make a donation, as much as they can afford. Then we can bring in someone really good."

"Mr. Phillips, I can't countenance murder."

His face flushed. "It ain't murder! It's self-defense. Look, I might be first on Wheeler's list, but others will soon follow. I heard him threaten you, and anyone could see he meant what he said. He'll squash you like a scorpion under his boot heel and won't think twice about it either."

"I'm not frightened of him."

"Well, you should be! There's only one way to stop a man like Wheeler; either you kill him yourself or you have him killed.

This isn't just my fight, Miss MacGreggor. If you want to stay on this land, eventually you'll have to take a stand. If we don't do something, soon every sheepherder and homesteader will be driven out of Arizona. There's only strength in unity."

She hesitated; what Phillips said did make a lot of sense to her. If they united together, perhaps they could get Wheeler to yield. But she did not like Phillips' idea of hiring professional gunmen.

"Do you have any idea who you want to hire?" she asked bluntly.

He smiled at her, realizing that she was at last considering what he had to say. "There's a man in Denver named Rondo Leston. He was recommended to me by a friend. Man was once an army scout and later a Pinkerton detective. Lately, he struck out on his own as a bounty hunter. The stockmen's association in Colorado hired him on, but he's got no particular loyalty to cattlemen. He likes to live well and would work for whoever could afford his expensive fee. I'm told he's between jobs right now. He could kill Wheeler for us, and then it would all be over without any more trouble."

"No one would mind that you had Wheeler murdered?" She raised her brows in disbelief.

"You think it's too simple a solution? Well, I think it just might work. Anyway, I'll be having that meeting on Friday at my place. You and yours are welcome to come. Good day, Miss MacGreggor."

Elizabeth joined her after the sheep rancher left.

"Were you listening?" Mary asked. She knew that Elizabeth had been careful to remain in the other room and had kept the girls with her.

"Some of it. I don't approve of eavesdropping. But yes, I got the general idea. Mary, are you going to involve yourself in stopping Mr. Wheeler? I have to say, I don't like any of this at all."

"Nor do I. I'm very bitter that Wolf is dead because of their foolish disputes. It seems to me that grown men act no better than little boys squabbling at recess. Only there I can set them aright. But there's always a bully who needs standing up to, isn't there? I just don't like Mr. Phillips's solution to the problem. I really don't approve of cold-blooded murder regardless. I can't in good conscience give him money to hire a killer."

"I agree completely," Elizabeth said. "I think it's time we left this place for good. It seems that everyone is fighting for land that really isn't worth having anyway."

Mary went to sleep that night still thinking about the situation, wondering how Cal Davis would be involved. Jack Phillips had mentioned that Cal tried to end the hostilities. Perhaps she had been wrong to be so down on him. Had her judgment been hasty? But it was too late now. She had condemned Cal Davis, blaming him for Wolf's death, and she was certain that he would never forgive her for that.

CHAPTER TWELVE

Mary awoke the following morning to what sounded like an argument. There were loud voices, and she could hear Elizabeth's high-pitched whine rising shrilly. Then in turn, there was Rebecca's young, softer voice speaking with urgency. The cacophony crescendoed as Mary quickly got out of bed and stood facing them dressed in her flannel nightdress.

"What's wrong?" Mary asked.

"It's Rebecca. You will not believe what she wants to do," Elizabeth said.

"Perhaps you should tell me."

"She wants to take our horse and ride off somewhere by herself. Can you imagine? First words out of her mouth in weeks and that's what she says."

"There must be more to it than that," Mary responded, growing somewhat impatient with her aunt. She turned to Rebecca, whose gaze was cast downward. "Where is it that you want to go?"

"To meet Billy."

Mary raised her eyebrows. "Has he been in contact with you?"

The girl kept her eyes fixed on the ground. "Not exactly, but I know he's thinking about me."

"Do you know where Billy is?"

Rebecca shook her head, the fine mane of blond hair falling into her face. "No one would understand."

Mary put her hands firmly around the girl's slender shoulders.

"You must try to explain it so that we can comprehend."

"All right. It just came to me, like a vision. Billy's in Prescott."

"Now why would you even think that?" Elizabeth interrogated sharply.

"What was the vision like?" Mary asked in a gentle voice.

"It was like a dream. Last night, I had this special dream, only really I was awake. Billy was calling to me and he asked me to meet him in Prescott. He said if I could meet him there, then we'd be able to be together and everything would be all right for us."

Elizabeth threw up her hands in a gesture of despair. "Do you see what I'm up against? The girl is a lunatic. I'm ashamed to admit it. My own child, and she's absolutely insane!"

Mary was aware that Amy was standing on the far side of the room listening intently. She would have liked to end the argument here and now, but both Elizabeth and Rebecca were too upset.

"I'm not crazy. I'm not!" Rebecca cried out. "I know that's what you think of me. I know how ashamed of me you are. I knew I should have just sneaked away because you'd never believe me. No one understands. In the Bible, they talk about dreams of prophecy, don't they, Cousin Mary? Well, that's what I have sometimes, only I'm awake when I get them. Why can't you understand?"

"You're impossible, Rebecca. I wish you had never been born!"

Mary put a restraining hand on her aunt. "Please, Elizabeth, don't say things you'll regret later."

"It's just the truth, Mary. I'm admitting how I honestly feel." There were bitter tears in her aunt's eyes.

Mary had to admit that she believed what her aunt said was true. When Elizabeth had given birth to Rebecca, she was young. The birth had been difficult, and later on, the baby's incessant crying had tried her as well. Mary distinctly remembered how hard it had been for her aunt. No, Elizabeth never had felt much affection for her firstborn.

Rebecca had been rather wild as a small girl and hard to discipline. Elizabeth might have forgiven that in a son, but not in a daughter. Unlike her aunt, Mary had always been very fond of the child and enjoyed reading to her. Unfortunately, all that had changed with Rebecca's accident.

One day, Rebecca had decided to take a ride on a neighbor's horse without asking anyone's permission. The animal had a mean disposition, and although the ride started out well enough, the horse became excited and began to gallop. The child tried to restrain the animal, but it was used to its master's strength and weight. As a result, the horse ran wildly, faster and faster, until it threw the small girl.

The injury and subsequent unconsciousness left Rebecca's mind clouded. Where once there had been a vibrant, active girl, there was now only a shadow of her former self. When the doctor talked of damage to the brain, Elizabeth had cried with grief. After that, it was as if Rebecca were dead to her. For Mary, if anything, the girl had become dearer.

Elizabeth was ashamed of Rebecca; Mary was as certain of that as was Rebecca herself. When visitors came, Elizabeth generally found some reason to exclude the girl, and eventually, Rebecca came to prefer seclusion. Mary tried to spend time with Becky whenever she could, but it was not the same as having her mother's love and support. And as the years progressed, Mary had been more occupied taking care of her father.

"Please, Cousin Mary, may I come to town with you today? I need to borrow the wagon and drive to Prescott."

"You really believe in this vision, don't you?"

"It was a dream of prophecy. Everything in it was real and true. Billy's going to be there. I know it! And I can find him. I promise we'll bring the wagon back to you."

Mary put her arms around the small, slender body of her cousin. Then she held the girl away, pushing the long, straight blond hair back from the cobalt eyes.

"Sometimes when we have a strong enough wish that cannot be satisfied in real life, we dream that it will come true. Such dreams seem real, but they are not."

"You're wrong about this. The dream is true. Mama says I'm touched in the head, but truly, it is the Lord who touched me. I returned to life like Lazarus from the dead and I was given the gift of second sight."

"It may seem so, but, dear, I believe this is just your longing for Billy making you think that you can find him. He was so frightened when he left here, I can scarcely believe he'd be as close as Prescott. Chances are he's headed south or to a different territory or state entirely."

Rebecca began to cry. "Nobody ever believes me!"

Mary studied the girl's round, innocent face. "All right, you can leave me in town and take the wagon, but I'm going to have your brother go with you. There's no way I'd let you travel alone. It is much too dangerous."

"Oh, Cousin Mary, thank you so much!" Rebecca hugged her.

"Really, this is ridiculous," Elizabeth said.

"Rebecca does have an uncanny awareness of what may come to pass. It's an eerie sensitivity. She won't be satisfied unless we let her go. Jeremy could use a day off from plowing anyway. Elizabeth, you may come to town with me today."

They hurried through breakfast, with Elizabeth glowering at both of them. "The whole idea is stupid. I don't know how you could let her talk you into it."

"It will be perfectly all right," Mary insisted.

Just as they were getting ready to tell Jeremy of the plan,

Mary heard pounding hooves beating in the distance. Horses were quickly approaching the farm. Mary grabbed her revolver and held it in readiness. She looked out from the window and saw that there were just two riders, dusty and dirty as if they had been on the trail for a long time and had been riding very hard.

"Anybody at home?"

Mary opened the door and stepped outside, her gun carefully pointed at the strangers.

"Who wants to know?" she asked in a clear, strong voice.

She was staring up at a man who was tall and lean, with a thick, dark mustache and cold eyes.

"How do, ma'am. Name's Tom Horn. I'm a scout for the army. We're warning folks in your area that Apaches are raiding hereabouts. General wants everyone to know. You can come to the fort where you'll be safe until this blows over."

"That's quite a distance for us. Is it really necessary?"

The man looked impatient. "Look, ma'am, you can do whatever you want. It's your scalp. But you'd be crazy to stay here. You folks are a real easy target. I can't give you an escort though. There's other people got to be warned. That rancher, Cal Davis, intends to stay. Since he's your neighbor, you might go over there. He said anyone would be welcome, and his place has fair protection."

Then the man who called himself Tom Horn and the other scout who hadn't spoken at all rode away. Mary walked back into the cabin and turned to Rebecca.

"I'm afraid there won't be any trip to Prescott today," she told Rebecca. "There's a problem with Indians, it seems."

"What is it? What's wrong?" Elizabeth asked anxiously.

Mary explained what she'd been told by the scout.

"Then we'd better go over to Mr. Davis's ranch," Elizabeth said. "We'll be safe there."

"You and the children go. I would rather remain here."

Elizabeth stared at her as if she were crazy. "Mary, that is the most ridiculous thing you've ever said. Of course, you're coming with us. We have no protection here."

"Maybe we should try to find the fort."

"I have no idea where it is, do you?"

Mary shook her head, realizing that she was trapped. Mr. Horn's message had been very convincing. But how she hated the thought of going to Cal Davis for help! Would he give her a smug, superior smile or just glare at her coldly out of those eyes bluer then the sea and sky? The thought of having to face him after she'd accused him of responsibility for Wolf's death was the worst torture imaginable. It really might have been easier to face the Apaches.

There were several other families at the Thunderbolt ranch when they arrived. All of them were small property owners like themselves. The men looked anxious and the women solemn. There was a sense of foreboding in the air, and Mary became aware that everyone was waiting for something horrible to happen. But she decided it was silly to be frightened, especially when no one knew for certain if the Apache were even going to be in the vicinity.

Doc led them into the main house and Mary began to look around, curious to see how and where Cal Davis lived. The house was one level of sturdy adobe construction and the furnishings appeared quite Spartan and masculine, but the pieces of quality pine showed fine craftsmanship. There were colorful rugs of native design on the plain wood floors serving as the only form of decoration.

Cal Davis came toward her, silver spurs jangling. "So you accepted my invitation," he said, his face showing no emotion whatsoever.

Elizabeth moved toward him, placing her hand on his arm. "Thank you for your hospitality. I hope we're not imposing on you."

"Not at all."

"You have a lovely home," Elizabeth said.

"Nothing fancy." But he seemed pleased with the compliment.

"You should see the place over at Rancho Royo," Doc exclaimed. "Now that's a house!"

"You have another home as well?" Elizabeth asked with both surprise and curiosity.

"It's not really my home," he responded, giving an annoyed look at Doc for bringing up the subject. "My father built a house in the style of a Southern mansion so that my mother wouldn't be unhappy. He tried to make it as much like the home she'd grown up in as possible. It was their house. My father lived in it even after she left him and went back East. I inherited it after he passed away and I renamed it."

"So no one lives in that house now?" Elizabeth asked.

"Not that I know of. The hands have a good, solid bunkhouse. No one needs or wants the old place."

"How unfortunate. Such a waste."

Mary thought that the rancher seemed uncomfortable with the subject and decided it was best to change it. After all, why should they know anything personal about the man? Surely, he had the right not to discuss his personal life with strangers.

"Do you actually expect that the Apache will show up here?"

His eyes stared into hers with unblinking directness. "It's possible."

"Are they really going to try to kill us?" Amy asked him, her eyes wide with fear.

Cal smiled down at the little girl. "I only know what the scouts said, just like you. But I'm glad you came here. I promise we won't let anyone hurt you."

"Mary was all for staying at the cabin," Elizabeth confided.

"Well, it's good you talked her out of it." His face took on a somber look.

"Couldn't this be just a scare blown out of proportion?" Mary queried.

His level gaze met hers. "Not likely. We got word that the Parkers were wiped out."

"What? I can't believe it!"

"It's true," Doc substantiated. "Every last one of them. So we figure there's reason to worry."

"Are you certain that the Apache were responsible?"

Cal looked at her questioningly. "Who else could it have been?"

"I don't know, but Mrs. Parker made it pretty clear to me that there were others trying to drive homesteaders off their land. In fact, she was rather outspoken about it."

His tanned face reddened. "So now you think not only am I responsible for Wolf's death but I'm some sort of monster who'd go around murdering innocent homesteaders?"

"I never said that!" She felt her own face begin to burn. She had been thinking of Sam Wheeler but realized Cal Davis could not have known that.

"Well, ma'am, if you was to see those bodies, you'd know it was Injuns what done it," Doc said. "The scout described it to us, and I can tell you that only the Apache kill that way."

"I suppose white men never take scalps?"

"You want all the details?" Cal Davis asked through clenched teeth. He looked as if he wanted to strike her.

She was suddenly aware that everyone in the room was staring at them, listening to their confrontation. She could feel the heat rising throughout her entire body. How she wished she could have avoided coming here!

"Perhaps it would be wise if we discontinued this conversation," she said. "There are young children in the room. I'd rather they weren't frightened."

"Fine," he said, "but if you ever want to know the details, just ask." His voice and eyes challenged her.

"Those poor, good people," Elizabeth said in a shaken voice. "I hate this place, I really do! Now we have bloodthirsty savages to fear. What do they want from us?" she asked.

"The land," Doc answered. "Same as lots of other folks."

Elizabeth began to cry and Peter Jenkins, who was there with his wife and children, tried to comfort her. "There, there, Mrs. Stafford, don't take on so. My wife and I were just discussing it too. She asked why good people like the Parkers should die such horrible deaths. She even blasphemed and said she doubted the Lord was watching over us. Ain't that right, Sarah?" Jenkins turned to his taciturn wife who nodded her head sadly.

"And what was your answer to her?" Mary inquired.

Jenkins removed his low-crowned plainsman's hat with its straight brim and turned his eyes to meet hers.

"I know the Lord has a plan for all of us. It ain't our place to question His will. We gotta be rock-solid like Job."

"Best be saving that kind of talk for Sunday, Reverend," Doc told him.

"Think we need it more now," Jenkins replied with the hint of a smile.

At that moment, a tall cowboy hurried into the main room of the house.

"Cal, we got trouble. Our outriders just came charging in saying that Apaches are heading in this direction."

"How many, Tiny?"

"They don't think more than a couple of dozen in the entire raiding party."

"That's more than enough," Doc remarked. "They're mean

fighters. For every one of them gets killed, at least two soldiers die, maybe more."

"Time we got ready," Cal Davis said, his expression grim.

Mary watched as he opened a large gun case and began passing out rifles to anyone who did not have his own.

"May I please have one for myself," she asked.

He stared at her in surprise. "You know how to use it? I wouldn't want you hurting yourself."

"I think I just might manage," she said in a dry tone.

He smiled indulgently and handed her a weapon.

"Tiny, I want you to see to it that the men are spread out around the bunkhouse and the barns. Make sure every man has a safe position. I don't want to lose a single man, animal, or building if we can help it."

Mary noticed that the main room of the house had many windows facing the front approach to the ranch. The men positioned themselves so that each had a view outward. Mary did the same while the rest of the women remained back.

"Damned evil creatures," Doc said. "The quicker we get rid of them savages the better."

"I'm certain they consider us intruders on their land," Mary observed. "Mr. Davis, you should understand that kind of thinking."

He flashed a hostile look in her direction. "The difference is, I wouldn't murder anyone for a piece of land."

"That's comforting to hear," she said, dripping sarcasm.

"Maybe the Apache will want the land you're squatting on," he snapped. "Would you just hand it over to them?"

"If their claim was genuine."

"And who would decide that?" he confronted her, his eyes fixed on hers with a piercing stare.

"I am trying to be open-minded," she countered.

"Are you? I hadn't noticed. For a tenderfoot, you sure think you know an awful lot."

"I've picked up a newspaper or two in my time, Mr. Davis, so I'm not as ignorant about this situation in the West as you might imagine."

"I see. Since you seem to think you know so much, how would you handle the Apache?" His tone was a direct challenge.

"A little humanity, kindness, and understanding on all sides. Some show of good faith on our part perhaps. No broken treaties."

"A little late for that now. Should I be showing them this kindness and understanding before or after they burn down my ranch and murder everyone on the premises, including you?"

"Couldn't you offer them some of your cattle? You have so many. Couldn't they just be hungry?"

"Animals may kill only to survive, but men are supposedly a higher form of life. We kill without any good reason."

"Cal's right," Doc concurred. "The Apache don't need reasons to kill. They'd take the beeves anyway, after we was all dead."

"I suppose you think I'm very stupid, don't you?" Mary asked, turning to look at Cal.

"Not at all. I just think you ought to think before you speak."

"I've read about Geronimo."

"Then you know he's a troublemaker."

"He hates the white man, certainly. But Mexican soldiers killed his first wife and three children while he was on a peaceful trading expedition back in the fifties. Since then, he's wanted to do nothing but kill. One can understand his desire for revenge without condoning it."

Cal frowned at her. "The reasons don't really matter. He feeds on hate and vengeance just like the other renegades. Usually the Chiricahuas raid close to the border, but they've been getting lots of rifles lately. There are those that benefit from this warfare, and they encourage the Indians in that regard."

"Is Geronimo a powerful chief?" Jeremy asked Cal.

"Not a chief at all. He's a medicine man, but they believe that he's got great power and so they follow him. The other renegade leaders are just as bad."

"I'm sorry we've imposed on you, Mr. Davis," Mary said to him. "We should have gone to the fort."

"You're wrong about that. You'd never have made it there. They'd have gotten you for certain. With all that pretty copper hair, I'm sure your scalp would have been of special value."

"If you're trying to frighten me, it won't work," she replied with a toss of her head.

His eyes darkened and looked deeply into hers; for just a moment she felt as if she were being buried in them.

"More's the pity. If you're not frightened, you're a damned fool." His voice was quiet and controlled, maybe a bit too controlled.

"We do appreciate your hospitality," Elizabeth reiterated nervously.

"Apparently, not everyone does," he replied, casting a brief glance at Mary.

She did not respond, and it was just as well. The first assault began quickly. Nobody had expected that the raiding party would actually attack the ranch, but that was what occurred.

There were blood-curdling whoops and yells as the bronze figures in their multicolored war paint began the attack. Some of the Indians had rifles while others shot flaming arrows. It was a brief attack, lasting only five minutes at the most. Then the party of Apache withdrew.

Mary breathed a sigh of relief; no one had been hurt. "Thank goodness it's over!" she said.

"Well, not exactly, ma'am," Doc said, his wrinkled, leathery face wearing a grave expression. "You see, that was just to kind of feel us out, discover what shootin' power we might have. Now that they know, they'll make their plans. It's gonna be a full moon tonight, an Apache moon. They'll come at us then. Gives them every possible advantage."

"I thought Indians didn't attack at night," she exclaimed.

"Depends on the Injun. These fellas come any time they think they'll win. So now we gotta just sit tight and wait."

"Not quite," Cal said. "We have to get a proper welcome ready for them. I'm going to check on the men."

She watched him leave the house through the back, which seemed to lead to the kitchen.

Amy put her head on Elizabeth's lap. "I'm scared," she said. "I don't understand why they want to kill us." She buried her face in her mother's skirt.

"They're not going to hurt us," Mary said. "Don't you worry. We're all safe here, just like Mr. Davis said."

She observed that Elizabeth looked just as frightened as her daughter. Rebecca sat by herself, silent and showing no emotion at all. The girl rocked back and forth, hugging her body. Perhaps she had slipped back into her private world, as she so often did when she found the environment around her threatening or unpleasant. Maybe she was better off that way, Mary decided. Jeremy in contrast sat with a rifle across his legs, primed for whatever would come.

Mrs. Jenkins had gone out to the kitchen and prepared some food for everyone. It was late afternoon and the food seemed to relax those present in the ranch house. She passed around cornbread, molasses, and strong coffee.

Mary wondered if Cal ate many meals in this house; probably he ate with his cowhands, she thought. This was not much like a home really; it lacked any sense of warmth, and like the man who had built it, it was strong but aloof.

When Cal returned to the house, he looked worried. She

watched as he took Doc aside and they began talking in whispers, serious and concerned. She came toward them.

"What's wrong?" she asked.

"Nothing that need worry you." His patronizing tone irritated her.

"Might I be the judge of that?"

Cal Davis let out a deep sigh, removed his Stetson from his head, and ran his fingers through wavy, sun-streaked hair.

"All right," he said in a loud voice, "guess I best make a general announcement. We don't have as much ammunition in reserve as I thought we did. There are a lot fewer boxes of shells than anticipated."

"Mr. Jones never did get that last shipment," Doc observed.

"Let's hope the Apache didn't lay hold of it," Cal responded.

"How much is there?" Mary asked.

"Enough," he asserted. "But it does mean we've got to make every bullet count. We can't afford to be wasteful. That doesn't mean we won't be able to shoot at them. Fact is we got to convince them from the start that we're too strong for them. And we have to keep them away from the house so they don't burn us out. Once we got no shelter, they've get the upper hand. So fight like hell! We have to cover all the windows somehow. They'll be no lights in the house once it gets dark. So move around as little as possible, and when you do move, keep low. I want all women and children in the root cellar under the house. It's not the most pleasant place, but you'll be real safe there in case anything happens." He spoke forcefully, taking command like a general. In spite of her hostility toward him, Mary was impressed.

The other women did as they were told, but Mary remained by a window.

"Why aren't you joining the other ladies, Miss MacGreggor?" Cal sounded irritated with her.

"Because I can be more useful here. I can handle a gun with a certain amount of skill, and I'm not afraid."

"Could you bring yourself to shoot a man?"

"If he were planning to kill me, I could. We Scots are known to be fierce fighters, Mr. Davis."

"Knowing you, I don't doubt it." His lip curled in the slightest smile, but it was only momentary. "One thing. That handgun of yours? Save some bullets in case it comes to that."

"What do you mean?"

"Let's just say that there are all kinds of ways to die. Some are worse than others."

She hoped that his statement was merely made with the intention of frightening her, but somehow she didn't think so. They waited in silence and time passed slowly. She could feel every muscle in her body twitch in anticipation.

And then it was dark. Doc was right; there was a full moon. She tightened her grip on the box of shells by her side and took a deep breath. In the distance, she could hear the sound of horses approaching. Clouds passed over the moon, floating like the gossamer cobweb of a spider.

The sounds grew closer, and soon the second wave began much as the first had started, with frightening yells and menacing screams from the braves. She could barely see them charging across the open expanse of land. Their leader signaled them with the motion of a lance. She could view them moving forward like a driving force of nature. She shuddered.

"Keep down!" Cal warned.

The shooting began. Mary took careful aim, supporting the rifle against her shoulder; still the recoil sent her sprawling backward.

"Not bad," Cal called out. "You got one. Must be beginner's luck."

She didn't even bother with a reply, repositioning herself to shoot again. By the time the second wave had been repelled, everyone looked tired but relieved. It was suddenly eerily quiet.

"Are they gone for good this time?" she asked hopefully.

"Not likely," Doc replied.

"Afraid Doc's right," Cal agreed. "They won't give up that easy. The scout told us these aren't the Apaches from the San Carlos Reservation. They're Chiricahuas led by Chato."

"Is he as bad as Geronimo?" Jeremy asked.

"Probably worse," Cal answered. "He's one of the wildest and most vicious of the Apache renegades. When General Crook settled the rest of the Apaches back in seventy-three, that bunch headed for Mexico. They claimed they had lived as free men too long to submit to the indignity of living on a reservation. Natchez, Chato, and Geronimo all come up this way from time to time to rob, loot, and murder."

"It's a way of life for them," Doc observed with obvious bitterness.

"Those reservations must be dreadful places though," Mary said.

"True enough," Doc agreed. "San Carlos got nothin' but hot, dry flats. A body can't farm worth a damn there. Not that the Apache ever was much for farmin', but they was promised better. I hear tell they want their Grey Wolf Chief to come back. That's what they call General Crook."

"And will he return?" she asked.

"Not unless it gets really bad," Cal answered.

"Wouldn't exactly call this a Fourth of July picnic," Doc remarked. "And I wouldn't have so much sympathy for them devils if I was you, ma'am. They'd soon as murder you as look at you."

"We're all the Lord's children," Peter Jenkins admonished.

The third wave began with more ferocity then the other two. The Apaches had torches and they were throwing them at the corrals. Now they were much more daring than in the two prior assaults. The blood-chilling yells froze her marrow. Mary glanced around the room, noticing that the faces of the men were taut and grim. She could see as well as the rest that there wasn't much ammunition left.

Suddenly, she noticed that Peter Jenkins had fallen, blood gushing from a bullet wound in his chest. She crawled over to where he was and applied pressure to the wound. Doc crawled along beside her and took over.

Mary went back to the window, keeping low, and picked up her rifle. Her eyes readjusted to the darkness. She could see them on their ponies, dressed in shirts, leggings, and blankets. She began shooting at the figures who glowed silver in the moonlight. Slowly she pulled the trigger and a brave fell from his horse to the ground. She was simultaneously pleased with her success and yet horrified by the fact that she had found it necessary to harm another human being. But there was no time for further reflection. They were coming again! She could not afford to be squeamish.

Mary took a steady grip on the weapon and readied herself, then pulled the trigger, aiming with concentration. And then there was a terrible pain in her arm. The agonizing ache made her drop her rifle. Cal Davis hurried to her side, a concerned expression in evidence on his face.

"Doc! Need you over here!"

The pain was excruciating. She looked over and saw an arrow protruding from her shoulder, blood saturating her dress.

"It's not serious," Doc reassured her. "I'll tend it as soon as there's time."

The assault continued for only a few more minutes. Then the Indians rode away and there was silence.

Cal stared out into the night. "They've taken horses and probably quite a few head of cattle. But it looks like it's over. I guess they finally figured we weren't worth losing any more braves over. They like it quick and easy, and we sure weren't that. Anyway, they got what they really wanted. The animals are what they prize. Killing us would have just been a little something extra thrown into the pot."

He leaned over her and caressed Mary's cheek. "You all right?" he asked, his voice actually tender.

She gave a quick nod.

"Doc, you take special care of this lady. She really is a good shot and brave besides. I'd better get out there. We gotta put out those fires and check on our losses."

The rest of the night was a confused blur for Mary. The pain and weakness she felt left little room for anything else. Doc made her drink whiskey before he would remove the arrow from her shoulder. Afterward, he cleaned the wound with the same alcohol. She endured her suffering in stoic silence. After all, she was going to be fine. But she soon learned that Peter Jenkins and several of the cowhands were not so fortunate.

She must have fallen asleep or lapsed into unconsciousness, for when she opened her eyes, she found herself in a bed. She looked around and there, sleeping in a chair just inches away from her, was Cal Davis. He must have been sleeping lightly because as she stirred, his eyes opened.

"How are you feeling?" he asked.

"I'll be fine," she said, more disconcerted by his concern than she had been by his anger.

He rose and came to the bed, sitting beside her. "I've given you my bed," he told her.

"You didn't have to do that. I really can sleep anywhere." She felt mortified.

"No, I want you here." He bent over and brushed her lips lightly with his own.

She brought the blanket more loosely around her and, looking underneath, discovered that she wasn't wearing her dress anymore, only a chemise and petticoat. She gasped.

"What's wrong?"

"Who took my dress?"

He laughed softly. "It wasn't me, if that's what you're thinking. Elizabeth helped you out of it. She wanted to get the bloodstains removed before they set. She said something about it needing mending as well. We can loan you some clothes in the morning." His eyes swept over her. "Would you have liked it if I said I had undressed you?"

"You are a wicked man," she responded, but couldn't help smiling.

He laughed deeply. "If only that were true." He kissed her forehead and went back to sit in the chair. "Get some more rest. You need it."

She didn't understand Cal Davis. His feelings for her were clearly ambivalent. But were hers for him any different? Mary soon fell asleep again, this time, with a smile on her face.

CHAPTER THIRTEEN

They stayed on as guests at the Thunderbolt for nearly a week. Mary was in no condition to argue the point. Besides, Elizabeth and the children were perfectly content to remain. A few days after the Apaches attacked, soldiers in dusty blue uniforms arrived from the fort to tell them that the army had chased the Apache back into Mexico and the danger was past.

Yet for Mary, there was another kind of danger, just as real. Every time she spent a few moments in Cal Davis's company, her heart began to hammer. She wished he didn't have that effect on her but couldn't deny it to herself anymore.

On the second day, she was sitting in the parlor when Cal came into the house. He looked hot and tired, as if he'd been working hard.

"How are you doing?" he asked.

"My wound hardly hurts anymore," she replied.

"Not much for complaining, are you?" The dimple winked in his cheek as he smiled.

"Complaining doesn't make anything better," she said. "You look worn out. Was there a lot of damage?"

"Three of our men dead. That's the worst of it. Doc did a good job patching up the rest. One barn's gone, burned to the ground, and quite a few head of horses and beeves stolen. It'll be a while before things are back to normal, but it could have been a lot worse."

"It's too bad there can't be peace," she said with a sigh.

"Why must this be a killing land?"

"As long as the Indian Ring's making itself rich selling supplies and ammunition to both the army and the Apache, there's going to be trouble for the rest of us."

"What's the Indian Ring?" she asked.

"Some greedy merchant traders. No one seems to know exactly who they are."

"Or maybe they know but just don't do anything about it because there's so much money involved."

He arched one patrician brow. "Bribes, you mean?"

She shrugged. "I don't pretend to know. It's just a thought."

He stared into her eyes. "I'm just glad you weren't hurt any worse."

"Would it have mattered much to you?"

His eyes caught hers and held them. "A lot more than you realize."

She looked away. "Elizabeth and the children like it very much here. You have a lovely ranch."

He laughed. "I've never heard it called 'lovely' before. Still, this place is all right—not as fancy as Rancho Royo, but it suits my simple needs."

She would hardly have called the ranch simple, but then she had not seen his other property.

"Hello, Mr. Davis," Elizabeth said, entering the room.

"I wish you'd both call me Cal. It seems like people who've suffered through the intimacy of an Indian raid together ought to be on a first-name basis."

"Then you'll have to do the same for us," Elizabeth said. "And I hope you don't mind, I've been doing some cleaning and cooking, just to repay your hospitality toward us. I have lunch ready, if you'd do us the honor of eating with us."

Cal seemed pleased. "That would be nice," he said. "I generally eat with the men, but you ladies are much more attractive company."

"Well, I don't mind telling you it's very nice to cook at your fine wood-burning stove instead of over a hearth for a change."

Elizabeth had gone to some trouble to put together a substantial meal for the occasion, and she was at her charming best.

"I hope you will stay on a while," Cal told her.

"Actually, I'll be well enough to travel in a few days," Mary commented.

For a moment, Mary thought she detected a look of disappointment on his face. Probably he would miss Elizabeth and the children, she thought.

"Must we go?" Amy asked. "I really like it here."

Cal did have a way with children, she acknowledged. Even the cowboys were being pleasant to them, probably by Cal's orders.

"I believe it was Ben Franklin who wrote that fish and visitors smell after three days. We don't want to overstay our welcome," Mary admonished.

"You shouldn't feel that way," Cal said. "An old bachelor like me isn't much used to having womenfolk around, but it's kind of nice. This house is too big for just one person to rattle around in."

"I'm surprised you aren't married," Elizabeth said, her eyes keen with interest. "I can't believe a man like you is still single."

He looked uneasy. "I almost did marry once, but things didn't work out." His eyes darkened visibly, taking on an almost haunted quality, and there was a scowl on his face.

Mary couldn't help but wonder. Why hadn't he married? There was something ominous about his frown.

That afternoon, Doc came by to check on her. "Cal said I ought to have another look at your shoulder. Leastwise, I can clean it and change the bandage."

"You really don't have to bother," she said.

However, Doc insisted, and so she pulled her dress off the shoulder and let him examine her. As he worked, she began thinking of what Cal had said during lunch.

"Doc, could you tell me about Cal?"

He eyed her warily. "What do you want me to tell you?"

"Do you know why he didn't get married?"

Doc gave her a funny look. "What do you want to know for?"

She chewed on her lower lip. "Just wondering."

"Well, I'm no old lady gossip like Emmy Jones."

"Of course not. I just want to know him better."

Doc shrugged. "I reckon it ain't no secret. Twelve years ago it was, when Cal was just eighteen. He was still living at Rancho Royo with his pa. He was seeing the younger daughter of one of the neighbors. She was a pretty young thing and I believe he loved her. Anyway, the families were good friends too. Cal's father and hers were best friends so the marriage was arranged between them. Trouble was the young lady wasn't so keen on the match. She got herself involved with her father's foreman, who had a wife and children of his own. Cal found them together one day, and that's when the wedding was called off."

"That must have hurt him a great deal."

Doc, working on her shoulder, did not look up. "More than that. It practically destroyed him. He was wild with anger and grief. One day, he ran into that foreman in a saloon and the man said some things to him. I guess they'd both been drinking pretty hard. Anyway, they got into a fist fight. It got out of hand and Cal beat him to death."

Mary gasped. "How horrible!"

"Don't think Cal was ever the same. He never trusted a woman after that. Never trusted himself neither. He holds himself tight in control and he never drinks much. He's lived with a lot of guilt and sorrow over the years and vowed he'd never kill another human being unless he had to do it."

"But he has to realize that all women aren't like his former fiancée."

"I don't think he does. You see, it wasn't just her. It was his mama too."

"I don't understand."

Doc scratched his grizzled beard. "Well, his mama was a genuine beauty, a Southern belle, an aristocrat. I never saw nor met another woman like her. Cal's pa came from old money too, but he was a third son and not going to inherit anything. That's why he came out here and started ranching. It was a terrible existence for a fine lady like Mrs. Davis. She was used to a life of wealth, comfort, and elegance. You can just imagine how much she hated ranch life." Doc paced the room. "Whatever Cal's pa did for her, it was just never enough. I think she even grew to hate him after a while. Anyway, I worked as a hand at the Royo in those days and couldn't help but hear the two of them go at it. When she left, it was like she deserted Cal just as much as his pa. I think Cal figures that all marriages are pretty much like the one his parents had. It does take a special kind of woman to survive out here. Aren't many got the strength of character and endurance. I don't think Cal ever intends to get hitched. Women have hurt him too much."

What Doc had said made Mary feel sad and disheartened. "But he was willing to marry once."

"His pa urged it on him, and he was young and thought he was in love. But Cal's older now and careful, and maybe a tad bitter. Also, when a man gets older, he gets set in his ways."

Doc finished dressing her wound, and then patted her shoulder.

"Thank you for telling me about him," she said.

"Just don't let on to Cal what I said. He'd be right angry at me. He's a private sort of cuss."

"I promise I won't."

After Doc left, she thought over what he had told her. She wished she could have known Cal before he changed. No wonder there were times when he looked so cold and hard. Yet there were also times when he was kind and considerate of her and her family. But she must not let herself care about him too much because that would only lead to hurt for her. She could think rationally, as long as he didn't come too close to her.

That evening, visitors stopped by the ranch. Jesse Wheeler, accompanied by her daughter, Lorette, dropped over, ostensibly to visit with her and Elizabeth, but Mary soon became aware that the real object of interest was Cal Davis.

Jesse was at least five years older than Cal, probably more, but she seemed to have a very particular interest in him. Perhaps they were just good friends; however, Mary was suspicious. Jesse seemed to want to encourage a relationship between her daughter and Cal. That was evident.

Elizabeth, who had made a fresh pot of coffee and baked cookies that afternoon, served the company as if she were the lady of the house. For a man with no wife, Mary thought, there were a lot of women interested him. And he acted the part of the chivalrous gentleman very well, all politeness and courtesy to each of them. Mary tried to keep a cool, detached distance, deciding to merely act as an observer as much as possible.

"I must get your recipe for these cookies," Jesse said pleasantly to Elizabeth.

"Oh, it's nothing special, I just used whatever Cal had in his cupboard," she said.

"My Lorette is like that too," Jesse interjected. "She can cook up a fine meal from almost nothing."

"Ma!" the girl said, as if embarrassed.

Mary conceded that Lorette was pretty. She had her mother's

fair coloring and slim figure, but was tall like her father.

"You are all very fine cooks, I am certain," Cal said with a gallant, southern drawl.

Elizabeth and Jesse smiled happily. Mary hoped that would be the end of it, but it wasn't.

"We should have you over for supper," Jesse said to Cal. "And Lorette can do the cooking. Then you can decide if I'm just being a boastful mama or not."

"You must come out to the farm as well," Elizabeth added. "After all your kindness to us, I intend for the women in our family to make you a very special meal in thanks."

Cal looked pleased with all the attention the women were giving him. "All offers cheerfully accepted. I just hope I don't put on so much weight that I won't be able to sit on top of my horse anymore." He patted his flat stomach.

"You need some spoiling," Jesse said sweetly.

Mary could hardly stand to listen to the gamesmanship between the women; she excused herself as early as possible and went to lie down. How foolish to vie for the affections of the man! How demeaning to try to impress him! She wanted no part in it.

Cal was spending a pleasant enough evening in the company of some very attractive women. They were all going out of their way to be friendly to him, except for Mary MacGreggor, who had been distant and chosen to go to bed early.

"Cal Davis, are you listening to me?"

"What?"

"Just as I thought. You men are all alike. When a woman talks, your thoughts begin to wander. Isn't he awful, Elizabeth?"

"I don't much mind," Elizabeth replied.

"Sorry, Jess. It's been a long day."

"Well, you can walk me out then," she said.

He'd known her for so many years that he was fully aware she was not actually offended. It took a great deal more to hurt Jesse's feelings. She looked delicate, but Cal knew full well Jesse was strong-willed. The only person she deferred to was Sam, though why she let the man dominate her the way she did, he had never understood.

At the door, Jesse told her daughter to go on and she'd soon meet her by the buggy, then she turned to him. "Cal, I wanted you to know that I heard from Linda."

The mere mention of that name brought him pain. "I really don't want to hear about her, not now, not ever."

"Of course not. I can't blame you after what she did. None of us ever saw her again after she left here. You know Pa disowned her. But I thought you ought to be aware that she wrote to me from Denver. I knew she'd worked in a saloon for a time. She wrote to say she's married to a miner now and finally happy. She wrote she feels bad about what she did to you and hopes that you will someday find it in your heart to forgive her. I'm sorry, Cal. I don't mean to open old wounds, but I just thought you ought to know."

He nodded his head but didn't look at her. "None of what happened was your fault. Maybe I just started loving Linda because she was your sister. You know I always had a crush on you, Jesse. I admired you so."

Jesse stood on her tiptoes and kissed his cheek. "Why, Cal, you never said anything!"

"You were older, and I was just a kid. Come on, Jesse, you always knew that I worshipped you. I do believe that's why I fell in love with your kid sister in the first place. It's too bad Linda wasn't more like you in ways other than looks."

Jesse took his hand and held it. "That's what I come about too. I want to make things right for you after all these years, Cal. You've seen Lorette. She's seventeen now, a real good age for a girl to get married. That's how old I was when Sam made me his wife. Anyway, Lorette likes you a whole lot."

"Does she?" Cal stared into Jesse's pretty face with surprise.

"Sure, she does. You're the most eligible bachelor in the entire territory. Any girl would be thrilled to become your wife. All you have to do is say the word, and Lorette will marry you."

"And what would Sam say about that?"

Jesse smiled, showing teeth as white as fine porcelain. "He'll do what I want. He might fight you on ranch issues, but he also knows you'd make a wonderful husband for his only daughter. Just think it over, Cal. I'll come around next week to discuss wedding plans if you've a mind." Her voice was half-serious, half-joking, but he wasn't certain which half to believe.

"I don't think I'll ever get married," he told her.

"That's the hurt talking. You'd get over that right quick with Lorette. She's a sweet, innocent child and she'd never treat you like Linda did. I've seen to it that she was brought up proper. You come by and visit with us. You'll find out that what I'm telling you is true."

He walked Jesse to her waiting carriage and helped her in. Lorette gave him a warm smile as they pulled away. He couldn't pretend that he hadn't noticed how attractive Jesse's daughter had become. Maybe that was the answer for him. Then again, maybe not. He hardly knew his own heart or mind anymore.

There was also Mary MacGreggor. What did he feel for her? He wasn't certain about that either. They didn't get along at all. She was so fierce and independent. She didn't need or want any man. Well, maybe she had loved Wolf, and he probably would have been fine for her, just as wild and passionate as she was. It was strange that what so attracted him to her was the very thing he'd sought to kill in himself.

CHAPTER FOURTEEN

For the next few days, it seemed as if Cal Davis were deliberately avoiding her. Mary couldn't help but wonder about it, but he was such a moody and complicated man that she hardly knew what to think. Sometimes he acted as if he liked her a great deal; other times he was cold and did his best to keep a distance between them, as he was doing now.

It was time for them to return to the farm anyway, she reasoned. Elizabeth honored her request somewhat regretfully. When she told Cal that they were leaving on the following day, he actually seemed unhappy.

"Is there anything I can do for you before you leave the Thunderbolt?" His eyes looked deeply into Mary's.

"Well, there is one thing," she responded thoughtfully. "I would like to try to grow trees around the cabin. It might help the land to retain water. It would also provide some shade for summer and insulation during the cold nights. I was wondering if I might have your permission to come and take some seedlings and young trees from your high country."

"Why, sure, if you like. I'll take you up there today for a look around if you feel up to riding. But there's one thing I got to warn you about. Those trees likely won't do well in the lowlands. It's just too hot and dry for them to take. Still, I don't suppose there's any harm in experimenting. Maybe even try out some cottonwood first. They should survive okay, but not the fir or pine."

He was so serious in his consideration that she couldn't help but smile. "Thank you. I would like to take that ride, if it's not too much trouble."

"I'll set aside the time for it and be back in a little while."

After he left, she wondered at her own audacity. She had suggested spending time alone with him, and that could be nothing but a mistake. Was she looking for trouble? But she really did want to grow trees; the venture seemed worthwhile. Besides, he had no real interest in her. She had offended him too often. If he were to become romantically involved with any woman, it would be Lorette Wheeler—or possibly even her aunt, who obviously liked Cal a great deal. She must put out of her mind the few occasions he had taken her into his arms, for she was certain that they were all but forgotten by him.

It was past noon when he returned, carrying some men's clothes.

"If you don't want to wear these, you don't have to. I know ladies like to wear gingham and frills, but it can get mighty cold up in the high country, so you might want to change."

She thanked him and accepted his suggestion. He had brought her a flannel shirt, woolen pants, a heavy canvas jacket, warm socks, a cowboy hat, and narrow leather boots. Even buckskin gloves were provided. Of course, she felt self-conscious in men's clothes and rather foolish besides, but he had guessed her size with amazing accuracy and the garments proved a good fit, although the shirt was somewhat snug in the bosom and the pants a bit tight in the hips. She decided to carry the jacket for the time being.

He surveyed her as she came toward him, his head cocked to one side in a gesture of appraisal, as if she were a gold mine he'd just discovered. "I wish all cowboys looked as good as you do," he said with a wide grin.

She did not look at him or bother to reply. The horses were

waiting for them when they left the house. He had selected a chestnut mare for her, which seemed to have a more gentle disposition than his stallion. She rode beside him along the trail until they got to the high ground, where the trail was narrow and she was forced to follow behind.

"Before we choose any trees," he said. "Let me take you for a ride up in the mountains. I think you'll enjoy it."

He was right. She couldn't imagine anything nicer. He was also right about it being much colder in the mountains; but it was also beautiful. The trees were magnificent, tall and regal. And high above, the mountaintops were crowned with snow. For a moment, tears came to her eyes as she remembered the winters in New Jersey and how she had taken the lovely forest land for granted. Still this country had its own special identity, beauty, and charm.

They continued upward through the wild, rugged foothills. Grass grew in every open patch of ground, some of it still green in spite of the season. The cottonwoods were now giving way to pine and spruce trees. She could hear birds singing and squirrels running upward into the trees at their advent.

"It's really remarkable how different this is from the land we're farming."

"You'll find some amazing contrasts out here," he agreed. "I love it all. This country is the one place a man can feel free."

"My uncle agreed with you. He thought he'd finally feel free coming out West. He came here for that reason."

Cal Davis pulled his horse up beside hers. "And why did you come?" he asked.

"To start a new life—to begin living finally."

"No other reason?"

"To help out my relatives."

Without warning, her horse reared. Her instincts told her that something was wrong. Cal reached out to calm the animal, but the mare remained nervous.

"What's the matter?" she asked uneasily, watching him reach for his rifle.

"Tell you in just a minute. Keep a tight rein on that mare 'cause she's real scared." He looked around, his eyes narrowing. Then he aimed his rifle. One shot rang out after the other.

For a moment, she thought she saw something high above them moving quickly away. Mary's horse reared again and she nearly fell off. Cal dropped his rifle. His strong arms came around her, holding her protectively.

"Are you all right?" His jolting blue eyes caught hers, and she felt overwhelmed.

"I'm all right now, thank you," she replied in a breathless voice. Then she moved away from him.

"Mountain lion," he said, dismounting to take back his rifle. "Horses sense them. It's gone now. The gunshots frightened it away. Why don't we stop for something to eat? You look a tad peaked. I brought some stuff along that Cookie threw together for me. No need to miss lunch."

She consented gladly. It was much later then she normally ate, and the business of the mountain lion had been disconcerting. She also realized that her full strength had not as yet returned as she'd hoped.

Cal took time to calm both horses. "The mare's a mite skittish, but she'll be fine."

It was apparent to her that Cal was completely at home in the outdoors. He set up a small campfire with speed and efficiency, preparing a pot of coffee. He obtained the water from a cold, clear mountain stream that ran downhill over large rocks. From a saddlebag, he removed biscuits and cold beef. There were also tin plates and cups.

"Hope this isn't too primitive for you," he said. "I know Easterners don't think much of how we live out here."

"It's fine," she responded and thanked him politely.

After they had finished, he washed the dishes in the stream and put them back into the saddlebag. She lingered by the fire and he came and rejoined her.

"I meant to tell you that I thought you handled yourself right well when Doc took that arrow from your shoulder. Most women would have carried on something fierce, but you showed real courage."

Mary realized she should say something, but she found it difficult to handle compliments. She also felt awkward being alone with him. Finding herself unable to face him any longer, she looked away at the scenery.

"The view from up here is breathtaking," she said, admiring the grandeur of the mountains.

"There's something I ought to tell you. I want you to know that I'm really sorry about Wolf. He was a good man, and he would have made you a fine husband."

She bit down on her lower lip. "I shouldn't have said those things to you that day. It wasn't fair. The truth is I don't know that I would have married Wolf. I certainly liked him a lot, but I didn't love him. I don't think you should marry without love. Marriage is difficult enough even with it."

Cal took her shoulders and forced her to face him. "You really didn't love him?" His eyes searched hers like torches.

She shook her head and was about to say something when she felt several raindrops on her face. Placing the cowboy hat on her head, she looked up at the sky, which suddenly seemed ominous and dark. Strange how she hadn't noticed it until now, but then her mind had been on Cal.

The rain became heavier and the wind more forceful. Cal pulled her to her feet. "This may go on for a while. I wasn't expecting a storm, but this time of year, weather can be unpredictable. There's a line shack not far from here. We can stay there for a time until the storm blows over."

They got on their horses and she followed him as they climbed even higher, carefully picking their way over the slippery rocks. It was raining very hard by the time they reached the cabin he had told her about. She was soaked through and felt chilled.

"Go on inside," he told her. "I'll take care of the horses."

She entered the cabin cautiously, but soon discovered it was clean and dry, and there were blankets tucked away on a bed near a fireplace. She removed her hat and wet jacket and started to place some logs and kindling into the fireplace. When Cal entered the cabin, he joined her, helping to set up the fire and get it started.

"You're turning blue," he said. "Better get those clothes hung near the fire and put yourself into one of those blankets. Everything here is clean because this place gets used a whole lot." When she hesitated, he went and got her a blanket and insisted. "I'll turn my back so as not to embarrass you."

She changed, pulling a blanket around her cold body. He did exactly the same, removing his wet clothes and placing them near the fire to dry.

"Be glad it's not time for snow up here yet. Then we'd have a real problem."

"Is it snowing higher up?" she asked.

"I'm certain it is," he told her. "I don't think this rain will last long, so you needn't worry. I won't compromise your virtue."

"I didn't think you would."

He let out a deep laugh. "I don't think that's much of a compliment somehow."

"I only meant that I consider you a gentleman."

His brow lifted questioningly. "I believe you told me that I hadn't behaved in a gentlemanly manner toward you."

She felt her face flush. "I was angry at the time."

"You seem to get angry at me an awful lot," he observed in a soft, silky voice.

"Only because you don't like me very much," she replied, being honest with him.

"If I gave you that impression, I am sorry."

He sounded gallant and chivalrous at that moment, she thought.

"Maybe I've misunderstood you," she conceded.

There was a warmth in his eyes that was not to be denied.

"So tell me where this fierce, passionate nature of yours comes from," he said, drawing closer to her.

"Probably from my father's side. His mother was a Highlander and she had a proud, spirited personality. I loved my grandmother a great deal. She used to teach me all the Scottish ballads, and we'd sing them together. I inherited my hair color from her as well."

"Did your father fight in the war?" he asked.

"Yes, he served the Union."

Cal smiled faintly. "My father went and fought for the South. He didn't have to, of course, but he wanted to do it. Jefferson Davis announced that Arizona was a Confederate territory back in sixty-two, and old Jeff was a distant cousin of my pa. My pa came back with some hair-raising stories, worst of which was that the South as he'd known it was totally destroyed forever. It really tore him apart."

"I'm sorry," she said.

"You're not sorry that the North won, I don't suppose."

"I never really thought about it too much. I was pretty young at the time, as you must have been."

"Was your father wounded?"

"No, but he was injured later on. You see, he was a civil engineer, a builder of bridges, and part of what he was building collapsed and crushed his spine. He spent the rest of his life as an invalid, and I did my best to care for him."

He nodded his head as if he understood. "I guess your life hasn't been too easy," he said.

"I loved my father a great deal, so I never minded taking care of him. He was a good man and he loved me as well."

"But still, it couldn't be a good life for you," he reflected.

"Has yours been good?" she asked, studying his handsome face.

"Not particularly. I guess I've been lonely for a lot of the time."

"Maybe it's time that you think about making some changes then."

"I don't think I'd know how," he responded almost regretfully.

She hesitated for a moment, took a deep breath, then plunged forward. "There's something I've been meaning to ask you. Do you think there's going to be a range war? I've been hearing some talk."

"Who from?"

"Does it matter?" She had no intention of telling him about her conversation with Jack Phillips.

"No, I just hope it doesn't come to that. I made an effort to arbitrate, but neither Sam Wheeler nor Jack Phillips will budge an inch. They're equally pigheaded and obstinate. By the way, I respected the way you stood up to Sam."

"You did? Well, I can't say that I'm all that pleased with myself. I let my temper get the better of me. I should have thought before I spoke. It's one of my worst faults. I'm afraid my pupils will be paying the price for it. He seemed quite serious about seeing to it that I lose my teaching position."

"I have just as much, if not more, to say about that as he does. I'll see to it that no one fires you."

"I wouldn't want you on bad terms with a neighbor because of me."

"Wheeler and I don't agree on much in general."

"He could see to it that the children stop coming to school," she observed.

"That would be a big mistake," Cal responded. His eyes were warm and admiring.

She cast her own gaze modestly to the floor. Cal Davis really could be a very appealing man. He was staring at her. Glancing down to where his gaze was drawn, she realized with a start that the blanket had slipped open a little and her breasts were partly exposed.

"No, don't cover up. You're such a wonderful sight," he said. "Do you know that your skin is so translucent, I can see blue veins right at the surface?" His hand went out and touched her skin, and where he touched, her skin began to burn.

He pulled back from her for a moment, his eyes dark with passion. "I want you real bad," he said. "Maybe it's wrong, but I do want you."

The Apache raid had taught her one thing: life in the West was uncertain and could change radically from moment to moment. She was just as drawn to Cal as he was to her, and she no longer wished to deny it. She stared at him. The powerful hunger in his eyes seduced her without a word or a touch. His look was raw, honest. Boldly, she pulled his blanket away from him and viewed his body just as he had looked at hers, no longer afraid or ashamed. She had never imagined that a man could be so wonderful to look at. There was no fat anywhere, only rippling muscle. His body was as strong and spare as a rawhide whip. His skin was tan, as if he'd spent time working outdoors without a shirt, but the coarse mat of hair on his chest was golden and godlike. She dared not look much lower, although he seemed to dare her to do so.

"How do I compare?" he asked teasingly.

She looked away trying to hide her blush.

"As opposed to whom?"

"Your other lovers."

"Oh, the multitude," she replied with a wry smile. "I really couldn't say. It wouldn't be polite, would it?"

He lifted her into his arms and carried her to the bed, pulling the blankets over both of them. His lips covered hers, pressing, parting, probing, and demanding insistently. She felt his tongue touch hers. His hands reached to her hair and pulled the pins from it, so he could rake his fingers through the cascading curls. He held her head and kissed her deeply. His lips kissed her throat and then move to the soft curve of her neck.

"Do you want me?" he asked. He pulled back from her momentarily, his eyes dark with passion. "I want you so bad," he said, "but if you want me to stop while I'm still able . . ."

"No, don't stop."

He kissed her lips gently, tenderly. His magic hands caressed her body. He excited her. She felt an urgency building, and then his hardness pushed into her body like a velvet fist. Her virginity shattered like fragile crystal. She bit down on her lower lip and did not cry out, determined to reach beyond the pain. His thrusts continued and the pain lessoned. She began to writhe under him, trying to match the rhythm of his body with her own. She realized that he was trying his best to hold back, but as his movements became more frenzied, she began to feel spasms of pleasure overwhelm her. He took her higher and higher still. Then he collapsed beside her breathlessly. She felt good and right when he pulled her back into his arms. He kissed her forehead and then her cheek.

"I'm sorry I hurt you," he said. "Why didn't you warn me you hadn't done this before?"

"Because you assumed I had. Besides, I wanted you too. So

it's all right."

She tried to move away from him, but discovered the blood between her thighs. So this was what it was to make love with a man, she thought. Well, it had been like heaven until the pain forced away her pleasure, but even that had been only a temporary drawback.

"You'll never have that pain again," he said, as if he could read her mind.

"I guess you've had a lot of women."

"Not many," he told her. "I've tried to stay clear of involvements."

"Am I an involvement?"

He smiled but didn't answer her right away. "I think for me you're real trouble."

"Don't worry," she said. "No one is going to chase you with a shotgun and force you to marry me." She kept her voice light and teasing.

"I wasn't thinking about that. I don't plan on getting married." He went to the fire and put some more kindling on.

Somehow that admission hurt her more than the loss of her virginity had. But then why should she be surprised? He had talked of wanting her. He never said a word about loving her. There was a considerable difference.

She was lost in thought when he rejoined her, brushing her cheek with his callused finger.

"The rain's stopped," he said. "And I think our clothes are just about dry."

Reluctantly, she dressed and followed him out of the line shack, knowing that she had left behind a part of herself that she could never regain. The odd thing was that she no longer really cared.

CHAPTER FIFTEEN

Cal helped her select some seedlings and young trees to bring back and tied them down carefully.

"Best chance for them to thrive is in the spring. So if these don't happen to take, I'll bring you back here in early spring to get some more—if you're still around."

She gave him a questioning look. "What does that mean?'

He shrugged. "If you haven't gone back East by then is what I mean."

"Why do you think I would?" Her eyes met his without flinching.

"It's just what I expect," he replied, lips tight and square jaw jutting out.

She felt anger begin to rise in her. How could he possibly say such a thing to her after she had given herself to him totally and unconditionally? The man infuriated her. They didn't talk much on the return ride to the Thunderbolt. Mary wondered what he was thinking, but Cal seemed reserved and contemplative. His mood made her tense, and she was glad when they finally arrived back at the ranch at dusk. The jaunt into the mountains had been very tiring for her and hard on her nerves. What was he thinking about her now that they had been together intimately? It had not seemed wrong at the time, but now she had to wonder. He was obviously having second thoughts about it. If only he would open up and talk to her!

Elizabeth was waiting for her when Mary came into the ranch

house, and there was a questioning look on her aunt's face. Mary told her aunt and cousins how she and Cal had been caught in a downpour in the mountains and decided to wait it out. She said little else, but somehow got the feeling that her aunt understood the situation far better than she was letting on. Perhaps Rebecca was not the only one of the Stafford women with intuition.

"We're just glad you're back," Elizabeth said gently. "We'd begun to worry something was wrong."

"No, I'm fine." But she didn't feel fine at all. Her body was wracked with chills.

"Are you feverish?" Elizabeth asked, noticing her tremor. "Your cheeks and lips are flushed. Perhaps you'd best lie down."

"I think you're right," Mary agreed without further discussion.

"Maybe we should plan just one extra day here. Then when we return to the farm, everyone will be fit."

Mary excused herself, undressed, and went straight to bed, worn out. She fell into an exhausted sleep almost immediately, but a few hours later awoke to discover that her flannel nightshirt was drenched in perspiration. She removed it and went back to sleep.

In her dreams, she felt the warm touch of a hand stroking her hair and the faint feathering of a kiss on her forehead. She reached out to touch the solicitous presence only to come awake, knowing the touch was real and not part of a dream at all. Her eyes snapped open.

"Cal!" she said in surprise, her heart beginning to beat more rapidly.

"Right here." His face was a series of shadowy silver planes in the moonlit room.

"But why are you here?"

"Elizabeth told me when I came back to the house earlier

that you were running a fever. I didn't want to bother you. Just thought I'd come in quietly and check on you. Go back to sleep. I didn't mean to disturb you."

She took his hand. "You're very thoughtful."

"Not really." He was looking into her eyes and still stroking her hair. "I wanted to apologize to you about what happened earlier." He sounded embarrassed. "I shouldn't have lost control of myself that way. I didn't mean to take advantage of the situation. I didn't mean to do you harm. I'm real sorry."

She turned away from him. Was that all he felt? Regret?

"I've hurt you, haven't I?"

She didn't answer.

He could see her bare, white shoulders in the moonlight only semicovered by the quilt, and he was rock hard, throbbing with desire for her. He'd only come to make certain she was all right because he kept thinking about her and couldn't sleep.

"I believe I love you," she said.

He brought the pillow back behind her head and lay beside her for a time, caressing her long, curling hair, which spread like silk tendrils on the pillow. When he finally heard the regular sound of her breathing, he left quietly to let her sleep. He was troubled by the strong feelings she stirred in him. Never before had being with a woman brought him to such heights of passion. The woman made him lose his self-control. No, he didn't like that one little bit. She'd said she loved him, but he didn't believe she really meant it.

When Mary awoke, she discovered that she had slept much later into the morning then she ever had before in her entire life. But she did feel much better physically and mentally. Frowning deeply, she wondered if it had been unwise to tell Cal of her feelings for him. She didn't want to scare him away by being too intense. Still, it was not in her nature to be secretive; she much preferred openness and honesty in human relationships. She realized he probably did not reciprocate her feelings. She talked of love while he likely felt only lust. She understood his wariness regarding emotional involvements. Doc had explained why Cal was shy of marriage, and she could sympathize with his hurt.

She got up and decided to wash, feeling the need to cleanse her body and freshen herself. After dressing, she went to the kitchen. Elizabeth had saved bacon and toast for her breakfast and she found herself possessed of a healthy appetite. The two of them had a pleasant conversation while she ate.

"Mary, you look much better today. Did you rest well?"

"I seem to have slept away the chill I took. I'm much stronger now."

"Then perhaps we will return to the farm tomorrow—unless you've changed your mind and wish to stay here longer." Elizabeth gave her a thoughtful look.

"No, that will be fine."

Her aunt poured coffee into a cup and handed it to her. "I've noticed Cal taking a very active interest in you. I'm happy for you, dear," she said. "You deserve a fine man like him."

Her aunt's generosity of spirit touched Mary deeply. "Thank you," she said, reaching over to hug Elizabeth. "I find I have feelings for him. I'm not certain he returns them."

"He certainly looks at you as if he does," Elizabeth observed.

"Do you really think so?"

Her aunt smiled, looking sagacious. "Yes, I believe he truly cares for you."

The rest of the morning, Mary felt happy, her spirits soaring as they never had before in her life. She had not seen Cal, but Tiny came by to tell her that the chestnut mare had been saddled for her in case she wanted to take a ride later, and

Mary could only think that it was done at Cal's suggestion, which meant that he had to be thinking about her. She helped Elizabeth tidy up the ranch house, singing "Barbara Allen" with a soft Scottish burr as she worked.

It was almost noon when Doc came by the ranch house looking for Cal.

"You haven't seen him?" Doc asked.

"Not at all today," she replied.

"You don't know where he could be?"

"No," she replied. "He could be anywhere. But if he comes here for lunch, I'll tell him you're looking for him. Is there a message?"

"Just tell him that Jesse Wheeler stopped by. She was looking for him and when I said he wasn't around, she just said that he should remember to see her soon. Something about wedding plans for him and Lorette." Doc scratched his head uncomprehendingly.

"Wedding plans?" Mary choked out the words in disbelief.

"That was my reaction too. Has to be a mistake, maybe a joke."

"Maybe not," Mary responded. She backed away from him.

How could she have been such a fool? She had thrown herself at Cal, offered herself up to him like a steer to be roasted on a spit. Naturally, he felt nothing for her; he was committed to Lorette Wheeler. Mary was furious with him and disgusted with herself. He had lied to her, she realized, telling her that he never intended to marry, and she had thought him too hurt by his previous engagement to do otherwise. Now she learned that he intended to marry the Wheeler girl? Damn him for a liar and herself for a fool!

Was Doc speaking to her? She hadn't heard what he said. She shook her head and walked hurriedly out of the house, holding back the tears that threatened to break free. No, she would not cry over him. She would not! She willed the tears and pain away.

Mary caught sight of the chestnut mare saddled and waiting for her. She called to Doc, who was standing just behind her. "Tell everyone I'm going back to the farm today. I'll see that the horse gets returned." With that, she mounted quickly and began to ride away.

Doc called after her, trying to get her to stop, but she ignored him. She couldn't bear to be with anyone right now. She especially didn't want to see Cal, didn't want to lose her temper with him or hurl any accusations. That would be beneath contempt. She had given herself willingly, without promises or commitments from him. He was free to do as he wished, free to love anyone he liked and marry any woman he chose, but she never wanted to see him again as long as she lived!

CHAPTER SIXTEEN

Returning to the farm turned out to be an unpleasant experience. The Apaches had visited here too. The sight that greeted her was disheartening. The cabin had been partly burned. Their milk cow was dead, a great lance forced through the animal's stout heart. On seeing the destruction, she broke down and cried. It was the final blow.

But then she remembered that the others would return soon and that she must make an effort for their sake to repair whatever she could. She began working and felt the better for it. There was always great comfort in doing useful things.

As she cleaned up the mess inside the cabin, she heard riders approaching and hurried to the window, pulling back the oil cloth that served them well enough until they could afford glass. There were three men on horseback, and at first she could not make out their features. The men rode quickly in, making straight for the cabin. She rushed to bolt the door, but the bolt had been broken. It took all her strength to move the table and chairs up against the door.

She had no idea who these men were, only that they didn't look like Thunderbolt hands, nor were they Indians. Mary glanced around for her handgun, and it was at that moment she realized the weapon wasn't there. In her upset and haste to leave after hearing Cal was making wedding plans with Lorette Wheeler, she had ridden off, completely forgetting to take her pistol with her, oblivious to any thought of danger. How stupid!

She was furious with herself for behaving so impetuously. If only she had one of Cal's repeating rifles! But, she reasoned, these men might represent no harm at all. She might just be worrying about nothing.

Just the same, Mary glanced around the kitchen area and located two sharp knives. One was a small, sharp weapon used for skinning, which she wrapped in leather and slipped into the good-sized pocket of her dress. The other knife, a huge butchering tool, she held tightly in her hand in plain sight.

They were at the door now, banging at it. "Who's there?" she called out.

"Mrs. Stafford?"

The man's voice had a rasp to it which made him sound sharp and hard.

"She's not here. What do you want?"

"We come for Mary MacGreggor," the same voice said.

A chill traveled silently down her back.

"She's not here. Go away!"

"Reckon we'll just wait for her."

She wished now that she had tethered the mare at the rear of the cabin so that she might have slipped out a back window. Everything she'd done today was a mistake. How she wished she'd thought before she acted.

Rifle shots tore through the door, and she threw herself to the floor. They were heaving at the door, and as it flew open and she saw the men standing there.

She looked at them, seeing every feature as if in a dream. One man had carrot-red hair and a beard; a second had the strangest, light blue eyes she had ever seen; and the third was swarthy and leered at her with flashing gold teeth. This third man made for her directly, waving a gun in her face. He didn't seem at all intimidated by the large knife in her hand and started to aim his pistol. She knew who they were, remembering every word of Elizabeth's description, and now she was filled with terror. But rage welled up in her, too. These were the men who had viciously murdered Uncle Isaac and raped her aunt! It was the rage that gave her a surge of courage. She lunged at the swarthy man without a moment's hesitation and shoved the knife violently into his chest. The man stared at her, his mouth gaping wide, his coal black eyes wide in disbelief. Then he fell, and Mary made for his revolver, trying desperately to grab it from the dying man's hand.

Before she could aim the gun, the man with the light blue eyes hurled his body into hers. She grappled with him for the revolver, and both she and the weapon landed on the floor. He slapped her hard across the face, sending her sprawling away from the gun. Stinging tears of pain formed in her eyes. Still she tried again, only to find his hands restraining her, his finger digging painfully into the flesh of her arms as he lifted her.

"My, you are a feisty female!" He brought her body tightly back against his as she struggled against him.

The redheaded man made no immediate comment, but pointed the barrel of the shotgun at her face. "I think she'll stop fighting now. That is, if she wants to live past this minute."

The hard, emotionless expression convinced her he meant exactly what he said. She stopped struggling and stood rigidly still. The second man still held his arm around her waist, but his grip eased.

"You got any menfolk around here?" the redheaded man asked.

Mary's mind raced feverishly. "No, I'm alone here, but I expect the marshal momentarily."

"That so?" he replied in obvious disbelief. "But there's no one here right now, is there?"

"No," she admitted, her voice thick as clotted cream.

He smiled as if her answer had pleased him mightily. "Hear

208

that, Luke? Ain't we the lucky ones? We can do this job quick and easy."

"I don't know what you want here, but we have absolutely nothing of value. You can see that for yourselves."

"I wouldn't say that," the redheaded man replied with a crooked smile. "You're forgettin' yourself."

Inside she was shaking with fear, but she resolved to keep as outwardly calm as possible. "I'm here alone because I have the spotted fever," she said. "And it's very contagious. Anyone can catch it, so I suggest you leave right away."

Luke finally released her, she noted with satisfaction. "What do you think, Rusty? Is the gal lyin' or tellin' the truth?"

Rusty had small, mean eyes, and the expression on his face was sinister.

"She's lyin'."

"No, it's true! I swear it! I'm really sick."

"You just killed a strong, healthy man, and you expect me to believe that?" Rusty spat on the floor in disgust.

"If you're smart, you'll get out of here and leave me be," she persisted.

"That so? Why don't I just shoot you now and put you out of your misery like I'd do a sick cow." He brought the shotgun closer, and in spite of herself, she let out a small gasp.

"There's an incubation period on such diseases. We won't know for a while whether or not I'll come down with it."

Luke laughed, pulling her around to look at her closely for the first time. "It don't matter none. We'll take our chances. You're comin' with us."

"I'll do no such thing," she protested loudly.

He seized her by the wrists. "You'll be comin' with us," he said in a voice that brooked no disagreement.

"You'll be catching the spotted fever."

Luke studied her thoughtfully.

"I was a soldier. I'm used to takin' risks."

"I refuse to leave this cabin."

Luke said nothing. He brought his fist back and smashed it against the side of her face. It was a hard, painful blow that sent her lurching to the floor.

"You won't be talkin' back to me, woman! Nobody does. Now you get yourself off that floor and walk out of here while you still can. Otherwise, I'll see you get a lot more grief."

The pain was excruciating; Mary stared at this vicious, violent man in shock and disbelief. Still she didn't move. The strange blue light of his eyes drilled into her and suddenly he was heaving her over his shoulder as if she were a sack of potatoes and carrying her out of the cabin. As she tried to protest, he slapped her hard on her backside.

"I don't like this," Rusty said. "She killed a real good man, one we needed. If we hadn't been paid to bring her to him alive, I'd prefer to shoot her here and now. This woman's nothing but trouble to us."

"Well, we'll be rid of her soon enough," Luke said, "though in a way, I'm sorry, 'cause she's mighty good to look at. And I never seen a woman with quite as much grit. Would be my pleasure to break her spirit."

He set her down again and the look he gave her was frightening. Who would have sent the Harrises to get her—and why? Surely not Cal Davis? She couldn't imagine him capable of such an act.

"What do you intend to do with me?"

Rusty shoved her forcefully toward her horse. "Don't ask any damn questions!" he shouted at her.

She was forced to mount the mare and ride between the two men. Her heart thumped. If she could just think rationally, maybe she'd be able to plot a course of action that would deliver her from her captors.

Her hand involuntarily went to the pocket of her dress. She had forgotten about the smaller knife. Mary slipped her hand into the pocket and touched the knife, just to reassure herself that it was still there. Yes, she did have in her possession a formidable weapon, and when the right opportunity afforded itself, she would use it without hesitation or qualm. Mary willed herself the strength to do whatever was necessary to be free.

As they began to ride, she heard Rusty begin cursing loudly. He called Luke's attention to dust rising in the distance.

"I think it's that damn posse! Would you believe that hard-nosed marshal is still after us?"

"I heard some big rancher hereabouts, name of Davis, put a bounty on our heads, so naturally, there's gonna be plenty of men in this territory lookin' for the reward."

"Damn! We'll have to take her with us. We can't deliver her or the other one until we're free of that posse." Luke pulled Mary off her horse. She tried to fight him, but his arms, like bands of steel, pressed her in front of him. "You'll ride with me, 'cause I don't trust you to ride alone right now. Give me any more trouble and I'll lay you down across my saddle."

Rusty took the reins of the mare and brought the horse along with them. Luke held her tightly around the waist so that she could hardly breathe. His huge brown horse was strong and did not seem the least bit burdened by the extra weight.

They rode hard across the desert country under the blazing azure sky. Clouds hung low overhead like tufts of cotton candy. Mary was hot and dusty by the time the outlaws rode into their camp, and her face ached badly. Luke Harris pulled her roughly from the horse.

She took a deep breath, looked around, and to her amazement, she saw Billy Travers! She couldn't control her expression of dismay. Billy looked different, no longer the boyish optimist. His face was gaunt and weary, covered with a mustache and beard. But it was most certainly Billy. She felt sick at heart. How could such a fine young man come to associate with vicious outlaws like these? Then she noticed that he wore no sidearm.

He recognized her immediately and came toward her. He seemed about to say something, but she made a sign to him, a motion indicating that he should remain silent, her fingers going to her lips. It was best the outlaws knew as little as possible about them being acquainted.

There were three other men besides Billy, all of them Mexican, and all of them heavily armed. Rusty Harris gave orders to them in rapid Spanish and everyone quickly mounted while Luke and Rusty watered their horses at a creek.

Luke took a canteen, filled it with water, drank some, and then surprised her by passing it to her. After she took a quick drink, he handed her a red bandanna.

"Soak this and put it against your face. It'll take the swelling down some."

She didn't bother to thank him, considering it was his fault that her face was so badly bruised, but she did wonder why he was being nice to her. The next moment, he was forcing her to mount up again, this time on her own horse, but he kept beside her as they rode out again.

It wasn't until well into evening that they finally made camp, and then only after Rusty Harris was satisfied that they had eluded the posse.

"What do you think, Rus? Where should we head?" Luke asked his brother.

Rus Harris scratched his scraggly beard thoughtfully. "You know the word is that our old friend Belle has a hideaway over in Indian Territory with that new husband of hers. We got the money to pay her. Maybe we go up there for a week or so, things'll quiet down. Then we can go back to business and finish with the boy and the woman. I don't want them on our hands any longer than necessary."

"Sounds good," Luke affirmed.

Mary was hoping they would say more about her, but they didn't. She also thought that perhaps during the night, she might be able to sneak away and escape. With that in mind, she seated herself as far away from the others as possible.

But Luke Harris had not forgotten about her. "Just so there's no misunderstanding, this here woman is mine and mine alone until I say otherwise," he announced.

"I don't want her," Rus Harris responded in a cold voice.

Luke pushed her to the ground. He pulled off his weather-beaten hat, which had a snakeskin band around it, and tossed it down beside her. Black hair dark as a raven's wing fell forward across his forehead as the strange, light eyes took on a demonic glow. He grabbed her wrists and held them tightly, forcing her down on her back. When she tried to get up, he brought his knee up against her chest.

"Don't you move!" he said. "I'll be gentle with you as long as you obey me."

She would not give in to him, no matter how afraid she was. She was not about to submit to this brute of a man without a struggle. She did not want to be touched by another man. Allowing Cal Davis to make love to her had only brought her grief. And this man was nothing like Cal. At least her first experience with a man had shown her how pleasurable lovemaking could be. But Cal had duped her! Fury rose within her even as she thought of him at such a critical moment.

No, she was not about to yield. Luke Harris was like a primitive force of nature ready to wreak destruction on anyone or anything that crossed his path. But she was not going to let any man touch her again; least of all a man like this, a creature who had raped her aunt and murdered her uncle!

Had she been a religious person like her mother, Mary would have prayed for a miracle of deliverance, such as Daniel had experienced in the lion's den. As it was, Mary subscribed to the old adage, "God helps those who help themselves." She was prepared to offer this demon considerable resistance.

His fingers pressed painfully into her arms, holding her tightly, while his mouth came down hotly on her own. Then his hands ran over her breasts, squeezing, pressing. She tried to pull free of him but his body was over her own and his strength was too great for hers. He began to thrust his tongue into her mouth. Disgusted, she countered by biting down as hard as she could. He yelped and released her, but only for a moment. Then he was back on top of her, trying to force her thighs apart.

It was at that moment that Mary reached for the knife. Unfortunately, the man had the uncanny instincts of an animal. As she brought up the knife to plunge into his chest, he pulled her hand back, deflecting her aim, so hard she thought it might be snapped like a twig. During the ensuing struggle, Mary managed to free one knee. She brought it back, and with all the strength she possessed, thrust it into his groin.

He let out a howl of pain and surprise, then recoiled. As she scrambled to her feet, he came striking back at her like a poisonous rattler. The expression on his face terrified her, but she refused to give in to her fear. She saw her knife on the ground and snatched it up again. In an act of desperation, she lunged toward him, but he moved fast, and she only grazed him. With a hard chop of his outstretched palm, he dislodged the knife from her hand, then hurled her to the ground.

"I could cut your throat with this," he shouted at her, holding up her knife. Moonlight zigzagged crazily on the steel blade of the weapon. "You deserve it."

"If you think I'm going to allow you to rape me, you're very much mistaken!" she shouted back, rising from the ground. She was every bit as enraged as he was. He used his foot to shove her down again, his boot heel resting on her stomach.

"I'll take you when I want you, woman! You'll learn to accept me. I never seen a female fight me like you." Luke shook his head.

Billy's eyes were wide open and his face was pale. "You can see she's a proper lady. Can't you just let her be?"

Luke punched Billy once in the midsection, and he doubled over in pain. "Don't you talk disrespectful to me, boy. I don't take no sass. This matter don't concern you."

Billy was on his knees, holding his stomach when Rus walked over and kicked his backside.

"Kid, I didn't figure you was too smart, but I thought you had enough sense to keep your mouth shut. You best not anger Luke again. Next time, he'll likely shoot you. Count yourself lucky to still be alive."

Mary's eyes met those of Billy as Luke dragged her to her feet.

"Before you die, woman, you'll know what it's like to be with a real man. I killed me near a hundred men, and I ain't yet forty."

She faced him furiously. "And I would have killed you if I could. What does that prove?"

"You would have killed me, wouldn't you?" Luke smiled as if he found the thought amusing. "A regular wild puma, ain't you?" He tangled his hand in her hair and pulled her toward him, forcing an unwelcome kiss on her lips. "I especially like a woman who can mix pleasure with pain. Gets my blood up. Still, if you fight me anymore, I'll kill you here and now. I ain't never killed a woman, but you might just drive me to it."

"That's right, you only rape and beat women. How kind of you."

He raised his hand as if to strike her, but Rus put his hand on his brother's arm. "Luke, she's gonna die anyhow. Wheeler wants the pleasure of killin' her, remember? And he's paid us for that privilege."

Of course! She should have known it as soon as she saw Billy. Sam Wheeler was a vengeful man; he had obviously paid these animals to find both her and Billy. She could hardly believe that Wheeler intended to kill them with his own hand, but that was what Rus Harris had said, and there was no reason for him to lie.

"He don't get this woman until I'm done with her. Be real nice to have me a virgin," he said.

"What makes you think she is?" Rusty questioned dubiously. "She ain't that young."

"Didn't you see the way she fought me, brother? No woman who wasn't a virgin would act that way."

Luke started to move toward her again and she backed away. She had to find a way to stop him.

"The first man to have me is going to die a swift and terrible death," she cried out, saying the first thing that came into her head. "It's been foretold."

Luke Harris began to laugh. "Am I supposed to believe such foolishness?"

Having once said it, she decided to tough it out. "That's right! My cousin Rebecca has the second sight, and she told me so."

Billy rose to his feet, still holding his midsection. "Miss Mary's tellin' the truth. I worked at the farm for a time and I know Becky right well. She's got the gift. She knows things that other people don't. And what she says is always true."

"That so?" Luke questioned. "That girl a gypsy or somethin'?"

"No, but she's special. Some folks think she's crazy, but she ain't. She just sees things different than most people. She was touched by the Lord."

Mary was grateful for Billy's support.

"People used to say I was crazy when I was a boy, but I reckon I was smarter than all of them." The outlaw had a peculiar, faraway look in his eye for just a moment. "Maybe I'll just let someone else be your first, little lady."

"Luke, let me tend to your shoulder," Rus said, looking as if he thought the entire conversation was idiotic, but was relieved that his brother seemed to be calming down.

"Hell, it ain't nothin' more than a scratch. She only knicked me. Some whiskey'll clean it out right and proper. I've had plenty worse."

The two brothers walked away and left her there. She would have liked to run to a horse and ride far away, but she found herself unable to move. Her legs wobbled when she so much as tried to walk. One of the Mexicans came and got her, tying her feet and hands tightly with buckskin thongs. He pushed her down next to Billy, who had been bound in the same manner. It was only after she was sitting quietly on the ground that she realized her dress was soaked with perspiration. Every part of her face and body ached, but she was alive.

For the time being, the Harris brothers seemed to lose interest in Billy and her. She listened to the three Mexicans talking and wished she understood their language. The one who had tied her up was named Jose, and he never smiled. The second man, Miguel, was small and agile, while the third and tallest of the three was called Esteban; he rarely spoke at all. Miguel began building a fire and eventually frying some meat. She noticed that they kept their rifles handy at all times. While the men were busy eating, Mary turned and spoke quietly to Billy.

"Thank you for helping me. I don't know how long it will work, but maybe Luke will leave me alone until we figure out a way to escape from here."

Billy shook his head, his eyes cast down, his expression forlorn. "I've been looking for a chance to get away from them right from the moment they caught up with me. You might as well know it's near impossible. They watch me closer than a hog does a corn crib. That Rus Harris might not look it, but he's a right clever fella. He's always one step ahead of a body. In my case though, I guess it ain't so hard. It's Luke that really scares me. It's like being with the devil himself. Don't know how you managed to stand up to him like you did."

"Neither do I," she admitted. "Billy, you and I have to find a way to escape," she reasserted. "We cannot just accept what's happened to us."

"I believe it's hopeless, ma'am." He slumped dejectedly.

"Well, I don't," she snapped. "And you shouldn't either." She realized she was exuding more confidence than she felt. "If for some reason I get away, I'll see that the marshal comes back for you, and I hope you'll do the same for me."

"What do you plan on doing?" Billy asked fearfully.

"I'm not sure, but I'll work out something."

Billy looked around and then spoke in a soft whisper. "Luke's crazy. I've seen him do things I can't even tell you about, mean, cruel things, and he don't even show any remorse. Just be careful!"

"I will be," she promised.

"Tell me about Rebecca," he said. "How is she?"

"Lost to us again. She misses you very badly. You were the only person who reached her."

Billy hung his head. "I acted real stupid, and now she's paying for it along with me."

"Rebecca wanted to go to Prescott about a week ago because she thought you were there."

Billy looked at her excitedly. "I was there! That was where

Luke and Rus found me."

Mary stared at him, too surprised to speak. Maybe Rebecca did have some special intuition, at least regarding those she loved, and it was obvious to her that the girl did love Billy Travers.

"There ain't a day goes by that I don't wish Becky and I was together. I wish I could change things."

Mary studied Billy's face; it was as round and undeceiving as a cabbage. There was nothing that smacked of deceit in those simple, gentle eyes.

"Rebecca truly loves you," she said.

"If I get out of this alive, I'm gonna make it all up to her somehow. I promise."

Their conversation came to an abrupt halt as Jose approached. He pulled Billy to a separate place so they could no longer talk.

She lay back on the cold ground, suffering pain and discomfort in stoic silence. Her mind moved at a feverish pace, thinking up and analyzing different plans for escape. She was resolved to act later in the same night, before they rode any farther away from Expectation.

Chapter Seventeen

Cal deliberately avoided being anywhere near the ranch house for most of the day. First, he rode over to Rancho Royo to check on any damage from the Apache, but mercifully, the Royo had been spared renegade incursions. When he returned to the Thunderbolt, he decided to work with Tiny, Nat, and Buck near the high country border, checking on stray stock.

The last thing he wanted to do was think about Mary MacGreggor, because his feelings for her were damned confused. He'd made love to her. And he realized that if he were honest with himself, all he wanted was to be with her again. Hell, he'd felt that way about her from the first moment he laid eyes on her. But it was surely a mistake for her as well as him. It was as if all his efforts to model himself into a controlled, reasonable person were going up in smoke because of his desire for her. He wanted her more then he'd ever wanted Linda. He'd been a green kid in those days. He'd known nothing about the depth of passion a man could feel. It could destroy him. The best thing was just to keep away from Mary and hope that he could forget those feelings. She'd be gone in a few months anyway.

By the time he returned to the ranch house, long shadows had formed and afternoon was turning into evening. He washed up outside, sweaty and tired from hard hours of physical labor. He was feeling better now, more like his old calm self.

Elizabeth was the first person to greet him as he walked into the house. "Everyone wondered where you were," she said, a warm smile on her face.

"Everyone?" Did that mean Mary?

"Why yes. Doc came by around noon because he had some message for you."

"Know what it was?"

Her hazel eyes opened a little wider. "No, he told Mary, not me. But, according to Doc, she's gone back to the farm, so I guess you'll have to see him about it."

What she said suddenly registered. "Mary went back to the farm—alone?" Why would she do something as dangerous as that? And why without telling anyone? Somehow, he was certain her precipitate action had to do with him. But she'd seemed fine when he left her during the night. Was she hurt that he had left without a word to her this morning?

Just then there was a knock at the door and he called out for the person to enter. It turned out to be Doc, and he was relieved. Now he could find out why Mary had left so abruptly. It shouldn't bother him but it did.

"They told me you was back. I need to talk with you," Doc said, rubbing at his watery eyes.

"That makes two of us. Why did Mary go off?"

"Don't know exactly. I came by to tell you about Jesse."

"What about Jesse?" He was growing impatient with Doc but trying hard not to let it show.

"Well, she dropped by looking for you, but when you wasn't nowhere to be found, she just said to remind you that you was to see her about making wedding plans for you and Lorette."

"She said what?" He remembered now the conversation between Jesse and himself the last time they had spoken. Knowing Jesse, of course, she had come by to follow up. "Doc, did Mary hear her?"

"No, but I told Mary what Jess said so that she could pass

221

the message along to you."

Cal felt a pain in his heart. He could only imagine what Mary would have thought when she heard Jesse's message. How betrayed she must have felt! He had to go out to the farm and find her, tell her it was all a misunderstanding. He had no intention of marrying Lorette Wheeler. He knew that now for certain. With a violent start, Cal realized that if he were to ever take a wife, it would be Mary MacGreggor and no one else.

There was a small, white hand on his tanned arm and he turned to see who was standing there. It was Elizabeth's daughter, Rebecca, the pretty girl who never spoke and often looked troubled or lost. She was staring into his face almost as if she were in a trance.

"Mary needs you," the strange girl said in a soft, dreamy voice. "She's in bad trouble. They came back again."

A shockwave went through him, because he believed she spoke the truth. But how could the girl know such a thing? He was seized by fear; he had to find Mary and bring her back to the ranch.

"Doc, come with me. I'm going out to the Stafford farm." His stomach clenched in a tight knot.

They were out the door and mounted in a matter of seconds. He rode as fast as he could, but the time passed so slowly that he could hardly stand it.

What they found at the farm only convinced him that the words Rebecca Stafford had uttered were true. Mary had been taken by the Harris gang, and that meant she was in terrible danger. He blamed himself, knowing it might have been prevented if he hadn't acted like such a cowardly jackass this morning.

"Damn it!" he said, looking down on the dead man lying in front of him. "Mary must have killed him. I wonder what they've done to her."

"Well, since she ain't here, you can be sure they've taken her with them. I wonder why."

"I've got to find her!" He tried to think what to do.

"Maybe we could find the marshal and get ourselves a bunch of men together."

"That would take too long. No, I need to get started right away. We'll get Tiny, and I'm gonna have to find a tracker. We'll make sure to bring plenty of provisions, fresh horses, and ammunition. There's no telling how long this is going to take. But we're going to find those bastards and take care of them once and for all!"

"Calm yourself, son. I ain't seen you like this in many years."

"Can't do it," Cal said. "Not until I know Mary's safe. This is all my fault, Doc. I was so busy thinking about myself that I never even gave a thought to her feelings. I've got to find her and make it up to her."

Doc put his hand on Cal's shoulder. "Steady. We'll do what we can, but you know them Harrises. We may not be able to save her."

Cal studied the grim expression on Doc's face, understanding the truth of what the old wrangler said, but refusing to accept it.

"Let's get going." Cal was making an effort to ignore the fear that tore at his throat like a wild coyote.

He would have liked to start tracking down the Harrises immediately, except he realized he needed to go back to the ranch first. Then he could return armed and prepared to take on the Harris gang.

Elizabeth had to be told about Mary, and he didn't look forward to that. When he got back, the Staffords were waiting for him. Elizabeth's face was pale and pinched with worry. He wasn't going to hold her in suspense; that would be unfair.

"Where's Mary?" she asked, immediately fearful.

"It appears Rebecca was right. The Harrises have taken her. Leastwise, that's the way it looks now."

"Oh, my God, no!" Elizabeth began to sob. Cal put his arms around her in what seemed a futile gesture of comfort. "Oh, Cal, I'm so afraid for her! They're such horrible vermin. I can't even call them men! They're like demons from hell. What will become of her?"

"I'm going after her, Elizabeth. I won't rest until she's safe. Meantime, I want you and your children to remain at the ranch. I don't want you in any unnecessary danger."

"I'm grateful to you," she said, and kissed his cheek.

Elizabeth was so cooperative that he felt at least one worry was off his mind. But he could not stop thinking about Mary and worrying about what might be happening to her.

Mary waited until the camp became relatively quiet, knowing that Jose was still tentatively watching her.

"I need some privacy," she said. "I have to take care of my personal needs. You've got to untie me."

At first, Jose ignored her, and she feared he spoke no English. But she repeated her comments, this time with more urgency. Finally, she realized with a sigh of relief, he was doing as she asked.

He followed after her, but she waved her hand as if to send him back and have him turn around. When he finally accommodated her, she frantically looked for something she could use as a weapon. There were a lot of large rocks and boulders. She felt around, eventually locating the largest one that she could manage to lift up. Ever so quietly she moved around Jose and smashed the large rock down on his head with as much power as she could manage. But he was only dazed for a moment and so she had to hit him a second time and eventually a third. She looked down, thinking he seemed unconscious, and that would give her at least a few minutes' head start. Stealthily, she moved around to where the horses were tied up. Was it worthwhile to try to scatter all of them? But time was precious, and she could be discovered at any moment.

There was no saddle on the mare and no time to bother with one. She climbed on bareback and held to the horse's back and mane, keeping low. First, she rode quietly and slowly, but as soon as the camp was behind her, she rode as fast as she dared, hoping not to fall off. Her heart was beating so hard, she was certain anyone within ten miles must be able to hear it.

She rode in the direction they'd come from and prayed she would not get lost in the dark. There was no way to know for certain how long she'd been traveling before she heard the hooves of a horse coming along fast from behind her. She sped up, but she could hear the other horse gaining on her.

And then strong hands reached out and seized her. She struggled against the iron grasp to no avail and was lifted from her horse and on to another, her own horse looped around the neck with a rope and brought beside his.

"Be still!" Luke said. "I don't much like racing after you in the dark. Damn fool woman. Horses could have broken their legs."

"You didn't have to come. Just let me go!" She brought her elbow back into his ribs and he tightened his grip so hard around her waist that she cried out.

"I'll be gentle if you behave," he said. "You went and knocked Jose unconscious, you know that? No one's gonna trust you again."

"I don't want to be trusted. I want to be free!"

"Well, you can't be! Just accept that, and it'll go a lot easier on you."

She wasn't going to accept it, not now, not ever. But fighting him at the moment would be futile. He was too strong and too mean. She held her back as rigid as she could and tried to stay clear of his body, not an easy task considering that he kept one hand tightly fixed at her waist.

Rus and the other men seemed to be waiting for them when they rode back into camp.

"I told you she was nothing but trouble. Can't wait to get rid of her! If it weren't for that nuisance of a marshal, we'd be rid of them both by now and on our way."

"I'll handle the woman. Don't worry. She won't get away again." Luke pulled her off the horse, half dragging, half carrying her to a place where he had set up blankets near the shelter of some scrub pines.

"Take off your dress," he ordered gruffly.

"What? I will not!"

He brought back his hand as if he would hit her and she held her hands over her face in a protective gesture. But the blow did not come as she had expected.

"Take it off!" he snarled. "Otherwise I'm ripping it off your body and you can ride naked from here on in."

She immediately removed the dress, neatly folding it on the ground away from him. He began binding her hands and feet with the same kind of rawhide thongs that had been used on her before. Then he lifted her, placing her on the ground and tying the end of the leather stripping around a scrub tree so that her hands were over her head. She felt completely defenseless lying in this manner. He must have realized what she was thinking because he smiled at her in a self-satisfied manner.

"Just in case you still got any ideas, I'll do one better. Recognize this?" He held up her knife, the blade glinting in the moonlight.

Did he intend to stab her with it as she lay there? He brought the blade down and she turned her head, closing her eyes. In the next moment, she heard the sound of material rending and felt her underwear being ripped from her body.

"Never could understand why women wore those stupid corsets and petticoats anyhow. From now on, you wear only a dress, and at night, it comes off." He forced her head to turn toward him, so that their eyes met, his own glittering with unnatural brightness. "I don't remember people's names anymore. They all kind of blend together after a time. Maybe I don't want to remember them. But I'll call you Beauty. I won't forget that." Then he wrapped her in a blanket. "Get some sleep now. You'll need it. You ain't goin' nowhere 'cept with me."

Luke woke Mary as dawn broke, kicking her with the toe of his dusty boot. Then he untied her, allowing her to dress and wash up. Miguel then gave her some dry beef jerky and coffee for breakfast. She took it eagerly, realizing how terribly hungry and thirsty she was. She'd eaten nothing since the previous morning. If there was any chance for escape, she must keep up her strength.

They were riding out again before the sun had fully risen. At least she had her bonnet, which had been left tied to the mare's saddle. It gave her face some protection from the hot sun and constant wind.

It was a long hard day of riding and her back ached miserably as they broke for lunch at noon.

"There's a two-bit town up ahead. Want to stop there?" Rus asked Luke.

"Could use some supplies and a drink or two."

"What'll we do with them?" Rusty indicated Billy and Mary.

"Take 'em in with us. They know what'll happen if they cause trouble." Luke tossed her a menacing glance.

An old man was sweeping in front of the general store as they rode into what looked like even less of a town than Expectation. A fierce wind blew off the desert, cutting across the man's wizened face like a knife blade. He looked up and caught sight of them and stared. The expression on his face told Mary he knew who the Harrises were. The old man dropped his broom and went running up the street. Could it be that there was a law enforcement officer in this town? Maybe finally they would get some help. She began to have some hope.

Esteban waited with Billy and the horses while Jose and Miguel went into the general store. Luke led her into a seedy saloon, wiping the trail dust from his mouth with his red bandanna. Rus scratched his growth of carrot-colored stubble and approached the bar. Luke surveyed the room with a quick jerk of his head, and then brought his attention back to the bar.

"We don't serve no women here," the barkeep said, staring at Mary.

"She's with me," Luke said as if that settled the matter. Luke's pale, cold eyes studied the barkeep's hands. "Somethin' wrong with them fingers of yours?" Luke's voice hammered out the words like metal on a forge.

Mary looked down. The man's fingers were twisted and gnarled like twigs on an old tree.

The barkeep looked down with some embarrassment. " 'Spect it's my rheumatics."

"Just leave the bottle," Luke ordered, but the barkeep had already begun to pour. "I said leave it, damn you. And don't touch it again!" Luke's eyes flashed blue fire.

"Let's just finish our drinks and go," Rus urged. Mary noticed the look of concern in his eyes.

"Didn't have nothin' else in mind, brother."

A thin man with a pinched face walked stiffly into the saloon. A sheriff's badge was pinned to his worn, leather vest. She could see Rus watching him out of the corner of his eye. Luke kept one hand on her; with the other, he reached for his holstered Colt.

"You best come along with me," the sheriff said sharply

through thin lips. Mary observed the sheriff's hand resting on his gun.

Luke spat on the sawdust floor contemptuously. "What's the problem? Ain't we peaceable enough?"

"You caused trouble here before." The lawman's voice was tighter than the tension on a fiddler's newly tuned instrument.

Luke didn't speak. He just smiled, his grin crooked. Rus nodded his head as if he knew exactly what the smile meant. Mary braced herself. She thought she knew as well.

Luke Harris pushed Mary to the floor as he whipped his Colt out, aiming and cocking it with a flowing movement. The lawman was no match for Luke. She watched in horror as two bullets were pumped into the sheriff's chest in quick succession and the man fell close by her. Blood shot from the chest wounds.

The barkeep tried to reach for his rifle, but his arthritic hands were a study in slow motion. Luke was still smiling his strange smile as he shot the bartender in the head. The silence in the saloon was palpable. Mary rose unsteadily to her feet and felt her stomach sicken as she stared at the two dead men.

"Wish you hadn't done that," Rus said.

"Couldn't be helped, Rusty." Luke went back to the bar and poured out a generous drink for his brother and himself. "Wasn't much of a lawman, was he?" Luke poked the tin star on the sheriff's vest with his booted toe.

"Reckon not," Rus agreed.

Luke's light eyes were distant now and when he spoke, his voice seemed to be coming from far away. "When I was young, killin' bothered me, but I traveled a far piece since then." His eyes were almost glassy, vague. "Be glad, Rusty, you wasn't old enough to go to war. At Shiloh, I was just a raw, green recruit like them others. Could scarcely hold my rifle steady, let alone shoot it. You remember all those times I took abuse when Pa beat on me? I didn't know no better then. But in that first battle,

I got to see men dyin' all around me. General Johnston hisself was right near when a main artery in his leg was cut open. He bled to death in minutes before a surgeon could even get to him. I seen it, and I wasn't scared no more. I filled up inside with righteous wrath. I knew then I was gonna kill every Yankee I could! When that day ended, my hands was caked red with blood. I rejoiced in it! I knew why the Lord had seen fit to put me on this earth. I was one of the chosen. He elected me to do his work, to smite His enemies. And I was able to do His work because He gave me the power."

"The power?" Rus questioned.

"Over life and death." Luke held up his Colt, eying it worshipfully as the well-shined barrel caught the glint of the fleeting sun's rays from through the swinging doors.

Rus shrugged, gulping his last drop of whiskey. "Guess we better get out of this town right quick."

Luke glanced around the room. "I'm not hearin' any complaints, are you?" The silence of the dead seemed to engulf them.

Rus let out a deep sigh. "Seems like I'm always the one needs to tidy up."

He handed Luke four bottles of whiskey from behind the bar, then, taking another, he uncorked it and poured alcohol around the room, finishing at the swinging doors. As they departed, Rus threw a lit match into the alcohol. It took several tries before he got the desired result. Luke took her arm and forced Mary forward to where Esteban waited with the horses.

They were joined by Miguel and Jose, who were tying provisions on a pack mule. As they rode out of town, Mary heard an explosion and turned back. Luke did the same.

"What a sight," he said. "Reckon the fires of hell don't burn no brighter."

"Afraid we just might get to see them firsthand," Rus muttered.

They made camp several hours later after more hard riding. Miguel began working with the provisions.

"I'm gettin' sick of his cookin'," Luke said.

Mary didn't hesitate. "I can cook for you," she said.

Rus burst out, "Oh sure, and find a way to poison us all? Forget it!"

"Never stop, do you?" Luke said, but there was a twinkle in his eye as if the thought of her trying to poison them was something he found amusing.

The men did quite a bit of drinking after they ate and Mary listened and watched keenly. Luke and Rus talked about how they were going to kill Jack Phillips once they returned to Expectation. She wondered if the sheepherder was making similar plans for Sam Wheeler. Men who plotted violence were themselves prone to die violently, she reminded herself, finding she felt little compassion for either man at present.

Any hopes of escaping that night were soon dashed when Luke came to her and demanded that she remove her dress as on the previous night. She turned her back to him, feeling demeaned and degraded, pulling off her dress and quickly pulling the blanket he held out to her around her body. He again forced her to lie down on the ground and bound her hand and foot.

"Must I be humiliated this way?" she said, finding it difficult to contain her rage.

"You brought it on yourself. Don't expect any sympathy from me." He left her then and went back to the other men. She tried to see what Billy was doing, and saw he was also bound just as she was, although at the other side of the camp. She realized with something akin to despair that Billy had been right;

it was nearly impossible to escape these evil men.

Mary finally fell into an exhausted sleep. But in the middle of night she woke to find Luke's hands on her body. She gasped and tried to pull away from him.

"Stop that carryin' on," Luke said in a gruff voice.

She smelled the whiskey on his breath. Mary realized that he was drunk, but instead of reassuring her, the knowledge made her that much more fearful of him. Drunks were volatile and unpredictable. Luke Harris was insanely violent even when he wasn't drunk. She shuddered.

"Once the little matter of your virginity is taken care of, I intend to have you all the time, and you're goin' to love it." He pulled her into his arms. "I seen you kill. Don't forget that. You're just like me. We're alike. And a woman who's got the spirit of a wild bronc only needs proper breakin' to be the best there is."

He eventually fell asleep with his body tightly against hers. She managed to turn her back against him but could feel the stirring of his erection. Although he made no actual attempt to force himself on her, she still slept very little for the rest of the night.

CHAPTER EIGHTEEN

In spite of his decision to go it alone, Cal had sent a man looking for Marshal Wade. He got the information that the marshal had chased after the Harrises and eventually lost them. Now Wade was at Apache Junction rounding up suspects in a Wells Fargo holdup. He sent word back that he would help Cal hunt for the Harrises again as soon as possible. Cal had no intention of waiting around. He knew it was up to him to find them. He couldn't imagine why the Harris gang had gone back to the farm or taken Mary with them. But it wasn't worthwhile to spend any time or thought in speculation. He could only hope they hadn't killed or raped her by now. Even if they had raped her, it wouldn't matter any to him because he wanted her back regardless.

Doc urged him to take more men with him, but Cal really wanted to do this on his own. He took Doc because Mary might need his services and Tiny because there was no one stronger or more dependable. He still needed an expert tracker. He knew the army would help him, yet he did not want to take time to send to the fort and ask for one of their scouts. The longer those bastards held Mary, the worse her chances for survival. He talked the matter over with Doc, since the old cowhand always seemed to have sensible ideas.

"Reckon I know every man in these here parts. There's a half-breed name of Joseph Cloud who done some trackin' for the army against the Apaches some time ago. Then he settled hisself on a homestead not too far from here. We could get him. Offer to pay him enough, and I'm sure he'll come with us pronto."

"Is he any good?"

"One of the best," Doc replied without hesitation.

Cal quickly consented. He had intended to go himself for the tracker, but Doc talked him out of it, and Cal realized he was right. There was a lot of preparation to be made before they left. He sent Buck to get the tracker. It was late at night before Buck returned with Joseph Cloud.

Cal's first impression was of a quiet man with intelligent eyes who carried himself with pride and dignity, a man just a few years older than Cal himself.

"I hear you know some about tracking," Cal said.

Cloud did not speak, but merely nodded, his eyes betraying no expression.

"Joseph's respected for his resourcefulness and courage. Ain't that right?" Doc said.

The bronze-skinned man merely grunted in response.

"I'll be payin' whatever you think right. When will you be ready to get started?" Cal asked.

"At first light," the tracker responded. "We must sleep now."

Cal found he could not sleep. He was too wound up, too worried about Mary. What had the Harrises done to her? Would he be too late? Would he find her dead? His mind was tortured by fears and doubts. He pictured her in his mind's eye. God, but she was a beautiful woman! It wasn't just her outward looks that made her special; it was the radiance of her soul, the glow of her inner self. Surely, even men like the Harrises must have seen that about her. But did they even have souls?

He could no longer deny the depth of his feelings for Mary, and if that meant laying himself open to hurt again, then he would have to run that risk. He wasn't going to hide from his feelings any more or continue to act like a coward. He hadn't for a moment forgotten Mary saying she loved him.

At the crack of dawn, he mounted up with Doc, Tiny, and Joseph Cloud. They took extra horses, pack mules, and plenty of weapons and provisions. Elizabeth was waiting to say goodbye to him. The iridescent lavender shadows beneath her eyes testified to the fact that she hadn't gotten much sleep either.

"Please bring her back to us," Elizabeth said.

"I'll do my damnedest!"

Jeremy Stafford stepped forward. "Mr. Davis, I want to go with you. Mary's my cousin and I love her. I want to help you hunt down those outlaws. I haven't forgotten how they murdered my pa." The boy's eyes were dark with hate.

"Son, you got every right to go with us, but you're needed here. Your pa would want you to take care of your womenfolk."

Jeremy seemed to accept that and stayed behind. They rode out, heading back to the Stafford farm, where Cal hoped Joseph Cloud would pick up the trail of the Harris gang.

When they got to the farm, Joseph spent a good deal of time looking and searching. Doc and Tiny watered the horses at the creek. Cal kept his eyes on the tracker.

"I have found the trail," Joseph told him, eyes sharp and alert. "They are not difficult to follow."

"Mount up!" Cal called out to the others.

As they rode along, Cal asked questions of the tracker. Talking helped to ease his tension, although the tracker was not much for conversation. Cal did learn a few interesting pieces of information about the man. Joseph Cloud was a Papago on his mother's side. He had never known his biological father, who was a white man. His mother had raised him with her tribe. He'd been brought up as a Catholic, taught by Jesuit missionaries outside of Tucson. He told Cal that his people disliked the Apache every bit as much as the white settlers did.

"The Apache are our hereditary enemies. When they raid our village and steal our cattle, we follow them into the desert, even to the mountains. When we are through, they know that the Papago do not lack courage." Joseph Cloud spoke with fastidious severity. "This woman you are seeking, does she mean much to you?"

"Very much," Cal admitted tersely.

"Then we will treat these men like the Apache, and we will find your woman."

The man's words somehow reassured Cal. Joseph spoke no more, but went ahead, following the trail the Harris gang had left through the sagebrush and into the desert. The purple light had turned to gold with the rising of the morning star as they rode on relentlessly through the open country.

Mary had hardly slept all night. Her mind continued to be active, thinking of ways that she might escape. There must be something she could do. Yet she could think of nothing. Toward dawn, Mary dozed off into a troubled sleep, only to be awakened a short time later by Luke, whose hands were traveling down her body.

"That's what I want to feel when I get up in the morning," he said. He pulled her against him and kissed her neck. She was becoming uneasy, but then he stood up and unbound her hands and feet, tossing her dress to her.

He held his head with both hands. "I reckon I must have drunk too much last night," he said.

He staggered away and Mary quickly set about the task of dressing herself. Unfortunately, Mary found that her hands and feet were almost numb and it took great effort to so much as button her dress.

Miguel served strong coffee and tortillas. She welcomed the food, eating as slowly as she could manage. Rus was in a hurry and they soon were riding again. Luke allowed her to ride her own horse now, and she was grateful for that. She did not want him putting his hands all over her body again. It disgusted her.

Up above, the sun sailed through the deep, ocean-blue sky with clouds like the sails of a clipper ship at full mast. A strong desert wind blew across the open land while the sun warmed the ancient Arizona earth. The smell of sagebrush mingled with the scent of leather and horse sweat. She wasn't certain where they were headed, but it seemed that they were moving in a northerly direction.

At noon, they made camp near a clump of cactus. Billy was allowed to sit near her and they got to talk again for a few minutes. He pulled his sugar loaf sombrero up so that his eyes met hers.

"He botherin' you much?" Billy indicated Luke, who was busy talking with his brother.

"Not yet," she said quietly. "But he has plans. I want to be away from him before that."

"I'll keep my eyes open," he promised.

Mary noticed that her mare had pricked up its ears nervously. "Easy girl!" But the horse reared suddenly and Mary moved back, startled.

She heard the sound before she actually saw it, like the ominous jingling of a gunman's spurs. Luke was suddenly beside her, whipping out his Colt. He shot the rattler twice as Mary calmed her horse, gently petting the lathered mane of coarse brown hair.

Luke got down to examine the rattler. Handling it carefully, he got out his knife and skinned the snake, handing the meat to Miguel.

"Save it for tonight," he said, then turned to her. "Rattlesnake cooked over a campfire will be tender and tasty as chicken."

"You do that often?" she asked.

"Kill snakes? Sure, that's how I got my hatband. I killed, skinned, and ate my first diamondback rattler when I come out here. The Injuns believe if you eat a snake you take on its characteristics, and that's just what I wanted. So I guess you might say I'm deadly as a rattler and just as treacherous."

She observed his smile and said nothing. Luke left her alone with Billy again, much to her relief. They sat down side by side on the ground.

"What did you do when you left Expectation? We all wondered what happened to you."

Billy shook his head. "Nothin' much to be proud of, Miss Mary. I worked around Yuma and Tombstone for a while, careful not to hang around too long. No one seemed to be needin' much help. Autumn and winter's not the best time of year for ranchers to be puttin' on extra hands. Spring's best for the round-up. I made my way toward Phoenix, lookin' for work and not findin' much. I was scared to use my real name and disguised myself by growin' this beard and mustache.

"The only work I managed to find in Phoenix was as a swamper in the Palace saloon. It wasn't exactly what I had in mind, but I figured it was only going to be temporary. I just sort of drifted through my days, existing, but nothing more. That was when I decided to move on to Prescott. Funny how Becky knew I was there. The thing of it is I was never really in danger until I got there, and it was like she could tell."

"Yes, she knew," Mary agreed. "Were the Harrises actually looking for you?"

"I don't think they were at that very moment. I did a pretty good job of disappearing. But I was cleaning out a brass cuspidor when a wrangler I used to work with seen me and called me out by name. I was sure no one would recognize me, but that wasn't the case. It just so happened Luke and Rus were in that saloon and they heard what was said. I think they asked

Fat Frank about me."

"Fat Frank?"

"He was the bartender. Never did like him much, with his piggy face and short fat body. Not much ever happens in Prescott that he don't know about. Anyway, I put down the spittoon I was emptying and decided to get out of there fast. I tried ducking through the back door. I'd headed to the livery stable to get my horse when they caught up with me.

"I'd just swung onto Blaze when Luke grabbed me and pulled me down to the ground. I throwed a wild punch and then before I knew what happened, a gun butt came crashing down on my skull. It's real lucky I got such a hard head." Billy rubbed the back of his head.

"I asked them what they wanted with me when I was fully conscious again. It was dark in that stable, but I could see the expressions on their faces, and I knew enough to be scared. They said Sam Wheeler had put out the word on me. He was going to pay in gold coin for anyone who brought me to him. I begged them to let me go, but they just laughed in my face. They had me slung over my saddle like a side of beef. I've been livin' in fear ever since. They was bringing me to Wheeler, but they left me with the Mex and went on to see him first. I guess that's when he told them about how he wanted you as well as me."

Mary nodded her head, understanding just how Billy felt. She was about to say something when Rus Harris walked toward them.

"Hope you're not planning any more escapes. There's a limit to my patience. You're gonna be with us till we don't want you no more. That's the way it is. Better accept it and you'll save yourselves a lot of grief. See them Mex we got? Trained them ourselves. Esteban, he's a powerful feller and can wrestle down a bear. I seen him snap a man's neck like it was nothin' stronger then a green bean. Now Miguel, he's small, but he's an expert with a knife. And Jose, he's got deadly accurate aim with a pistol. Don't underestimate any of them. See Miguel's mouth? Them front teeth wasn't lost in any accident. He did something Luke didn't like once. Hope you don't make that mistake. It's hard to say what might set Luke off. He ain't quite like most folks. That's why nobody crosses him. My advice to both of you is not to do anything that riles him. Best stay on his good side. Hate to see you dead before your time." Rus's mouth formed a smile, but it did not extend to his eyes, which continued to look cold and mean like a hungry rattlesnake.

Mary studied the man's face. Rus Harris's face was a maze of orange freckles. His nose was slightly crooked and out of alignment, as if it had once been broken and never properly healed. He was a creepy figure, but not as eerie as Luke. Mary couldn't help but wonder how long she and Billy were destined to survive. Still, she refused to give in to her fears. As long as they were alive, there was still hope.

Rus walked away from them and gave the signal to break camp.

"If I had any sense, I'd have clean left Arizona Territory," Billy said, rising to his feet. "Ma always told me how dumb I was, and I'd get mad. Appears she was right about me. I got my life into a terrible predicament. Seems if there's a mistake to be made, I manage to blunder into it."

It was late afternoon when they heard sounds up ahead of them. At first, Mary had no idea what she was listening to; then she realized that it must be a wagon of some sort.

Luke immediately rode on ahead, and when he returned, he seemed excited. His light eyes were crystal bright, like mountain lakes. "Come on! We're gonna rob us a stagecoach." Luke let out a wild rebel yell and was soon joined by his brother.

They were forced to ride fast and hard as the gang passed by the stagecoach at some distance, only to locate themselves at an advanced point. Rus carefully chose a spot for an ambush that provided sheltering rocks. It was near an old stagecoach stop, an adobe building that had once stood solid but was now in a state of ruined decay. Luke told Jose to bind Mary and Billy's hands and keep an eye on them as he and the other outlaws prepared for the attack.

Mary observed everything around her with sharp attention to detail. Old rock walls rambled across the mesa between thick stands of mesquite and greasewood.

"Billy," she whispered, "we might just get our opportunity now if things go right. Let's watch carefully."

The youth nodded his head in agreement and they waited in tense silence. They didn't have long. The old stagecoach came to a halt near the ruined building. It seemed that in spite of its deserted appearance, this was still used as a watering hole because a deep well existed here.

Jose kept back with Mary and Billy, his gun drawn. The four other men raised their bandannas, covering their faces and went out into the road.

"Move a muscle and you're dead men!" Luke shouted out. "Drop all your guns and ammunition to the ground. Then one at a time, get down from the coach. My men are gonna search everyone."

The driver did as he was told, but the man riding shotgun raised his rifle. It was the last move he would ever make. Luke Harris let out a volley of bullets that blasted the guard off the coach and rendered him motionless, sprawled in the dust. Mary saw the strange gleam in his eyes and felt sick.

"Anyone else plan on tryin' something?" Luke called out.

There was no reply. The passengers quickly threw their weapons on the ground and left the stagecoach one at time, as they had been told to do. There were three men in all, and they were carefully searched for valuables. None of them seemed to be carrying very much.

"Where's the strongbox?" Rusty asked the driver.

"Ain't any on this run."

Luke pistol whipped the man, smacking the barrel of his six-shooter across the driver's face twice.

"Stop! I'm telling the truth! Look for yourselves."

Rusty signaled Miguel to go through all the luggage. Just as the driver had said, there was no strongbox.

Luke was incensed. "Damn Wells Fargo! I ought to kill every last one of you." For a moment, he looked as if he would actually murder the driver and passengers.

"Come on," Rus urged. "Let's not waste any more time and effort here."

Rus called for Jose, who left the captives for a moment and went to help the others collect the weapons and tie up the men. That was when Mary started to ride away, with Billy following behind her. She rode in the direction they had come from, hoping they would have enough of a start to escape.

They had managed to ride several miles before Luke caught them again. He had a rifle aimed at them. Esteban was at his side with a drawn handgun.

"Turn the horses around! I'm gettin' right annoyed with you, woman. Surprised at you too, Billy boy. Don't you have no more sense than to follow this wild female?"

He didn't bother to untie their hands, so they were forced to ride in an awkward manner. They made camp late in the day and there was little festivity.

"Fifty dollars and a broken gold watch," Luke stormed. "Hell, that's chicken shit! Thought there might be a mine payroll on that coach." Luke kicked over a metal pot that Miguel had set up for cooking.

"Probably be on the next run," Rus said, seeming eager to

appease his brother.

"Well, Rus, we ain't got time to hang around for that. Besides, after this, they'll arm the next shipment real heavy." Luke was in a foul mood, Mary realized. What would happen when he got around to her?

She was not long in finding out. She and Billy were given no supper and were forced to sit bound hand and foot while Luke paced in front of them, his face darker than a thunderstorm.

"There's lots of things I could do to the two of you. But I'll make it real simple. Wheeler's gonna pay us extra when we bring you both to him, so he can hang you with his own hands. Of course, if you could make me want to keep the both of you, I might just reconsider. Now Billy, you already killed one man. I'd consider lettin' you ride with us if I could trust you."

"I'm no killer. I just done it one time in self-defense."

"Well, boy, one time's enough for a hangin'. Ol' Sam Wheeler sure sees it that way. But if you turn out all right for us, I might just save you from him. You understand? Let me share some wisdom I learned long ago. It don't matter how many men you kill or how you kill 'em, 'cause they can only hang you one time. So free yourself, boy, 'cause you're above the laws of ordinary society now. There's only one rule that counts: not gettin' caught. You think on it. Advice to live by, you might say."

Luke turned to her. "And now for you, Beauty. You're my real problem. I got to think real hard about you." He pulled her to her feet and led her away from the others. In spite of her determination not to show fear, she trembled.

"I know you got the boy to go with you. I know how you are. But once I've had you, you won't want anything but to be with me. And I promise that'll be soon. Just so you know, I've made myself a promise that if you try to escape me again, I'll do something drastic. I don't know that I could bring myself to kill you with my own hand, so I just might have to trade you off.

Years ago back in Texas, there was this woman who was a mighty shrew, and her husband traded her off to the Comancheros, who didn't much like her either and give her to the Comanches. Them Injuns do value a white-skinned female as a captive. By the time all the braves got through passin' her around and takin' their turns with her, she was a mite less feisty, I hear tell. Then the squaws went to work on her, burning off her ears and her nose, all painful and slow."

Mary bit down on her lower lip until she felt the blood well up. She didn't say a single word, but Luke's eyes were burning into her very soul.

"I'm not tellin' you this to scare you. It's just facts. Nowadays what's left of the Comanche have got themselves stuck on a reservation, thanks to the army. But there's still the Apache. I once seen a cut-nose squaw wearin' the strangest necklace. When I asked about it, I was told the Apache remove the finger bones from their victims and the women collect them and make them into necklaces. It ain't unusual for them to hack a man apart and keep the limbs as souvenirs. Fact, I heard somewhere that the Sioux took the trigger fingers of sixteen of Custer's men and made them into a necklace."

Mary was unable to stop shaking.

"The Indian Ring are just as eager to trade as the Comancheros ever were. 'Course mostly they trade whiskey and guns to the red heathen, but I bet a woman with coppery curls like yours would make a real nice captive. Them squaws are powerful inventive in the ways they mutilate whites. I could tell you lots more stories, real grisly ones. You'd think I was a saint after knowin' what the savages would do to you. Me, I'd always treat you good. As long as you're with me. So you think on it real careful, Beauty, because the next time you try to run from me, my feelings will be so hurt, I might just arrange for you to find out about the Apache firsthand."

His eyes held hers with frightening power. It was fortunate she hadn't been given any supper, because at that moment she felt like retching. However, Luke didn't come near her that night, so at least there was something to be grateful for.

The following day, the two brothers began to talk about committing yet another robbery before they traveled any farther north.

"We're close to the railroad," Rusty said. "Trouble is, I'm not sure we can handle a job like that. Don't think we got enough men for a train robbery."

"I like the idea," Luke responded. "A man who don't dare can't win."

That was enough for them to go into action. They chose a location and prepared to wait for the next train. Six hours later, the locomotive came rumbling down the track, clouds of steam puffing from its stack. The tracks began to tremble. Luke Harris lit sticks of dynamite and threw them in front of the train, then he hurled Mary to the ground beside him to wait for the expected explosion. The impact shook the earth.

Mary saw the dynamite had worked, and the train was derailed. In the confusion that followed, the outlaws boarded the train. Billy was forced to join them, although he had no sidearm. Luke held Mary beside him so that she could do nothing but watch helplessly. Moving swiftly from car to car, the outlaws disarmed the passengers and herded everyone out of the train.

Although Rusty did most of the talking, there was no mistake that Luke was the leader and the man in charge. They removed all of the passengers' valuables, looking mainly for money. Then Jose and Miguel were left to guard Billy and Mary as well as the passengers while Luke, Rusty, and Esteban went to the back car. She could hear another stick of dynamite explode. The ground shook as if there had been an earthquake. There was an exchange of gunfire, and she saw that Esteban had fallen from the train to the ground.

When Luke and Rusty returned, they looked solemn. When they made camp that evening, the two brothers talked about the train robbery and examined what they'd collected from the passengers.

"Wasn't worth losing a good man," Rusty said.

"Did you see the surprise on those two soldiers' faces? What a pleasure shootin' bluebellies again."

Rusty just shook his head.

"Too bad the train wasn't carrying an army payroll," Luke said.

"Just as well. We don't need the whole United States Army chasin' after us."

Luke turned to Billy. "Son, when I was your age, I'd already killed me twenty or thirty men. I got this scar down the side of my face in hand-to-hand combat. There's no better feeling. You got yourself the power. There's nothin' that compares to holdin' the power of life and death in your own hands just like you was the Lord Hisself."

Luke removed his pistol from its holster and pointed it at Billy's head. "Get on your knees and pray to me, boy. I am your God. I am your savior, your salvation. I decide whether you live or die. Worship me!" Luke's eyes had that strange light in them again and he seemed worlds away.

Poor Billy got down on his knees as he was told, wretched and resigned, fear etched in his features.

"Luke, let's have us some supper," Rusty said in a quiet voice. He seemed accustomed to his brother's disturbing moods.

Luke holstered his gun. "We got cause to celebrate tonight. Earned us some money. We got us any lemons? I'm in the mood to suck one now, just like ol' Stonewall Jackson used to do before his battles. Now there was a man for you. Wish I could have served with him."

"No lemons, Luke, but Miguel's got a melon."

"Ain't the same. Suppose it'll have to do for now."

Chapter Nineteen

Mary was shivering in her dress as they rode north. The weather had become chilly now, and she kept a blanket tightly wrapped around her body for warmth. The temperature was around fifty degrees, she estimated. They were still in the lowlands, and with relief, she noted that they weren't headed for the mountains. For the last day, Luke had forced her to double up with him again. He kept his hands around her waist and often talked about what he planned to do with her. She tried very hard not to listen to him and did not respond at all to his words, sure it would only encourage him.

That morning, they turned and began riding in what she thought was an easterly direction.

"Best thing for us is to head through New Mexico and right into Indian Territory," Rusty told his brother as they rode.

"You think it's worth our time?" Luke questioned.

"Sure is. We'll be able to relax for a while. And when we finish our business with Sam Wheeler in Expectation, we can go down and stay in Mexico, maybe buy ourselves a hacienda and live like kings."

Luke smiled at his brother. "Sounds real good to me, though I'm still more partial to southern Arizona. It wouldn't be a half bad place if the climate were a tad cooler."

"You could say the same thing about hell," Rusty said.

Mary had not for a moment forgotten that the unfinished business in Expectation referred to the deaths of herself and

Billy Travers. Yet she would have welcomed returning to Expectation, for in spite of her fears, she felt her best chance of escape would be in a place she knew and where people knew her.

They stopped to buy provisions and warmer clothing in a small, dusty town. Mary's dress was torn and dirty, but there were no ready-made women's clothes for sale. Luke decided she would dress like a cowboy. Mary really didn't mind, as she hoped that would help keep a rein on Luke's amorous attentions. It did seem to help. Once they wore the new, warmer clothing, she was allowed to ride her own horse again.

New Mexico, it seemed, was just as arid as Arizona. She was grateful for the cowboy hat she now wore and pulled it well over her face against the perpetual stress of sun and wind. They made camp that evening by a watering hole. Just as she was helping Miguel refill the canteens, trouble began. From out of nowhere it seemed, an Indian appeared and attacked Rusty Harris. The brave had nothing but a tomahawk, and as Rusty cried out, Luke came running toward the Indian and pulled him away. The Indian tried to gouge his eyes, but Luke kicked him hard in the groin. In one fluid motion his gun was drawn, the trigger pulled, and blood spurted from the Indian's head.

"Damn sneaky critter!" Luke hissed. He looked around quickly. "Where's the rest of them? There's got to be more. They never travel alone."

Luke signaled his brother and the Mexicans to fan out. The outlaws found the rest of the Indians hidden behind large rocks. When they returned, the party was with them, and Mary opened her mouth, gaping in surprise.

"Might as well kill 'em quick," Rusty said.

"Hardly worth our ammunition," Luke responded.

"You can't kill them!" Mary protested. "Look at them! They're just women, children, and old people. That man was the only warrior among them."

"All Injuns are the same," Rusty replied in disgust.

She turned to Luke. "Let them go! They can't do you any harm."

Luke gave her a very odd smile. "They'd kill us if they could." Luke turned to a young girl who carried a baby in her arms. "Come here!" he growled.

Mary thought that this small, bronze-skinned girl with almond-shaped eyes was no older than her cousin Rebecca.

"I seen you following what we said. What do you people want? Tell me right quick or I'll blow your head off, baby or not!"

"Food. We only wanted some of your food. Gray Fox thought to get some for us."

"And he'd of killed us for it if I let him. Where you from?"

Her black eyes would not meet his. "We come from far away. We still have much distance to go."

"In other words, you ain't gonna tell me nothin' you don't have to."

"Can't you let them have some food?" Mary found herself asking Luke. "The children in particular look pitifully malnourished. They're starving to death."

"Where do you come off, askin' a thing like that?" Rusty said to her, his eyes burning with anger. "You're nothin' but a captive yourself."

"If Beauty wants to feed these people, we'll do it," Luke said, smiling at her in what she could only interpret as an indulgent manner. Somehow his sudden willingness to humor her seemed almost as nerve-racking as his past hostility.

Rusty shook with rage. "What's wrong with you, Luke? You gonna listen to that do-gooder female? She's havin' a real bad effect on you."

"We can spare some food," Luke replied. "Miguel, Billy, you

help the woman give them somethin' and then send them on their way."

Mary quickly set about the task of supplying the group with whatever provisions Miguel thought they could spare. When she passed the women some raw jackrabbit meat, thinking they might want to cook it later, she was surprised to see them immediately cut it into small chunks with their knives, then pass it around to be quickly devoured raw. Mary then passed a canteen among them and watched as they drank thirstily and yet with restraint.

"Where are you from?" she asked the girl to whom Luke had spoken previously.

"We come from reservation by fort."

"Why did you leave?"

"We want to go home to our own lands."

"Why can't you live on the reservation?"

The girl held her baby tightly in her arms, pushing back one dull, black braid. "The land the white chiefs gave us is barren. We starve there. Many die. Soldiers would not let us go. They say they bring us food, but only brought us some bad oxen, black meat, bad smell. It made us sick. Better go hungry. I have to sleep with soldier from fort in return for food."

Mary looked again at the baby and understood.

"The soldier gave me something else too—white man's sickness." The girl cast her eyes downward as if ashamed. "We sneak off during the night while most soldiers asleep. But they will come after us."

"There are so few of you that I doubt it," Mary commented with skepticism.

The girl shook her head. "They make example of us for the others. If we get away, then others will try. They want all of us dead."

Mary stared at her in disbelief. "The army would not

251

deliberately set out to do you harm when you are at peace."

The girl did not answer, but took whatever Mary handed her in silence. The small band of ragged Indians departed as silently as it had come, resuming their slow hard trek across the barren land in the growing darkness.

Luke came to her after they were gone. He made her sit on the ground beside him in the twilight. "You know I only did that to please you, don't you?"

"It was the right thing to do," she said simply.

He laughed in a loud voice. "No, it wasn't! It was pure foolishness. That's why Rusty's so sore."

"Then why did you do it?"

He looked at her from under hooded eyes, his sooty lashes the same shade of ebony as his hair. "I already told you," he said. "I want you, all of you. You give yourself to me, and I will put you above me." His eyes were now fixed on hers, looking for some sort of response, but she remained impassive. "In time, I'll wipe away all your resistance."

He tied her up as usual that night, but he did not force her to undress, and she was grateful for being spared that bit of humiliation. He slept beside her, yet left her alone.

After they had eaten in the morning, they began riding again. It wasn't long before they came across a sight that made Mary stop dead. Soldiers had rounded up the small band of Indians, their rifles trained on them, as if ready to shoot.

Without thinking, Mary rode quickly into the middle of the group. "What are you doing!" she cried out.

The soldiers stared at her as if she were some sort of raving madwoman.

The officer in charge quickly found his voice. "Ma'am, you better ride out of here now. This is none of your concern. We're on official army business."

"What are you going to do with these people?" she demanded. "They're hostiles."

She noticed Luke was beside her now, his hand touching her arm.

"Think we best be going," he said sharply. "This ain't none of our concern."

"Didn't you see? They're about to kill these innocent people!" She trembled with outrage.

"Where you people going?" the officer asked. His brows lifted in suspicion.

"Just passin' through," Luke said quietly.

"Get on your way then," the officer said. He was young but his eyes were old and empty.

No one moved, least of all Mary.

"Why would you want to kill them?" she demanded, her voice hoarse.

"We're Indian fighters, miss. You people in Apache country ought to be mighty glad to have us around. Why, the hostiles would have wiped you off the face of the earth by now if we weren't here to protect you. They think this land belongs to them."

Perhaps it did. "These people aren't warriors. They pose no threat to anyone."

The officer turned to Luke. "Get your woman moving. Otherwise, we'll have to take her into custody for interfering with army business."

"We wouldn't want that now would we, darlin'?" Luke turned as if to go, but Mary saw him reach for his handgun and seconds later, the officer was lying dead on the ground, as were two of his companions. There were four other soldiers but their number was quickly decimated by Rusty, who took his cue from Luke. The astonished soldiers were simply not prepared for the blinding speed and accuracy at which the outlaws were able to use their firearms. The incident occurred in a matter of seconds. To Mary, the scene seemed unreal, as if she were dreaming. Yet she saw the carnage and knew it was real enough.

She sat astride the mare, staring at the dead soldiers as Luke turned to the Indians.

"Guess you can be on your way now," he said to the silent band. Luke led her horse and they rode on.

"That was hardly worth our ammunition," Rusty called back to his brother.

Luke merely grunted.

"I'm sorry the soldiers are dead, but you did save the lives of those poor Indians."

"Woman, you are a trial and a tribulation to me." Luke shook his head at her.

They didn't speak again until they stopped for a break at noon. Luke joined her in a spot shaded by some brush.

"Thinkin' on what happened today?" he asked her.

His intent gaze snared her own, and she thought that they were such an odd color, as light and delicate as the blue shell of robin's eggs. "It didn't bother you none when I killed those soldiers, did it?" He gave her a knowing smile.

"It should have."

"I was an instrument of the Lord's retribution, expressing the wrath of the righteous."

"Perhaps today, but not always," she replied coldly.

"I have been called the spawn of Satan on occasion," he said with a crooked smile. "I expect that's also true."

"How do you reconcile the two?" she asked.

"I don't even try. There's no need. I am what I am. The Lord has chosen to make me so."

"Don't you ever want to stop killing?" she asked him.

He placed his arm around her shoulder. "You are so innocent," he told her. "It's a shame you have to lose that, but I

intend that you will. I'm going to take your virtue from you."
He seemed to be waiting for some reaction from her.

"A woman's innocence can be taken, but not her virtue if it's
the real thing."

He laughed at her remark. "You really don't know anything
about people. I think I should give you your first lesson. See, I
knew what was going to happen to those Injuns you set such a
store by. There's one thing I learned early in life: people are
basically bad. You don't understand that yet."

"Giving those people food was probably the only decent thing
you've ever done. It had to make you feel good."

"Nope, I didn't feel anything. I know people only do decent
things to make themselves feel important. It's just another form
of selfishness."

"I don't believe that's true."

"Everything we do comes from bad. Man is corrupt and vile.
Unlike most folks, I'm no hypocrite. I admit it. You going to tell
me that you believe people are mainly good?"

She was thoughtful for a moment. "I was raised to believe
that man was born in sin and therefore corrupt, but I don't
really believe it. I think there's some bad in all of us, but no
one's completely evil. I even think the worst of people have
some good in them."

"Like me?" His gaze locked with hers.

She hesitated. "Even you."

He laughed again with a deep, rumbling sound. "Like I said,
you're still innocent. When I was a boy, I learned right quick
what life was about. My pa was a mean drunk who beat my ma
and us kids all the time. Ma had no gumption whatsoever, just
took it and cried. I got to hating her as much as I hated him.
When I come back from the war, I swore the first thing I would
do was kill the old man. But he outfoxed me even then, 'cause
he'd went and got hisself killed in a barroom brawl."

"Everyone's not like your father."

"Like those soldiers who would have killed your fine Injuns back there if I didn't stop them?"

She wouldn't answer him; she couldn't.

"I just want you to see the way things really are, 'cause you are mine. And the sooner you understand that, the better."

She became aware that he wasn't out to possess just her body but her soul as well, and the thought jarred her. Luke leaned over and kissed her lips in an almost gentle, loving manner, then he sat back looking at her and caressed her cheek. Mary knew she should feel revulsion toward him and yet she did not. In fact, she felt nothing at all. It would be better if she could still hate him as she had when he first kidnapped her, but she found that impossible too. The realization was more than a little disturbing. However, neither could she ever come to care for him. In fact, there was only one man whom she could love and she was unlikely ever to see him again. The thought made her sad and she felt emotionally dead inside.

Rusty came toward them. He had obviously seen the kiss that Luke had given her. "Why are you courtin' that damn female?"

Luke gave him a tolerant smile. "She's good to talk to and she listens right well. There's comfort in it. I never courted a woman, so I wouldn't know how, but I think it might be a nice luxury." He gave her a final, warm glance before walking away with his brother.

What troubled Mary most of all was what she perceived of as her own growing acceptance of Luke's violent behavior as if it were some everyday, normal thing. It alarmed her the way she had looked at the death of those soldiers and felt nothing at all. No, that wasn't true either. Luke was right; she had actually been pleased by what he'd done, pleased to see the soldiers die, because if they hadn't been killed then the unarmed Indians would have been massacred.

Yet she realized that the longer she was forced to remain with the Harris gang, the more likely it was that she would become like them. Luke had said that she was like him because she was capable of killing. She could only hope he was wrong. She did have a moral conscience, something he obviously lacked. But his current regard for her was a form of insidious seduction. She must always recognize it for what it was, never allowing herself to accept it. He was the devil incarnate. She must never forget that. Whatever happened, she must not permit Luke Harris to corrupt her, to possess her soul.

Joseph Cloud led them into a small town situated in the New Mexico desert. "They were here," the tracker told him simply.

Cal looked around and saw there wasn't much to this town; in fact, it looked a lot more dismal than Expectation. Still, there was a general store and that had to be a good place to obtain information. He told Doc to come with him; the old cowboy seldom missed much.

As they entered the store, a man with salt-and-pepper whiskers looked up from behind the counter, cocking a gray brow with interest. "Mornin', what can I do for you?"

"We got an order to fill. Coffee and flour to start."

As the man began to move, Cal cleared his throat. "By the way, did you happen to meet two Anglos, some Mex, and a woman? They would have been through here recently."

The man's eyes widened with recognition. "You might say we howdied, but we never shook."

"How long ago were they here?" Cal tried to keep the urgency out of his voice.

"They come a day or so ahead of you. Friends of yours?"

"Not exactly," he replied, offering as little information of his own as possible. "How was the woman faring?"

The man's eyes lit with interest, as if he were speculating

about Cal's interest in the woman. "She looked pretty, but her dress was all ragged and dirty. I guess that's why the man with her wanted to buy her another. He was plumb put out that we don't stock no women's clothes. But he bought her men's stuff instead."

"Was the man rough with her?" Cal tried to keep the anxiety he was feeling in check.

"Nope, it was plain to see that he thought highly of her. Told me to bring out the best shirts, boots, and such that I had."

"Was she bound in any way?"

The question seemed to surprise the old man. "Not that I could see, but he did hold her arm real tight while they was in here and he slipped his arm around her waist besides. I thought for certain she was his woman, him being so possessive and all."

The old man's response cut into Cal like a knife wound. "Did she happen to say anything?"

The storekeeper took his time answering. "I don't recall it. Oh, there was one thing though. Those men with her were mean-lookin' hombres, like desperados. The one with her scared me in particular. Fact, I was scared the whole time they was in here. Had the feeling that they might be fixin' to rob or maybe even kill me. But when they finished orderin' and the man with her commenced to puttin' his hand to his sidearm, the woman seemed to notice and she touched his hand real gentle-like and looked into his eyes. Well, he give her a smile, the kind a man might give his wife if he loved her and wanted to please her. Next thing I knew, he pulled out a fist full of money and handed it to me. Then they took their purchases and rode out."

Cal didn't like what he was hearing one bit. "What did the man look like, the one with the woman?"

"Black hair, light blue eyes, bad scar down one side of his face. Hard face, hard body."

There was no mistake here. It had been Luke Harris with

Mary. Somehow, he had hoped it hadn't been them. Cal was lost in thought while the storekeeper and Doc set about putting together the needed supplies.

So Luke Harris was treating Mary with respect, something completely out of character from all he'd heard about the bastard. If she had fought him, surely he wouldn't be acting that way, would he? Had she given herself to the outlaw? He wouldn't believe it! Yet what other possible explanation could there be? The thought tore at him. He could stand it a whole lot better when he thought the outlaws were abusing her, but he realized that might be selfish of him. People did what they had to do to survive. He had no right to pass judgment.

When they left the store, Doc spoke to him as if he could read Cal's thoughts. "Storekeep could have misunderstood what he saw, you know."

He avoided meeting Doc's gaze. "I doubt it."

"Mary's not the kind of woman to give in to a man like Harris, not without a real fight. You saw yourself she killed one of them back at the farm."

"He forces women. We know that as a fact. What if she just stopped minding? What if she even accepted him as her lover? That would explain why he acted the way he did in the store."

"Don't put yourself through this, son. There's no way for us to know what's goin' on with them. Everybody says Harris is real peculiar. Maybe she found a way to win him over somehow. She's a strong-minded, resourceful woman and a smart one, remember? Bet she could outfox the devil. No sense torturing yourself. Besides, seems like the important thing is she's alive and well. Ain't that so?"

Cal nodded. Doc was right and he knew it. Still, how did he know that she didn't kiss all men with as much passion as she'd kissed him? Of course, he was the one who had taken her virginity—no, he didn't take it, she'd offered it to him! And Mary told him she was in love with him. That had to mean something, didn't it? Or had he been fooled by yet another woman? Was she just another whore like Linda? His hands clenched into fists as anger and doubt seethed within him.

CHAPTER TWENTY

Mary was weary and worn out from what seemed like endless days of riding. Her entire body ached. Luke and his brother argued over whether or not they would continue on to Indian Territory after all.

"Luke, nobody's after us no more. I think we should turn back to Arizona and deliver the woman and the boy to Wheeler soon as we can."

"Why's that, brother?" The two outlaws faced each other. "Got some money. Don't we deserve a little fun? Belle's a fine figure of a woman. We can enjoy ourselves at her place."

"Some other time. Havin' this here woman around is bad luck for us. I think we need to get rid of her pronto."

Luke stared at his brother. "All right. We'll do things your way for now."

Rusty breathed a sigh of relief. As for Mary, she felt the smallest glimmer of hope at the thought that they were going to head back to Expectation. At the same time, she acknowledged the foolishness of her feelings, since Sam Wheeler waited there to seal her fate.

However, the brothers weren't finished disagreeing. Two days later, Luke told Rusty that he wanted to stop at a town called Dermont.

"Luke, we're only gonna find trouble there. You know damn well that town's wide open to everything. We'll have to watch each other's backs. Way I hear tell, they'll shoot you for your boots in Dermont."

"They have what I want there," Luke said. "Reckon we'll be stoppin' there."

Mary had no idea what Luke had in mind, but she knew it couldn't be anything good. As they rode into Dermont, she immediately had a sense of Rusty's description of the town being right. It seemed like a veritable Sodom with wild behavior at every turn. Several men were fighting in the street, others rode around recklessly while drinking, yelling, and shooting off guns. Luke led them into a large saloon. He went up to the bar and ordered whiskey. The barkeep cast a disapproving eye in Mary's direction.

"We have our own girls here," he said pointedly.

"She's with me," Luke said. "I want rooms for the night."

"We don't generally rent them out, but if you pay in advance, well, it's all right I guess."

Luke paid for two rooms. Rusty would share a room with Billy, Miguel, and Jose. Luke took a room with Mary. She was apprehensive, but said nothing.

Luke locked her into the room and told her to rest, that he would be back later. "Don't even think of running off. I'm posting Miguel outside the door while I'm gone."

Mary lay down and tried to rest, but she was too edgy to relax. The worst thing in the world was to be a prisoner to someone else's whim, especially a man as insane as Luke Harris.

An hour later Luke returned and thrust a garment into her hand. "Here, put this on."

It was a red dress, made of some velvet material. The bodice was cut low in the front and it reeked of cheap perfume.

"Where did you get this?" She held the dress away from her in distaste.

"Never you mind. Beautiful, ain't it? Just like you. Put it on. I want to see you in it."

"I'd rather not wear this," she said.

"If you want, I can put it on you," he said with a big, wide grin that chilled her.

She shook her head. "Wait outside. I'll change."

"All right, but don't take long. I ain't a patient man."

She trusted him least when he was being agreeable. What was Luke up to now? She shuddered.

He came back a few minutes later. Luke looked her over and smiled with a wicked grin. "You'll do right well," he said with a nod of approval. Then he took her roughly by the arm and dragged her downstairs into the saloon.

Mary felt a lot of eyes turn to look at her. She was conscious of how low-cut the dress was. Some of the men stared at her with venal interest. The painted women who worked in the establishment narrowed their eyes in hostility at what they perceived as unwelcome competition.

"We'll wait a little longer," he said, glancing around the crowded barroom appraisingly, "till the place fills up more."

"Wait for what?"

"Don't ask questions." He practically growled at her.

Luke sat her down at a table and ordered whiskey, which he proceeded to down slowly. His left hand never released the grip on her arm. He watched her the way a pirate might watch a treasure chest.

After some time had passed, Luke rose to his feet and shouted that he had an announcement to make. He had to use his gun and shoot at the ceiling in order to get the attention of the raucous crowd. Then he pulled Mary to her feet.

"I'm plannin' to sell this here woman for tonight. You can all see she's a real beauty, and she ain't even been with a man yet. So I expect to get some decent offers. Who wants to buy her for the night?"

There was a general uproar. Luke shot another hole in the

ceiling and plaster started to tumble down.

The bartender hurried up to Luke. "You can't just be sellin' a woman! This here's a free country. Lincoln done freed the slaves."

Luke shoved his pistol under the bartender's chin. "Who says I can't?"

The barkeep backed away.

Mary stood as straight and stiff as a statue carved from marble. Who but Luke Harris would think of doing something so evil, crazy, and bizarre?

"I'll make you a bid. Three hundred dollars in gold and silver coin." The room buzzed and several patrons gasped.

Mary's head snapped around at the sound of the familiar voice. She thought at first that she was imagining it. She came close to fainting. But there stood Cal Davis directly in front of her. For once, she was grateful that Luke held her arm so tightly.

"I might do better," Luke said, his eyelids hooded like a snake.

Cal smiled coldly. "Might at that, but I'll stay right here, and if you get a higher offer, I'll better it by fifty dollars."

"Then I reckon we got a deal," Luke said.

It was all Mary could do to keep from crying out. Cal was here! He'd come for her! But how and why? A look from Cal warned her that she must keep silent for now. She was careful to avoid doing or saying anything that might tip Luke off. All she could think of was that no one could be a more welcome sight right now than Cal Davis.

"Why do you want this woman?" Luke asked narrowing his eyes suspiciously. "You can get a whore here much cheaper."

"I like her looks."

"Got a room upstairs. Try her out. See if she suits you. I'll trust you to pay up in the morning."

Luke's smile chilled her. He led the way upstairs, never letting go of her arm until they were at the door of the room.

"Goodnight," he said, looking from Cal to her. Luke licked his lips and left.

Once they were inside the room, Cal listened until Luke's footsteps receded down the hall. Carefully, he locked the door behind them. "I don't know how much time we've got," he whispered, "so I think we better figure a way out of here as soon as possible."

"Cal, I'm so glad you came for me. I didn't think I'd ever be free of them!"

"Well, you're not free yet. We've got to get out of here and hit the trail."

She felt the urge to throw herself into his arms. Then she remembered what Doc had told her about Cal and Lorette making wedding plans, and all her ardor slipped away.

"You're right," she said in a dull voice.

"Get out of that dress and into something suited to ride in."

"With pleasure. Turn your back."

He sighed deeply. "I know what you look like. Remember? No need for modesty."

"It doesn't matter. Now that I know you're engaged to another woman, I won't have you staring at me."

"About that—"

She interrupted him. "I don't want to hear it. I don't expect or require any explanation. After all, you're free to marry whomever you wish. You never gave me any reason to think you cared for me, and what I did was done of my own free will. Let's not speak of it again. I do appreciate all the effort you must have gone through to find me." She spoke even as she dressed back into the men's clothing that was so much better suited to riding on the trail.

"We can go through this window," Cal said as she finished dressing. "Can you climb?"

"I don't know."

"Well, I'll be there to help you," he assured her. "It's just one floor down, and it's our only way out. I have a feeling Harris is going to be watching the door all night. We're lucky the window faces the back of the saloon. No one's likely to be in the alley."

Out on the window ledge, Cal looked for anything to take hold of. "Drainpipe," he said, indicating the object. "I'll go first. You place your feet on my shoulders and keep your hands wrapped around the pipe."

It wasn't as difficult as she'd feared. They were down in a matter of moments and running toward the stable. Cal's horse was ready, but the mare had to be saddled. In less than ten minutes, they had stealthily removed themselves from the town. Mary breathed a deep sigh of relief.

"Did you come for me by yourself?" she asked.

"Tiny, Doc, and a tracker are waiting for us at a watering hole. Tiny's normally strong as an ox, but he took ill with fever yesterday. So I told Doc to stay with him. My tracker and I came on alone. When we saw what kind of town the Harrises took you to, I sent him back to wait for me with the others. It's no place for a half-breed. They'd skin him alive. Don't worry. I don't see them catching us."

"They will come, though," Mary said. "Luke won't let me go so easily. He's relentless. There's something you should know. Sam Wheeler promised them a lot of money to bring Billy Travers and me to him. The Harrises still have Billy. Mr. Wheeler wants to kill both of us."

Cal turned to her in surprise. "Are you certain?"

"Absolutely certain. Mr. Wheeler also wants them to murder Jack Phillips for him. There's something else. I'm convinced Sam Wheeler hired the Harrises to kill my uncle and who knows how many others."

Cal stared at her. "It's hard to believe Sam would go that far to drive out homesteaders and sheep men."

"It's the truth just the same. I believe Mr. Wheeler is twisted inside with hate."

Cal was thoughtful. "This changes things," he said. "We'd better head south and go directly to Expectation."

"What about Doc and the others?"

"Our tracker's real good at his job. When we don't show by morning, he'll pick up our trail and follow us back. I can't afford to meet up with them now. We've got to get back and see about stopping whatever plan Sam's set in motion. I expect the Harrises will be bringing Billy to him even without you."

They rode mostly at night and rested in the heat of the day, talking very little, intent on returning to Expectation. It was growing warmer as they drew closer. She had come to consider the parched desert country as home. But Arizona was much more than desert. It was a land of great natural beauty and variety. Mary knew she wanted to remain here, whatever the price.

The closer they got to Expectation, the hotter it became, and Mary found the flannel shirt uncomfortable.

Cal saw how miserable she was. "Why don't we rest in the shade for a time? There's a good spot over yonder."

Mary was grateful for his consideration. Cal passed her a canteen and she drank deeply. "I was wondering about something. Did you really have the money to pay for me?"

"Not exactly. I had a hundred in gold and silver I took along for expenses, but that was it."

"Why did you offer Luke so much then?"

His cheek dimpled as he smiled. "I had to make certain of the high bid. Wouldn't want some filthy lowlife getting his hands on you."

"Good thing Luke didn't insist on the money right away. What would you have done if he had?"

"I'd have thought of something. Probably given him the

hundred right off and promised to get him the rest in the morning when I was satisfied." He winked at her.

Mary felt her cheeks begin to burn. "Maybe I ought to tell you that Luke thinks I never was with a man before, because I fought him so hard. Then I told him how Rebecca said the man who took my chastity would die a sudden horrible death. I thought it might get him to leave me alone. It was a desperate lie but all I could think of at the time."

"And he believed it?" Cal's eyes widened in surprise.

"He did, mainly because Billy backed me. He convinced Luke that Rebecca has the gift of second sight. Of course, Rusty Harris didn't believe it for a second. But Luke isn't like other people. He doesn't think the way we do. Anyway, I guess he decided if he got a man to sleep with me for a night, then he would have me afterwards. I suppose then he intended to hand me over to Mr. Wheeler."

"Sounds like they're both crazy, Harris and Wheeler."

"I believe they are," Mary agreed. "Both of them are obsessed with power and control. Luke does it through killing, and Wheeler does it by hiring men like the Harrises to kill for him."

"You look real uncomfortable," Cal said, studying her perspiring face. "There's a water hole right over there. Why don't you wash before we hit the trail again?"

The water felt so cool and refreshing against her skin. She put her entire head beneath the surface and felt renewed. When she came up for air, she saw that Cal was watching her.

"Do you have any idea how worried I was about you, how crazy I got? All I could think about was what if you were killed or hurt. I nearly went out of my mind thinking about Luke Harris putting his hands on you."

"Just what would your fiancée, Lorette, have to say about that?" Her eyes flashed fire at him.

"Hold on. Lorette Wheeler is not my fiancée. That was all

Jesse's idea. I have no intention of marrying her. There's only one woman I want to marry. Of course, I don't rightly know if she'd have me, seeing as she seems to get angry at me an awful lot of the time, always believing the worst of me."

"You really mean that?"

"Want me to get down on one knee?"

"Not at the moment," she said, throwing her arms around his neck.

He drew her against him and his mouth consumed hers. They were both breathless by the time they came apart.

"I love you, Mary. I realized just how much when you were taken. I blame myself for the Harrises ever getting near you. Only one man should ever lay hands on you, and that man is me."

She caressed his cheek; she'd never felt so happy in her life. They sat together in each other's arms, caught up in the pleasure of a passionate embrace. They were so involved with each other that neither one of them heard the movement behind them, until it was too late.

CHAPTER TWENTY-ONE

She heard the blow to Cal, turned to see what was happening, and then screamed. Cal fell forward, unconscious, blood on the side of his head.

Luke stared down at her, red-faced. "Might have known you'd convince the cowboy to help you run away."

She and Cal had been foolish to let their guard down, believing it was safe to indulge their emotions when reason indicated otherwise. Yet there never had been anything sensible about her feelings for Cal. She wanted to go to Cal and see if he was all right, but Luke's hands were on her shoulders now. She also couldn't help fearing that if she acted overly concerned, Luke's wrath would grow even greater.

"This fella was one slippery cowpoke," Luke said. He moved away from her, taking something from his saddlebag and tossing it to her. "Put this on," he said. "You can't wear those heavy clothes no more."

She saw it was her gingham dress and sunbonnet. She changed rapidly, aware that his eyes were hungrily following each of her movements. But she saw little point in modesty at the moment.

"I'm ready to go now," she said in a subdued voice, trying to reach for his arm.

"Go join the others," he said to her. "I got unfinished business here." He was looking directly at Cal's crumpled form. Luke appeared calm enough, but there was a tight set to his mouth and a glint in his eyes.

Mary's own mouth was dry with fear, and her tongue seemed to have swollen to twice its normal size. "Let him be," she said in a thick, choking voice.

"No need to ask if he done you. I see that plain enough." Suddenly, his hand lashed out and hit her cheek with a blow that sent her reeling. "Whore! You enjoyed it, didn't you?'

She felt rage well in her. "You sold me to him, remember?"

"Well, now I'm taking you back." His light eyes still glowed with their unnatural light. "You knew I'd be back for you."

"I hoped you wouldn't," she said truthfully.

"Doesn't matter. You're mine! I'm not letting any other man have you."

"If you leave him alone," she said, "I'll go with you willingly."

Luke laughed in scorn. "Doesn't matter whether you're willing or not, but you'll want me. I already know that."

"Don't be so sure," she replied. There was only one man she wanted, and he was lying stretched on the ground, very likely to be killed if she could not intercede for him.

"Your cousin was right. The first man to sleep with you is going to die a quick and violent death." Luke raised his Colt. As he aimed it at Cal's head, Mary rushed between him and the unconscious rancher.

"No!" she cried out. "I've seen you kill before, and God help me, I did nothing to stop you, but that won't happen now!"

"Get out of the way," he snarled at her.

She shook her head and he grabbed her roughly.

"I swear you'll have to kill me first if you think I'll let you have me after you've murdered him." The fierceness of her tone seemed to have some effect on him.

"All right, maybe women are foolish and sentimental about the first man who takes them. I won't kill him."

"You swear it?"

He gave her an indulgent smile. "I won't touch him. Now let's go!"

She started to move shakily to her horse, but he drew her to him.

"We'll ride together for a while."

He forced her to sit in front of him, his legs molding around her thighs. The others were waiting for them at a short distance.

"Miguel," Luke called out to the wiry Mexican. "There's a man back there. I want you to wait until we're out of earshot and then kill him, one bullet in the brain, another in the heart."

"No, you can't!" she screamed. "You promised me!"

"I'm keeping my word to you, Beauty. I didn't kill him in front of you in deference to your female sensibilities. That'll show how high a store I put on your feelings."

"You liar!" She tried to bring her elbow back and smash it into his ribs, but he caught her arm easily and laughed, amused by her resistance.

"I promised you I wouldn't kill the cowboy. I didn't. We can play games later," he said. "I expect we'll have a lot of fun tonight. You can put on that red dress for me again." He pulled her so tightly against him that she could barely breathe. "I brought it along for you."

She thought of Cal, of Miguel emptying his revolver into his head and chest. She began to sob.

"Stop that now! Do you understand me? I don't want to see you bawlin' over that worthless cowboy. If you keep on cater-waulin' that way I'm gonna be forced to really hurt you. Then you'll have reason for tears." He pulled hard against her waist and squeezed as a warning.

She struggled to regain control of herself, but the grief enveloping Mary ate into her heart like acid.

★　★　★　★　★

They had ridden for several more hours before Mary rose from her dazed state and realized they were just outside of Expectation. There was a creek nearby and Rusty decided that they would stop, have food, and water the horses.

Luke helped her dismount; Mary sat on the ground, motionless and unwilling to look at him or speak, clasping her knees to her chin. She was nearly out of her mind with grief.

Rusty approached his brother after he'd finished eating. "It's taking Miguel an awful long time to rejoin us. You think that cowboy got the better of him?"

"Don't see how. The man was unconscious. I dealt him a heavy blow."

Rusty shook his head, removing his sweat-stained Stetson. "Just don't seem quite right, is all." He turned and looked sharply at Mary. "All on account of her."

"Was my doin'. You know that."

"While you was busy knocking out that cowboy, I come and checked his saddlebags and took what he had. I didn't find but a hundred in coin. He went and lied to you. That's probably why he sneaked out of town so fast."

"Rus, all you think about is money."

"One of us has got to consider the practical end. Look, let's deliver the woman and the boy to Wheeler right away. Then we can do the job for him on the sheepherder, collect our pay, and be headed straight to Mexico. We can't afford the luxury of hangin' around this place too long. Otherwise that marshal's gonna be on our trail again."

"I agree with everything," Luke said, "except the part about the woman. I keep her."

Rusty ran his fingers through his unkempt thatch of carrot hair. "The hell you will! We got a deal with the man, remember?"

"She's mine, and that's all there is to it."

"You want this female to spread her legs for you, don't you? Look, why not just take her here and now and get it over with. Then you won't care no more what Wheeler intends for her."

"I don't want her just once," Luke said. "I want her with me down in Mexico."

Rusty openly showed his anger and disgust. "Luke, we hardly ever argue, but I got to say that this is the craziest thing you've ever intended to do. You can get all the willing women you want in Mexico, especially when they see our money. This makes no sense at all."

Luke's face was so livid that Mary thought for a moment he might strike his own brother. "Are you sayin' I'm loco?" he burst out.

"Right now, you ain't actin' right in the head. I swear you're worse than Pa was!"

Luke's slammed his fist into Rusty's jaw, sending the slighter man sprawling flat on his backside.

"Don't you say another word to me. Never call me crazy again! Now mount up!"

Rusty Harris rubbed his jaw and threw a murderous look in Mary's direction as they returned to their horses. Mary felt no emotion. She was dead inside.

Cal Davis had the worst headache he'd ever felt in his life. His eyes would barely focus, and someone was pouring water on his face so that he thought he would drown.

"Stop it!"

"Good, you're finally conscious." Cal recognized Doc's voice, but he couldn't see him very well.

"Where's Mary?" he asked, suddenly feeling much more alert.

"They took her back," Doc said in a somber voice.

"Hell, no!" All the grogginess was gone now, replaced by a hard pain in the pit of his stomach that felt a lot like fear. "I can't lose her again."

"We'll catch up. Joseph says it's an easy trail to follow. Fact, he says they're headed toward Expectation."

"That's right," Cal agreed, remembering where he and Mary had been headed and why. He pressed his hands to his head, willing his mind to focus. "I've got to get to the Bar W before they do. At least I know a shortcut that'll save us an hour or so."

Cal tried to stand, but as he did, his head began to pound and he nearly blacked out. Strong hands held him upright.

"Careful with him, Tiny. He's not himself yet."

Cal was grateful for the support, but he was determined to get to his horse under his own power. Still, he staggered slightly and then nearly fell over something. He looked down and saw the body of a dead Mexican bandit. Cal looked at Doc questioningly.

"Fella was sent to kill you. Joseph was the first one here and he stopped him with his skinning knife."

Cal looked to the tracker. "Thanks for saving my life," he said.

"No need," came the simple response.

They mounted their horses and Cal set the pace, accelerating so that the wind whistled by his ears and made him feel alive again. Inside, he was frantic with fear, afraid he might already be too late to prevent Mary's death. But the fear gave him courage and helped him ignore the throbbing pain in his head.

There was a strange inactivity at the Bar W, which was usually such a lively, bustling ranch. Cal noticed it the moment they rode up. He asked the others to wait for him outside the ranch house and knocked at the door.

It was Wheeler's housekeeper who finally answered. Maria was a plump, pleasant woman who spoke little English. He removed his brown Stetson, which was caked with dust, and hung it in the front hall only after asking Maria in his halting Spanish to get Mr. or Mrs. Wheeler immediately. He took the liberty of walking into the parlor and seating himself on a straight-back chair, feeling drained and exhausted. Then Cal glanced over at the big grandfather clock in the parlor ticking away the minutes. He swallowed hard, all too aware that time was something he did not have in abundance.

He had no idea what he would say to Sam Wheeler, but he knew he had to do something drastic. Mary's life depended on it. Maybe even the fact that Cal was going to confront him might be enough to put a halt to Sam's vicious plans.

He was finding it hard to wait and began pacing the room. Where was Sam or Jesse? He considered himself a patient man, but not today.

Jesse Wheeler came into the room dressed in a neat black dress. She didn't look well, her face drawn and pale, her fine blond hair undressed.

She surprised him by falling into his arms and starting to cry. He did his best to comfort her.

"What's wrong, Jesse? What happened?"

"You didn't hear? I thought that was why you came."

"I've been away for a time."

She turned away for a few moments as if to compose herself. Then she sat down on a large, overstuffed horsehair sofa.

"It's Sam. He was murdered three days ago along with my two oldest sons."

Cal stared at her in shock and then took a seat beside her. "I'm real sorry. I had no idea. Do they know who did it?"

She shook her head. "Nobody's been arrested yet. The marshal says it was a professional killer. In fact, he's certain of it. I suspect it was Jack Phillips who did the hiring. When Marshal Wade asked around, he found out that some fellow named Rondo Leston was at Phillips's place. Leston's got a reputation. I actually saw the man in town with Jack one day. I noticed him because he didn't look like most people. He had determined, calculating eyes and a narrow lower lip and moved like a man who knows his own worth, very self-assured. There was something about him, a dangerous look. I recall feeling chilled by the sight of him."

"You don't really know that it was this Leston fellow though, do you?"

"Not for sure, but when the marshal checked out where Sam and the boys were killed, he found evidence that they'd been stalked for some time. Spent rifle shells were found on high ground above where the men were camped. The marshal says Leston learned tracking and scouting from the Indians, and this murder looked like someone who knew Indian ways."

"Marshal Wade is a good man. He'll do something about this."

"Maybe I ought to do something myself. What do you think?"

"I can't say what I would do, Jesse, but if I were in your boots, I believe I would let the marshal handle it."

Her full lips contorted bitterly. "Would you, Cal? Would you really? I know for a fact that isn't what Sam would want."

"Have the Harrises been here yet?"

She looked at him in surprise. "You mean the outlaws? No, of course not, why would they come here?"

"Because your husband hired them. He wanted them to bring Billy Travers and Mary MacGreggor to him. And they're on their way here now to deliver them. They don't know about Sam being dead any more than I did."

"Billy Travers killed Ned, and Sam took that very hard, as I'm sure you know. It doesn't surprise me that he would get professional killers looking for Ned's murderer. I'm not defending it, but I do understand."

"Ned goaded Billy into a shoot-out. But let's forget about

him for now. What about Mary?"

Jesse stared at him through puffy, reddened eyes. "I don't know. He was wild with anger at being insulted publicly by that woman. She was awfully rude to him. She more than sassed him."

"It's Mary's way to be blunt and outspoken, but do you think she should have to die for it?"

"I never said that."

Cal smiled at her. "Then you can help prevent another needless tragedy. The Harrises are going to be here in a short while. We'll make certain men are posted all around you, and when those vermin arrive, you tell them that Sam's dead and all deals are cancelled. Be very firm about it and don't weaken. They'll ask you for money, but don't give it to them."

"I find it hard to believe those men would still expect me to pay them."

"They'd give no thought to robbing and killing you if they could, Jess. The Harrises are hard, violent gunmen, and greedy besides."

"I'm frightened, Cal." Jesse took his hand in hers and held it tightly.

He realized that he had special feelings for this delicate, lovely woman whose physical appearance of fragility was in contrast to her strong character. She would get through this, he knew. He planned to do his level best to help her. But his main concern was Mary and her well being.

"I'm so glad you're here with me. I know you and Sam were having your differences of late, but I hope you and I will always remain friends."

"A body can never have too many friends," he said with a warm smile. "Anything I can do for you, just ask."

"Well, I think I'm going to need help with the business end

of running the ranch. I need to choose a new foreman, for instance."

"Be happy to do what I can to oblige," he said. "But you know a whole lot more than you think."

"Sam never let me make a decision about anything important. Said it wasn't a woman's place to know about matters of business."

"That's going to change, and you'll be glad of it." As far back as Cal could remember, Sam was always undermining his wife; it was time for Jesse to build back her self-confidence.

"About Lorette—"

He interrupted her immediately. "There's someone else, Jess. I think I ought to tell you that."

She appeared undaunted. "That's all right. We'll just see what happens."

"Do you want me to wait with you for the Harrises?"

"Yes, please do. I don't think I could talk to them alone. Why I would likely have a fit of the vapors."

"I doubt that. Thing is, they already know me by sight. But I can be out of sight, and you'll have an armed escort all the time they're here. I'll see to that."

"Are you gonna kill them?" she asked.

He squared his jaw. "Will if I can, but my first concern is getting Mary away from them."

"Mary MacGreggor's the one, isn't she?" Jesse asked, her brow furrowing.

"Yes, she is."

Jesse let out a deep sigh. "I don't see why."

"All I know is when I'm with her, I feel like I'm on fire, and when I'm not with her, I can't hardly think of anything or anyone else."

Jesse smiled at him knowingly. "I guess you love her all right.

All I ever wanted was for you to be happy, Cal. I hope you realize that."

He gave a quick nod.

She hugged him. He moved away from her and held her hand.

"Jess, there's one other thing. Sam intended for these men to kill Jack Phillips."

"But you don't want me to let them go ahead with it?"

His eyes met hers. "No, it's best the trouble be over. Killing just begets more killing. Sam did start the whole thing with Phillips."

Jesse cast her eyes downward. "He still didn't deserve to die that way! My boys are gone too." Tears welled in her eyes once again.

"It would only make matters worse to have the Harrises working for you. They're evil killers."

"If it were your family, wouldn't you want revenge?"

He looked away from her. "I tried that once, if you'll remember, and the results have haunted me ever since."

"What if the Harrises were to kill Mary? I'd reckon you'd rake Arizona from the Little Colorado to the Superstitions hunting them down."

"Very likely."

She looked into his face. "But still you want me to send them away?"

"What if I promise to make certain that Phillips doesn't get away with what he did? The only difference is, I'll see that it's done legal and proper."

"You're going to tell me that law and justice are the same thing?"

He could hear the bitterness in her voice. "Maybe not, but I will do right by you and yours. You have my solemn vow."

"I trust you, Cal. I'll do what you want."

"Just remember, you'll never really be alone with them. So don't be afraid to speak up."

They didn't have long to wait. The Harrises showed up at the ranch that afternoon. Cal was watching from a window and clearly saw that neither Billy nor Mary were with the two brothers. He felt a wave of deep disappointment; what had they done with their captives? He had expected to take them back here and now, and then it would finally be over. He realized the Harrises were too shrewd to make it so simple.

He stayed out of sight in the small study Sam Wheeler had used at the rear of the parlor. In that way, he could hear everything that was said, even if he could not see. He heard Jesse lead them into the room. Cal had made certain that she was surrounded by armed men with rifles. There were six in all, Cal thinking that would be enough of a show of force to keep those lowlifes from trying anything violent with Jesse.

"You won't be able to see my husband," she was telling them. "He was killed several days ago."

"We were hired to do a job, ma'am. We done it, and want our payment. We got the man who killed your oldest boy. Your husband wanted him."

"I'm sorry, but we won't be needing your services anymore. You can just let the boy go."

"Now, just hold on a minute! We done work for you and expect full payment." Cal recognized Luke Harris's voice, a harsh voice with a clearly menacing undercurrent of violence to it. "Besides, don't you want revenge?"

"No. It won't bring back my family. So what difference will it make?" Jesse sounded firm and strong. Cal was pleased with her show of courage.

"If it were reversed, your husband would track your killers to hell." The other brother's voice was almost as disturbing as Luke's.

"I want no more trouble."

"Don't worry. We don't work unless we're paid. Oh, by the way, your husband wanted us to take care of a certain sheepherder for him. I don't suppose he's the one responsible for ol' Sam dyin'?"

"He might be." Jesse sounded as if she had lost her composure.

"Seems to me someone ought to do for this Phillips gent. And we come a far piece just on your husband's say. I think, widow lady, you and us should work out a new deal."

"I'm sorry. I can't do that," Jesse said. "My hands will see you out." Her voice grew louder as she summoned her men to do her bidding. "These gentlemen are leaving. Would you escort them to their horses?"

"An eye for an eye, Mrs. Wheeler, a life for a life. That's what it says in the Bible," Luke said.

"Vengeance is mine said the Lord," she replied in a subdued voice.

Cal could hear the triggering mechanism pulled back on a rifle. Then the Harrises began to leave. As soon as they were out of the house, Cal went to Jesse, who virtually collapsed in his arms.

"It was all I could do not to tell them to go ahead and kill Phillips."

"You were wonderful," he said. "You handled them just right. Never doubt yourself."

"Cal, those men really frightened me. Be very careful dealing with them."

He nodded and gently kissed her forehead.

As soon as he saw the Harrises galloping away, Cal went to Joseph Cloud. "Trail them for me. I got to know where they're going with Mary."

"Where will I find you?" Joseph asked him.

"I'll be at the Thunderbolt getting my men ready to ride. We've got to stop them now. It's got to be over with once and for all."

All he could think about was Mary; he must get to her, hold her safe in his arms, feel her body against his. He set his jaw with grim determination. He'd save her, no matter what it took.

CHAPTER TWENTY-TWO

Jose kept Mary and Billy tied up the entire time Luke and Rusty were gone. When the two brothers rode back, they looked angry. Billy stared at them in terror. Clearly, something was wrong.

"Did you see the army of men she had escorting us off the ranch? Too many for us to take on but I was itching to try." Luke's face was like a thundercloud.

"Someone must have warned her we was coming. Wonder who?"

"That woman's a bitch."

"I didn't think much of her neither," Rusty agreed. "Pasty-faced little woman, got cheeks as white as the belly of a dead catfish."

The two brothers shared a laugh.

"Never did understand the value these fancy ladies put on keepin' their skin pale all the time. There's sure no blood in that one! We offer to give her vengeance and she treats us like we was lower than gully dirt." Rusty spat on the ground for emphasis. "She owes us. I won't forget that, woman or no woman."

"What do you want to do now?" Luke asked.

It didn't surprise Mary that Luke looked to his younger brother for guidance. It seemed as if Rusty, always shrewd and calculating, was in charge of the business decisions, while Luke was in charge of their execution.

"I think maybe we could do one quick job before we head on

south, maybe make up for losin' out with Wheeler. I got my eye on something."

"What about the boy?" Luke gave a nod toward Billy.

"We could use an extra man, seeing as Miguel hasn't met up with us. I figure if it don't work out, we can always kill him."

Luke nodded in agreement and turned to Billy. "You hear Rusty, boy?"

Billy's eyes dilated with fear.

"We gonna give you a chance to be part of our gang. If you do this right, you'll never have to worry again. We'll take care of you." Luke looked at the youth with a smile on his thin lips. "But you turn on us in any way and you'll beg for death."

Mary shuddered, knowing that Luke did not make idle threats.

"What kind of job do you have in mind?" Luke asked, turning back to his brother.

"They got a nice fat little bank in Expectation. Got a feeling the money in it will make up for what we didn't get from ol' Sam Wheeler."

Luke shrugged. "Think it's worth our trouble?"

"Sure, it should be an easy job. So why not?"

They quickly got ready to ride out. Luke allowed Mary to ride her own horse and her hands were untied. She flexed her fingers until the pins-and-needles sensation left them. It wasn't until they were right outside of Expectation that Billy's hands were freed.

"Just remember," Rusty said to the youth, "you make good today and you'll be a full member of this gang. We'll treat you like family."

"How come you didn't hand me over to Wheeler for hangin'?" Billy asked.

"The old man's dead, boy. So we can either kill you ourselves or let you become one of us. What we do depends on you. You're still a wanted man, you know. Wheeler's widow could accuse you at any time."

Billy looked from Rusty to Luke. "Whatever you say."

"Good, then it's settled," Rusty said, slapping Billy on the back.

"Can I have a gun?" Billy blinked nervously.

Luke glared at him. "Boy, I wasn't at the end of the line when the Lord passed out brains. You'll stay outside the bank and hold the horses for us. Anybody comes along, you warn us right away. That's your job today. It's simple enough, and you damn well better do it right!"

They rode into Expectation, heading straight for the bank. Luke pulled Mary from her horse while Rusty handed all the reins to Billy.

"Beauty, I want you walkin' in the bank right in front of me," Luke said. "Just smile at the people like you come in to do business."

Mary took a deep breath and tried to clear her head. She was feeling dizzy but somehow managed to take hold of herself. She reflected that if she let Luke use her in the robbery and left Expectation with him, it would be all over for her. Then he really would own her body and soul, just as he thought he did. She couldn't allow that to happen. Even if Cal were dead—and she couldn't bear the thought of it—but even if he were gone, she still must not capitulate to this man. It would be like selling her soul to the devil.

Somehow she had to will herself to think intelligently. She couldn't let the Harrises succeed in robbing the bank; she had to take a stand. She reasoned that if she kept alert, her chance might come and she would seize it without a second thought.

They walked inside the bank, Mary in front, Luke with one hand tightly at her waist, Rusty and Jose behind. Mr. Pemrose, the banker, looked up at her with a smile of recognition.

"Why, Miss MacGreggor, nice to see you again." But his expression rapidly changed to one of alarm. "Are you all right? Didn't I hear that someone abducted you?"

Luke came around from behind her and pushed his rifle into Pemrose's face. The lanky bank manager raised his arms uncertainly.

"This is a hold-up," Luke announced. "Put all your money out here into these saddlebags." He threw brown leather saddlebags at the banker.

Pemrose stared at the three men for a moment, and observed that they were all well-armed with Winchesters and double-barreled shotguns.

Rusty was moving around the room. There were two other people in the bank: Mrs. Jones, who apparently had been in the middle of making a deposit; and the bank teller, Harley Witherspoon, a small, bald man with a scarlet complexion.

Witherspoon assisted Pemrose in filling the bags with money, his hands shaking violently.

"You move like snails!" Luke yelled at them. "Be quick about it, otherwise I'll kill you and take the money myself."

Mr. Pemrose's trembled as he finished gathering the bills.

"All right, now empty out the safe," Rusty ordered.

Pemrose's narrow mustache twitched, but he did as he was told. It occurred to Mary that her own money was deposited in this bank. The Stafford farm and many others like it would probably go into bankruptcy if the Harrises were successful in this robbery.

Rusty moved toward Mrs. Jones. "Gimme your purse," he said, snatching it from her.

It was the first time that Mary had ever seen the storekeeper's wife speechless. As Rusty pulled the purse from her hands, she dropped in a faint. While everyone's attention was momentarily drawn to the unconscious woman, Mary seized opportunity.

Realistically, it was probably the only chance she would ever get.

Luke's handgun was holstered and his attention was on the banker, the rifle pointed toward Mr. Pemrose's chest. She reached adroitly for the pearl-handled revolver in Luke's holster, her hand wrapping around the cold metal. She aimed the weapon at Luke's back, but strong hands grabbed at her. She and Jose grappled for the gun. She managed to get off one shot before the weapon was wrenched from her hands.

Luke let out a small cry. He was bleeding from the thigh and turned to look at her in amazement. "Why would you do a thing like that?"

"I have to stop you," she said, trying hard not to let her voice shake from the fear she felt.

"Damn you!" he shouted. "I warned you what would happen if you didn't behave!" He moved toward her as she stepped away.

If he were going to kill her, she wasn't going to make it easy for him. Mary could feel the blood vessel at her temple throbbing and her heart hammered as if it would burst, but still she managed to stand erect.

"You wanted to kill me, didn't you? Why?" There was a look of betrayal in his eyes.

"You murdered my uncle. You raped my aunt. God knows how many other lives you've taken or destroyed."

"Luke!" Rusty called out in an alarmed voice. "Listen for a second! Do you hear it?"

"Hear what?" Luke responded in a distracted tone of voice.

"Horses, damn it! Can't you hear them thunderin' into town. Must be at least ten, maybe twenty, riders. Why would they be movin' so fast?"

"Posse, I reckon. Let's finish this off right quick and get goin'." Luke waved his rifle in Pemrose's face, and the banker retreated back into his vault.

Rusty glanced out the front window. "Luke, I don't like it. There's cowboys out there talkin' to Billy."

"Relax, Rus, he ain't gonna tell them nothin'. Maybe he knew them from before when he worked out this way."

"I'm not so certain we can trust him," the red-haired man replied. "Wait! The cowboys are walkin' away from him now. Jose, get out there and replace the kid pronto! Then send him in here."

The small, ebony-eyed man moved like an agile trout.

"Come here," Luke said to Mary. He handed her a bandanna. "Tie it around my leg," he told her, pointing to his bleeding thigh.

"I told you no good would come of her," Rusty reminded Luke. "Rotten bitch! I'll see she pays for this."

Mary refused to give in to her fears, realizing that if she did, she was truly finished. Billy walked into the bank, and she could see how nervous he was by the way his body trembled.

"Who were you talkin' to out there?" Rusty demanded, pointing an accusing finger.

"Just my old boss, Cal Davis," the youth replied. He gave Mary a meaningful look.

She tried very hard not to smile. So he was alive! She had never been so glad to hear his name mentioned. And he knew they were here! Maybe there was hope after all?

"Why was he in town?" Rusty asked.

"He's with his men. They come in to drink some in the saloon."

"You tell him anything?"

"No, sir, I did not! Why would I? They'd hang me right along with you."

"That's correct, boy, and don't you forget it," Luke agreed.

"No more of this damn fool talk," Rusty said. "Let's get out of here. I still don't like it." He scooped up the filled saddlebags. Then he turned to the bank manager and the teller. "You walk out in front of us." He pulled Mrs. Jones to her feet, grabbing her by the arm. "Okay, lady, you too. Just in case someone starts shootin', it ain't gonna be me gets hit. Billy, you're first. Luke, keep your woman in front of you as a shield."

"Hell, Rus, you worry too much."

"Think so? I've learned one thing: it pays to be cautious. You can't trust nobody except yourself in this world."

They began walking toward the door and Mrs. Jones broke down, sobbing.

"Shut up!" Luke shouted. He slapped her once across the face.

When they got out into the street in front of the bank, Mary noticed something peculiar. The horses were gone and so was Jose. Billy broke free, running behind a wagon. Luke took aim but there was gunfire all around them now and it threw him off.

"Back into the bank everyone!" Rusty shouted. "They know," he said turning to his brother.

They pulled Mary and the other three hostages back into the bank. There was no more shooting, but she knew Cal and his men were out there, waiting and watching.

Back inside the bank, Rusty was in a rage. "Damn that kid! I hope they do hang him. We gave him a chance and he turned on us."

Mary was glad Billy had escaped, but it would not be so easy for her—or for the other hostages.

"You men in there!" She tensed, recognizing Cal's voice. "Got something for you to think on. If you turn those people loose, we'll let you ride out of here free and clear."

Luke took the butt of his gun and broke the glass out of the front window. "You listen, cowboy," Luke shouted back. "I got me a better idea. You give us back our horses right fast and we'll take the money and hostages with us. If you don't come after us, we'll release these people this side of the border. Otherwise, we're gonna kill them all. We got four people here, two of them women."

"We'll think on it some," Cal yelled back.

"Think quick, 'cause the first dead hostage is gonna be tossed out of here in exactly five minutes."

"If you kill those people, you're as good as dead yourselves."

"We'll take our chances."

Rusty turned to his brother. A concerned look furrowed his brow. "Luke, what if they don't care about the hostages? What if savin' the money means more to them?"

"Always worryin', aren't you, Rus? Think you better understand somethin'. They ain't gonna let us go if we hand these people over. They're lyin'. Smart fella like you ought to know better. Besides, that man out there, I recognize him. I know why Miguel didn't come back. That's the cowboy who had my woman! He really come for her." There was a smile on Luke's lips and an eerie light in his eye. "It's between him and me."

Mary watched Rusty. He was perspiring freely through his checkered shirt. There was little doubt in her mind that he was just as scared as she was. The only person in the room who appeared to be calm and unaffected was Luke. It seemed to her that he thrived on this kind of situation.

"What's takin' them so long to decide?" Rusty questioned.

Luke laughed. "Why, you're more nervous than a cat havin' kittens. They're probably just tryin' to figure a way to take us by surprise. Being a soldier taught me a thing or two. You got to figure what your enemy will do next and get one move ahead of them. Stay where you are and keep your rifle pointed at our hostages. I'm gonna poke around for a minute. I figure they'll try to rush us through the back way if they can."

There was total silence in the bank as Luke went to the back door. Mary waited breathlessly for something to happen. She knew Cal was not the kind of man to give up. He would be planning a strategic move. If only she could find a way to help!

There was a large clock in the bank. She found herself staring at it, watching the minutes ticking away. She hoped this would not be the end for her. It seemed as if she was just beginning a new life, and too swiftly it might be over. She yearned to be safe in Cal's arms, being loved by him. She remembered what Luke had said, that he would kill one hostage every five minutes. After what she had done to him, she expected to be the first. The ticking of the clock seemed to grow louder with every passing second.

She heard the sound at the back door almost at the same time Luke did. He began blasting his rifle through the door.

"Get away from here if you expect to ever see these folks alive again!"

Mary heard jangling spurs retreating from the door. Was it Cal? she wondered. Would he be any kind of match for a man like Luke Harris, who had no qualms about killing?

Luke turned to his brother. "That tears it, Rus. We gotta prove to them dumb cowpokes we mean what we say. The five minutes are almost up." He looked over each of the hostages.

Mary took a deep breath and stepped forward.

Luke pushed her down on the floor. "Damn it! Not you!"

Luke glanced at the two men. "You!" he said, pointing his rifle at the bank teller. Mr. Witherspoon's eyes opened wide, registering terror. He seemed frozen. Luke brought up his rifle. "You can die where you stand. It don't make no difference to me." He gestured with the rifle barrel and the small man stumbled forward.

Luke called out again. "Davis, I guess you need evidence that we mean business. Here's delivery of the first hostage." Without another word, he shot the bank teller before Mary's horrified eyes, once in the chest and once in the head. Then he lifted the teller's limp body and pushed it out the door and into the street. Mrs. Jones was weeping hysterically, and Mary moved to her, extending an arm around her shoulders in comfort.

Luke locked the bank's front door. He went back to the window where he had already smashed the glass. "Okay, Davis, that was number one. Five minutes from now, I'm shootin' a woman. Maybe it'll be your woman, maybe not. Hurry up and decide. I ain't got all day. And no tricks."

"All right, Harris, you win." Cal's voice sounded hoarse. "I'll have the horses brought around. Just don't shoot anyone else!"

She could hear the defeat in Cal Davis' voice. Something had to be done fast! But what?

Luke laughed loudly in triumph. "See, Rus? I told you. A man's always got to have courage, be audacious, never let nobody scare him. A smart gambler will tell you that any hand can come a winner if it's played right."

Killing the bank teller seemed to have put Luke in jubilant spirits. But he was limping noticeably. The bullet wound she had inflicted was bleeding. His faded jeans were covered with blood.

"I hope this works out," Rusty said.

"Just think on the good time we'll have in Nogales once we start spending this money," Luke responded with a cheerful smile. "We'll live like kings."

"I'd feel a whole lot better if we were already out of here." Rusty wiped perspiration from his forehead with the dirty sleeve of his tan shirt.

"It's all right. They're gettin' our horses."

"What's keepin' them?" Rusty questioned uneasily. Both men peered out the front windows.

Mary realized that if the horses were brought around, nothing would stop the Harrises from leaving the territory. There had to be something she could do. They weren't watching her now. She cast around desperately, looking for anything that she might use as a weapon.

Her eyes suddenly caught sight of a possibility. Kerosene! The container was there for the lamps, but it could be a useful weapon. Quickly, quietly, she inched over to it. She tried lifting it, her hands hardly able to behave as she wanted. At first, she nearly dropped the container. Her heart was pounding so loudly, she was almost certain everyone else could hear it. She managed to dump the kerosene across the back of the room, dousing everything she could. A box of matches lay near the lamp by the teller's cage. She snatched it up and quickly struck one.

Rus turned and saw her then. He came running at her just as she put the match to the kerosene. She prayed it would ignite, and it did. It was already too late by the time Rus took hold of her. A burst akin to an explosion occurred in the room. Fire leaped everywhere.

Mrs. Jones began screaming.

"Damn crazy bitch!" Rusty swore at her.

"Let's get the hostages out in front of us," Luke ordered. He turned to her then. "I'm not even mad at you. It's just what I would have expected. No matter what happens, I'm keeping you. You're mine for always. We'll just have to mix some pain with our pleasure." His smile was chilling. He took her savagely by the arm and threw the bags filled with money over his shoulder. Luke held his rifle in his free hand.

Mary's lungs were beginning to hurt; they were all coughing from the smoke they inhaled. Luke pushed her into the street. Rusty carefully kept Mr. Pemrose and Mrs. Jones in front of him as shields.

"Them horses, where are they?" Luke shouted out.

"Be right there." It was Cal's voice, but she couldn't see him. In fact, there was no one in the street. She comforted herself with the thought that he was out there waiting for just the right moment to save them. Then she caught sight of the unmistakable glint of a rifle barrel from the roof of the hotel. She looked down again, hoping that Luke hadn't noticed.

Something clicked in her mind. Cal was not going to simply let the Harrises go. She understood now why the street was deserted. Cal must have his men positioned all over town where they would not be easily seen. She tried to steel herself for whatever would come.

Rusty Harris cursed at her again. "That bitch forced us out here before we was ready, before they brought around the horses! I don't like being exposed this way. I don't care what you say, Luke, she's dead meat as soon as we hit the trail."

"Only I decide that, Rus, and I want her." Luke's eyes flashed blue lightening at his brother as his fingers bit into her arm. He turned to her. "If I die before you, I want you wearin' that red dress when they bury me. I kept it for you in my saddlebag." His lips punished hers for just an instant.

Mary looked up to see Cal leading the horses around himself.

"Better be no tricks, cowboy," Luke warned.

"We agreed to your terms. Just let the hostages go on this side of the border like you promised."

"All except her," Luke said. "Just like you, I figure she's worth the trouble. Now mount up, cowboy, I want you with us too. Take off that gun belt first though."

Cal took a few steps closer to Luke and her. He was beside Mary now.

"Sure, Harris, whatever you say. Just take it easy."

As Cal reached for his gun belt, he shouted out: "Now!" Then he grabbed Mary, knocking her to the ground. His big body covered hers as a volley of rifle shots opened up, blasting Luke. Without Mary in front of him, Luke made an excellent target. Rifle fire rained down from every rooftop. Luke fell to the ground mortally wounded, blood hemorrhaging from his body.

When Rusty saw his brother fall, he dropped his own rifle. "Stop shootin'!" he yelled out. "I'm givin' myself up." He still held himself behind Mrs. Jones.

Tiny was the first to lay hands on Rusty Harris. Mrs. Jones collapsed into Mr. Pemrose's arms, nearly bringing him to the ground, just as the lady's husband came running down the street. A general cheer went up among the cowhands.

Cal was still holding Mary in his arms, and he made no effort to let go of her; for her part, she was perfectly content lying on the ground as long as Cal held her to him.

"Are you all right, darlin'?"

She found her voice at last. "I'm fine now. I'm so glad you're here. I can't believe it's finally over!"

Cal helped her rise to her feet. Her unsteady legs were like those of a newborn colt. He stared at her with concern.

"I must look terrible, don't I?"

"I was just thinkin' the reverse." Then he kissed her deeply, passionately and she responded with every ounce of emotion that was in her. When they finally came apart, she could hardly breathe at all.

"Cal, I'm so tired," she said.

He put his arms around her. "I reckon you got cause."

CHAPTER TWENTY-THREE

Cal lifted Mary to his horse and seated her in front of him, pressing her back tightly against his chest. As they rode, he held her securely to him. He brought Mary back to his ranch and walked her to his bedroom. He knew how worn out she was and he felt exhausted himself. He looked into her rich chocolate eyes and saw the weariness there. So he merely kissed her gently and told her to get some rest.

"I don't want to put you out of your bed again," she said with a guilty frown.

He touched her cheek and smiled. "You aren't. Believe me, the place I want you is in my bed. You'll hear more about that tomorrow."

"Is that a promise?" she asked, her eyes lighting with a smile.

"Count on it." He left her then, because he knew otherwise neither one of them would get any rest.

He thought that he would sleep well now that it was all over with the Harrises, but he found himself restless. During the night, he woke several times, thinking of Mary, realizing that she was just a few rooms away from him and safe in his house. She needed a chance to recover as much in mind as body. They hadn't really spoken, but he understood how it was. He considered the ordeal she had suffered would surely have broken a person with a lesser spirit.

The following morning, Cal rose before anyone else was up in the house and joined the hands in the bunkhouse for breakfast. The men immediately began coming to him with problems, and he had to make quite a few decisions, things that had been put off in his absence. There was a lot to catch up on, he realized. He was kept busy almost until noon. Then he could stand it no longer and went back to the house.

He found Elizabeth out in the kitchen. She and her little daughter Amy removed muffins from the oven, which made the entire room smell of the delicious aroma of cinnamon. The homey scene made him feel warm inside. Elizabeth turned and saw him, immediately making him welcome with a big smile.

"We're so glad that you're back," she said. "And you brought our Mary home to us."

"And Billy too," Amy added. "Thank you, Mr. Davis."

"My pleasure," he said.

The child hugged him.

"Amy, you let him be! Cal, you just come and sit down right here and have some fresh coffee and muffins hot from the oven. I think you'll like them. They're made from a special recipe my mother taught me and her mother taught her. Just put a little butter or honey on it."

He did as she suggested, sat back, and enjoyed her good baking. "This is very nice," he said, appreciating the cozy atmosphere.

He couldn't help noticing how meticulously clean and neat the house was since the Staffords had been staying with him. He liked Elizabeth a lot. Like Mary, she was a very attractive woman, even if she lacked her niece's spirit and vibrancy.

"What will happen to Russell Harris?" Elizabeth asked, her expression becoming serious.

"They'll hang him I expect."

"They won't let him get away with what he's done?"

Cal sensed the repressed anger behind her question and sympathized with it. "No, they won't do that. Of course, I wish we had a hanging judge out here the way they do in the Indian Territory. I visited Fort Smith when the Harrises were in the vicinity. They got a new judge there name of Parker who don't hold with outlaws killing anybody. They say he always brings in a verdict for hanging."

"I just wish you'd been able to shoot him like you did his brother."

"It's not my way," Cal said. "Lord knows, the man deserves to die, but I couldn't take it upon myself once he was unarmed. I've had enough of killing and violence to last me a lifetime. I just want to live in peace with my neighbors. We've got to trust in the law. I told Jesse Wheeler the same thing."

"I hope the law proves worthy of our trust. But I will come forward to testify. Russell Harris and his brother were responsible for killing my husband, and I won't be satisfied until the man is dead."

Cal took her hand and held it in a gesture of comfort. Elizabeth took a deep breath and forced a smile back on her face.

"You know that Jim Bailey took over church services after Mr. Jenkins passed away. I do believe he has a lot of emotional fervor, talking about whopping the devil and such."

"Maybe we can all go together," Elizabeth said. "I think it would do Mary a world of good too."

"How is she this morning?" he asked.

"She had breakfast with us earlier and we talked for a little while. Then she went back into the bedroom. She's exhausted."

"Think I would disturb her if I were to go to her now?"

"That would be the best thing for her."

Cal finished drinking his coffee, savoring the fragrant aroma. As he rose from the table, Billy Travers entered the kitchen hand in hand with Rebecca Stafford. They were smiling at each other, and there was no mistaking the look that passed between them.

"Well, you seem to have adjusted just fine to being back at the ranch," Cal said to Billy.

The young man grinned. "Thought I was a dead man for sure. You saved my life, Mr. Davis."

"Mine as well," Rebecca said. She threw her arms around Cal and kissed his cheek.

"Fact is, I'd like you all to hear this." Billy turned to Elizabeth. "Mrs. Stafford, I want to formally request to marry your daughter. I love her very much. I don't have a lot to offer, but I plan to work real hard—and I'll never go near a saloon again as long as I live. You have my solemn word."

Elizabeth was all smiles. "If Rebecca wants you—and I know very well she does—that's all that matters. You're welcome to our family," Elizabeth said. She hugged both her daughter and Billy.

Cal left the happy scene, thinking he would bring Mary back to share in the good feelings. He knocked at the bedroom door and heard her call out to come in. He was all ready to draw her into his arms when he saw her and let out an involuntary gasp.

Mary stood near the window looking out, her hair neatly combed and swept upward, and on her body was a crimson, velvet dress, cut very low and showing the creamy, smooth skin at the top of her breasts to advantage. He remembered that night in the saloon when he'd been forced to buy her from Luke Harris. Magnificent as she looked in that dress, he absolutely hated it. The sight of Mary in that dress repelled him.

"Where did you get that dress?"

"Billy said that one of the hands dropped my things off early this morning. They were in Luke's saddlebags along with some of the stolen money you plan to return."

"Why are you wearing that dress now?" he said, his voice tightening.

"Luke asked that I wear it when they buried him. Billy told me that he was buried yesterday after the shooting without any funeral, so I thought to wear the dress for a little while today."

Cal felt angry with her, but strove to keep his temper under control. "You'd do that honor to a cold-blooded killer, the bastard who murdered your own uncle?"

He saw the color rise to her cheeks.

"There was nothing cold-blooded about the way that man killed. I saw him do it. It was like a love affair for him. Love and death were twisted up together in his troubled mind."

"So you'd honor a man who enjoyed killing? A sick murderer. That's even worse!"

"I don't expect you to understand. Maybe I don't myself. All I know is that Luke Harris in his own peculiar way cared for me."

That was too much! He was overcome with anger. It seemed to him as if the ghost of Luke Harris were standing there beside Mary, laughing at him with contempt, mocking him. There was only one other time in his life that he had been this consumed with rage. He wished he could resurrect Luke Harris so that he could kill the sonofabitch right now with his own two hands!

"You sound as if you loved that man," he said through clenched teeth.

She stared at him in surprise. "No, I didn't love him at all. In many ways, he disgusted me. I even tried to kill him. But I felt sorry for him because he never had a proper start. He told me how his father used to beat his mother, himself, and the rest of the children. They were terrified of the horrible man. And then in the war, when he was only sixteen, he started killing for the Confederate cause and began to think that killing was a good thing."

"You're making excuses for him. I don't believe this! You

really had feelings for that snake. Did you let him make love to you too?"

Mary's eyes flashed. "You know I didn't!"

"How do I know that? He had you with him for quite a while."

Mary pursed her lips as if she'd swallowed an insect. "There's only one man I've ever known in that way and it happens to be you."

He saw the look of hurt on her face but it didn't mitigate his sense of betrayal. "Take that dress off, Mary. Take it off now!"

"I will when I'm ready and not before."

God, how he hated her stubborn disposition. "I want you to burn it," he seethed. "I don't ever want to see it again. In that dress, you're his whore."

She slapped his face so hard that the sting brought a tear to his eye. He reacted without thinking. His hands went out to grab her body into his arms. Then he tore at the front of the gown, ripping it violently apart from the bodice down. She stood before him in a thin, clinging chemise and silky drawers which hid none of her obvious attributes. He felt the stirring of desire rise unbidden. He wanted to pull her into the bed with him, strip her naked, and take her. It took all his force of will to stop himself. Cal told himself that if he did that, he would be no better than Luke Harris.

Mary didn't move. She stared at Cal, wondering how he could behave this way after his tender consideration of the previous day. His expression, so intense and hard, outraged her. He looked as if there were some sort of a war raging within him.

He came toward her. His mouth came down hard on hers. The kiss was meant to punish, but it drew from her a jolt of need that made her respond to him with all the passion pent in her. She pressed her body against him, bringing her hands upward to caress the strong sinews of his shoulders. But just as suddenly as he had forced his kiss on her, he pushed her away. She felt an overwhelming sense of disappointment and frustration. All she wanted was to be held in his arms again, to be loved by him, and he was rejecting her.

"I can't stand thinking of you grieving for that bastard. You loved him, didn't you?"

She was so hurt, so wounded by his unfair accusation. How could he think that of her?

"Cal Davis, I should never have given myself to you, but I'll remedy that mistake in the future. I'll be leaving your house today, and I hope never to see you again. Now leave this room!"

Mary stared at the bedroom door as it slammed behind him, and then she burst into tears of heartbreak. How could he have acted that way? She stared at the ripped dress and tossed it away. She would throw it out; she never wanted to see it again. After all they had been through, she so looked forward to seeing Cal this morning, to being with him, and he had ruined it with his absurd accusations.

There was a knock at the door and for a moment Mary thought that Cal had returned to apologize for his cruel behavior toward her.

"May I come in?"

It was Elizabeth, she noted with disappointment. She told her aunt to enter and then began to cry again.

"What's wrong?" Elizabeth asked in alarm. "I saw Cal go storming out of the house as if he wanted to murder somebody."

"Me," she replied. "He's furious with me. He's got this stupid notion that I loved Luke Harris. I tried to tell him it wasn't true, but he wouldn't listen. He saw me in the red velvet gown Luke bought for me and it was like a bull seeing a matador's cape. He went completely wild."

"I expect he was jealous," Elizabeth observed.

"Jealous? I never thought of that."

"Of course not, you're personally involved."

"Maybe I did say the wrong things," she conceded regretfully. "But I only spoke the truth. I know Cal thought it was strange that I should spend so much as a moment mourning for an evil man like Luke, but I thought he was more sick than evil. Though he would have beaten me just as easily as make love to me, I knew he cared."

"You just might be giving that vicious outlaw more credit then he deserves. I can't believe that the creature who raped me and murdered Isaac was capable of caring for another human being at any level."

"You forget that I was with him for quite a while. I tried to kill him, you know, and he respected me for fighting him. He said we were alike. I hope we aren't."

"In no way are you anything like that horrible man. But I can see why Cal was troubled when you spoke kindly of Luke Harris. That would bother most men, let alone Cal, who's had bad experiences with women in the past. You can see why he wouldn't understand, Mary. Frankly, I'm not certain I do myself. Luke Harris was a monster."

"I was with him too long, I guess. It did something to me, something I can't explain. I felt something for him, but I know it wasn't love."

"Somehow you've got to make Cal understand. Otherwise, I'm afraid you'll lose him and that would be terrible for both of you."

Mary shook her head, looking at her aunt's face filled with kindness and concern. "I think it's too late. I think I disgust him now and he hates me."

"We'll see about that," Elizabeth said. Her aunt held her in a comforting embrace, patting her arm.

Mary was forlorn. It was hopeless; she had seen the hard set of Cal's mouth as he left the room. Whatever he might have felt for her was gone. After Elizabeth left the room, she cried until there were no more tears and then she got herself ready to leave Cal's ranch forever.

They did not let her leave alone. Her family left with her, and so did Billy Travers. It was a silent journey, but at least she took it with her family. There was comfort in that.

The condition of the farm was downright depressing, but everyone began working immediately. The effort of putting the farm back in order relieved some of the sorrow she was feeling. Mary welcomed the weariness of being so tired at night that she couldn't think of Cal.

Billy and Rebecca planned to marry in a month. It seemed as if her cousin had come alive again. Billy stayed on at the farm and Rebecca worked alongside him out in the fields for a portion of each day. Elizabeth put in a special order for white silk material, and when it arrived, she began making a wedding dress for Rebecca. Mary was pleased to see that mother and daughter were finally getting along.

Rebecca was making a real effort to relate to Elizabeth, and Mary knew that it had everything to do with Elizabeth's warm acceptance of Billy. The thought of the upcoming marriage made everyone at the farm feel good. She could be angry at Cal for his harsh attitude toward her, but she could only be grateful that he had delivered Billy and her. For her family, it made all the difference.

Spring touched the farm; the creek was like a river. Jeremy was doing what his father taught him. With Billy's help, he carefully controlled the water, using it to irrigate the arid land. Everyone pitched in for the planting.

When the planting was completed, Mary was forced to think about many things that she had been keeping from her mind.

She took an early morning walk, trying to sort matters out. Observing with some pleasure that the mesquite had opened its leaves, she also noticed that the catclaw acacia were as yellow as Rebecca's hair. She could feel the quickening in the earth. The dormancy and sterility of winter were finally over, and the miracle of rebirth had begun. They had been in this new land a full year, she realized with something akin to surprise. She had wanted a different kind of life and had found it, though sometimes the harshness had been shattering. Yet in spite of all the pain, she had survived and endured, even the agonizing disappointment of losing Cal.

Except for herself, the family was in good spirits. Jeremy had grown several inches and put on some weight and muscle. Rebecca was blooming just like the acacia. Mary watched Billy pull her cousin into his arms and kiss her lovingly. She could feel great happiness for them. Elizabeth and Amy were looking forward to Rebecca's marriage, just as she was.

Billy came to find her. "Miss Mary, I just want you to know that I've asked Cal Davis to be my best man, and Rebecca wants you as her maid of honor. I hope that won't be uncomfortable for you."

She shook her head. "Mr. Davis and I have had our differences, but we both wish you and Rebecca well."

Once in a while, she would see Cal in church and their eyes would meet, but then he would quickly look away. She wanted to go to him and say that she was sorry, but he always seemed angry when he glanced at her. Besides, wasn't he just as much at fault? She might be proud, but he was foolish. And yet she yearned for him so.

He was always with Jesse and Lorette Wheeler these days, and that served to make her feel worse. One bright Sunday morning, Mary found herself talking to Jesse alone after the service, much to her displeasure. She expressed condolences at the woman's loss and thought to leave it at that, but Jesse seemed determined for them to talk further.

"It's good that Cal could bring you back safely," Jesse said to her. "He's a fine man."

She felt her cheeks start to burn. "He's been kind to our entire family."

"Yes, Cal's told me about your cousin getting married and how he plans to stand up for Billy. I think it's time that Cal was involved in another wedding as well, one of his own." Jesse cast her eyes meaningfully to where her daughter was standing talking with Cal.

Mary bit down on her lower lip, feeling too much anguish to speak.

"I know Cal has feelings for you, but I also know that it hasn't worked out. I hope in time he'll come to care for Lorette. She'd be a very good wife for him. My daughter has a sweet disposition. Cal deserves to be happy. He's suffered a lot in his life. Lorette could change all that."

"I don't doubt it." Mary quickly excused herself. She did not want to speak further with this woman, who was obviously in Cal's confidence. She could only imagine what he must have said about her.

If only she could forget about Cal Davis! But the truth was, she loved him and doubted she ever would stop loving him. For her, there was only one man; very likely he would never know it, and if he did, he no longer cared.

Cal accompanied the Staffords to Prescott and made the wedding arrangements for Rebecca and Billy. He intended this as his final courtesy to the family. He rode ahead at a distance from the family so he wouldn't have to constantly look at Mary or talk to her. He wanted as little to do with the woman as possible. He couldn't stop desiring her—that seemed impossible—but maybe with time, he would forget how she had felt in his arms or how giving of herself she had been. She had made him feel that she wanted him as much as he wanted her; now he realized that was just a lie, a woman's trick.

Every time he looked at her and began to weaken, all he had to do was remember her in that red dress, mourning the likes of Luke Harris. Then his heart would harden toward her and his rage would burn as hot as if he'd been consigned to an inferno.

But at the wedding ceremony, it became increasingly difficult to remain angry at her. Mary stood beside him wearing that green silk dress he had so admired her in at the dance a long time ago. He remembered how badly he'd wanted her that night, in spite of all the dictates of reason or logic. God help him, he still felt the same!

As Rebecca and Billy took their vows before the clergyman, he was hardly aware of anything except Mary standing beside him, her face as radiant as that of the bride, the stamp of character and quality there plainly to be seen. Of course, Luke Harris had fallen in love with her! How could he help himself?

After the ceremony, they all had lunch at the hotel where they had stayed the night before. The clergyman was included and seemed content to share a meal with the family. Cal kept looking at Mary and found that he had no appetite whatsoever for food.

Elizabeth sat beside Cal and chatted agreeably. "I'm glad we came to Prescott. What an interesting place!"

"Just like Expectation, it's got good ranch and farming country, gold mines, and plenty of desert. But it's a whole lot bigger."

"It's good to see a bustling town with lots of people again," Elizabeth told him.

He tried to listen to her, but found himself preoccupied with Mary.

"I'm thinking of returning East," Elizabeth commented.

He looked at her in surprise. "I thought you were getting used to it out here."

"I am, but with Rebecca and Billy getting married, I don't think I'll be needed at the farm. Billy and Jeremy are going to work the farm together. Rebecca and Billy will want to start their own family soon enough. I feel that my presence would be unnecessary. Maybe you were right, Cal, when you said I was like your mother. I do find life out here hard. I thought I might take Amy back home with me—and Mary too, if she wants to come. I don't imagine there's really anything here for her anymore. Mary likes it out here, but she's been very unhappy lately."

Elizabeth's observation severely jolted him. Mary going back East? But wasn't that just what he always thought she would do? Still, Mary wasn't weak or genteel like his mother or Elizabeth. Mary was made of sterner stuff—or so he'd thought.

Now he turned to her. She was talking with Billy, Rebecca, and Jeremy, but he interrupted their conversation with an abruptness he knew bordered on rudeness. And he didn't care.

"What's this about you going back East, Mary?"

His words seemed to catch her by surprise. She exhaled sharply.

"That's Elizabeth's idea. She thinks we might both be better off back in New Jersey."

"And is that your opinion too?"

Her head turned to one side as if she were trying to read his face. "I don't know. What do I have out here?"

"Me," he answered.

Her mouth fell open in surprise. He wasn't behaving like the rational, calm man he tried so hard to be, not when he was forced to be in her presence. He turned to the clergyman, whose name he couldn't even recall at the moment.

"Reverend, could you perform another ceremony today if you have the time?"

"Sure could!" The reverend gave Cal a knowing smile.

"Fine, because this lady and I are getting married right here and now." He took Mary's hand in his and held it tightly.

She stared at him in disbelief and shook her head. "You're as crazy as Luke Harris was."

"Good, then I suppose that means you might just be willing to have me." His retort had been sharp with sarcasm, he realized, and it had not gone unnoticed by her.

"You can go straight to hell!" she shouted at him. She pulled her hand free of his and hurried out of the dining room.

Chagrined, he noticed that everyone in the room was staring at him.

"Reverend, we'll be back in a few minutes. I expect the lady needs some courtin'."

"Son, take all the time you want," the reverend said. Cal thought he heard the clergyman mutter under his breath, "You'll likely need it."

He followed after Mary. She stood outside in front of the hotel, and as she turned around to face him, Cal could see that there were tears in those large, luminous eyes of hers.

"I guess I didn't handle that right, did I?" he said.

She gave him a withering look. "I don't understand you," she said. She tapped her toe against the wooden boardwalk. Not a good sign.

"I reckon that puts us just about even. This past month, I felt like a stallion with a bur under its saddle. It would have been easier living if the Apache had staked me to an anthill."

Cal snatched Mary's hand. "I feel things for you that I never felt for any other woman. You make me crazy. All I know is that

I love you and I can't stand to live without you anymore, even if you did have feelings for that lowlife scum, Luke Harris."

"I never loved the man. I don't understand why you think I did. You don't have any idea what's inside my heart. Luke wanted me. That's true enough. And there were moments when it would have been easy to accept him, but I didn't! I fought him. I kept free of him any way I could, even when I thought you had used me and didn't really care for me. The truth is I always loved you and only you, no matter what!"

Cal was moved by the earnestness in her voice. He took her into his arms and kissed her. She had always been honest with him, always told him the truth; he could see that now. Why had he ever doubted her?

"Please marry me today, right now. We've got the minister and everything. I'm sorry, Mary. I've got flaws. I'm far from perfect. But I do love you. I promise never to act like a damn fool jealous jackass ever again."

"You probably will, but I'll forgive you. In case you haven't noticed, I've made some mistakes myself. I'm not exactly perfect."

She threw her arms around his neck and kissed him with so much passion it took his breath away. He held her away from him for a moment.

"We better get married right quick," he said, "or we're going to end up embarrassing ourselves out here in public."

Mary's face glowed with radiance. "Can't think of anything I'd rather do than marry you."

ABOUT THE AUTHOR

Multiple-award-winning author **Jacqueline Seewald** has taught creative, expository, and technical writing at the university level as well as high school English. She has also worked as both an academic librarian and an educational media specialist. Fifteen of her books of fiction have been published including the Five Star novels *The Inferno Collection, The Drowning Pool, The Truth Sleuth, Death Legacy,* and *The Third Eye.* Her short stories, poems, essays, reviews, and articles have appeared in hundreds of diverse publications.

Head
Over
Heels

Center Point
Large Print

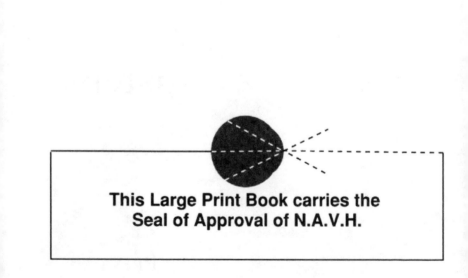

**This Large Print Book carries the
Seal of Approval of N.A.V.H.**

Head Over Heels

Hannah Orenstein

CENTER POINT LARGE PRINT
THORNDIKE, MAINE

To all the athletes who spoke up about the abuse in gymnastics, I'm in awe of your strength, bravery, and perseverance. Thank you for making this sport safer.

• Author's Note •

Head Over Heels was inspired by my love for gymnastics. I spent fifteen years training as a gymnast and always knew I wanted to write about the sport someday. In August 2018, the idea for this novel hit me and I quickly emailed my agent. "What *perfect timing* for summer 2020!" she wrote back. I was thrilled my editor agreed: the book would come out just in time for the 2020 Olympic Games in Tokyo. It never crossed anyone's mind that the event wouldn't happen.

Two days after I finished the final page proof review of this novel, the International Olympic Committee announced the 2020 Olympics would be postponed by a year due to the coronavirus pandemic. Since the modern Olympic Games were founded in 1896, the competitions have only been canceled for World War One (in 1916) and World War Two (in 1940 and 1944). While a postponement was undoubtedly the safest choice, it's also a devastating one for some gymnasts. Athletes have a very narrow window of opportunity to compete at their prime, and delaying the Games by even a year could mark the end of some gymnasts' Olympic aspirations.

This is hardly the first blow elite gymnastics has suffered in recent years. In September

2016, the *Indianapolis Star* reported that two former gymnasts had accused Larry Nassar, the former USA Gymnastics (USAG) national team doctor and an osteopathic physician at Michigan State University, of sexual assault. Since then, more than 265 women have come forward with accusations dating back to 1992. In July 2017, Nassar was sentenced to sixty years in federal prison after pleading guilty to child pornography charges; in 2018, he received two additional sentences of 175 and 40 to 125 years in state prison for sexual assault charges. As of February 2020, the United States Olympic & Paralympic Committee have proposed a $215 million settlement to current and former athletes who survived Nassar's abuse, but some top gymnasts have noted the settlement would prevent further investigation into USAG's role in the scandal.

In *Head Over Heels*, both Avery and Hallie's lives are shaped by the pursuit of Olympic glory. This book is a work of fiction, but top gymnasts' dedication and sacrifice, even amid terrible suffering, are not. As the sexual abuse scandal continues to unfold and the coronavirus pandemic pushes the Olympics off schedule, my heart goes out to the real-life Averys and Hallies. I invite readers to escape into a world in which the coronavirus pandemic does not happen, the Olympics go on as planned, and gymnasts deserving of justice chase their dreams.

OCTOBER
2019

• *Chapter 1* •

The flight attendant thrusts a box of snacks under my nose without hesitation. I dab at the half-dried tears on my cheeks with the crumpled-up tissue I've been clutching ever since we left Los Angeles an hour ago and peer at the options.

"Popchips, Sun Chips, Doritos, pretzels, or trail mix," she recites, snapping her gum.

Everything is processed and full of salt, sugar, or both. "Thanks, but I'm all set," I say.

"The beverage cart will be coming next," she says, ignoring my sleeping neighbor and swiveling to the passenger on the other side of the aisle.

The thirty-something woman next to me, whose iPhone lock screen is a selfie of her in Minnie Mouse ears kissing a man wearing Mickey ones at Disneyland, took an Ambien the moment she sat down. I'm grateful, because I'm not up for a conversation right now. It's been two days since Tyler broke up with me, and I don't want to talk to anyone, much less a stranger.

There was no question that I'd leave the apartment we shared. The lease was in Tyler's name, and even though I had always promised that I'd be able to pay half the rent someday, I'd never been able to afford my share of the luxury high-rise condo. I didn't have any friends I felt comfortable crashing with while I waited out my two weeks' notice at work, which they didn't really need anyway. I coached a preteen girls' recreational gymnastics team only a few afternoons a week, mostly to have something to do while waiting for Tyler to return from football practice and games.

Packing was simple because Tyler owned almost everything: the gleaming set of pots and pans in the kitchen, the oversized flat-screen TV he liked to watch *SportsCenter* on, the sprawling sectional he'd bought under the guidance of the decorator he hired the first time he cashed an obscenely fat check and thought he had an image to uphold. I threw the remnants of my old life—clubbing dresses and stilettos collecting dust in the closet—into the trash, then stuffed the remaining T-shirts, leggings, and sneakers into two suitcases. I left pieces of me behind: my favorite dog-eared cookbook, the heating pad I used when my back pain flared up, a pair of silver earrings he had given me. Anything else I needed would be waiting for me at home in Greenwood, Massachusetts.

I don't know if "sad" is the right word to describe how I feel. Maybe more "dazed." Or "lost." Or *What the fuck do I do now?* I'm not devastated or even angry. I love Tyler—or loved him, I guess. At first, I loved learning his quirks:

12

the way he'd look over his shoulder after running onto the field, searching for my face in the crowd; the goofy way he grinned after his third beer; the polite, Midwestern way he always called my parents Mr. and Mrs. Abrams instead of Bill and Michelle. I admired his ease and modesty in the spotlight, traits that came naturally to him but never felt within reach for me. But I don't know if I necessarily *love* him. Not anymore.

To say that I didn't see the breakup coming both is and isn't a lie. I guess I didn't want to look hard enough at what our relationship had become, not until he forced the issue and announced we were done. Because that would have required examining all of it—everything that'd happened since that day in San Jose, California, when I was nineteen—and admit that Tyler has a life to move on toward, and I don't.

After what happened at the Olympic Trials seven years ago, it was too late for me to apply to any colleges for that fall. I spent a miserable "gap year" slumped on the couch in my parents' basement, "exploring" and "studying" the way the TV could slide from morning talk shows to daytime soaps to the six o'clock news to prime-time sitcoms to the worst dregs of late-night movies.

I worried that twenty was too old to start college, but I had been recruited to one of the country's top gymnastics programs at Los

Angeles State University, and it seemed a waste not to go. I had assumed that my reputation would precede me, that I'd be the star of the team. But I had been out of practice for more than a year by that point, recovering from my injury. I was flabby and weak, soft both physically and mentally. The other girls kept their distance; at first, I think they were intimidated to talk to me, but by the time they realized I was no queen bee anymore, they had already formed their own cliques. Practice was lonely and humiliating as I struggled to whip myself back into shape without my coach, Dimitri's, help. His methods had been extreme—punishing exercises, a cold shoulder if you didn't perform your best, rage if you failed—but I found myself missing them. My new coach asked us to call her Miss Marge. She began each workout with a mandatory dance party to get our hearts racing, and ripped open bags of Twizzlers as parting gifts at the end of every practice. The other girls loved her. But none of them had what it took to be truly great. Without training under the intensity of a legendary coach, how were any of us supposed to become champions?

I wound up randomly assigned to live with a scarily peppy girl named Krista. She was an LA native who claimed to be "ob-*sessed*" with every-thing, including my near brush with fame as an almost Olympic gymnast. She begged me to join her at the campus gym, where she clutched three-pound dumbbells while strolling on the treadmill, and stocked our room regularly with boxes of Franzia Sunset Blush she bought with her fake ID. Krista walked in on me in the shower one day by accident; she's the first person who brought it to my attention that normal girls shaved their legs with their foot propped up on the ledge of the tub, not at eye level, pressed against the shower wall.

I floundered through Psych 101, Intro to Mass Communications, and Human Physiology before my GPA dipped low enough for me to get kicked off the team. I watched myself fail with a perverse sense of curiosity: I had pushed myself to superhuman lengths for years; I had never seen myself falter before. Letting go was easy when you didn't care.

With Krista by my side, I fell into the world of dorm parties, then house parties, then bacchanalian nights at clubs. I learned the hierarchy of low-cal cocktails (vodka-soda, then vodka-tonic, then sugary vodka-cran as a last resort), the way to convince a club promoter to let you past the red velvet ropes for free, and the art of determining which men were game to flirt and which only wanted to grind their sweaty bodies against yours on the dance floor. I had finally unlocked the way regular girls got to feel powerful, beautiful, and magnetic: buzzed, carefree, gussied up in black Lycra dresses with men's hungry eyes locked with yours, moving to the beat of a soaring pop remix. Here, in the normal world, I didn't need to stick the landing. I could stumble—out of a club, into a cab, under the covers.

When I failed out of school midway through sophomore year, I barely registered it, other than to note that I could finally stop showing up hungover to my 12 p.m. lectures. I had some savings—bat mitzvah money and birthday money I had been given over the years and had never had time to spend—and so I rented a room in a three-bedroom apartment in Westwood. I lined up a series of odd jobs (dog-walking, babysitting) that supported my habit of ordering flimsy minidresses from NastyGal.com, and kept faithfully showing up at 1OAK, Argyle, Supperclub, or wherever my best club promoter, Angelo, would have me.

That's how I met Tyler. The way ESPN later described it, our encounter sounded like an athlete's happily-ever-after: a former elite gymnast just so happened to meet a rising football star one twinkling night in Los Angeles. That's the romantic spin. Tyler and his friends bought a table at 1OAK and Angelo brought me and two other club rats over to sit with the guys. Tyler offered to pour me a drink from the glass pitchers of vodka, cranberry juice, and orange juice. Back then, Tyler was just a rookie—the backup quarterback for the LA Rams; the life-changing season that catapulted him to· real, mainstream fame as a quarterback was still a year ahead of him—but he probably expected me to be impressed. Instead, I volleyed that I had been a top athlete, too, a few years back. We talked and danced and made out in the club for hours. When it was closing down for the night, he shyly invited me back to his place. On any other night, I would've said yes. But something came over me; maybe I recognized a kindred spirit, someone I could find common ground and an equal playing field with. Instead, I gave him my number and told him to text me if he wanted to go out sometime. Sure enough, he texted the next morning and invited me out for dinner.

That was four years ago. Dinner turned into a string of dates, which soon led to a bona fide relationship. We fell for each other fast—it was giddy and disorienting in the best way possible. He liked that I understood and supported his strict training regimen, unlike other girls he had dated in the past. And with his encouragement, the messy pieces of my life took shape. The more time we spent together, the more my diet shifted from fruit-flavored vodka to real fruits and vegetables. I started working out again. Tyler was the one who suggested that I seek out a part-time coaching job. By our third month of dating, I was smitten. By our fourth, I was confident enough to say "I love you" out loud for the first time. He said it back.

Moving into his apartment was a no-brainer. We spent almost all of our free time together anyway. Growing up, I had never allowed myself to really dream past the podium stand; when you believe you're on the edge of Olympic history, fantasies about boyfriends seem frivolous. But there I was, twenty-three years old, playing house with a hunky football player, lingering just a little too long over a bridal magazine in the checkout line at the grocery store. I had found myself living a dream I'd never known I wanted.

The next season, he threw the winning pass in the Super Bowl, and he became a household name. But the cozy closeness of our relationship thinned. We saw each other less, and when we did, it was often squeezing a date night into a football banquet dinner or charity event. I saw for the first time up close what it meant to be a champion, and I hated having my nose pressed up against the glass like a dirty onlooker; I still wanted that glory for myself. I couldn't admit that to Tyler; that meant giving him unfettered access to the haunted way my brain still taunted me with the word "failure."

It would be easy, I think now, as the airplane cuts through a gloriously white cloud and descends into a fog, to leave the breakup at that. I'm flying to the other side of the country, where Tyler knows no one. I could pretend we broke up because he got caught up in his own fame, and I

18

didn't want that kind of life. Nobody would know the difference. Nobody but me.

There was an afternoon a few months back when Tyler came home unexpectedly early; he wasn't feeling well. It was around 3 p.m. on a Thursday, one of my days off from the gym, and I was sitting on the kitchen floor with my legs splayed out in a lazy straddle, organizing the new spice rack I had ordered online. Around me, there was a mess of little plastic bottles: saffron, nutmeg, coriander, star anise, red pepper flakes. I had accumulated so many, splurging on whatever I needed to make a recipe sing. I'd discovered, once I moved in with Tyler, that I liked to cook; the process kept my hands and mind busy. And after an adolescence of grilled chicken and microwaved Lean Cuisines, the rich flavors I created felt like a gift. So I alphabetized the spices, sipping a generous pour of sauvignon blanc.

"Oh, you're . . . still home?" Tyler had said, a note of surprise in his voice, taking in my ragged pajama pants and the afternoon glass of wine. He looked past my shoulder, toward the living room I had vacuumed, dusted, and straightened up earlier that day.

"Hi! I didn't know you'd be home so early," I chirped. I tilted my chin up so he could give me a kiss, but he didn't. "Do you want something to eat? I can whip something up really quickly if you're hungry."

Tyler shook his head and turned on *Sports-Center*. The open-floor-plan layout of the apartment meant I could stay in that same spot on the floor and see him on the couch in the living room. But a few seconds later, he turned off the TV.

"You don't want to, I don't know . . . *do* something?" he asked, voice dripping with disgust.

"I'm doing this," I said, gesturing to the spice rack.

"You're practically a housewife," he said. "Minus the husband and kids."

I gave him a sour look. We'd talked about marriage as a possibility someday, because it seemed impossible to be living together in a years-long relationship in your midtwenties and *not* talk about it.

"I work," I said evenly.

"Part-time," he clarified.

"You're the one who suggested it," I reminded him.

"I didn't think you'd be happy with that little to-do forever," he countered.

"So, what? What do you want me to do?" I asked, slumping against the refrigerator and resisting the urge to grab my wineglass, lest it make me look even more like some awful cliché.

He sighed. "I don't know, have a . . . passion? Have some kind of ambition?"

"You know I do. You know I *did*," I said defensively, thinking furiously: *How dare he.*

"It's been a long time, Avery." His words drip out carefully, like he's been churning over the best way to say this for a while.

I was tempted to rattle off all the things I do all day that I genuinely enjoy: cooking, coaching, trying new workouts with my ClassPass. But that wasn't what he meant.

"Is this about money?" I demanded. "Do you want me to pay more in rent? Because I can make it work if you want me to."

"It's not about the money." He sighed. "It's just . . ."

He trailed off and looked critically at my bed-head, my shrunken sleep shirt printed with the name of a gymnastics meet I competed in more than a decade ago, and the overhead kitchen cabinets I'd flung open without bothering to close.

"It's just I expected a different kind of life with you, that's all," he said quietly.

And then he turned the TV back on.

There were more fights like that in the months that followed. Sometimes, I'd be honest enough to admit that long ago, ambition was all I'd had. And when the one thing I had built my world around collapsed, I didn't know where else to turn—I didn't know *how* to turn. Maybe I never fully recovered from the depression that hit like a truck seven years ago. I never found a reason to.

The plane enters a rough patch of air and gives

a sickening jolt. As the turbulence jostles us, a clear *ding* rings out through the cabin, and the pilot makes an announcement over the PA system. "At this time, we ask that you return to your seats and fasten your seat belts. Thank you." The neon seat belt sign flashes on; there's an uneasy groan from some of the passengers. While my neighbor continues to doze, the man across the aisle from me crosses himself and downs the remainder of the Johnnie Walker he's been nursing. In front of him, an infant starts to wail in her mother's lap.

The turbulence up here doesn't bother me much. I'm more afraid of whatever lies ahead, once the flight lands back at home.

• *Chapter 2* •

Mom and Dad meet me at the arrivals gate at Logan airport with faces scrunched in concern.

"That's all you brought?" Dad asks, taking the two bags from me.

"Oh, honey," Mom says, pulling me in for a hug. She kisses my hair. "We'll get you fixed up."

I had returned home plenty of times since moving to LA, but this time, it has a sense of finality. I'm not here for a quick Thanksgiving visit—when Mom hits the clicker and rolls her Honda into the cold, musty garage, I'm returning for good. I take a suitcase in each hand and trace my old, familiar steps through the house.

A corner of the living room serves as a shrine to what once was. There's a life-sized cardboard cutout of me, frozen forever at seventeen years old, in a red-white-and-blue spangled leotard with chalky thighs and a pile of medals around my neck. Trophies, medals, and competition photos fill the floor-to-ceiling bookcase behind it. I heave my suitcases past the living room, up the stairs, and into my childhood bedroom. It's still painted a childish shade of pink, and there's a smattering of glow-in-the-dark stars stuck on the ceiling. Once-glossy posters of gymnastics greats like Nadia Comaneci, Mary Lou Retton, and Shannon Miller cling to the walls.

I flop on the bed. Compared to the king-sized one I shared with Tyler, this twin-sized mattress feels like a flimsy pool float. I'm no longer a hundred pounds of pure muscle; I don't fit here anymore. I look at my phone with a sigh, wishing desperately for any sort of distraction. I have no texts; barely anyone knows I've moved.

I open Twitter. At first, it's a mindless stream of news, memes, and snippy comments from people I can't remember following in the first place. I see missives about gratitude and accountability from Krista, my old college roommate; according to her tweets, she's been sober for a year now. But then a headline catches my attention. My heart lurches as I open the story on TMZ: *TYLER ETTINGER NEWLY SINGLE? SPOTTED COZYING UP TO A SWIMSUIT MODEL.*

I read it over—once, twice, three times—but the words seem to swim on the screen. Someone on Twitter recognized Tyler at Bootsy Bellows, a celeb-studded club in LA, and took a grainy video of him grinding up on a woman that TMZ identifies as model Brianna Kwan. She apparently had a four-page spread in the *Sports Illustrated* Swimsuit Issue this year. In a fit of self-loathing, I hit play on the video. He nuzzles her neck as his hand trails down the front of her dress; she tilts her head back to whisper something in his ear. Paparazzi caught them outside the club, too, striding hand in hand from the back door to a waiting black car. Tyler knows what he's doing—he knows better than that. He's the one who taught me how to ditch the paps or throw them off the trail: don't show affection or even walk within the same photo frame when photographers are around unless you want the attention. He never did. He said he didn't like too much publicity around his personal life, but now I just wonder if he didn't want it with me.

TMZ concludes that Tyler has likely split from Avery Abrams, his ex-gymnast girlfriend of four years. "Or if not, he's sure to hear from her soon . . ." the site snarked.

I shove my phone under my pillow and bury my face in it. While Tyler is moving on, I'm spiraling into the worst version of myself: lethargic, self-pitying, aimless. The same way I felt after Trials. The version of myself that he didn't want anymore. I want to scream. I feel full of bitter rage in a way that makes me tear up. I went so many years without crying: not when Dimitri assigned me triple sets of conditioning because I talked back one day; not when a fall off beam knocked the wind out of me; not when I developed a stress fracture in my spine at fourteen. The Olympic Trials failure opened up a floodgate I couldn't close. Ever since then, the littlest things set me off. It's embarrassing, how quickly hot tears spring to my eyes now.

This isn't little, though. I wish it were.

I pull up Tyler's Instagram on my phone and scroll down, scanning for the occasional photos he posted of me or of us together. There should be one from a month ago, when we attended his cousin's wedding together—but it's gone. So are the pictures from our anniversary getaway to San Francisco. It's like he's erased me. My stomach drops when I see he's unfollowed me, too. Worse, still, I see he just recently followed that swimsuit model.

I feel sick. I can't remember the last time Tyler touched me the way he touched Brianna in the club, like my skin gave off the oxygen he needed to breathe. I knew our relationship had its issues, but Tyler always said that if you love each other, you stick it out the whole time, no matter what. Nothing a person could say or do would push you away forever. I believed him, because he was the first guy I'd ever really dated, and he had had a serious girlfriend in college. He knew. He and Megan had the kind of relationship where they went on summer vacations with each other's families and talked about future baby names. It only dawned on me later that he eventually left Megan, too.

When the phone rings at dinner, I'm grateful for anything that cuts through the conversation.

Mom plated an endive salad and asked probing questions about why I think Tyler broke up with me; she served grilled tilapia and suggested jobs I could apply for; she refilled our water glasses and peppered me with updates about childhood friends I haven't seen in fifteen years. She can't do silence or stillness. She picks up the call on its second ring.

"Abrams residence, Michelle speaking."

I push a bite of fish across my plate and try to shut out the unwanted image of Tyler's fingers snaking down Brianna's taut abs. Mom listens, draws out an elongated "ummm," and cocks her head toward me.

"Sure, I'll put her on." She covers the receiver with one hand. "Avery, phone for you."

I can't imagine who it is. Nobody knows that I'm here. I take the phone from Mom and wander into the living room.

"Hello?" I ask uncertainly.

"Avery, hi," a male voice says. "I'm sure you don't remember me. It's been a million years. This is Ryan Nicholson."

Of course I remember him. His name is seared into my memory; you never forget the name of your teenage crush. Ryan was a top gymnast around the same time that I was. He trained in Florida, and like me, he was homeschooled for most of his teenage years. Because we both competed on a national and international level, we crossed paths at meets a few times a year. When my best friend Jasmine and I made lists of the cutest boys we knew, his name was always on them. To be fair, we were both homeschooled and knew of just eight or ten boys who didn't sport rattails—an unfortunately popular fad among male gymnasts in the 2000s—but still. His thick, dark hair; chocolate-brown eyes; and nicely muscled arms and abs made a lasting impression. He went to the Olympics in both 2012 and 2016.

"Ryan! Hi. Wow. It's been a minute."

"It sure has been," he says.

"Um, so . . ." I say.

It's like all normal social niceties have completely fallen out of my brain.

"I hear you're in town again," he says.

"How?" I blurt out.

I wonder if he read the TMZ story and drew his own conclusions.

"Winnie told me she ran into your dad at the grocery store yesterday."

Now *that*'s a name I haven't heard in a long time. She's the office manager at my old gym, Summit. I loved her.

"Oh! Right," I say, relieved. "What have you been up to all these years?"

"Has it been that long?" he asks. "Wow. I mean, well, a lot of things. Training. I went to the University of Michigan for gymnastics, and competed in London and Rio. Did some traveling for a while. And I've been coaching, too. You?"

"Well, I just moved back to Greenwood," I say, hoping that covers it.

There's a beat of silence on the line.

"Uh, you're probably wondering why I'm calling," he says.

"Yeah," I admit.

Years ago, if Jasmine and I could've chosen a personal phone call from Ryan Nicholson or Ryan Gosling, we would've picked Nicholson every time. I pace the width of the living room and wind up face-to-face with my cardboard cutout. I swivel to dodge her.

"I'm working at Summit Gymnastics now," he says. "I know you trained there for years with Dimitri Federov before he left."

"I did."

Dimitri put Summit on the map in the 2000s by producing more Olympic gymnasts there than any other training facility in American history—Lindsay Tillerson, Jasmine, and plenty of others. But after 2012, he left Summit to found his own gym, Powerhouse. Summit was taken over by one of its own longtime coaches, Mary Li, but I haven't heard much about her. It sounds like she prefers to stay behind the scenes these days, running the business, rather than training athletes on her own.

"I'm training this girl Hallie for Tokyo," he explains, referring to the 2020 Olympics. "She's amazing, especially on bars. Hardworking and determined like you've never seen before, real natural talent, total star quality. Maybe you've heard of her?"

"Um, believe it or not, I haven't been keeping up much with the sport lately," I say.

The truth is that if 2012 had gone differently for me, I might not have the hard feelings that I do now.

"I'm optimistic about her chances," he says. "Bars is on lock. She's strong on vault and beam, too. But floor is a weak spot for her. Her routine has an impressively high level of difficulty, especially when it comes to tumbling, but she keeps getting dinged on execution. Her artistry could be better."

I know what he means. There are two types of gymnasts: the powerhouses who nail sky-high tumbling and have so much energy, they nearly bounce out of bounds, and the delicate dancers who captivate fans with beautiful choreography, but never attempt the toughest tricks. I was among the latter. You can't choose—you work with what comes naturally to you. At five-foot-three, I was relatively tall and elegant for a gymnast, and my flexibility put the famously bendy Russians to shame. Floor was where I shone—I had a sense of poise and presence to my artistry that's almost impossible to teach. You either have it or you don't.

"I'm looking for an assistant coach to come on board to lead her training on floor," Ryan continues. "There's only so much I can do to help her."

Gymnastics is split by gender: women and men compete on both floor exercise and vault, though women also do balance beam and uneven bars, while men do parallel bars, high bar, rings, and pommel horse. But even though Ryan and I both did floor, the event is drastically different for men and women. We both performed difficult and exciting skills, but his focused on brute strength while mine were interwoven with dynamic choreography. It doesn't matter that Ryan earned an Olympic gold team medal, a gold on high bar, and a bronze on parallel bars. His skills don't fully translate to women's gymnastics, although plenty of men coach women. That's how it's always been. The greatest coaches in the sport's history—like Igor Itzkovitz and, yes, Dimitri Federov—are all men.

"I'm wondering if you would want to come by the gym this week and meet Hallie," he says. "See if you'd want to work with me to train her."

I can't help it. I actually laugh.

"I'm serious," he presses.

"Ryan, I'm flattered, but this isn't a good time for me," I explain. "I just moved back, and I'm

31

not really looking for coaching jobs. I mean, I've never coached at that level before."

"So you're not interested?" he asks. "I mean, Avery, we're talking about the Olympics. I promise you, this girl has what it takes. She just needs to be polished up a bit. That's where you'd come in."

I hesitate. It's dark outside now, and the row of gold trophies on the top shelf gleam menacingly in the living room window.

"I can't," I say.

He sighs heavily on the other end of the phone. "Why don't you take my number in case you change your mind?"

"Uh, sure," I say.

I add his number to my own phone, even though I know I won't use it.

"It's not like there are dozens of qualified coaches with Olympic experience running around this town," he jokes.

His words make me pause. It's like UCLA all over again, when my name was bigger than my actual achievements.

"Just Olympic Trials, actually," I say curtly. "I never made it any further. I have to go; my family's having dinner. Take care, okay?"

I say goodbye and hang up. When I turn back to face the kitchen, Mom and Dad's eager faces already look hungry for news.

"It was nothing," I say, taking my seat. "Just

a call about whether I'm looking for a coaching job. I'm not interested right now. I just got back, you know."

They exchange glances.

"It could be a good opportunity," Dad ventures.

"And you should have something to do," Mom adds. "It'd be good for you to get out of the house."

They're eager because that's all they know. Gymnasts don't ascend the ranks to become Olympians unless the whole family is committed from the start. My ambition burned out, but theirs never did.

"It's really no big deal," I say. "Let's just eat."

That night, I can't sleep. The TMZ video loops cruelly in my head, interspersed with my most romantic moments with Tyler. I see him hand-delivering a bouquet of two dozen white roses and lilies, just because it was Wednesday and he missed me. I flash to his eyes shut tight, head bopping to the beat of the club's house music. I remember the sexy, sleepy way his hair stuck up in bed when he woke up on Sunday mornings, and the time he bought out an entire theater so I could see a showing of *Stick It* on my birthday. My brain cuts to the way he slipped his hand into Brianna's as they exited the club, heads ducked from the flashing cameras. And then there's Mom's voice: *You should have something to do*. Something other than this: lying sweaty in a twin-sized bed in a room decorated by an eight-year-old.

Fuck it. If Tyler can move on, so can I. I download a dating app and throw together the bare bones: a full-body photo from my skinny days before the Freshman 15 set in; a close-up from Tyler's cousin's wedding, when my hair and makeup looked good; and no bio at all, because what's there to say? I set my location radius to thirty miles. Even after all this time, my name is easy to recognize in this small town. People still think of me as that girl who almost made the Olympics.

It's past 11 p.m.—probably too late to swipe without looking like I'm only here for hookups. But I feel a morosely intoxicating combination of sadness and loneliness, so I swipe anyway. I reject the first seven men right off the bat because once you've dated a pro football player on *People*'s 50 Most Beautiful list (number forty-one, but still), it's tough to recalibrate your standards. But I find a groove eventually, indicating interest in a local firefighter, an accountant, and a middle school math teacher I vaguely recognize as someone who grew up in Greenwood a couple years ahead of me. I match with the teacher—Lucas—and involuntarily shudder. He's not Tyler. It's disorienting to actively seek out other men. I don't know if I really feel ready for this.

Hey, Lucas messages me. *What's up?*

Not much, I write back. *Just moved back here this week from LA, actually.*

You grew up here? he asks.

I hold my breath. *Yeah,* I write.

But miraculously, he doesn't seem to recognize me. Instead, he asks what I'm up to tomorrow. When I answer truthfully that I have nothing major going on, he invites me out for a drink tomorrow night. I hesitate, then swipe quickly through a few more potential matches. Nobody else stands out to me. So I say yes. It's not like I have anything better to do.

Jade Castle is a mediocre Chinese restaurant with one of the few liquor licenses in this formerly Puritan dry town. My family never came here; we always preferred to eat at Ming's House—not that I could ever have anything besides the steamed chicken and broccoli—because Jade Castle has always attracted a less family-friendly crowd. When I arrive at seven thirty tonight, I spot the father of one of my middle school class-mates sitting at the bar with a girl half his age, and a large round table crowded with boys in matching lacrosse team jackets, probably using an expired ID swiped from an older brother. I take an empty bar stool; I'm not sure if Lucas intended for us to eat or not. When a bartender asks if she can get me a drink, I awkwardly decline. It's been a very long time since I've been on a first date, and it feels like the muscle has atrophied. I felt optimistic setting up the date on the app, but now my confidence has evaporated.

Lucas walks in at seven forty, when I'm on the verge of losing my nerve and leaving.

"Avery?" he asks, tilting his baseball cap up to reveal a baby face and a smattering of freckles. He has a narrower frame than I expected; a Boston Red Sox jersey hangs from his shoulders.

"Hi," I say, unsure whether to rise and hug him.

I make an attempt to stand, but my feet get tangled behind the leg of the bar stool. He slouches onto the seat next to me instead and leaves his phone faceup on the bar.

"You want a beer?" he asks, not quite making eye contact.

"Uh, sure," I offer.

When the bartender glances our way, he holds up two fingers, and mouths, "Two." I get the distinct sense that he's been here on plenty of dates. He drums his fingers on the bar in a staccato rhythm, then visibly relaxes once he sees her returning with our drinks.

"So, LA, huh?" he asks finally.

"Yeah."

"Why'd you move back?"

The question makes me frantic. "Uh, I just needed a change."

"Must be wicked nice out there," he comments. "Warm. Beautiful. You go to the beach a lot?"

I feel stupid telling him I spent six years in LA and can count my number of beach days on one hand because I wasn't confident enough to wear a bathing suit.

"Yeah, all the time," I lie.

It's obvious that this date is not off to a strong start. And what's worse, it's not a stretch to imagine my future as a string of evenings just like this one, probably at this exact bar, probably while Lucas conducts a similar string of dates a few bar stools down.

"So, you teach? What are the kids like?" I ask, turning the conversation to him.

"The kids are fine. Bunch of Goody Two-shoes, a couple of class clowns, mostly smart kids," he says. "You know how this town is."

I do. The suburb's strong public school system attracts a wildly overachieving, goal-oriented population. When I was in elementary school, nobody thought it was weird that I spent sixteen hours after school every week training in a gym because everyone else spent that amount of time on horseback riding lessons, piano lessons, theater classes, or all three.

I don't know what else to say, so I cast around for anything we might have in common.

"Is, god, what's her name? Mrs. Marcotti? Is she still teaching math these days?"

He nods and rolls his eyes. "Yep. With a stick up her ass."

"She was a tough teacher," I say, ignoring the rude comment.

"You had her?" he asks.

"Yeah, in seventh grade? Eighth, maybe?"

"Me, too. What year did you graduate?"

"Uh, 2010? I mean, technically. I was kind of homeschooled the last few years."

He cocks his head and really stares at me. For a few stretched-out seconds, neither of us speak.

"You're that girl," he says, squinting like he's trying to recall the details. "The gymnast."

"Yeah," I say quickly, sipping my beer in an attempt to shut down this line of conversation.

"You were that girl in that *video!*" His voice gets louder.

My blood runs cold. In my most pathetic moments, I've watched the damn video alone. But Lucas is jubilant, leaning in closer but talking louder than ever.

"I *knew* you looked familiar!" he says cheerfully.

I feel cornered. I shrug and try to cast around for another topic of conversation to distract him.

"So, do you ever—"

Lucas opens YouTube on his phone and starts to type in "worst gymnastics crashes." It doesn't take him long to zero in on the clip he's searching for. He gleefully hits play, and I hear the familiar roar of an athletic arena cut through the bar's din. I can hear the faint, singsongy chant of my name—"Let's go, A-ve-ry, let's go!" I don't need to watch; I know it by heart: me, nineteen years old, in a shimmering red leotard and a ponytail, performing the sharply sultry opening dance moves of my floor routine at the 2012 Olympic Trials. Even all these years later, the music stirs my muscles; *this* is where I pirouette; *this* is where I roll my hip. I ground myself back into reality on the bar stool, willing myself into stillness.

But I can't forget what I know is playing out on-screen: the younger version of me launching into my first tumbling pass. It's the most impressive one of my routine: round-off, back hand-spring, whip, back handspring, double-twisting, double back somersault. I had performed it a thousand times before. But this time, I under-rotated and came crashing down onto the blue spring floor while I was still spinning. There was a horrific shredding sensation in my knee before my hands even hit the ground.

"Gnarly," Lucas says emphatically, shaking his head at the screen. "I used to watch this all the time. Sick."

My floor music continues as the audience gasps. I scream. Lucas taps the screen to watch the crash over again, cutting short the moment when Dimitri rushed onto the floor to carry me

39

away in his arms. My stomach lurches as I watch Lucas lean even closer to the video.

I clear my throat. "Please turn that off," I say.

"I can't believe this is you," he says, glancing from me to the screen. "You were so tiny back then."

He makes no move to stop the video.

"Can you—?" In a jolt of frustration, I grab the phone out of his hands and shut the video off, leaving the phone facedown on the bar.

I do my best attempt at a smile, but I can sense it comes out all thin and strained.

"Whoa," Lucas says, holding up his hands as if to prove he's harmless.

"I don't like to watch that," I try to explain as calmly as possible. I swallow. "That right there? That was the end of my gymnastics career. And a lot of stuff changed for me after that. It was hard, okay? So, please, let's stop watching it."

"No need to be so intense," Lucas says defensively. He slurps down his beer. "I got it."

Somehow, I have a hard time believing he's "got it." I had trained for that moment since the time I was four years old, when my ballet instructor complained I had too much energy for dance and suggested I switch to gymnastics instead. By age eight, I was practicing four times a week. At twelve, I sat in a straddle on my living room floor, transfixed as Lindsay Tillerson won the all-around gold—I knew I could follow in her footsteps. Two years later, I convinced my parents to let me drop out of school and study with a tutor so I could train full-time under the legendary coach Dimitri Federov. In this sport, it's outrageous for anyone to claim an easy path to Olympic glory. But everyone from Dimitri to Jasmine to the girls who sent me fan emails all said the same thing: I had a better chance than any other athlete out there.

I was furious that I'd just missed the cutoff to be eligible for the 2008 Olympics. Sixteen is the minimum age to compete, and my birthday fell just weeks after the Beijing games at the end of August. So I threw myself into the next four years of training, desperate because I had dreamed of this one moment for nearly my entire life.

The Olympic Trials for gymnastics are held just seven weeks before the actual Olympic Games. Trials and the Games are held closely together to limit the likelihood of anything disastrous happening in the middle; god forbid a gymnast sprain an ankle, or worse, develop. In 2012, fourteen athletes competed for just five spots on the team, plus three alternates. I performed beautifully all day long, and floor was my final event of the competition. I liked the idea of finishing on a high note.

And then I crashed. It was over. All of it. Gone. Recovering from surgery was tough because it seemed as if there was nothing to recover *for*. I was nineteen years old. Even if my knee healed well, I was too old to seriously consider the prospect of training for Rio in four years. The cruel reality of the sport is that you train your entire life for one event, and then the moment disappears in a flash. By twenty-one, twenty-two—forget about twenty-three—your body has taken beatings for too many years.

So, the same night my career ended, Jasmine's took off. She didn't just make the Olympic team—she became the star of it. While she competed in London, I watched the competition on the couch, recovering from knee surgery. In lulls between performances from the American gymnasts, the commentators noted that Avery Abrams, widely considered the front-runner, the shoo-in, hadn't made the team due to a last-minute injury. They rattled my name off like a fun fact, the same way they commented on the architecture of the stadium and the number of Swarovski crystals sewn onto competition leotards. Jasmine won a gold on bars, a silver on beam, and a gold team medal.

I had imagined that I'd return home from London as America's sweetheart. I'd model for Wheaties boxes, chat up talk show hosts, and land *Sports Illustrated* covers for a few months. Then, once the mainstream interest in my athletic prowess had died down, I'd enjoy a revered career within the world of gymnastics. I'd be a commentator on TV, design a collection of leotards for GK, and give motivational speeches to aspiring athletes across the country. There was no plan B.

Meanwhile, Jasmine was on the Wheaties box. She was on the cover of not only *Sports Illustrated*, but *People*, *Seventeen*, and *Essence*, too. She was invited to New York Fashion Week and the Grammys. She won *Dancing with the Stars* and seemed to be Ellen DeGeneres's new best friend. Little girls across the country did cartwheels in leotards she designed. We had been best friends, training side by side for six years. At first, she called often, asking sincere questions about my knee surgery and saying she wished I could be there with her. She even sent me a care package of souvenirs from London— British chocolate bars and a commemorative mug stamped with Prince William and Kate Middleton's wedding portrait, taken the year before. I could barely stand to reply, and I let our friendship wither to monthly texts. I saw her in person just once after the Olympics; it was her twentieth birthday dinner, and I couldn't come up with a plausible excuse to turn down the invitation. It felt like all the comfort had been sucked out of the air between us. She didn't bother texting at all after that.

Lucas makes a show of sliding his phone into his pocket. I don't know what the protocol is for ending a bad date early, but I sense with absolute clarity that I should leave. I saw a woman on TV once slap money on the bar and saunter away, which looked supremely classy, but I'm not carrying any cash. I don't want to leave Lucas—as awful as he is—with the bill, just on the matter of principle. Instead, before I lose my nerve, I clear my throat and tell Lucas I'm leaving.

"I'm going to head out, but have a good night," I say.

I signal the bartender. As I wait for her to come my way, I stare straight ahead, not brave enough to even glance at Lucas.

He sputters, "You're leaving? Now?"

I hand my credit card to the bartender. "Just for the one drink, please," I tell her. Then I turn to my date. "I'm sorry, yes, I'm leaving. It's been a long night."

I grab my purse and jacket and stride through Jade Castle to get to the parking lot. I've only had a few sips of beer; I should be fine to drive home. Before I back the car out of the spot, my fingers find the preset for the angriest indie rock channel on the radio. The presets haven't changed since I was in high school. I take the familiar turns through the town center, replaying Lucas's moronically cruel behavior on a loop in my head. If I had to venture a guess, this is not how Tyler felt after his first night out with Brianna.

When I reach my driveway a few minutes later,

I'm still too angry to get out of the car. I know that when I walk into the house, Mom and Dad will probably pepper me with questions about how the night went, and I'm not ready to face that.

I look up Ryan's phone number in my contacts. The unfamiliar area code is proof that he's an outsider—a fresh start. He saw me in the context of the sport, where career-ending falls are unfortunately more common than you might think. They're par for the course, not a local tragedy. Unlike Lucas, Ryan—hopefully—doesn't look at me and think, *train wreck*. He's seen me draped in gold medals. And it's not like I have anything else going on. I dial his number.

"Avery?" he asks, sounding confused.

"I've thought about your offer," I say, voice shaking with remnants of anger. "I'd like to take you up on it."

• Chapter 3 •

Arriving at Summit hurls me back in time. On Thursday afternoon, I swing open the front door in a daze, but no one else seems fazed by my entrance. Moms congregate in the windowed lobby, watching their children's practice. The office is still home to racks of leotards with matching scrunchies and warm-up shorts available for purchase. The entire building has the mingled scents of chalk and sweat. The only clues to the passage of time are the selection of photos hung in the front hall. There used to be a larger-than-life print of me at a competition with my signature in black Sharpie. It's gone now, and in its stead are a series of framed team portraits. I recognize a few of the faces—the younger siblings of the girls in my age group. The last time I saw these kids, they were seven or eight years old. Now they're teenagers.

When I enter the locker room, I feel the acute sense of no longer belonging. The narrow space is crawling with skinny kids who don't yet know that the scrunched cotton underwear hanging out the sides of their leotards makes them look like amateurs. The middle of the room is occupied by stacks of cubbies stuffed with gym bags, grips, sweatpants, and Uggs. My usual one is occupied, so I find an empty spot to store my socks and sneakers. I tighten my ponytail and steel myself to find Ryan in the main training area.

I open the glass door that separates waiting parents from the gymnasts and coaches and scan the gym for Ryan. The room is thick with memories. Everywhere I look, I flash back to younger versions of myself: six and crying because I just straddled the beam when I was supposed to land a cartwheel; twelve and high on the adrenaline rush of my first giant on bars; eighteen and prepping my floor routine for Nationals. I spot Ryan and a girl I assume to be Hallie sequestered on a stretch of mats by a mirror. They're conditioning—the full-body workout designed to build the strength necessary to perform. I used to do an hour a day of crunches, push-ups, squats, rope climbs, and more, just to stay in competitive shape. Ryan's in track pants and a T-shirt, holding a stopwatch as Hallie does V-ups with weights strapped to each ankle.

I call his name as I approach. He glances at me, then down at the stopwatch.

"Thirty more seconds, Hal," he says. She grunts in recognition and keeps working. "Welcome back, Avery," he says, giving a firm handshake.

"Thanks for having me," I say.

It's odd to see him all grown-up now, and I

wonder if he feels the same way about me. In some ways, of course, he looks exactly the same: chocolate-brown eyes, high cheekbones, a dimple in his left cheek, a thin scar over his right eyebrow, an impressively strong physique. But his thick, dark hair is longer on top—I guess he can wear it like that, now that he's no longer competing—and there's a smattering of stubble on his sharp jaw. Up close, I can see a colorful sliver of a tattoo peeking out from the sleeve of his T-shirt. *Of course.* He has the Olympic rings, just like his teammates do. Just like I would have, if things had gone differently.

"What do you think of being back here again?" he asks.

I take in the view of the gym, catching sight of coaches I recognize from way back when. "It's weird," I admit. "But this place feels like home."

"That's one of the reasons I thought you'd be perfect for the job," he says, clearly pleased that I feel the same way. "I want to take today slowly. Get to know each other. Have you meet Hallie. See how it goes."

"You know, I don't know if you and I have ever really hung out," I say. I feel like one of us has to note that this is our first proper conversation—we've always been in each other's orbit, but that doesn't mean we actually know each other.

"I'm pretty sure I asked you for directions to the vending machine at some competition once," he says, shrugging like he's just taking a vague stab at a memory.

But he's not. Because I remember it, too.

He's talking about Nationals the year I was sixteen, when the competition was held at an arena in Houston, Texas. The space was large and confusingly laid out; I must have walked in circles for five minutes on my way to finding the bathroom. I was returning from the women's restroom when I spotted Ryan—or Cute Ryan, as Jasmine and I called him. We had seen each other around at other competitions before, but hadn't ever spoken. Still, I was pretty confident that he recognized me.

"Hey, Avery—it's Avery, right?" he had asked.

I was secretly thrilled that he knew my name.

"Yeah," I said, trying not to blush.

I wanted to project the façade that hot guys spoke to me all the time. Totally normal. Yawn.

"Any chance you know which way the vending machines are? This place is like a maze," he said.

Luckily, I had just walked past them. I pointed him in the right direction. I won the gold all-around medal later that day, cementing my status as a gymnast to watch. But when I think back to that competition, what stands out is the twinkling, giddy adrenaline rush from Cute Ryan knowing my name.

All these years later, I feel vindicated, knowing that I'm not the only one who remembers the interaction.

"You know there's a machine in the lobby here, right?" I tease.

"Yeah, this one, I got covered," he shoots back.

The stopwatch beeps. "Done!" he calls to Hallie. She collapses on the mat. "Come over, I'll introduce you," Ryan says.

Hallie sits up, clutches her stomach for a moment, and undoes the Velcro straps securing her ankle weights. I'm sure that whatever set of reps she just completed was no joke, but she leaps to her feet. Her auburn ponytail swings over her broad shoulders. She's muscular and compact; the rippled outline of a six-pack is visible through the fuchsia Lycra of her leotard.

"Hallie, this is Avery. She's going to be coaching with me today," he explains. "Avery, Hallie."

She gives me a shy smile. "Hi. I'm sure you don't remember me, but I was a level four when you were training here. I remember you." She must have been one of the skinny kids running around in the locker room years ago.

"Oh, really? Wow," I say, unsure what else to add. Back then, I was so focused on my own training, I barely noticed the kids.

"Your poster was in the lobby," she recalls. "I wanted to be just like you someday." Instantly, her cheeks—already pink from exertion—flush red.

"Well, I'm sure you can aspire to loftier goals," I say.

"No, you were great," Ryan says confidently.

I don't want to tarnish his perception of my life since then, so I let the subject drop. "What are you working on?" I ask brightly.

"Finishing up conditioning," Ryan says. "We have fifteen minutes left. Then we'll move onto floor, cool?"

"Cool," Hallie and I say in unison.

Ryan alternates between leading Hallie through her remaining reps and filling me in on the situation. Hallie is sixteen now; he moved here to coach her three years ago, not long after he competed in Rio. The Olympics are the long-term goal, of course, but the next hurdle is the World Championships, held later this month in Stuttgart, Germany. She's very strong on bars and vault, and pretty solid on beam. But she's feeling less confident when it comes to floor. He wants me to watch her routine and see how I can help her polish it.

"Warm up your tumbling," he instructs Hallie, once she finishes conditioning.

She refills her water bottle, takes a slurp, then trots to one corner of the blue spring floor to practice her tumbling passes. She's diligent, efficient, and polite; she bounces in diagonal lines

51

from corner to corner, letting other, younger girls tumble across her in between passes while she catches her breath. The other gymnasts defer to her with an obvious sense of reverence. Hallie's skills are strong, and she moves with a powerful sense of energy. It's too powerful, in fact—at the end of each tumbling pass, she bobs and stumbles to control her motion.

Next, she warms up the other elements of her floor routine: leaps, jumps, pirouettes, smaller acrobatic elements. Here, I see why Ryan is concerned. She has talent in spades, but lacks poise. The one lesson coaches drill into gymnasts from the first lesson is to *always point your toes*. Hallie points hers—but not with the sharp lines or intense muscular focus that she should. Until you've felt your thighs quaking as your toes curl toward your heels, you haven't really pointed your toes.

The problem, I realize, is presentation. Her chin needs to be a fraction higher, her shoulders should pull back by two inches. Her posture is stiff and strong, lacking grace. She goes through the motions of each skill in a technically accurate way, but that's it. She's moving, not performing. If I could teach her how to do that, she could be a champion.

If. I don't know if I can. I don't know if anyone can. It's a lot of pressure.

"What do you think?" Ryan asks.

I get the sense he's been watching me take her in to gauge my reaction.

"She's good," I say truthfully. "Really good."

"But . . ." he prompts.

I hesitate. "She could be better," I admit.

He nods and silently watches his charge work. She squats with one leg extended, then winds up to perform a clunky pirouette with her foot maneuvering inches above the ground. It's an awkward spin—known as the wolf turn—but the Olympic code of points awards it an insanely high difficulty score, so almost every top gymnast attempts to squeeze it into their floor and beam routines these days. I'm glad the move wasn't in vogue when I was competing.

"How would you want to train her?" he asks.

"I'd want to see her perform a full routine first, just to get a better sense of where she's at," I say. "But already, I can say that she needs to focus on her performance. She's talented, and her skills are impressive, but she could look a lot more polished. And her tumbling needs to get under control—she needs to stick those landings."

Ryan nods in agreement, and that gives me the confidence to keep going.

"It all boils down to one problem, really," I explain. "She needs to be sharper. More in control. Clean lines, solid landings, more intentional movement—that's what's missing."

I pivot to face him, and I'm grateful to see a

bemused expression on his face. "Maybe you're right," he says. He calls out across the gym, "Hallie, ready to run a routine? Let's show Avery here what you can do."

Ryan connects his phone to a stereo system and calls for the other gymnasts to clear the floor. They scatter, giving Hallie a wide berth as she makes her way to a spot a few feet from one corner of the floor. She freezes into a pose with her left leg extended and her right arm above her head. Then, a tinkling flute leads into a sweeping piano melody, and her body comes alive. The structure of her routine is familiar: a few brief dance steps, an impressive tumbling pass, followed by a series of hastily executed acrobatic movements and artistic elements designed to propel her into a new corner of the floor, where she launches into another tumbling pass. The structure repeats again, giving her exactly ninety seconds to pack a lifetime's worth of training into a single performance.

There's no denying it—it's a good routine. But it's not the kind of show that brings home Olympic medals. Here, too, her posture is rigid; her motions seem rote and uninspired. The elegant music she's chosen doesn't fit her style at all.

"How long has she been competing with this routine?" I ask Ryan.

"It's changed a bit over the years, but basically,

she's been doing this for forever," he says.

I nod. "She needs an upgrade," I say.

"New music? New choreography?" he asks, looking concerned. "Now? With less than a year to go?" We both look back to the floor as Hallie lands her final tumbling pass, throws her arms into a dramatic flair, then sinks into her end pose. She holds it for a second, then flops down on her back, chest rising and falling hard with the intensity of her breath. Floor is an endurance test; the best gymnasts make it look effortless, but that's just an act.

"Yeah, now," I say. "This is okay, but it doesn't play to her strengths. And there's so much to refine. It could be better for her to start from scratch and learn something she loves, rather than beating a dead horse here."

Ryan grimaces and rolls his neck, letting the vertebrae crack. Reflexively, I rotate my wrists until they crunch and push each knuckle into a satisfying *pop*. The sport is brutal on our joints.

Hallie joins us by the stereo. She has her hands on her waist and she looks like she's trying not to appear out of breath.

"What'd you think?" she asks, biting her lip.

"Awesome," Ryan gushes. "Great height and rotation on the double Arabian; that's really come a long way. The wolf turn looks tighter today, too. Your left hip isn't dropping as much anymore."

His comments aren't the full picture. Of course

her double Arabian had fantastic height—she excels at tumbling, even the forward-rotating flips requiring superhuman power like that one—and she knows it. Her wolf turn was passable, but that's hardly the most pressing item to critique. I don't know Ryan well enough to determine if he's a softy or if he just lacks the gimlet eye necessary to pick apart the subtleties of a women's floor routine. But either way, he's shortchanging Hallie. He's letting her slide by without the grueling feedback she needs. If Dimitri ever saw this routine, Hallie would never hear the end of it.

"Avery? How did I do?" Hallie asks.

She radiates desperate energy; I can feel how badly she craves my approval. I was just like her once.

"That was very good," I say honestly, steeling myself to be straight with her. "But there's room for improvement, and I'd love to work with you."

Her jaw sets with disappointment. "Yeah?" she asks.

She shifts her weight onto one hip and crosses her arms across her chest. The muscular curves of her triceps jut out proudly, and for a split second, a wave of doubt washes over me. My triceps are soft and flabby. Seven years ago, sure, I could do what Hallie just did. I could do it better. But now? Who am I to tell this lean, powerful dynamo how to improve?

Hallie's hazel eyes narrow, and in them, I

recognize a self-conscious flicker. I see her swallow hard. If I'm guessing right, she's gifted, hardworking, but anxious. I bet she knows her natural talent and ambition can only take her so far. Ryan knows it, too. That's why I'm here. In my experience, a coach can't only be your friend—they have to push you, too. Ryan doesn't seem like the type to zero in on a gymnast's insecurities and manipulate them into motivation, the way Dimitri did. But if he's an effective coach on bars, beam, and vault, then maybe I could be the bad cop on floor. Gymnastics is classified as an individual sport, but it's not really. No gymnast can succeed without a coach shaping them into the best version of themselves.

"Yeah," I say, straightening up to my full height.

I take a deep breath and try to plaster on the front of calm confidence I used to wear in competitions. I'm out of practice.

"Don't get me wrong, you're incredible," I say. I explain what I've already told Ryan. "But your execution is sloppy and rushed. Your landings aren't clean. Your posture is stiff. Your toes aren't even one hundred percent pointed."

"I *point* my *toes*," she fires back. "I'm not a baby."

I'm stunned into silence. If I had given Dimitri so much sass, I would've suffered through an extra hour of conditioning alone.

"You have the skills of an Olympian, but you don't look like one," I sum up. I sound cold, but I don't care. She needs to hear it. "I'm being straight with you because I know how hard you've worked for god knows how many years, and I don't want that to be a waste. You have a shot. Let me help you get there."

She gapes a little and turns to Ryan. He shrugs and juts his chin out at me.

"Show her what you mean," he says. "Go ahead."

I think for a moment. I could run through feet stretches until she learned what it *really* means to point her toes, but that feels low-impact, unimpressive, and possibly a sore spot. Instead, I tell her to follow me to a mirrored wall along one side of the floor.

"Show me the very beginning of your routine," I instruct. "Just the dance elements before your first tumbling pass."

She gets into position, pauses, then launches into motion. Her arms swing, her legs bend, her head tilts. She pivots and shimmies into place. The entire thing takes five seconds. When she's done, she looks up at me with a flat, expectant look.

"Okay, no," I say. "The start of your routine is where you draw people in. It's an opportunity to showcase what you've got—not a time to rush through a few steps of choreography before getting to the big, flashy stuff. Instead of that, it could be this."

I copy her movements, but amp them up. Each arm movement ends in a sharp flick of my fingers. Each step is taken with perfectly pointed toes. I pivot with a dramatic bump of my hip. As I spin, I catch my reflection in the mirror, and feel another crashing wave of nostalgia.

"See? Your turn."

She resumes her position, then dives into the first step.

"No," I say, cutting her off.

I squat down next to her and push her foot into the arched position it needs to be. Her ankle stiffens at first, then reluctantly turns to putty.

"Like that," I say. "That's your first step. It's not just about moving your foot from point A to point B—it's about creating an intentional shape. Dance can be powerful, too."

"Like this?" she asks, rocking back and forth from her initial pose into the step.

She watches herself in the mirror and bends her knee experimentally.

"That's better," I say. "Again, from the top."

We work like this for ten minutes, dissecting each step of choreography until she understands exactly when and how to move each muscle in her body. I bet she'd rather be practicing a new skill or drilling tumbling passes until she can stick one perfectly, but she lets me train her.

When I demonstrate a move for her, she studies me carefully. And when she regurgitates the choreography back at me, she attacks it with new energy. As she hones in on the right motions, she looks closer and closer to the way I would've performed this choreography when I was her age. It breaks my heart. But it's not my time anymore. The only way I can belong to elite gymnastics now is like this, as a mentor.

Ryan had been watching quietly from the side-lines, but now he steps in with a suggestion. "Try the whole routine again," he says. "Throw all that in there."

I'm skeptical—you don't relearn how to move your entire body after just ten minutes of instruction. You can't simply "throw all that in there" and expect real change. But Hallie takes her usual place on the floor and winds up for another routine.

When the opening notes of her music ring out, she flies into action. The first few steps of choreography are sharper now, but soon enough, her poise falters. Her shoulders slump forward, her chin drops, her toes go slack.

"Hip!" Ryan roars over the music, as she sinks down into a wolf turn.

In response, her body flinches into position. She pulls off the turn well and bounds into the home stretch. When the routine is finished, she walks back to us, panting.

"Better?" she asks.

"The beginning was much better," I admit.

"Looks great," Ryan says.

I wait for him to give her notes on the rest of her lackluster routine, but he doesn't. Instead, he claps her on the shoulder. This gymnast-coach dynamic is one hundred and eighty degrees opposite from what I was raised on—I'm not sure I understand it.

"Let's break on this for now. Grab your grips, and meet me at bars in five," he instructs.

" 'Kay. Thanks, Avery! This was cool," she says, giving me an exhilarated high five.

It's not my place to argue coaching strategy in front of her. Ryan and I watch as she scampers away toward the locker room.

"Nice work today," Ryan says, turning toward me and shoving his hands in his pockets. "Thanks for coming in."

He catches me off guard. I didn't realize I'd be dismissed so quickly.

"Oh, that's it? That's— Oh. Thanks for having me."

He nods at the door leading out toward the lobby. "I'll walk you out," he says.

My chest tightens at the prospect of leaving behind this musty haven of adrenaline and ambition. I don't want to *leave*—I want to dangle from the bars, tiptoe across beam, and launch myself eight feet high above the white trampoline.

"So, I'll see you tomorrow?" I ask awkwardly. My cheeks flush.

His eyes stay glued to the floor. "I, uh, I don't know. To be honest, I'm interviewing another coach, too. We'll see how things go."

"Who?" I spit out.

"Does it matter?" he asks. He hesitates, then adds, "She wasn't ever at your level herself, but she has a decade more coaching experience than you do. I think she could be good for Hallie."

"I really feel like I can make a big difference here," I insist, pushing past the insistent lump that's beginning to form in my throat. "I know I can."

He doesn't respond. This is humiliating. I'm surprised at how bold I am with him, but I have nothing left to lose. I'm lucky enough that this gig fell into my lap; finding another one that would make me feel even a fraction as excited as I'd be coaching at Summit doesn't seem possible.

We're at the door now. Ryan places his hand on the handle. Parents lined up in gray plastic folding chairs peer at us through the waiting area window. Their passive boredom in Lululemon leggings and zip-ups is so familiar to me.

"Avery, I like you. I respect you. I want to be honest with you—I don't know if this is going to work," he says apologetically. "Worlds is so close, and then there are just a few more months until the Olympics. I don't know if your approach is the right one. I think she needs to polish what's she's got—not start over."

A mental image appears in a flash: me slipping underwater, slumped on the couch in my parents' basement, with nothing to look forward to tomorrow or the next day or any day at all. I don't have to imagine it; I know it intimately. This gym is the only place I've ever felt truly at home; this job feels like it should be mine. I can't fathom Ryan giving it to anyone else. But I don't know how to succinctly explain the territorial greed I feel for this coaching gig and how badly I need it without sounding desperate.

Ryan opens the door handle, and I mutter "Thanks" as I propel myself through the waiting area, down the hallway, and into the locker room, where Summit gymnasts who aren't quite good enough have always gone to break down into silent tears.

NOVEMBER
2019

• Chapter 4 •

A familiar voice blares from the TV. I crunch an apple noisily between my teeth to block out the sound. My parents are sprawled out on the couch in the living room with their feet kicked up on the ottoman, passing a single glass of red wine between them as they watch the World Championships on TV.

"Hon, you're sure you don't want to watch with us?" Mom calls from the room next door.

"It's Jasmine!" Dad adds. "She's doing great."

I groan.

"I'm fine in here!" I call back.

Jasmine has been a regular commentator for televised gymnastics competitions since the last Olympics. As jealous as I am, she does a fantastic job. Her deep knowledge of the sport, status as a household name, and pretty features make for good television.

It's been two weeks. Ryan never called. I assume he must have gone with the other coach. I bet the coach is even there with Ryan and Hallie in Stuttgart right now. Truly, I can't imagine a worse evening than watching a person who knocked me out of the running for a job while listening to commentary that—had life gone differently—I could be delivering instead.

I chomp on another bite of apple while swiping left on three more dating app profiles. I haven't been out with anyone since my Jade Castle date with Lucas. In fact, I've barely done anything at all. I've half-heartedly cobbled together a résumé and scanned job boards. I know I can't coast like this for much longer—my bank account is running low—but I can't get the thought of the Summit job out of my head. Nothing else compares. I've been slightly more proactive on the dating front; I have a handful of conversations going with different guys, though honestly, I'm too wary to meet up with any of them. Another profile pops up.

Cali > Mass, the profile reads. *Love football, hockey, and 420.*

I flick disinterestedly through the guy's photos, if only because we've made the same geographic move. In his third photo, he's wearing a Rams jersey with Tyler's name stamped across it. I swipe left and, in a fit of frustration, delete the dating app from my phone.

"Ave, you gotta come in here!" Mom shouts. "That girl from Summit is coming up next."

"And this coach, remind me, what's his name?" Dad asks.

I won't get any peace in here.

"Coming!" I shout back finally.

I trudge into the living room and perch on the arm of the couch. There's a glare on the TV from the overhead lights reflecting off the trophy case along one wall. I've told my parents to move them. Jasmine and a decorated male gymnast from the '90s are on-screen. In some ways, she looks the same: her eyes still sparkle with a hint of the glittery eyeliner she's always loved, and her warm, brown skin pops against a tight, long-sleeved, magenta top that looks vaguely reminiscent of a leotard. But now, dolled up for the cameras, she's wearing bright lipstick that matches her outfit, and her hair is smooth.

A banner running across the bottom of the screen lists the commentators' names: Barry McGuire and Jasmine Floyd-Federov. I always forget she works under her hyphenated married name. That was the other thing that happened during my downward spiral in LA: Jasmine and Dimitri. They got *together*. The news felt like the most violent hangover of my life. I turned down the invitation to their wedding, citing a family reunion that same weekend. It was a lie.

Nothing about it feels real. For starters, he's more than twenty years our senior. He called us each "girl" interchangeably, like it would've been too much effort to learn or use our names. And between me and Jasmine, he was always harder on her. When he mocked my vault, chided me for running like a girl, and made me do laps around the gym with weights strapped to my ankles, I could get through it. I knew his next compliment was just one good routine around the corner. But when Jasmine wobbled through a beam routine and he screamed that she was a "sloppy cow," everyone knew that he really meant it. His abrasive demeanor, stormy mood swings, cruel nicknames, and outsized punishments were intended to mold us into champions, but they left me with pure distaste for him. I can't fathom how Jasmine survived all that and could stomach marrying him. If we were still friends, maybe I could ask her. Maybe I'd see a different side to him. But my chance is long gone.

"Now, Hallie always has very strong showings on vault and bars, and today was no exception. Her beam routine was fairly decent, but floor hasn't historically been her strength," Jasmine explains. Her tone is authoritative but sympathetic—she knows exactly how it feels to be the underdog.

Barry tuts in agreement, launching into a list of her floor scores from the past year.

"But I hear she's been training hard on floor recently, so let's see how she does," Jasmine adds diplomatically.

She tucks her hair behind her ear, and I catch a flash of a diamond ring glinting on her left hand. I just can't fathom how or why she's with Dimitri. I certainly can't imagine her *loving* him.

The camera pans to Hallie lingering by the edge of the floor, awaiting her turn. She rolls her toes under her foot, bites her lip, and tugs on her ponytail to tighten it up. She's alone. Jasmine and I at least always had each other. Before every competition performance, we'd huddle up, arms looped around each other's shoulders. We'd chant something encouraging, like, "We got this," or, "You're gonna nail it." It made us feel confident, centered. And as we approached each performance, we'd call out the same singsongy chant for each other: "Let's go, Avery, let's go!" *Clap, clap.* "Let's go, Jasmine, let's go!" *Clap, clap.*

A high-pitched beep rings out across the arena, indicating that Hallie is permitted to start. She strides to her spot on the floor, settles into position, and waits for her music to begin. I watch carefully as she hits the opening steps of choreography. Her movements aren't quite as elegant as they should be, but at least her chin is lifted proudly and her toes reach toward a sharp point. Her first tumbling pass is sky-high, but there's too much power in her landing; she bobbles out of place, and then out of bounds. She takes three separate steps as she winces and struggles to slow her inertia. Not good.

Mom and Dad gasp and squint. Old habits die hard—they still get anxious and overly invested, even as unattached bystanders, rather than parents with skin in the game.

"Three steps, that's a three-tenths deduction," Jasmine notes.

Hallie slides down into a one-legged squat to wind up for her wolf turn, looking determined. She pushes off the ground into a hasty spin, but her left hip drops like usual, and her left heel drags across the floor—another deduction.

"Oof!" Barry says. "She's struggling."

Duh. I really could do better commentary than this.

I feel a prick of pain in my hand, and realize I'm biting my knuckle out of nerves. It's tough to watch her sloppy execution and stiff style while powerless, stuck here in my parents' musty living room.

Hallie drags herself through the rest of the routine and sheepishly salutes the judges before trotting off the floor. Ryan wraps his arm around her shoulders and walks with her quickly away from the cameras. He's muttering something under his breath.

"So, that routine probably knocks Hallie off the podium for all-around, but she still has a shot at medaling on individual events," Barry says.

"Let's go back to that gorgeous double Arabian, though," Jasmine suggests.

Sure enough, the channel plays back that impressive tumbling run. Jasmine walks the viewer through exactly what makes it so special to fill the time as the judges deliberate on Hallie's score. When it finally arrives—12.475—Hallie furrows her brow and looks away, dejected.

I feel myself tunneling back in time to every shaky routine I performed at a competition. I remember the raw horror that seized my nerves, the way my frenzied brain taunted me on a loop—*You're never going to make it. Just give up now.* Failure is inevitable in this sport; it happens to everyone at some point. But there's no room for failure, not if you want to make the Olympics. Not if you want to win. The paradox is crushing.

"Poor girl," Dad says. "She's talented, but that routine didn't do her any favors. What'd you think of her?"

I sigh and slide off the couch. "I think I'd do a better job coaching her than whoever Ryan hired."

I know Hallie and Ryan won't stay in Stuttgart for long. There are just eight precious months to go until Olympic Trials—no time for a European vacation. I figure they'll travel home on Sunday and start practice again on Monday. I give myself one extra day, just to be sure, and on Tuesday night, I drive to Summit. I back into a parking spot under a maple tree and stay in the driver's seat so I can watch the last few gymnasts stream out the front door. They have pink cheeks and messy buns, with bare legs stuffed into Uggs. I listen to Kiss 108, the Top 40 station, as I wait for Hallie to emerge.

I dressed carefully tonight: no-nonsense black

leggings and white sneakers paired with the red, white, and blue hoodie every member of the US elite women's gymnastics team received during training in 2011. The once-bright cotton has faded, but my name is still embroidered on the sleeve—proof that I once belonged.

Sure enough, Hallie trudges out of the gym with a phone in one hand and an electric yellow bottle of Gatorade in another. A navy canvas gym bag hangs from one shoulder. She spots what must be her dad's car and makes her way toward it. I dip my head and pretend to fiddle with the radio dial; I don't think she sees me. Once she's buckled up and her dad has pulled out of the parking lot, I get out of my car and walk toward the gym before I can lose my nerve. It's dark, and a chill nips at my ankles.

Inside Summit, the fluorescent lights are still on in the lobby, but the parents have all cleared out. I take a deep breath and venture around the corner to the office. For a split second, the cozy familiarity of the charcoal-gray-flecked carpet and the neat rows of paper schedules thumbtacked to the wall make me slip back in time. I could be here to give Winnie my parents' check for the quarter, or to kill time before practice by flicking through rows of plush velvet and slick Lycra leotards. But it's late. Winnie's gone home for the night. Instead, Ryan is hunched behind the desk, one fist clenched tightly in his hair, the other propping up an iPhone, the sound turned all the way up.

"Yes!" he whispers. "*Yes!* No!"

Then, sensing my presence, he snaps his head up.

I give a belated knock on the door frame.

"Hi. Can I come in?" I ask.

He gives his phone screen a pained glance, then pauses the video he's watching.

"I wasn't expecting you," he says.

"I know."

I take a couple of hesitant steps toward him. There's nowhere convenient to sit, so I hover a few feet from the desk.

"Watching anything good?" I ask, nodding toward his phone.

"Football," he says, tapping the screen. "You a fan?"

"Not really," I say.

"I'm watching the Rams slaughter the Giants," he explains. "They have this quarterback—"

"Yeah, I know about their quarterback," I say curtly, cutting him off.

This feels like a sign that I shouldn't even be here at all. I wonder what Tyler would think if he knew I was returning to the gym to beg for a job. He'd probably nod encouragingly with puppy-dog eyes, like, *That's great, Ave!* and then go throw a winning pass or whatever. I clear my throat.

"I was hoping you'd be here tonight," I begin. "I watched Worlds, I saw Hallie . . . and Ryan, she's so close. She has so much potential, but she's not quite solid enough. I know she can do better. You know it, too—that's why you were looking for a new coach in the first place."

"Worlds was tough for her," he admits, looking away.

"Look, I don't even know who you hired. It's nothing personal. But watching her flounder like that on floor? It was painful."

"And you think you can do better?" he asks.

I nod. "I really respect you, Ryan. You're doing an amazing job with her. But she needs extra help on floor. Remember how quickly she picked up what I was teaching? What if we could do that every day? Just imagine how much we could accomplish together, you and me and her."

My heart is racing. Everything rests on his reaction. Ryan leans forward onto the desk and rests his chin on his interlaced knuckles. For a moment, he doesn't speak.

Then finally, he says, "It didn't work out."

"The other coach?" I ask.

He shakes his head. "Svetlana Morozova. You know her?"

"The name rings a bell," I say.

"Russian. She's, like, sixty, super old-school. She and Hallie didn't really click."

"Oh."

He lifts one dark eyebrow. "She likes you, though."

"I like her, too. I get her. I mean, I think I do," I admit.

"She kinda reminds me of you, way back when," he says. "Super determined, ambitious, follows every rule."

I laugh; I had no idea he knew me well enough to think of me in any particular way, much less like that. I could volley back a joke about how *that* didn't last so long, but it feels too sad, given the reason I spiraled out of control.

"She sounds easy to coach, then," I offer instead.

Ryan nods wordlessly. He holds my gaze for a beat longer than is comfortable. I want the job so badly.

"I can do it," I blurt out. "I was in Hallie's exact shoes seven years ago. I know what she's going through. I know how to take her to the next level. Floor was my thing—it's what I did better than almost anyone else in the world."

"I remember," he says, leaning back in his spinning chair and kicking his sneakers up onto the desk.

"If I trained Hallie, I'd go back to basics and focus on her poise and her posture. I'd find her new music and give her new choreography that plays to her strengths."

Pitching my plan to Ryan reminds me exactly

how deeply I need this job. I'm on the verge of choking up, but I take a deep breath and force myself to hold it together.

"She's gonna shine—I know it. Just . . . please. Give me a chance."

Ryan runs a hand along his stubbled jaw and squints at me. I feel too exposed now; I curl my fingers around the sleeves of my hoodie and fold my arms tightly across my chest.

"I'll talk to Hallie's parents," he says finally. "If they sign off on you working with her, then the job will be yours."

I'm grinning so hard, my cheeks hurt. "Thank you," I say.

The gravity of Ryan's decision fills me with a giddy sort of delight; my mind glosses right over the fact that the Conway family has to approve of me first and skips straight toward a blur of practice, choreography, and chalk dust. I throw my arms around Ryan in a hug, and to my surprise, he actually hugs back. He promises he'll let me know when he's had a chance to speak with Hallie's parents. When I exit the gym, I don't even feel the crisp night air. I feel the way I felt about leaving practice a decade ago: pink-cheeked, high on adrenaline, blood running hot.

As I cross the parking lot, I feel this primal urge to cartwheel across the smooth pavement. I turn to check over both shoulders before letting my arms stretch down and my feet pinwheel over the top of my head. I feel weightless when I sink into the driver's seat of the car and turn up the radio. It's late, and the roads home are empty at this time of night. I wish I had somewhere to go or someone to tell about my exciting news, but my only real option is home. I drive a little faster than I should, and for the first time, the glittering green traffic lights in the town center and the dark pine trees along the back roads feel like exhilarating markers of what could be my new life, not dull reminders of my old one.

The house is quiet when I walk in. Mom's probably watching TV in bed, and Dad is probably reading in his office. I slump down on the couch in the living room, feeling restless but unsure what to do. That old life-sized cardboard cutout of me in a leotard is propped up against the mantel. There are visible shadows marking each individual ab and the muscular curve of my thighs, but even so, I'm slender and lithe. The cardboard version of me has one hand on my tight waist and the other casually holding the gold medal dangling from my neck. I don't want that old image of myself haunting me anymore. I get up from the couch and fold the cardboard stand in the back into the cutout. I pick it up and see a soft gray coat of dust on the floor. I carry the cutout to the garage and prop it up by the recycling bins, facing the wall. Then I grab the vacuum from the front hall closet and suck up a decade's worth of dust bunnies. I'm glad to see them go.

• *Chapter 5* •

Two days later, Ryan arranges a meeting with Kim, Todd, and Hallie Conway before practice. I want Hallie to like me, of course, but I've already done my best to win her over. Now, it's crucial that I can convince Kim and Todd to trust me with their daughter's career. My nerves jangle with anticipation as I slog through rush-hour traffic in the town center. I used to dread being up this early, but today I'm wide-awake. This morning will make or break me.

Summit is still sleepy when I arrive. The practice space is empty; the fluorescent lights are off; there's no hum of Top 40 radio over the sounds of creaking bars and coaches' shouts. I meet Ryan and the Conway family in the office. Walking into that room makes my heart pound; I wish I had more professional experience to bolster my confidence.

"Hi, it's so nice to meet you," Kim says warmly, reaching to shake my hand.

She has bangs brushed across her forehead, and she's dressed casually in jeans and a faded, oversized button-down. I wonder if she still works, or if—like so many moms at this level—she quit her job to support her daughter's gymnastics career.

"Hi," Todd says, extending his hand, too.

Like his wife, he looks as if he's in his midforties. He's in a charcoal-gray suit, like he's heading straight to some office job after this meeting. Hallie gets her square face and hazel eyes from him.

I take the open seat between Ryan and Hallie.

"I'm sure you don't remember us, but I remember watching you train here years ago," Kim says.

"Oh, really?" I say, flustered.

"You were a beautiful gymnast," she says. "Really incredible to watch."

"Thank you," I say.

Kim's sunny demeanor turns slightly strained. She glances at her husband and continues, "Don't get me wrong, I'm excited to see that you're so passionate about helping Hallie here, but I also do want to know for sure that you're one hundred percent qualified to get her through 2020."

Hallie slumps back in her chair, like she's heard this complaint one too many times.

"Mom, I need help on floor," she mutters.

Todd clears his throat. "We'd like to hear more about your experience as a coach."

"It's not that we don't trust you," Kim rushes to add. "It's just, you know, Trials are only eight months away, and this is a once-in-a-lifetime shot."

"Of course, I understand," I say.

Families make enormous, life-changing sacrifices to give their kids a chance in this sport, and I don't fault them for wanting nothing less than the best for their daughter. Otherwise, those sacrifices aren't worth it.

"Hallie's sixteen now, and if we wait another four years, she'll be . . ." Kim makes a helpless gesture with her hands.

"Maybe too old," I offer.

"Twenty's not *old,*" Hallie groans.

"In this sport? Honey, it's a long shot," Kim says, ruffling a hand through her bangs.

"Do you want to try for 2024?" I ask.

"That'll be where, Paris?" Todd asks.

Ryan nods.

"Of course!" Hallie says. "And then after that, college, maybe law school, who knows?"

It's impressive that she has the next dozen years of her life mapped out, but I'm not surprised. Since childhood, her entire life has revolved around a singular, far-off goal.

"But 2020 is your best shot," Kim reminds her gently. "And the Olympic team will be smaller and more selective than ever before."

She's right. In 1996, the US gymnastics delegation included seven athletes, nicknamed the Magnificent Seven. But the rules have changed over time. By 2012, the year I tried to make the Olympics, only five gymnasts competed, known as the Fierce Five. Another five girls, the Final

Five, competed at the 2016 Olympics, but by that point, the Worldwide Organization of Gymnastics had already ruled that team sizes would dwindle to four spots each in 2020. Making the Olympic team this year will be harder than ever before.

"I'm very confident in Avery's abilities," Ryan says smoothly. "I wouldn't bring her in if she wasn't right for Hallie."

"Pardon my saying so, but that's exactly what happened last month," Todd counters.

I have a flash of Hallie's disastrous floor routine at Worlds.

"Mr. and Mrs. Conway . . ." I begin.

"Please, call us Kim and Todd," she offers.

I take a deep breath to steady my voice. "Kim and Todd, I coached gymnastics while living in LA, and before that, I was the top gymnast in America when I was Hallie's age. Barring an injury, I would've made the Olympics, and I don't mean to brag, but I would've medaled on floor. I know floor. I've watched your daughter perform, and I have a good grasp on how to help her improve."

They lean forward hungrily. As much as Hallie has her eyes set on the Olympics, so do they—maybe even more so.

"I'd like to choreograph a new routine for Hallie, one that plays to her strengths," I explain. "It sounds like she's been performing the same routine for years, and it isn't serving her well anymore. Once she learns the new routine, it'll be a matter of finessing her performance: we'll work on controlling that extra power she gets on her tumbling passes, sticking the landings, moving with more poise and better posture, and polishing her dance elements. Her skills are all there. But her execution could be more graceful and dynamic, and that's where I can help."

Todd sits back in his seat. Kim bites her lip. They look at each other.

"Hmm," Kim says.

I can't tell yet if they're fully convinced.

"If you're able to find another floor specialist who can work well with Hallie with just eight months to go until Trials, by all means, please do," I say. "But more than anyone else out there right now, I get exactly what Hallie is going through and I know how to help her. So, please. Let me help your daughter."

Todd rubs his jaw. Kim swallows. I feel the same way I did during competitions, back when I had finished a routine I felt unsure about and had to wait torturous minutes for the judges to reveal my score.

"Mom, Dad, I really need help," Hallie adds. "Come on."

Her parents exchange glances.

"You really want this?" Todd asks.

She throws her arms up, exasperated. "I don't have time to waste. I'm going to go warm up."

Hallie heads to the locker room to drop off her bag.

"Let's give this a shot," Ryan says. "Trust me."

Kim sighs. "All right, but if the new routine doesn't come together soon . . . we'll have to have another conversation about what's next."

Todd gets up, closes the button on his suit jacket, then shakes hands with Ryan and me again.

"Let's make this work," he says.

I can't tell if that's a promise or a threat.

Kim and Todd leave, and Hallie and Ryan enter the gym. I tell them I'll join in just a minute, and make it to the bathroom just in time. Locked in a stall, I slump against the cool white tile wall, clap a hand over my mouth to muffle my sobs, and break down silently. I've never felt such intense relief in my life. I felt aimless in LA and completely lost back in Greenwood; once I had my heart set on this job, nothing else remotely measured up. I can't believe it's mine. The tears come in hot and fast. My shoulders shake. There is still so much of my life to figure out—I can't live in my childhood bedroom forever, and the loneliness I'm facing in the wake of my breakup is awfully isolating—but this is a start. This is good. I will be okay.

After wiping away my tears, I find Hallie warming up on floor, running through the same rote cardio exercises and stretches every gymnast has burned into their memory. Ryan flicks on the lights and the radio for her, then joins me to watch on the sidelines. I'm still buzzing with adrenaline.

"Nice speech in there," he says, clapping me on the shoulder. "You're good under pressure."

All gymnasts are.

"Thanks," I say.

"Her parents aren't really so bad," he says. "Todd's a little intense, but he just wants the best for her. They both do. Kim used to work in marketing, but now volunteers part-time at the library so she can mostly be around for Hallie."

Ryan pulls a three-ring binder from the shelf under the stereo. "I have her training mapped out for the next eight months, but I want to get your take on it," he says, taking a seat on the floor. "Sit. Let's look at this together while she finishes up."

We sit side by side. I try not to notice the way his white T-shirt stretches across his broad chest, though it's not easy. He flips through the stuffed binder, showing me the Code of Points, which assigns a different level of difficulty to each skill and changes every three years; a practice schedule; a list of goals; Hallie's emergency contacts and list of doctors. He finds the calendar section, outlined with what he and Hallie will be working on every month until Trials. It's crammed with his spiky handwriting—notes to himself.

"When it comes to vault, she's solid. She does an Amanar and a Mustafina," he explains.

Those are two of the most difficult vaults in the world, both named after the first gymnast to perform each, as is the sport's custom. The Amanar is a round-off, back handspring onto the board, with a two-and-a-half twisting back layout off, while the Mustafina is a round-off and half turn onto the board with a full-twisting front layout off.

"Her right ankle bothers her sometimes, so we've mostly been drilling them into the pit these days," Ryan continues. "I don't want to push her too hard on the landings. But the thing is, she gets a ton of power off the board, so she has a tough time sticking it. So one thing we're focusing on is keeping her ankle strong, so we can get those landings in consistently good shape."

"Got it. I'll be careful about her ankle."

"On bars, her routine is already excellent, but I'd like to upgrade it over the next few months," he says. "Like, right now, she does a Tkatchev into a giant into a Pak Salto, but she could cut the giant."

It's been a long time since I've spoken the language of gymnastics, and I'm relieved that it all comes flooding back: the Tkatchev involves flinging yourself up and over the high bar backward in a straddle position; a giant means swinging around the bar in a full circle with body outstretched; a Pak Salto is when you swing off the high bar, arch into an elegant back flip, and catch the low bar.

"Which means a higher difficulty value," I say, mentally mapping out the combination in my head.

Because the Tkatchev and the Pak Salto are both release moves, Hallie would earn more points for connecting them back-to-back, rather than separating them with a giant, which is considered an easier (and less risky) move.

"Exactly. We'll play around with it. And we're working on some other cool stuff. Have you ever heard of a Seitz?"

"Maybe?" I cock my head. I've been out of this world for a long time.

His eyes sparkle. "It's a transition move. Imagine a toe-on circle on the low bar with a full twist to catch the high bar."

"Wow."

"Yeah, *wow*," he says, exhaling. "That's our girl. We just gotta get her the recognition she deserves.

"She's not bad on beam. Her acrobatic skills are all there—a back handspring, back whip, back layout combo you could die for, a solid front aerial. But there are places she could tighten up, like that goddamn wolf turn."

"She does that on beam, too?"

"The way the Code of Points is these days, you basically have to. She does hers as a double, but I'm hoping we can get it to a two and a half."

"That'll be tough."

"Right." He closes the binder and drums his fingers on the cover. "And then there's floor. That's in your hands now."

"Thanks for letting me do this," I say.

Ryan smirks and taps on the binder again. "I mean, you gotta come up with a *plan*," he says.

I already know I want to choreograph a new floor routine for her, and that includes selecting new music for her to perform to. I know the rest will come in time.

The next hour of Hallie's workout slips away— for me, at least. I can tell *she* works hard. She doesn't skimp on tough ab work or mind-numbing reps, like some kids do. On the contrary, I get the sense she deepens her squats and tightens up her plank form when she notices me watching. I'm honored she considers me worthy enough to impress. When she's finished with conditioning, she takes a water break, then meets Ryan and me on floor. She places her hands on her hips and looks from him to me, waiting for instructions.

"I'm all yours," she says. "Put me to work."

"Trust me, I will," I say. "But first, we should talk."

I'm nervous, but know I have to drop the bomb anyway.

"Hear me out on this: your floor routine is good, but it doesn't play to your strengths. I would love to create a new routine for you—mostly the same tumbling, but new dance, new music, maybe some new skills."

She flinches and recoils, crossing her arms over her chest. "But—but we—there are—we have just eight months to go," she sputters.

"So why waste those months on a routine that's not working?" I shoot back.

"I've been using this routine forever. You want me to throw it away now? I'll never learn a new one in time."

"Of course you will. I see how hard you work. You got this."

"I'll be rushed, I'll forget the choreography, I'll mess it up—probably *in* competition, and then I'll fail out of gymnastics without even a high school diploma and I'll be stuck living at home with my parents forever."

I'm sure it's just a flippant comment, but the cruel reality of her words cuts me deep.

"Hallie . . ." Ryan admonishes.

"There's no need to be so dramatic," I say, breezing past her insult. "Please just trust me with this."

"I'm on board," Ryan tells her.

She bites her lip. For a moment, she's quiet, considering the prospect.

"Okay," she says finally. "Then so am I."

I pick up the binder and rifle through it until I find the section that lists every floor skill with value in the Code of Points. To test her capabilities, I rattle off different acrobatic and artistic elements and ask her to perform them, starting with tumbling. Her double Arabian is fantastic, but her triple twist isn't doing her any favors—that tumbling pass might work better as a double-twisting double back layout. Hallie diligently follows my instructions and swivels to gauge my level of approval after each tumbling pass—so she's sassy but ultimately obedient. I can work with that.

Fifteen minutes in, I notice her grimace and roll her right foot carefully from side to side.

"Ryan, hey," I say, catching his attention. He looks up from his phone. "It looks like her ankle is bothering her."

"Yeah, let's take a break," he says.

"Hey, hey, Hallie, stop," I call. "How's your ankle?"

She winces. "It's starting to hurt again," she admits. "It's really not that bad, though, promise. I'll keep going."

"No, let's rest for a sec. I'm going to grab you some ice, okay?"

She exhales, clearly frustrated with herself. "Fine. Thanks."

I retrieve an ice pack from the cooler and wrap it in a paper towel so it doesn't freeze-burn her skin. By the time I make it back to the floor, Ryan is already wrapping up her ankle with gauzy prewrap and white athletic tape to keep the joint stable.

"Thanks for the ice," Hallie says glumly.

"How long has this been going on?" I ask.

She sighs. "On and off for, like, two years."

"I think it's time to see that sports medicine doctor again," Ryan says.

"Dr. Kaminsky?" Hallie asks.

"Yeah."

She makes a face. "I'm fine."

Every gymnast racks up injuries like these, but they're nearly impossible to heal while actively training for competition. I pushed through my stress fracture at fourteen and wound up with back pain that flares up for weeks at a time, even more than a decade later. I sometimes wonder: if I could go back in time and make different choices, would I avoid a lifetime of pain? Even in my worst moments, I don't think I would. As debilitating as the flare-ups can be, what I gained from gymnastics—identity, discipline, commitment—is worth so much more. But just because I've made peace with that choice doesn't mean that Hallie needs to.

"A doctor might be able to really help," I say. "Why don't you go just once, just to check in?"

She juts out her chin like she's going to protest, but Ryan's reaction stops her.

"Hal, you don't want to mess around with an injury this year. Be smart about this."

"Fine. I'll go."

"Let's take it easy today," Ryan says. "After your break, we'll do bars. No dismounts, nothing crazy, just to play it safe."

She pouts. "But that's such a waste of a training day."

An idea hits me. "What about this—while you ice your ankle, why don't we listen to new floor music? Pick something out?"

Ryan backs me up, and Hallie reluctantly agrees. He steps out to grab some coffee, promising to be back in just a few minutes. This is the first time that Hallie and I have ever been alone, and I want to make the most of it. I need to get on her good side—and right now, that means finding the perfect song.

Floor music needs to be exactly ninety seconds long and contain no lyrics, so you can't use just anything. I start by rifling through the collection of CDs and cassette tapes still stacked under the stereo, but these have all been here since before even I was a gymnast. When my search turns up nothing fresh or interesting, I pull out my phone and Google new options.

"We need something powerful, something fun," I say, scrolling through a list of song titles. "Nothing dainty, nothing boring."

"Maybe . . . jazz?" Hallie asks. She looks up at me nervously.

"You like jazz?" I ask.

She shrugs. "Yeah, it seems fun to perform to."

"Jazz!" I practically yelp. "Let's find you something. You need something you'll *enjoy,* whatever that is."

For the next fifteen minutes, we listen to snippets of songs and debate their merits. When we land on a track packed with energetic trumpets, we know we've got it right. It's a big band number called "Jazz Fling." Hallie bops her head along to the melody. When Ryan returns, I play it back for him and watch his expression.

"You like it?" I ask hopefully.

He gives a bemused smile. "On floor, I defer to you. Do *you* like it?"

This is my first big decision as a coach. The right song can make or break a routine. I know the upbeat tempo and playful sound are a strong match for the powerful physicality of Hallie's movements. She has just enough bravado to pull it off.

"I do. Let's do it."

At noon, Kim returns to the gym to pick up her daughter for her midday break for lunch and homeschooling before she comes back for a second practice. It's completely unnecessary for Kim to actually walk into the gym and chat with us; Hallie could easily head out into the parking lot on her own. I get the sense that she's probing to see how well I'm doing. She instantly notices Hallie's taped ankle.

"What's going on here?" she asks.

"It's been an okay day, but I'd get that checked out soon," I suggest.

Kim sighs. "I'll make an appointment with Dr. Kaminsky."

"I'm *fine,* Mom," Hallie protests. "And hey, the other big news is that Avery is redoing my floor routine, and we picked new music. I'll play it for you in the car."

"See you this afternoon," Kim says, ushering her daughter toward the exit.

"Are you staying here or heading out?" Ryan asks me once they're gone.

It didn't actually occur to me that I'd need to figure out a way to spend the afternoon.

"I usually take my lunch in the office, help out around the gym, that kind of thing," Ryan offers.

I'd be happy to help other coaches with whatever they need, but the prospect of eating lunch alone with Ryan makes me nervous. Aside from Hallie, I'm not sure what we'd talk about. I grew up exclusively around fellow female gymnasts, gossiping about cute boys we saw at competitions, trading compliments on new leotards and scrunchies, and quoting *Stick It* to each other ("It's not called gym-*nice*-tics"). I've never had any platonic male friends; the only times I've ever hung out one-on-one with guys were dates. Freshly heartbroken or not, I still can't ignore that Ryan—formerly a cute boy—grew up into a highly attractive man. It's not smart for me to let this crush of mine fester. The last thing I need to do is let my feelings get in the way of this job or dump my broken heart on Ryan's plate.

"I, uh, I think I'm going to head home. But I'll be back later this afternoon, cool?"

Ryan fist-bumps me. "Cool, see ya."

I head into the parking lot and sit in the driver's seat, but don't want to go home just yet. Now that I'm alone, I can't help but dwell on Hallie's tossed-off comment from this morning—the one about failing out of gymnastics and being stuck living at home forever. Out of curiosity, I look at Craigslist for houses or apartments with spare rooms nearby. I've never looked for a place to live outside of LA before, and the tiny selection of results makes me nervous. There aren't that many people like me in Greenwood—the town is mostly filled with families raising kids in big, beautiful houses, not single people who need to rent out a spare bedroom. Rent here is more affordable than it was back in LA, but not by much. I'll need to work for a few months to save up enough money to move out. It's a daunting goal, but I know I can do it. I haven't had much faith in myself these past few years, but I have faith in this: my ability to work hard.

It's lunchtime. I could drive into the town center to pick up a sandwich or a salad. There's a new Italian place that opened up since I've last lived here that looks delicious. But that's money I don't need to spend. Instead, I drive back to my parents' house, thinking all the while about the day I'll call somewhere else home.

• *Chapter 6* •

After practice ends that night, I get ready to leave the gym. But the prospect of heading home is unbelievably depressing—I love my parents, but moving back into what is essentially a shrine to my failed childhood dream is unbearable. They hover. They ask too many questions about my plans for the future. I'm grateful that they let me stay with them (rent-free, even), but I'd be fine spending as little time there as possible. So, halfway through crossing the gym's lobby, I turn around and head back onto the floor. It's late, and the gym is empty; this is a golden opportunity to start choreographing Hallie's new routine without gymnasts and other coaches gawking.

I choreographed all the girls' routines back in LA, but this is a different beast. With Hallie, there are no physical limits; anything I can dream up, she can do. That doesn't mean I have entirely free rein, though. The sport's scoring system is laughably complex. It used to be simple: a perfect performance earned a perfect ten. But now, according to rules instituted in the 2000s by the Worldwide Organization of Gymnastics, a routine's total score is made up of a difficulty score and an execution score. On floor, only the top five hardest tumbling skills and top three most challenging dance skills are allowed to count toward the difficulty score, though additional points can be earned by connecting multiple elements. Points are docked if you miss out on certain skills. I take Ryan's binder from the shelf under the stereo and flip through it until I find the section of the Code of Points that details the requirements: I'll need to include a leap or jump series, a front flip, a back flip, a flip with a full twist or more, a double flip, and a final tumbling pass with a difficulty value of at least a "D" (skills are ranked alphabetically, with the easiest ones labeled as "A"). In other words, choreographing a winning floor routine isn't just an art—it's a science, too.

I hook up my phone to the stereo system and roll my head and ankles out in a light stretch as I find "Jazz Fling," the piece of music we've chosen. I play the first ten seconds to jog my memory—*Dun dun dun . . . dun-dun-dun dun dun dun*—and experiment with movement on the floor. I could start with this pose, or that one. There could be a flashy kick, or a spin, or a flick of my wrists. I watch myself carefully in the mirror as I string together a sequence of dance, and try it out to the beat of the music. It's good. But what if I squeeze in a jump series before the first tumbling pass? I rework the choreography three different ways before I settle on a version I like. I try it out—and this time, I'm pleased.

The next section of the melody soars, and I make a mental note to reserve that for Hallie's first tumbling pass, the impressive double Arabian. I listen as the music unfurls and try to imagine what could come next. The song has flaring trumpets and a sassy beat. You don't just dance to this music—you strut. I pop my hip, flick my fingers, shimmy my shoulders. I let myself get lost in the song, leaping and pirouetting with abandon. It's been close to a decade since I've allowed myself to indulge in this way, and I can practically feel my heart glowing with joy.

That is, until I catch sight of the mirror across the floor, reflecting stiff joints that don't bend the way I envision. It's cringeworthy. I hear echoes of Dimitri's criticisms: the split in my leap isn't crisp enough; my Shushunova doesn't get enough height; the routine would really look better if my thighs were thinner. I thought I was done mourning the loss of my ability years ago, but fresh grief springs up again. It's overwhelmingly sad to know that no matter how hard I train, I can never regain the body I once took for granted.

I take a break, letting the music play out as I take an ice-cold slurp from the water fountain. Then I tighten my ponytail, take a deep breath, and queue up the beginning of "Jazz Fling" again.

Over the next hour, the bones of the routine begin to take shape. I'm reminded of one of the many things I loved about gymnastics: if you work hard, you can become a superhuman version of yourself, at least for a time. If I were in prime shape, I could spiral like a ballerina, contort myself like a circus performer, catapult myself like a soldier, and defy gravity like a goddess. There would be no limits on what I could do. Outside the gym, that's never been true for me—I couldn't make it through college, and I couldn't make Tyler stay in love with me. But here? This is my world. Or at least it was. Until I went to Trials.

I run through the light version of the choreography—I cartwheel across the floor where Hallie will tumble for real; I spin on my butt where she'll do a wolf turn. I don't want to overextend myself and trigger another flare-up of back pain, so I take it easy. Watching the choreography gel together is satisfying, and I get so lost in performing it that I don't hear the soft creak of the door on the other side of the gym. When the song finishes, there's a beat of silence, then the sound of applause.

I whip out of the dramatic final pose—chest thrust out, back arched, arms outstretched—and turn toward the noise. I'm mortified to see Ryan walking down the vault runway toward the floor.

"Impressive," he says.

I cross my arms over my chest, embarrassed. "I had no idea anyone was still here."

"I was in the office. So, will that be Hallie's floor routine, or are you just playing around?" He looks bemused.

"That depends," I say. "Do you really like it or are you just being nice?"

"Come on, Avery," he says with a smirk.

Ryan doesn't seem like the kind of guy who'd joke around when it comes to work. The stakes are too high. *I* genuinely like the routine: the choreography is playful, energetic, and suited to Hallie's strengths. But I'm not so brazenly confident to expect Ryan to like it right off the bat.

"It's great," he clarifies. "I love it."

"You know this isn't actually the real, final thing," I warn him. "I just can't perform at that level anymore. So Hallie will kick up the difficulty level by, like, five notches."

"Yeah, that's fine. I figured. Show me the beginning?" he asks. "I missed it."

I jog to the stereo to restart the song, then scamper into place for the opening steps of the routine. I'm terribly self-conscious of his gaze on my unmuscled arms and soft stomach, but that leaves me with only one choice: I *have* to throw myself into the choreography and perform it to the fullest extent, because otherwise it'll look lackluster. It's fine for him to think I'm out of shape—but he can't think I'm bad at my job.

"Nice, nice, nice," he calls over the music as I

sashay through a section reserved for a tumbling pass. "I got it."

Relieved, I turn off the music.

"So?" I ask, trying not to let on that I'm close to panting.

He crosses the floor to join me near the stereo. "So! That's it."

I laugh. "No, I mean, do you have any notes? Suggestions?"

"Mmmm . . . no? Not now, at least? Let's see how Hallie does with it. Avery, you did an amazing job."

He shakes his head, grins, and looks away.

"What?" I ask, suddenly self-conscious.

Now that he's just two feet away from me, I realize he can probably see the sheen of sweat on my forehead and the halo of frizz that always escapes my ponytail when I dance.

"I just . . ." He trails off and laughs quietly. "Do you remember Worlds in 2010?"

"Yeah."

The memories of that weekend snap into focus. My scrunchie flew off my head during my bars routine. That was the first day I heard whispers about me as a likely contender for 2012. Jasmine cried that night in our shared hotel room when Dimitri pointed out that maybe the reason she slipped off beam was because her ever-expanding hips and ass threw her off balance.

"I'll never forget seeing your floor routine

that day. I mean, I remember watching from the sidelines and thinking, *Damn, that girl is going places,*" he recalls. He gazes off into the distance, then snaps back toward me. "And now you're here."

The words should fall flat, but he says them with a sense of wonder. His face lights up. I don't know what to say.

"If I had known, all those years ago, that we'd end up working together, I think I'd be kinda starstruck," he adds.

I can feel my cheeks flush pink. "Starstruck?!" I yelp.

"Hundred percent," he says, nodding.

A panicked thought flashes by—is he *flirting* with me? Am I imagining the coy warmth behind his words? I take in his casual stance and the impressive curve of his biceps straining at the sleeves of his T-shirt. He looks good without trying.

"Well, I was pretty starstruck, myself, when you called," I admit. My voice is just a touch more honeyed than usual. "Olympians don't call me every day, you know."

I'd assumed my ability to flirt had dried up after I started dating Tyler, but I'm pleasantly surprised to find it's still there. My hands find my hips; I straighten up and suck in my stomach.

He waves away my comment. "You should've been one, too. It was just bad luck."

"Yeah," I say, shrugging. This isn't my favorite subject. I'd rather change it. "So, you spend all your evenings here?"

"Ouch, are you telling me to get a social life?" he shoots back.

"Hey, all I'm saying is that you spend an awful lot of time in a gym that smells like feet," I say, holding up my hands.

I briefly weigh the pros and cons of what I want to say next, and spurred by a rush of adrenaline, I toss it out there.

"What, no hot date tonight?" I tease.

A flicker of surprise crosses his face. He recovers by shoving his hands into his pockets and looking away, laughing.

"Not tonight," he says softly. "But I'll take that as my cue that you want the gym to yourself to finish choreographing."

He starts to walk away, but I realize I don't want him to.

"Wait!" I call. "I didn't mean it that way. Stay?"

He wavers. "You want me to?"

It takes me a split second to think of a plausible excuse. "I need someone to film what I've choreographed so far, right?"

He turns back toward me with a smile. He pulls his phone out of his pocket. "Let's do it."

DECEMBER
2019

• *Chapter 7* •

By the time Hallie's ankle is strong enough for her to learn the new choreography, the radio plays holiday shopping jingles between every song. The town center is decked out in blue and white lights. I have to throw a parka on over my sweats just to make it from the parking lot to the gym. Christmas break is three weeks away, and most of the gymnasts and coaches are buzzing about holiday plans and winter vacation trips to visit grandparents in Florida. But not us. Ryan, Hallie, and I will spend the week between Christmas and New Year's here. There's no sense in wasting a week of prime training time. I have been practicing the routine every night after Hallie leaves practice, ensuring the choreography flows flawlessly and I've maximized every moment to squeeze out the highest possible difficulty score. I've been waiting until she's gone so she doesn't catch a glimpse of it until I'm satisfied it's perfect.

"Let me show it to you first before I teach it to you, okay?" I tell Hallie.

She's just finished warm-ups, stretching, and conditioning, and is happy to sit on the sidelines for a ninety-second break. I give her my phone so she can control the music.

"If you check out the Notes app, you'll see the entire breakdown of the choreography," I explain. "You can follow along, so you can see where, for example, I spin around on my butt, but you'll actually do a wolf turn."

"Got it," she says, peering at the screen.

"And when I do a switch leap with a full turn and it sucks, you'll do a switch leap with a full turn but make it look good," I say in the same matter-of-fact tone, hoping she'll laugh.

She snickers. "Understood."

I unzip my hoodie and kick off my sneakers. They'll only get in the way. I hear the bars creaking on the other side of the gym; Ryan is doing pull-ups. His muscles bulge cartoonishly. I force myself to look away.

"Ready?" she asks, once I've struck the starting pose on the floor.

"Ready!" I say.

"Jazz Fling" fills the room. To the extent that I can, I perform the hell out of the routine with the same passion and intensity I used to give the judges. I need to sell Hallie on this routine. It strikes me—while upside down, midway through a cartwheel we're all kindly pretending is Hallie's third tumbling pass—that the thrill of this performance isn't so far off from the adrenaline high I used to get from doing my own routine during competition. Maybe there can be real joy on the sidelines as a coach and a choreographer.

When I'm finished, I retreat toward her, trying desperately to catch my breath.

"Okay, cool, teach me," Hallie says, bouncing up to her feet.

"You like it?" I ask.

"Well . . ." She fidgets, scratching the back of one calf with the other foot. She looks at me with a shy gaze. "It's different. I'll give it a try."

She's clearly skeptical, but not strong-willed enough to challenge my judgment. I'm relieved she doesn't reject the routine flat out, but I know I can't let my expression waver. The coach-gymnast relationship is sacred and built on a concrete foundation of respect and trust; she can't catch on to the fact that I'm anxious and have feelings that can be hurt, just like anyone else.

"Whew, okay. Let's break it down from the top. Start here, a couple feet out from this corner," I instruct, pointing to the spot in which she needs to stand.

From the other side of the floor, I see Ryan watching us with a smile.

I walk Hallie through the choreography step by step, focusing on teaching her the broad strokes of every move. We can sharpen each motion later on, once she's gotten the hang of the routine. She hasn't warmed up her tumbling yet, so she goes for lazy, easy passes, like a round-off, back handspring, back tuck instead of the real deal. With Hallie toning down her skills and me performing to the fullest extent of my abilities, the playing field is almost level.

She picks up the routine fairly quickly, delighting in the creative combinations I've thrown together for her. Not everything runs so smoothly, though. I planned a switch ring leap connected to a switch leap with a full turn. A switch leap involves scissoring your legs back and forth, so you hit both a left split and a right split in midair before landing; each variation is tricky on its own, but the two moves back-to-back are even more complicated. That's the point, of course—the more difficult the series is, the higher the payoff is from the judges. Hallie fumbles the combination three times in a row. It doesn't matter how powerful or energetic she is—the move requires an absurd amount of precision.

"You have to use your arms for momentum in between the two leaps so you can have enough height on the second to make the full rotation," I explain.

She exhales and tries it again. It's sloppy, and she knows it. The moment her feet touch the floor, she shoots me a frustrated glance.

"More height," I remind her, demonstrating the way she needs to swing her arms. "Try it again."

She takes a few steps backward and screws up her face. I can tell she's trying to visualize the move in front of her. She sashays into the combination, but the series looks more like a jumble of flailing limbs than real gymnastics. If we had a stronger relationship at this point, I'd feel comfortable pushing her to work through it. But right now, I don't want to bring down her mood. Today, her confidence is worth more than the difficulty value of that leap series.

"Or maybe we put something else in that spot," I suggest. "Moving on . . ."

When we make it through the end of the routine, I give her a celebratory high five.

"Let's do it again," she says, bouncing up on her toes. "For real, this time, to music."

"You think you have all that memorized already?" I ask.

I know she's good, but she can't be *that* good.

"Not *all* of it, but most," she says proudly.

"Okay," I say, chuckling. "One more walk-through together, then you do it by yourself for real."

We repeat the choreography. This time, she deftly slides into most of the right moves, though she does spend half the routine with her neck craned toward me. Her switch leap series is a flop, but she pushes through to make it toward the final tumbling pass and the simple last bit of dance. (By the time you hit the fourth tumbling pass, you're flat-out exhausted. Even waving to a crowd cheering your name feels impossible. So I kept her last few motions easy.)

Ryan drops down from the bars. "How's it going over there?" he calls, wiping sweat from his brow.

"Good!" Hallie and I shout at the same time.

"Jinx, you owe me a soda," she says quickly. As Ryan approaches, she lowers her voice. "Not that I even drink soda, but, you know."

"I'll get you a Gatorade," I reply.

"Can I see how it's going?" Ryan asks.

"What do you think, Hallie? Are you ready for music?" I ask.

"Yeah," she says, jutting out her chin. "Let's do this."

She scrambles over to the starting spot, settles into the first pose, then peeks back at me, as if to ensure she's doing it right. I nod and turn on the music. On her own for the first time, her performance is rough and uneven. She nails certain sections of choreography, though I'd still like to tighten up the way she moves and performs; other bits, though, she stumbles through, or forgets entirely. I watch her face freeze when she realizes she has no idea how to transition from upright and standing to down on the floor for the wolf turn. She doesn't have enough time to figure it out; the music has already moved on. So she spasms and drops to the floor, shouting an apology as she goes.

"That's part of it?" Ryan deadpans.

"Yeah, doesn't it look great?" I joke back.

Hallie flits through the rest of the routine, shouting a dramatic "Ta-da!" as she hits the final pose.

"Needs some work," Ryan suggests kindly.

"But we're on the right track," I insist.

"I'll run through it twenty more times today," Hallie promises.

"That's not necessary," I say. "Let me buy you that Gatorade, and then we'll drill the choreography until it's muscle memory."

Hallie skips through the gym, leaning on one balance beam as she kicks up her feet and clicks her heels in midair, making her way toward the vending machine in the lobby.

"Motivating her with treats? Interesting coaching strategy," he points out.

"Effective coaching strategy," I correct him.

I head toward the lobby. Ryan makes a soft noise like he's clearing his throat, and when I look back toward him, his mouth is half-open, like he's about to say something.

"Yeah?" I ask.

He presses his lips together and dips his gaze away from mine. "Nothing," he says. "I was going to say something, but it's nothing."

I look at him curiously, but he just crosses his arms over his chest and nods toward the door of the gym.

"Go catch up with Hallie," he says.

• *Chapter 8* •

I want to believe that I've grown up a lot since I was Hallie's age. It would be nice to think that I've blossomed into a mature, confident, graceful adult. But then Ryan will make a particularly charming joke or simply breathe in my direction, and I'm forced to remember that I've been harboring the same teenage crush for a full decade. So maybe not much has changed.

"Heading out?" Ryan asks.

It's a Wednesday in the middle of December; we've just wrapped up our morning practice, and we're scattering in different directions for our midday break. Kim picked up Hallie for lunch and homeschooling, Ryan is retreating into the office for a meal, and per usual, I'm on my way out. Even though I've worked at Summit for a month now, I've never quite been comfortable spending the lunch break hanging out with Ryan. I know he stays here. I don't want to intrude on his personal space—and if I'm really honest with myself, the prospect of regular alone time with him sounds like a nervous thrill. What would I say? So I typically eat at home.

"Yeah," I say, a little embarrassed.

He gives me a bemused smile. "You know, you're more than welcome to hang out here," he says. "Even when you're off the clock."

I look at the door, then back at Ryan. "Do you want company?" I ask.

"That'd be nice," he says. "Unless you have other plans."

That'd be nice, I replay in my head. Between clubbing in college and a high-profile relationship with a famous athlete in my twenties, I eventually got comfortable around men—even intimidating ones I was attracted to. I could flirt, banter, relax. But maybe because Ryan is from a completely different era of my life, back when the prospect of interacting with guys point-blank terrified me, I lose my cool around him.

It's time for that to change.

"Do you have food here?" I ask.

"I brought a ton of leftovers, if you want to share," he says. "It's just some chicken and rice and veggies."

The offer is very sweet. "Sure, why not? Thank you so much."

He heats up the leftovers in the office's microwave and clears space off the desk for us to sit and eat.

"Did you make this?" I ask.

The chicken is a little bland, but it's not bad.

"It's basically the one meal I know how to make, yeah," he says.

"I ate a version of this pretty much every single day back when I was training," I say. "It's like comfort food."

"Exactly, same," he says.

There's a moment where neither of us says anything. I could change the subject to something completely professional, like Hallie's floor routine—but I recognize it wouldn't hurt for Ryan and me to get to know each other on a friendlier, more personal level, too.

"I actually love to cook," I tell him. "My first few years in California, I lived in dorms or these tiny apartments with bad kitchens, but eventually, I moved into this place with a huge, awesome setup for cooking. For the first time in my life, it was like I had both the space and the lifestyle to actually enjoy food."

"Oh, wow," he says. He looks down and pokes a piece of chicken with his fork. "I wish I had known that before serving you *this*."

"No, no, don't worry, this is good," I lie. "And it's so nice of you to share. Maybe I'll cook something for you sometime."

I can't tell if I'm overstepping a boundary, but he doesn't seem to flinch.

"It's funny that you say that you could enjoy cooking more once you left gymnastics," he notes. "That's how I felt about working out."

"Yeah?"

"It turns out, once the pressure of winning medals isn't hanging over your head, you can chill out a little more," he says.

"No kidding," I deadpan.

"I used to get so bored with conditioning when I was a gymnast, but after I retired, I realized I missed that kind of workout. So that's why I started lifting weights just for me—not for the sake of the sport."

"Ha, see, I felt the opposite way. I've done enough conditioning for one lifetime," I say.

"Fair enough," he says.

"How'd you get into coaching?" I ask.

"Back in high school, I coached kids' classes, just to make a little money during the summers," he explains. "So I knew I liked it. And then around the time I was thinking of retiring, my old coach from Michigan connected me to Mary here at Summit. The timing was perfect, since Hallie was leveling up and wanted to work one-on-one with a coach. The Conways looked into Powerhouse, but Dimitri didn't have room for her at the time." He explains that Dimitri's hands were full with other gymnasts: Emma Perry, Skylar Hayashi, Brit Almeda. "And the Conways were pretty reluctant to find another coach in another state because of Todd's career. So I was the best option—better than nothing."

"They took a pretty big chance on you," I say.

He knocks his knuckles against the wooden windowsill behind him. "Trust me, I'm grateful for that every single day."

He already knows that I coached a preteen girls' gymnastics team back in LA, and we trade coaching stories back and forth. He's had more than his fair share of dealing with sassy thirteen-year-old gymnasts and their uptight parents, but so have I. This is such a niche profession, it's rare that I meet someone else who understands it completely; even in the close-knit gymnastics circle, I don't know any other coaches around my own age. I'm glad I got over my nerves about eating lunch with Ryan at Summit. It's good for us to be friends.

• *Chapter 9* •

While the rest of the world counts down to the clock striking midnight on New Year's Eve, or the ball dropping in Times Square, we're more focused in the gym. Chalk dust hangs in the air as Hallie Sharpies a red X over the day in the calendar in Ryan's training binder. There are 175 days to Trials.

Hallie's floor routine has been my singular obsession for most of the month. I sometimes catch myself tapping out the steps while rinsing my hair in the shower, or humming the music while I refill my water bottle. She has the choreography down pat by now, and we've settled on which tumbling passes go where. We still have a ways to go when it comes to her actual performance—but I know the nuanced details, like the sassy tilt of a head or the satisfying *thunk* of a cleanly stuck landing, take time to develop. She'll get there. I'm optimistic.

So, today, Ryan wants Hallie to prioritize bars and vault. He told me I could take the day off, but the prospect of a weekday stuck in the house with Mom and Dad was too dull to consider. Instead, I spend hours lolling about by the chalk bins between the bars, fluffing the dismount mats, sucking down water bottles while wielding a whistle and stopwatch through Hallie's conditioning reps.

When Hallie heads home for dinner at six thirty, the sliver of night sky I can see through the gym windows is navy blue and studded with stars. New England winter nights are frigid, and this one is no exception. I'm gathering my stuff by the stereo—phone, socks, hoodie—when Ryan sidles up and leans nonchalantly against the plastic shelves.

"Are you going out tonight?" he asks.

I have no plans. Three days ago, as I slathered peanut butter on a banana and slid out the side door to the garage, Mom and Dad suggested that we all watch the ball drop on TV, like we used to. That's how I spent almost every New Year's Eve as a teenager, back when I lived at home and had no social life outside of the gym. My new life mirrors my old one all too well. If I were still living in LA, I might try to slither into a sequined minidress, pulled down tight around my thighs, and dance while clutching an overfilled champagne flute as the clock struck midnight. I can't do that here. I have no clue if Boston even has clubs, and if it does, there's no way I want to brave the line outside with bare legs on a winter night.

"Uhhh . . ." I try to stretch out the word in order to buy myself time to generate a response that saves me from looking like a loser with no friends, but nothing comes to mind. "Well . . . not really?"

I'm grateful that his expression doesn't flicker with pity.

"My friend is having a party tonight," he says.

"Oh," I say, exhaling and feeling my cheeks flushing pink. "You don't have to invite me out just because I have nothing better to do."

"No, no, I'm saying . . ." He chuckles and looks down. "I'm saying you could come? If you want to."

The way his voice lilts, I get the sense that he's not just being nice. He sounds nervous, like he's actually hoping I say yes. I've never seen a hint of vulnerability from him before, but I like it. Part of me wants to spit out a reassuring answer quickly so he doesn't have to feel flustered; part of me marvels at seeing him like this.

"Or, you know, if you'd rather do something else, that's cool, too," he rushes to add.

It's funny, I guess, the way we've spent hundreds of hours together at this point, and yet we're still not quite comfortable around each other. Our lunch two weeks ago was a good step forward, but we have a ways to go.

"That sounds like fun," I say, aiming to sound cool and confident, instead of overly eager. I'm not sure I land the right effect. "I could swing by."

"Sweet," he says, knocking the side of the

stereo with his fist. "I'll text you the details."

A million questions start to unfurl on my tongue: *What should I wear? Should I bring drinks? Who's your friend? Where's the party? . . . Is this a date?* But by the time I work up the courage to spit out even the most basic ones, Ryan is already straightening up and heading across the gym.

"See you tonight!" he calls, stretching up to slap the top of the door frame as he disappears into the lobby.

Once I'm sure he's gone, I turn to face the mirror that runs along one edge of the floor. I'm bare-faced, with a lifeless ponytail that probably should've been washed yesterday. Chalk dust and foam pit particles cling to my clothes. I have no idea what kind of party I'm in for, but I can guarantee that this look isn't going to cut it. I head home, checking my phone at each red light, waiting for Ryan's text.

There's a message on my phone when I step out of the shower. I wipe the fog from my screen against the blue terry cloth of my towel and read Ryan's text: a Somerville address I don't recognize, 10 p.m., BYOB. Many of my former classmates moved to Somerville after college, especially the ones who stayed local for school. From what I know of it, it's the kind of place with fixed-gear bikes and all-organic markets, not far from Harvard. It's just bustling enough to feel hip—I think. I've never actually been.

I clutch the towel to my chest, shivering a little at the shock of cold air outside the shower, and head into my bedroom to find something to wear. My flimsy clubbing dresses are gone, but any of them probably would've looked desperate and out of place, anyway. Instead, I find a pair of pleather leggings and a silky black cami. I hesitate, wondering if my black knit sweater would be more appropriate. I rummage through a dresser drawer until I find it. The fabric feels comfortably thick under my fingers. Ryan is my coworker. But arms are just arms, aren't they? And it's New Year's Eve. I push the sweater back into the drawer.

I blow-dry my hair, put on a tasteful layer of makeup, grab a bottle of wine from the liquor cabinet downstairs—though I need to blow a coat of dust off of it first—to stash in my purse, and then . . . wait for time to pass. It's barely after eight. There was a time in my life when going out before midnight seemed lame. Now, the prospect of even making it to midnight seems questionable. I pad into the kitchen to scrounge for leftovers.

"You're going out?" Dad asks, looking up over his glasses. He's eating a plate of pasta with one hand and reading a magazine in the other.

"Yeah, if that's . . . okay?" I ask tentatively.

He tilts his head. "I guess I can see how sitting around with your parents tonight probably isn't your idea of fun."

"Oh, come on, Dad," I say, trying to force a laugh.

He shrugs. "Pasta's in the fridge," he says.

I make myself a plate and pop it into the microwave, trying to figure out what to say to him as the appliance hums in the background.

"Ryan invited me to his friend's place in Somerville," I explain. "I'll take an Uber there."

Dad reaches for his wallet and fishes out two twenties.

"No, Dad," I say, laughing. "Uber doesn't take cash. But I got it. I'm good. I'm making money now, you know."

After Dad and I finish our pasta, we join Mom in the living room to watch TV. The crowd packed into Times Square looks miserable in tonight's frigid, slushy weather. Their "2020" glasses are a jarring reminder that the Olympics are just months away. Between the countdown clock in the corner of the TV screen, ticking away the minutes to midnight, and the uncomfortable sensation of my pleather waistband digging into my stomach when I normally sit here in sweats, it's impossible to forget that I have somewhere to go. I'm anxious to leave; I'm nervous about the prospect of heading into a party where I only know Ryan, and I'm curious to see how the night will unfold. The year ahead feels like a fresh start, and I want it to hurry up and arrive already.

Mom and Dad encourage me to leave at nine thirty, but I force myself to wait at least another twenty minutes before I dare call the Uber. I don't want to show up embarrassingly early. When my driver arrives, he grumbles about traffic but plays a comforting mix of pop hits from the '80s and '90s as the car whisks me through the suburbs and into the city. If I were meeting Tyler at a party, I'd text him a heads-up: *On my way.* But I don't know Ryan that well. My finger hovers over his name in my phone. I do my best to resist the urge.

Finally, at ten thirty, the car stops in front of a three-story house with a strip of a snowy front lawn. A group of people cluster in the wide bay window of the first-floor apartment; that must be it. I scurry up the front walk, climb the short set of stairs to the porch, and take a deep breath before ringing the buzzer.

A trim, dark-haired guy comes to the door a few seconds later. His mouth parts halfway, and he gives me a quizzical expression. "Hi?"

I glance past his shoulder to see if I can spot Ryan, but I'm not tall enough to see beyond this guy's bulky frame. "Hi, uh, Ryan invited me?"

"Oh, hey, c'mon inside," he says, stepping back to welcome me into the apartment. His expression softens. "I'm Goose. This is my place."

"Goose?" I ask.

"Mike Guzowski, but everyone calls me Goose," he explains, gesturing to the group of people gathered in his living room.

The room is dim, illuminated by a strip of lights along the window that emit a soft glow that rotates through the colors of the rainbow. There's a massive sectional along one wall where an assortment of thick-necked, muscled guys sit with their dates, facing the TV. The screen is turned to the countdown in Times Square, but mercifully, it's on mute. Instead, ambient electronic music floats through the room. The party is dominated by a dining room table set up for beer pong with teams of two facing off at each end. The kitchen island is entirely covered with empty beer bottles, flattened six-pack cartons, open bags of chips, and a Tupperware full of lopsided, homemade chocolate chip cookies.

Ryan is perched on the arm of the couch, sipping a beer. He pops up when he spots me.

"Hey, you made it," he says, approaching me and Goose.

He hesitates for a split second, then leans in for a hug. It's the first time we've ever been this close, and I can detect some kind of cologne. I lean into him for a brief moment, and his hand grazes the small of my back.

"Good to see you," I say.

Training was only a few hours earlier, but here, at the party, it feels like it could've been days ago. I unzip my black wool coat and shrug it off, tossing it on the pile of parkas and peacoats on the love seat.

"I brought, um, this," I say to Ryan, fishing the bottle of merlot out of my bag.

"Oh, sweet," he says, looking down at the label. "Thanks. Should we open it?"

The merlot seemed fine earlier that night, but now that I see everyone else nursing beers, it feels like an uncomfortably fussy choice.

"Maybe later?" I suggest. "I'll have one of whatever you're having."

Ryan grabs a beer from the fridge, scans the table for an opener, and snaps off the cap. We clink bottles ceremoniously.

"You look great," he offers sheepishly. "I've never seen you, you know . . ." He gestures to the slick pleather pants and looks like he's at a loss for words. "I've never seen you with your hair down before."

Was his comment flirty? It felt flirty—but maybe he only wanted to bring me along because the other guys here have dates.

"Oh, thanks, yeah. I figured, you know, I could look a little more presentable for a night out."

I don't know what else to say, so I mumble that he looks great, too. It's not a lie; he's in a charcoal-gray sweater that looks like cashmere and slim-fitting black pants. Away from the gym's harsh fluorescent lighting, dressed in real clothes, he looks more like a *GQ* model than any real person has a right to. He may be my boss, but I'm not immune to the fact that he's hot. I like that while he's tall for a gymnast, he's much closer to my height than, say, Tyler. It's nice not to have to crane my neck to have a conversation with him.

"So, uh, how do you know Goose and everyone?" I ask.

"Goose and I grew up together in Florida," he explains. "He's been in Boston since college, and half the reason I was psyched to take the coaching job at Summit is because it'd mean seeing him regularly again. And then a lot of these guys are buddies from the gym. Here, let me introduce you." He gestures for two people on the sprawling sectional to scoot apart and make room for us. "Move."

A space opens up, and we sit, our thighs bumping as we get comfortable on the couch.

"This is Avery, the other coach," Ryan tells the group.

He reels off their names, though there are too many for me to keep track of them. His friends nod at me in recognition, like they've heard of me already and knew to expect me tonight. People say hello, then return to a heated conversation about the Patriots' chances of making the Super Bowl. The last thing I want to do is talk about football with another guy.

"So, you must have been a gymnast, too?" Goose asks.

Next to him, his girlfriend, a blond girl with meticulous highlights dressed in a clingy, metallic sweater dress—Melissa, I think?—looks up.

"Yep," I say. "I retired after an injury about seven years ago, so I'm just into coaching these days."

"That's sick," he says, shaking his head.

"So cool," his girlfriend adds.

The attention makes me slightly anxious. I know the next logical question is if I was ever in the Olympics, like Ryan, and that's a rabbit hole I don't want to have to deal with. So I jump in with a question of my own to divert the conversation.

"What do you guys do?" I ask.

Goose works in sales for a tech start-up, and Melissa teaches fifth grade.

"It looks like they're finishing up," Goose says, nodding to the beer pong table. "Want to play next?"

"Yeah," Melissa says, leaning forward. She clutches my wrist. "Girls against guys?"

"Let's do us against them," Ryan says, claiming me on his team.

"Are you any good?" I ask.

He gives me a cocky look. "Two world-class athletes against these two? We got this."

We wait a minute for the game to wrap up, and

then Goose sets up the table for another round. He throws the first ball and sinks it into a red Solo cup, but Ryan doesn't look worried at all. I expect him to step up to the table for the first throw from our side, but he encourages me to take the shot. I center myself against the table, focus on the exact spot I want the ball to land in, and steady myself. The precision reminds me of preparing for a vault—except here, my skills are shaky at best. Sure enough, my ball bounces off the rim of one cup and ricochets across the living room. I chase after it in a hurry before it disappears under the couch.

"Try a lighter touch next time," Ryan suggests when I return. He mimics the throw.

I chuckle. "Are you coaching me? You know, we're off the clock. This is just for fun."

He holds his hands up. "All right, you're right, I'm sorry."

"No, no, I don't mean you have to cut it out—I'm just teasing you. Show me how to make a shot."

Over the course of the game, between turns, he slowly but surely guides me. He's standing inches behind me when I finally land one, and he leans forward to wrap his arms over my shoulders in a celebratory hug.

"Yes!" he exclaims. "Great job."

When we win the entire game a few minutes later, it's all because of Ryan.

"Victory!" I cheer, throwing up both hands to punch the air.

"We're a great team," he counters.

"That one point I scored definitely helped," I say faux-seriously.

He doesn't argue with me.

We relinquish the table to the next group of players and get another round of beers from the fridge. The party has gotten crowded.

"So, Avery, beer pong champion," he begins, "I know we spend all this time together at work, but please don't take this the wrong way—can you tell me about yourself?"

I laugh. "Like, first date style?"

"First date style," he echoes.

"Is this a date?" I ask, suddenly feeling emboldened by the beer and the victory and the heady rush of New Year's Eve.

His shoulders creep toward his ears, his lips curl, and he cocks his head to one side. "Maybe?" he asks coyly, self-consciously, like my question caught him off guard. "If you want it to be."

Before I can formulate the right response—*do I want it to be?*—he clears his throat and rushes to add, "Or if you don't want it to be, that is absolutely okay, too."

"I wondered what you were thinking when you invited me out," I say, hedging my bets.

"I . . ." He falters. "I never heard you mention seeing anyone. Are you seeing anybody?"

"I'm not seeing anyone, no," I say. I hesitate, then decide to share a little more. "But that's kind of why I moved back to Greenwood. I was in a relationship in LA, and then it ended."

I consider telling him more about my breakup with Tyler, but decide against it. That conversation would require exposing too much of myself. I don't need Ryan to see the raw, messy bits of my life. It's better that he think of me only as a stellar coach or maybe even as someone he might start to like. There's no use ruining that impression.

Ryan nods and sips his beer. "I'm sorry to hear that."

Maybe I'm imagining it, but whatever glimmer of potential there was between us before, it's hardened now. His jaw sets a millimeter tighter than it did before. Is he calculating how long I've been back in town and how quickly a person can get over heartbreak?

"It was . . . it was for the best," I say. "It was time. We should've broken up long before we actually did."

I've never said that out loud, but it's the truth. I've always been conscious of the fact that Tyler pulled me out of a dangerous spiral; I know he was so damn good for me when we met. But we both changed. We grew apart. And just because I'm grateful for how he was back then doesn't mean I owe him forever. The idea is strangely energizing. I've been leaning one lazy hip against the kitchen counter, and I straighten up to my full height.

"You're a fighter," he says serenely. "You'll get back out there in no time."

A fighter. I can't remember the last time someone called me that. It's been ages since I deserved that compliment. It feels good to be seen that way.

"Yeah, I know," I say, testing out what it's like to accept praise. Not bad.

Ryan digs through an open bag of potato chips, and when he looks back up at me, he has a funny look on his face. His mouth twists to one side. I get the sense that he's weighing whether or not to say something, and I don't want to interrupt his train of thought. I pick lightly at the chips.

"For the record, I'm not seeing anyone, either," he says finally. "I haven't had anything serious for a while."

"Mmm."

I worry that if I say too much, I'll scare him into changing the subject—and I want to hear more.

"It was tough to date when I was training seriously, and then after, I jumped into a relationship, probably just to feel normal and fill all that time, you know? I figured, if I can't be a competitive gymnast anymore, maybe I could be someone's boyfriend."

I can't help but let out a short, harsh laugh. "Oh, I know that feeling. Maybe too well."

His face lights up. "It's weird, isn't it? Going from this thing that dominates your whole world to nothing at all. It's like, well, shit, can I even *be* anybody else?"

I exhale deeply. "I know what you mean."

"But anyway, that didn't pan out. Obviously."

"Obviously," I say.

He takes another chip and turns it over in his hand, considering it.

"So I guess what I'm saying is that, if this *were* a date, I wouldn't mind," he says.

I like the hopeful twinkle in his expression.

"Well, I—" I start to say.

"Hey, everyone!" Goose booms from the couch. "One minute to midnight. The countdown's coming."

He double-fists electronic devices, cutting off the music with his phone and using the TV remote to take the Times Square broadcast off mute. I hadn't even noticed Melissa bustling in the kitchen, but while Ryan and I had been talking, she must have poured champagne into two dozen plastic flutes lined up in rows on the counter.

"Here, help me pass these out," she instructs as she squeezes by me, clutching four to her chest.

I'm frustrated that my conversation with Ryan got interrupted. I grab as many flutes as I can carry and make my way into the crowd, passing them out. When I turn back to get more, Ryan is behind me, his gaze locked on the trembling, overly filled drinks. I hand three plastic flutes to strangers and keep a fourth for myself. I feel too self-conscious to take up prime real estate in a spot in front of the TV, so I move to the edge of the party, near the windows. There's a roaring, rhythmic cheer coming from the hordes of tourists in Times Square that signals the new year is mere seconds away. I wonder how many millions of people must be watching this same exact sight, and what unfathomable pressure that must place on whoever is responsible for lowering that massive crystal ball.

"Ten, nine, eight," the party chants.

I shrink closer to the windows, unsure whether or not to join in. They aren't my friends.

"Seven, six, five," they shout, growing louder.

Suddenly, Ryan slips between the couple to my left, and he's by my side.

"Hi," he breathes.

"Hi," I say, instantly feeling less alone here.

He places his hand on the small of my back.

"Four, three, two, one! Happy New Year!" everyone announces.

All around us, couples erupt in celebratory kisses. I turn to him just as he turns to me. A curious grin plays on his face. His fingers slide over my waist, keeping us close. I place my hand lightly on his chest, tilt my head up to look at him, and we kiss. I feel a giddy burst of adrenaline, and it's not only the festive energy radiating throughout the room. Despite harboring a crush on him for years, I never fathomed a world in which I stir up the same dizzying feelings that he creates in me. Ryan pulls back ever so slightly, and a smile curls on his lips.

"Happy New Year," I whisper.

"I think I like this year already," he says softly.

He rests his drink on the windowsill, then pulls me closer to him, sliding his hands over my hips. His embrace is warm and thrilling. I feel confident enough to let my hand roam from his chest to his shoulder to his neck, feeling the powerful muscles underneath his sweater. My fingers brush the plush edge of his hair. He nuzzles my cheek and trails kisses down the side of my neck. The sensation is electrifying, and my eyes flutter open.

Most of the crowd has moved on from making out; the music is back on. It suddenly hits me that I'm kissing *Ryan*—not just Cute Ryan from my teenage dreams, but Ryan, the coach I work alongside every day. The person who, like me, is responsible for molding an Olympic champion, and probably shouldn't be distracted right now. A thick blanket of self-consciousness settles over me, and I tense up.

"You okay?" Ryan asks, dropping his hands from my waist.

I stare out at the room of people. "I, uh, I . . . I'm sorry."

"For what?" he asks, looking concerned.

"Should we be doing this?" I ask, pushing my hair back from my face.

Anxiety creeps into my chest.

"Is this too soon?" he says, inching away from me.

I take a deep breath. It's hard to face him.

"I like you, but I didn't expect to like you like this," I say, fumbling for the right words. I'm not brave enough to say what I really mean, which is that I didn't expect to like him *this much*. Crushes never really work out that way—just because you think someone is attractive from afar doesn't mean shit when it comes to having a real connection. "Should we maybe, I don't know, think about this? I don't want to mess up what we have at work."

He rubs his jaw and doesn't look at me right away. "Sure thing."

"I should go," I say.

He doesn't protest.

The entire ride home to Greenwood, I replay that kiss in my mind and regret leaving.

JANUARY
2020

• *Chapter 10* •

Summit is closed on New Year's, but opens the following day. I pull into the parking lot with one minute until practice, although I don't get out of the car right away. Ryan's Subaru is parked, and I'm worried about entering the gym without Hallie as a buffer. I spent most of yesterday ping-ponging between desire and self-doubt; I want to let myself enjoy the memory of that tantalizing kiss, but I know I shouldn't. Without the heady buzz of the party clouding my judgment, it seems awfully stupid to jeopardize my professional relationship for the chance at anything romantic. We can't risk Hallie catching on; she's sheltered enough that a midnight kiss between her two coaches would sound scandalous, not festive. It would be a distraction she can't afford to indulge in right now. And beyond that, Ryan is the closest thing I have to a friend these days. I don't want to ruin that. The thought of explaining this tangle of emotions, responsibilities, and fears to Ryan makes me queasy—I'd rather simply pretend the kiss never happened. We were tipsy; I was lonely; that's that. So I wait until I see Hallie's mom drop her off before I dare get out of my car and enter the building.

Hallie is usually happy to chatter away the

143

first morning after a break, like a weekend or a holiday. But when I find her and Ryan on the floor, she's not dilly-dallying—she's already running laps. It looks like she doesn't want to squander a moment of practice.

"It's 2020," she pants as she cruises past me. "No time to waste."

Ryan turns ever so slightly toward me with his arms crossed over his chest. "Hi," he says simply, like he's testing out the vibe between us.

"Morning," I say, maybe a bit too businesslike.

"How was your day off?" he says evenly, turning his gaze back to Hallie.

I follow suit. It's easier to watch her than to look at him.

"Fine. Yours?" I say, aiming to sound slightly softer this time.

"Fine," he replies.

Hallie jogs past us again, and we fall into uneasy silence.

"Are you cold in here? It's cold in here," he says, sometime after her third lap. "I'm going to go fiddle with the thermostat."

He stays across the gym for longer than it takes to adjust the temperature.

It strikes me that even if I want to pretend the kiss never happened, he may not. Maybe he feels rejected, or embarrassed, or like he misread the situation entirely. Or maybe he came to the same conclusion that I did, that getting involved with each other can irreparably damage the work we're doing. If Hallie overhears our awkwardness, there's no way she wouldn't pick up on the fact that something is off.

I glance at Hallie—she's been doing a variation of this same warm-up routine since she was in preschool. She doesn't need me to hover over her and bark instructions. I leave my regular perch by the stereo and head to the back of the nearly empty gym to find Ryan leaning against the wall and looking at something on his phone.

"Hey, can we talk?" I ask quietly. "Like, for real."

We're far enough that Hallie won't hear us, but still, I'm nervous.

"Hi, what's up?" he says, making a valiant effort to appear casual.

I wring my hands and steel myself for a moment of terrifying honesty. "I had so much fun with you the other night, and I really appreciate that you invited me out," I begin. "It was all amazing, including the kiss, but I . . . I don't think it should happen again. I think we'd be better off as friends."

"Oof," he says coolly. "You're quick to turn me down."

"No! That's not it. I mean, if the circumstances were different, I'd want to give us a real shot."

He raises one eyebrow. "What do you mean?"

I take a deep breath and try to summon the

vulnerability I need to pull off this conversation successfully.

"I like you. A lot. I really appreciate that we come from the same world; it makes me feel like you understand me better than most people. I think that if we . . ."

This is mortifying to say out loud, but I have to keep going.

"If we got together for real, it would be incredible," I say. I'm fully emotionally naked in front of him now. "But that scares me, because we could get caught up in whatever's between us, and that could affect our ability to work together."

His face softens. He doesn't look angry—just sad.

"This isn't just about us," I remind him. "It's about Hallie, too. This is a once-in-a-lifetime shot for her."

I see his gaze drift over my shoulder, and I turn to follow it. Hallie is stretching in an oversplit—a split with stacks of mats under each foot and her crotch flush against the floor. She grabs the toes of her front foot and bends over to face her knee. The position requires superhuman flexibility developed over years, which sums up my point exactly. We all have to stay focused on our goal.

He sighs. "You're right. I get it."

"I'd still love to be friends, though, if you're open to it," I add. "Really."

His expression is tough to read at first, but it ultimately crinkles into an attempt at a smile. "Of course."

Me and Ryan, friends. There's something about the idea that's hazy and hard to picture, but maybe that's because *nothing* about my future feels completely solid right now. I've finally saved up enough money to move out of my parents' house, and I'm going to see an apartment this weekend. The idea of moving makes me feel hopeful.

"I'll see you around," I promise Ryan.

He claps his hands authoritatively and calls across the gym, "Hallie, how's that stretching going?"

For the rest of the morning, Ryan and I stay out of each other's way. I give him space while he works with Hallie on vault. When it's time for me to take over on floor, he tells Hallie he's going to head to the office to answer some emails.

"Tumbling, let's go," I instruct.

She warms up and practices each of the four passes we've chosen for her routine. After a hard landing, she sighs and rolls out her ankle, flexing her foot in different directions.

"Feeling okay?" I call across the floor.

She takes a few experimental steps, head cocked to the side.

"Yeah, yeah. That landing was weird, but I'm good."

"Did you get a chance to see that doctor?" I ask.

"Dr. Kaminsky?" she asks. "Yeah. He checked me out."

"What did he say? How are you feeling?"

She sighs. "Nothing major is wrong, but I can tape it up if it's bothering me."

"Did he order any tests? X-rays? MRIs?"

"It's all fine," she says. "I'm gonna tape up my ankle."

She retrieves gauzy prewrap and athletic tape from the supply closet and sits on one side of the floor with her foot in front of her, methodically winding the materials around her ankle and heel to stabilize the joint.

I sit and join her. She silently fumes when the tape is too tough to rip cleanly. I help her pull off a long strip.

She bites her lip. "I know he's a good doctor, but I don't know . . . I kind of got a weird vibe from him. And my ankle really feels fine, anyway. So it's not like I'd need to go back."

Something about Hallie's quiet, fidgety demeanor and insistence that everything is normal raises a red flag for me. She reminds me of Jasmine, back when we were kids, the way she'd pretend like Dimitri's behavior on bad days didn't bother her. She always cried later, when it was just the two of us. I remember the pressure to stay tightly controlled and focused on training, the way we would push down our feelings until we could barely notice them anymore. I don't want that for Hallie.

"If something's not right, you can tell me, you know," I say slowly, choosing my words carefully. "I'm always here if you want to talk."

She hesitates, glances at the door, and then back at me. Ryan is nowhere in sight. She absent-mindedly picks at the edge of the roll of tape.

"Both times I've seen him, he examines my ankle and shows me certain exercises I can do to strengthen it," she says. "But then he also says the reason I have trouble with it has something to do with my hips. So he has me roll down my leggings a little, and he holds my hips and watches me bend over."

She doesn't make eye contact. She keeps picking at the tape.

I don't know enough about medicine to know if she's describing a legitimate professional encounter or something far more sinister. But something feels off to me.

She pulls her knees up to her chest. "He's a doctor," she points out. "My mom was in the room with me both times. She didn't think any-thing of it."

When Hallie finally looks up at me, her eyes are bright and glassy with tears.

"It's never okay for him to make you feel uncomfortable," I say. "Not even if he's a respected doctor, and not even if your mom is in the room."

"Got it," she says. She digs her chin into her knee.

"I just want to make sure you're okay," I say.

She shrugs.

"It might be helpful to tell your mom," I suggest gently. "That way, she'll be sure not to bring you back to him."

I don't want to pressure Hallie into saying anything she's not ready for, but also, her parents should probably know—and I'm not sure it's my place to tell them. I remember how daunted I felt at her age by the prospect of being vulnerable with my parents. But I wish I had been more open with them.

"Maybe later," she says. "Not right now. And can you please not tell Ryan about this?" she asks.

She looks at me so expectantly, I don't know how to say no.

"Sure," I say, leaning forward to wrap her in a hug.

Hallie leans her forehead against my shoulder and lets me embrace her. I feel this odd wave of maternal instinct, and so I stroke her hair and rub soothing circles on her back. She exhales.

• *Chapter 11* •

On Craigslist, I found a spare room in an apartment on the edge of Greenwood. The person leasing it, a yoga instructor about my age named Sara McCarthy, was two years below me in Greenwood's public school system, though we didn't know each other as kids. Normally, this would make me wary; I wouldn't want a repeat of my disastrous date with Lucas. But as Sara gave me a tour of the cozy, colorful apartment, she didn't ask any leading questions or pry for uncomfortable answers. She seemed both bubbly and relaxed. The apartment spanned the top floor of a duplex; the living room was painted an electric shade of purple, like Rachel and Monica's apartment in *Friends*; the rent was affordable; the bedroom came furnished. I said yes on the spot.

A week later, I pack my things into the trunk of the Honda and drive across town to move in. Sara helps me carry my suitcases and laundry baskets of clothing out of the car and up the stairs.

"It's fine if you smoke, just open the window first," she says, miming holding a joint. "And I make kombucha every Sunday—you're welcome to have some."

I'm not particularly interested in either offer, but I appreciate her openness.

"Cool, thank you," I say.

She jostles open the door to the apartment and leans one of my suitcases against the couch covered by an enormous hand-crocheted afghan. A pink yoga mat hangs in a nylon carrier on a hook by the coatrack, and a trio of creamy white candles rest on the coffee table.

Despite my protests that there's no need for her help unpacking, Sara seems happy to. She brews us hot, fruity tea and carries it into the bedroom at the end of the hall—the one that's now mine. She lets me have what is clearly the better of the two mugs, printed with a faded graphic of a cat wearing bejeweled cat-eye glasses and only barely chipped. She sits cross-legged at the foot of the bed and folds clothes into neat stacks for me to place inside the old-fashioned armoire by the window, chattering easily as she works.

"So, I'll admit, I know who you are, obviously," she says, pushing her hair behind her ear to reveal a constellation of silver stud earrings.

"Oh," I say nervously.

Maybe I'd misjudged her.

"I mean, like, from years ago," she says. "My little sister went to Summit and practically worshipped you from afar. She'd flip if she knew you were moving in, but I don't know . . . You seem so normal? Is that a weird thing for me to say?"

"Um . . . I don't know? A little?" I say.

I get the sinking feeling that I've just moved

all of my possessions into the home of a woman who sees me as Avery, the athlete, not Avery, the regular roommate.

"I'm sure your life has moved on," she says graciously.

I'm grateful she said that—it makes me feel more confident that's true.

"I just recently moved back from six years in LA," I say, as if to prove that I'm not still the girl who grew up in Greenwood.

"I mean, *I'm* not the person I was a few years back, either," she says. "I went to UMass for psych, but then I got pretty into yoga there, and that led to me getting my yoga teacher's training certificate, and here we are. Just couldn't stay away from this ex-*ci*-ting town."

Her tone makes it clear she's kidding.

"I teach at Mind & Body Yoga," she explains, naming the yoga studio not far from Greenwood High. "Since I practiced there so often during summer breaks home from college, I couldn't say no when they offered me a job. I gotta say, I'm jealous that you moved away. I wish I could've done something cool like that."

"I mean, it's kinda like you said, one thing turns into another, right? And then you wind up in a place you never thought you'd be? After my gymnastics career ended, I moved to LA for school, then stayed because of my boyfriend at the time," I say, glossing over the manic years of partying. I'm not sure if she'd approve. "And then when that relationship ended, I didn't have much keeping me there. So I moved back, and luckily, a coaching job opened up at Summit."

"Okay, wait a sec," she says, lowering her voice conspiratorially, even though we are the only people around. "Your boyfriend. You dated that football player, right?"

As soon as she mentions Tyler, it hits me that I haven't dwelled on him in a week. I feel a little proud of myself for beginning to move on.

"Yeah, yeah, I did," I say, trying to downplay it.

I turn toward the closet and hang up my parka so I don't have to face her.

"*That* sounds totally major," she says. "What was that like?"

Her tone sounds hungry for gossip, but I'm not in the mood to give it. I get why some people might be starstruck by the prospect of dating a pro football player, but having actually done it, the sheen is lost on me.

"Uh, lots of muscles, lots of sweat," I say quickly. "But underneath all that, just the same old, same old."

"Huh," she says, chewing that over.

"We just grew apart," I explain slowly, testing out her reaction. "We both changed. We wanted different things."

She dramatically closes her eyes and places her hands together in prayer. "Preach, girl."

I laugh.

"I used to date this guy who . . ." she begins before cutting herself off. She shakes her head. "You know what? No. He's not even worth the breath it would take to explain it."

"Fair enough," I say.

I'm starting to like Sara.

I reach for the scissors on the nightstand to cut open my last box of things. We're both quiet for a minute.

"Actually, I like this new guy," I blurt, surprising myself, even.

"Yeah? Who?" she asks.

I run the odds in my head that Sara would have ever crossed paths with Ryan. Greenwood has just thirty thousand people, but he didn't grow up here, and they seem to run in different social circles. I don't think they know each other. I grab my mug of tea and sink down across from Sara on the bed.

"His name is Ryan. We work together."

"Ooh . . . another coach?"

"Yeah. I actually sort of knew of him when we were younger, and I always thought he was cute. We work pretty closely together now—it's just the two of us training this one incredible gymnast. We think she could have a pretty decent shot at making the next Olympics."

"So has anything happened between you two?" Sara asks.

Right—she is not here to listen to my thoughts on Hallie's athletic career. The question was about Ryan.

"We were work friends up until New Year's Eve, when he invited me out to his friend's party," I say. "We kissed at midnight. And then . . . I don't know, things sort of changed between us? I realized how much I liked being around him. It freaked me out. I don't know."

This is the first time I've ever told this story out loud, the first time I've had a person to tell it to. The events of that night have been playing on a jumbled loop in my brain ever since I left the party in Somerville, but that doesn't make explaining what happened with Ryan any easier.

"Not a good kisser?" she asks, wrinkling her nose.

"No, not that. Not at all," I rush to say.

God, how many times since New Year's Eve have I imagined the electricity of our kiss? Sometimes, I catch myself daydreaming about it at Summit when I know I shouldn't.

"You should go for him," Sara says clearly.

"What?"

"You like him. So tell him that. Go out with him. Do something."

I feel hot, like I'm under a spotlight.

"I can't do that," I protest.

"You can sit here in your discomfort, or you can step outside your comfort zone and try something new," she continues, slipping into what I assume must be a platitude from her yoga classes.

"We work together. It's complicated," I explain. "I told him we probably shouldn't do anything like that again."

"Life is short," she says.

She shrugs and scoots off the bed, then whirls around to face me. "We can be friends, can't we?" she asks.

"Of course we can," I rush to say.

"Good. I was hoping you'd say that," she says, grinning. "I have to get going. The studio does candlelit yoga on Sunday nights. I'm teaching at six thirty and eight o'clock. Wanna join?"

I glance around the bedroom, which doesn't quite feel *homey* yet, though it's shaping into something that feels like mine. This apartment feels like a fresh start. I don't want to leave it just yet.

"Maybe another day?" I suggest.

I don't mean it. It's the way I was raised—unless a workout involves a raised heartbeat and death-defying stunts, I'm not interested. Chanting mantras in downward dog doesn't seem like it'd do it for me.

"Free classes on me anytime," she says, heading around the corner into her own bedroom to get ready.

I sink onto the bed. First Summit, then whatever is going on with Ryan, and now this new place to live. For the first time in a long time, I feel the different elements of my life clicking together. I like this new life.

After Sara leaves, the apartment is quiet. I drive to the supermarket, pick up an armful of carrots, mushrooms, herbs, and rice, and make risotto for myself. Cooking dinner for one is an endeavor that requires a little too much time, energy, and money for what it's worth, but I need to do something to keep my hands and mind busy. I have to focus on drizzling the pan with precisely the right amount of olive oil and dicing the vegetables the right way so I don't have the bandwidth to think about Ryan. He's been on my mind more than I'd like to admit lately.

I didn't used to be like this—sappy, emotional, with a soft center. I used to pride myself on being able to block out distractions. It's a necessary skill in gymnastics: when you're four feet aboveground, balancing on a four-inch-wide beam, there's no room to notice the trilling of another girl's floor music or the flailing kid cartwheeling past you or the watchful gaze of your coach. There's you and there's the beam. That's it. Tonight, there's me and there's this meal. I wish that could be it. My mind keeps circling back to thoughts I shouldn't be having.

There's nothing worth getting distracted from Olympic glory, least of all a crush—that's what

Dimitri drilled into me years ago. But the truth is that however deeply I know Ryan and I can't hook up or date or whatever we were veering toward, I still want to kiss him again. I can't stop thinking about running my fingers through his hair and feeling his powerful hands pressing into the curve of my waist. I *like* him. I liked him back then, too, though I didn't think I could do anything about it. Now, though? I'm not sure. I'm in a new home. It's a fresh start. Anything could be possible.

• *Chapter 12* •

Monday's practice slips by in a flash. Hallie, clad in a blinding neon orange leotard sprayed with sparkles, whips through warm-ups and conditioning with alarming grit, charges down the vault runway like a sprinter, attacks her tumbling with gusto, and moves with an impressive sense of focus on beam. Nationals—the annual competition that brings together the country's top talent—is one of the most important events of the year, and it's just two months away. The upcoming competition sharpens the pressure. When Hallie's moving in top form, like she is today, practice never drags. It's impossible to look away from her.

She and Ryan have spent the final hour of the day together on bars, drilling her new Tkatchev–Pak Salto combo. It's coming together nicely; right now, she can pull it off just fine, though she has some work to put in before the combination looks effortless. That's the gold standard in gymnastics: making the impossible look not just possible, but *easy*. I've been sitting and stretching on the sidelines, watching Ryan tracking Hallie's movements as she arcs through the air. His arms are outstretched; he's ready to catch her if she falls.

"It's six," he says finally, after what must be her thirtieth attempt at the move.

"What?" she says, spinning around to look at the clock. She gapes. "No! I was just getting into it."

"Time to go," he says. "You know your parents like you out of the gym in time for homework."

"One more?" she pleads.

He laughs. "One more. Then you gotta get out of here."

"Avery, would you film this one?" she asks.

She likes to have video clips to post on Instagram—though, of course, only the most jaw-dropping ones actually get posted.

"Sure," I say, digging my phone out of the pocket of my fleece zip-up and getting ready to record. "Ready when you are."

She takes her position under the high bar. Ryan grabs her by her waist, and she jumps; he helps her reach the bar. She does a move called a kip to swing up so the wooden equipment is flush against her hips, then screws up her face in a look of pure concentration before launching into a handstand, giant, and finally, a Tkatchev followed swiftly by a Pak Salto. Her compact body flings over one bar, then between the two, and it's magnificent. Once the final move is complete, her knees bend, and her shoulders sag into a relaxed swing. She knows she's nailed it. She drops down and jogs over to my spot on the mat to watch the playback.

"I look pretty good, right?" she muses.

"You do," I admit. "I'll text this to you."

"Thanks!" she says. "Okay, now I can head out. I just wanted to nail it once."

She strips off her grips and heads across the gym to pack up for the night. Ryan jumps up to the high bar himself, swings back and forth, and drops back down to the mat.

"You leaving, too?" he asks.

I shrug. "I mean, I guess? My new roommate, Sara, invited me to another yoga class tonight, but I told her practice might run late."

"We never run late," he points out.

"Yoga seems boring. But I can't tell her that," I say.

He laughs. "Gotcha."

Ryan meanders around the bars and leans against one of the silver poles holding up the apparatus.

"So, if you're not doing anything, then, would you want to get dinner?" he asks. He clears his throat and hastily adds, "As friends."

If only he knew how I regret saying that I only wanted friendship.

"Yeah, let's do that," I say. "It'll be cool to catch up outside the gym again."

"Yeah? Awesome. Maybe a bite at Stonehearth Pizza?"

I know the place. Wood-fired pizza with surprisingly healthy toppings, which is a plus, but brightly lit and full of kids—less than ideal.

"I was actually planning to cook tonight. I could make us dinner?"

Too late, I realize that inviting Ryan over might feel too intimate.

"You love to cook, I love to eat," he says, like the decision has been made.

Maybe I'm overthinking it.

"Perfect."

"Cool, I'm just gonna go grab my coat from the office, then," he says.

As we walk together from the bars to the door, I try to pretend that everything is fine and normal, and that I haven't spent the past two weeks wishing for another opportunity to spend time alone with him. When I duck into the changing room to pick up my parka and purse, I spend an extra thirty seconds fixing my ponytail and putting on a coat of mascara from the tube I find in the bottom of my bag. *This is not a date,* I remind myself as I lacquer up my eyelashes.

I find Ryan in the lobby, leaning against the wall and looking at his phone. There's something casually intimate about the way he waits for me; it's something Tyler did when I met him after football practice. But I can't let myself think that way.

"Hey," he says, straightening up when he sees me. "I was thinking I can follow you in my car?"

"Sure thing. Let's go."

He tails me across town, and I try not to look back at his reflection in my rearview mirror too often. I also refrain from turning on the radio, in case he gets an embarrassing glimpse of me bopping my head along to the music. I try to remember exactly how messy the apartment was when I left this morning. I don't think there are any random bras tossed over the arm of the couch, but I could be wrong.

I meet him in my driveway, and we climb the stairs to my apartment together. *This is not a date,* I remind myself, as I unlock my front door and usher a handsome, funny gentleman inside. This is my first time inviting a guest over to my new apartment, and it's a little nerve-wracking. I distract myself by babbling to Ryan about the tortellini soup recipe I was planning to try out tonight.

"So, it's actually a good thing you're here, because it was so much soup to make for just one person," I explain.

"Glad to hear I'm good for something," he says.

I sift through my fridge and cabinets, picking out the right ingredients to make the dinner. Cooking will keep me busy in front of Ryan, which is a relief because it's jarring to see him sit on one of the yellow bar stools in my kitchen, watching me work.

"Hey, do you want some wine?" I ask.

I hope he'll say yes, so I can have some, too. It'll take the edge off.

"Yeah, I could do a glass," he says.

I find a bottle of red wine in the cabinet and give us each a generous pour. The first sip is so flavorful, that alone calms me down a notch.

There's a lull in the conversation as I start to peel and chop an onion. The apartment feels quiet without Sara here.

"Can I help?" he asks. "I'm no chef, but I can follow instructions if you tell me what to do."

I consider the recipe. "Do you think you're up for the challenge of chopping celery?"

He nods. I hand one to him along with a knife and a cutting board, and we get to work side by side at the kitchen table. Our knives *thwack* rhythmically into our respective vegetables, and I realize again that I don't know what to say that will strike the right balance between friendly and polite.

Ryan clears his throat. "Hallie was great today," he says. "Clean, on point."

I'm both relieved and disappointed that he brought up work. It's easy, safe territory—I don't have to worry about accidentally saying anything unprofessional or inappropriately personal. But on the other hand, well, it's *work*. I don't want to be just his coworker.

"Cheers to that," I say, raising my wineglass.

He clinks his to mine. "Cheers. Seriously. Let's

just hope she keeps up the good work," he says, sighing.

"I'm sure she will," I say. "You're a great coach."

"I do all right," he says, shrugging. "But you had Dimitri. The best. I'm jealous."

"You're jealous I had *him?*" I ask.

"Yeah," he says, his voice full of awe. "He's a legend. I tried for years to get him to take me on, but he only coaches women's gymnastics. What was he like?"

"Tough," I say honestly, moving on to mince a clove of garlic. "Really brutally tough. I like your style better."

"Really?" He looks skeptical.

"Oh, one hundred percent. Hallie loves you. Dimitri was . . . intense."

"What do you mean?"

"Eh, I don't want to get into it. Let's just put it this way: he had insanely high expectations, and it was impossible to meet them all."

"Huh. I'm sorry to hear you had a hard time with him."

"It's fine," I say.

"I didn't mean to pry," he says.

"It's fine," I say again, using a tone that I hope will shut down the subject. I stand up to start cooking the veggies in a pot on the stove. "I'm fine."

Luckily, Ryan doesn't keep digging.

"Coaching's really the only thing I'm qualified for at this point, so I better make the most of it."

"You went to college, though—what did you study?" I ask.

"I majored in business so I could always have the option of starting my own gym, if I wanted to," he explains. "But I don't think I was the most dedicated student. I went to school on a gymnastics scholarship, and that was mostly what I cared about."

"Would you really open your own gym?" I ask.

"Maybe far in the future. But for now, I've realized I'd be happier coaching than doing anything else, and you don't need a degree to do that—just experience, and obviously, these incredible muscles."

"Modest," I observe dryly.

"It's one of my best qualities," he jokes. "How long were you in college for?"

"Only a year and a half."

He snaps his fingers. "That explains it all, then."

"What?"

"Why you're so terrible at beer pong," he says, eyes sparkling with pure delight at delivering a playful burn. "Most people get a full four years to practice."

"Oh, very funny," I say, pursing my lips and pretending to be annoyed. "As I recall, we won that game. Mostly because of you, but still. We won."

"True, true. So, why'd you leave school?"

My answer tumbles out before I can second-guess myself. "I was completely, totally, and majorly depressed. And also, I partied too much to ever make it to class."

He lets out a low whistle. "That got dark fast."

I wince. "Too dark?"

"Nah, it's good to be honest," he says. "Sorry you went through that."

"Yeah, thanks," I say.

I shrug and turn my attention to the pot on the stove so I don't have to see what I assume is a look of pity. But when I look back at Ryan, he doesn't look like he pities me at all. He nods in a way that makes me think he understands.

"You spend all this time obsessively focused on this one thing, and it becomes your whole identity, and then it's gone," he says quietly. "And then it's like, well, what *now?*"

"Exactly," I say, relishing in the fact that he gets it.

"But you're doing all right now?" he asks.

"Kind of the best I've been in a long time, actually," I say, suddenly realizing just how true that is. "You?"

"Yeah, it's all good," he says.

This time, Ryan raises his glass and clinks it against mine.

"Well, cheers to that," I say.

I want to say something more, to come up with a clever idea to toast to, but I get tongue-tied when he makes eye contact over our drinks. Instead, I finish making the soup and ladle it into two bowls. I'm pleased with how it turned out— savory, hearty, bursting with flavor. It's a simple meal, but Ryan seems impressed.

"This beats Stonehearth, hands down," he says appreciatively, scooping up a tortellini with his spoon.

Over dinner, Ryan regales me with stories from his travels. Years of competing across states and countries sparked his love of seeing new places, and now he saves up for as many trips as he can.

"Next up, obviously, I'm saving to do a trip around Asia after Tokyo—*if* Hallie makes it to Tokyo, of course," he explains. "You ever been?"

"No, I haven't," I admit. "What's been your favorite trip so far?"

He thinks for a moment. "Traveling for gymnastics is always cool, but you don't get tons of time to actually explore or indulge in great food, so . . . hmm. I guess my favorite would be the summer that Goose and I backpacked across Europe together."

I wish I had done something like that.

"And obviously, we saw some of the best beaches in the world," he says.

"Why obviously?" I ask. "I'd think that would be, like, the Caribbean."

He leans in closer and stage-whispers, "Nude beaches."

"You perv!" I squeal. The wine has definitely started to go to my head.

He holds up his hands in protest. "Hey, I'm just a man."

"I don't know if I could ever do that," I muse.

"What, go to a nude beach?" he asks.

"Yeah. I mean, maybe years ago, when I was in shape, but certainly not *now*."

He raises an eyebrow, then looks down in intense concentration at his bowl.

"What?" I ask.

He sips his soup. "You could go," he says, coyly glancing up at me.

"Did you strip down?" I ask.

"When in Rome . . ." he replies.

I feel precariously close to the edge of saying something stupidly flirty, so I shove a tortellini into my mouth to keep myself from speaking. Discussing nude beaches makes me wonder what Ryan looks like naked, which is absolutely the very last thing I should be doing.

We linger after we finish eating. He tells stories about what Hallie was like when he first met her (apparently, "tiny, furiously hardworking, adorably wholesome, and too energetic"—or in other words, exactly like she is today). We go off on tangents about gymnasts we competed alongside a decade ago, musing about the few in the public eye today and the majority who faded into quiet lives. We try to gauge where we fall on the spectrum, and jokingly agree to not let the fame go to our heads.

Ryan runs a finger around the rim of his empty wineglass, and his mouth screws up to the side.

"What?" I ask.

"I was going to suggest another glass, but that's probably not the wisest idea if I have to drive out of here," he says.

"True," I say.

"But this was fun," he says, suddenly serious. "I mean it. I'm glad we did this."

"Me, too," I say.

"Let me pay you for half the groceries and wine," he says, reaching for his wallet.

"Oh, no, no," I protest. "I was going to make all this, anyway."

"Avery, it's fine, I don't mind," he says.

"No, really, I can't let you pay for this," I insist.

"Fine," he says heavily. "But next time, I'll win."

"Oh, next time?" I retort. "We'll see about that."

I like that we can match each other in competitive spirit.

"And in the meantime, let me help you clean this up," he offers.

"Now, that, I can accept."

We spend a few minutes clearing the table and loading the dishwasher. He takes the most annoying task, hand-washing the pots, of his own volition. For a split second, the rhythm of cooking and cleaning together reminds me of living with Tyler, and I forget that Ryan isn't my boyfriend. I feel a dull sense of loneliness, thinking ahead to the rest of the night, once he's gone. It only gets worse once the kitchen is clean and he grabs his coat from the hook by the door.

"I'll walk you to your car?" I offer, lingering by the couch, suddenly feeling shy.

"Oh, you don't have to do that," he says. "It's cold."

"I don't mind," I insist.

It's January in New England, which means that getting ready to head out the door requires serious effort: jackets zipped, scarves wound, gloves tugged on. Outside, it's pitch-black. The driveway is only partly lit by the golden glow of a street lamp. By the time we reach Ryan's car, parked behind mine, I'm not ready for the night to end. There's an easy comfort between us—a type of intimacy that only grows between two people who have lived the same kind of life. Ryan reaches for his car door. I don't overthink what comes next; it just happens.

I lean forward and I kiss him. It feels like the most natural thing in the world. He kisses me back, slipping an arm around my waist, and bracing us both with a hand against the car window. His lips are soft, and his embrace is sturdy and strong. There's a warmth radiating from him, even on this frigid night, and I like the way I fit in his arms. I could stay here happily forever, even if it's freezing, even if we shouldn't be doing this.

And then, suddenly, he pulls back. He pushes off the car and shoves his hands into his pockets. Even his eyes flicker away from mine. Without him hovering over me, I feel cold and exposed.

"Avery," he says softly. "We've talked about this. We know it's not a good idea."

I'm shocked by how much his rejection hurts. It's embarrassing to have to be reminded that my past self made a responsible decision that my present self is too emotional or tipsy or lonely to adhere to.

"I . . . I'm sorry, I just . . ." I stammer.

The easy banter over dinner, the fuss over paying for groceries, the comfort of cleaning up side by side—maybe this wasn't technically supposed to be a date, but it sure felt like one. And what happened next was simply a natural extension of the night. Wasn't it? I sigh, and in the cold, my breath becomes a visible cloud.

"I just thought that maybe you wanted this, too," I say.

He gives me a sad look that makes my entire body feel weighed down with two-ton anchors.

"So you don't want this," I clarify.

It's mortifying to say that out loud, but he has to understand how he made me feel tonight. I want him to recognize that he made me feel like there was possibility blooming between us again.

"I've really thought this through since New Year's Eve, and as much as I wanted this to work between us, you were right—it's just not a smart idea for us to jump into anything," he says.

I hate that he's using my own words against me. I'm afraid if I protest, my voice will come out thin and whiny, like I'm begging for his affection.

"Oh," I manage to squeak out, feeling very small.

He sighs. "I don't want to push you away."

"Right. I know we talked about being just friends," I admit. "I'm sorry if I crossed a line, then."

He looks down at his feet and doesn't say anything. I can feel whatever sliver of a chance of us being together evaporating, and it makes me feel frantic with desperation.

"Do you feel like there's something between us?" I blurt out. "Because I do. I'd be lying if I pretended otherwise."

"I . . ." He trails off and rubs his jaw. I'm overcome by a desire to kiss that spot, but I refrain. "I do. Of course I do, Avery. Come on. You're beautiful, and so unbelievably strong, and I feel so at home talking to you. I like that we're cut from the same cloth: competitive, hardworking, goal-oriented. It's rare to find someone like that who also has room in their life for someone else."

Against my better judgment, a thrill runs through my body. My brain feels like a jumble of confetti and trumpets and parades. And then I notice the way his voice lilts downward at the end, like there's a "but" coming. My heart races and then skids to a stop.

Sure enough, he starts with, "But—"

I have to cut him off. "Here's the thing, Ryan. Whether or not it's convenient, or whether or not it's a good idea, I can't just walk away from the fact that being around you makes me happier than I've felt in a long time."

I sound ten times braver than I feel. It's terrifying to be so honest with him, but I'm in too deep now to turn around. I have to keep going—I owe it to myself to at least try to win Ryan over. I take a deep breath and barrel on.

"And this isn't just about me. You have a great job and a great life, but I know you want more. I bet you've been lonely. That's why you jumped into a relationship right after retiring from gymnastics. That's why you flirt with me, even when you say you know better. I know what it's like to want a real connection and not find it, and it's awful."

Ryan is still just inches away. I take in the soft, dark depths of his eyes, the faint scar over his eyebrow, the smattering of stubble along his jaw, his tensed, broad shoulders. He swallows.

"You're right," he says quietly, not breaking my gaze. "About all of it."

"Okay . . ." I say, feeling hopeful, though not secure enough to relax just yet.

"I'm just not sure that's enough," he says. "Not when there's so much at stake. As long as we're responsible for Hallie, she comes first. There can't be any distractions."

Distractions. The word reverberates uncomfortably and settles into the pit of my stomach. That's what I'd be: a distraction. I can't look at him. I'm not a monster—I don't want my love life to stand in the way of Hallie's shot at Olympic glory. But I don't think it's quite that simple. She would never need to know. I fiddle with the zipper of my jacket.

"Look, I'm not saying no to this. To us," he says, reaching out to tuck a stray piece of hair behind my ear. "I'm just saying we need to think carefully here, because the Olympics are right around the corner. And you, more than anyone, can understand how devastated Hallie would be if she doesn't make it."

I'm sure Ryan didn't mean to do it, but linking my feelings for him now to the depression I felt years ago just crushes me. It's cruel.

"I have to go," I mutter, blinking back tears.

Ryan doesn't protest as I head back inside.

FEBRUARY
2020

• *Chapter 13* •

"Do you have a boyfriend?" Hallie asks at practice a week later.

I hold her feet as she dangles her upper body off the back of the vault, then muscles her way up into a sitting position. Her abs swell in size by the second.

"What?" I spit out, caught off guard.

I'm very careful to resist the urge to peek across the gym at Ryan. In fact, I've spent the majority of the past week avoiding him, because it's painful enough to replay our awful last conversation in my head every night before I fall asleep. I don't want to have to relive it in his presence, too.

"I asked if you had a boyfriend," she repeats, finishing another rep of crunches.

She rarely, if ever, asks about my life outside the gym. I don't share, either. Did she Google me? If so, there's a handful of tabloid stories about me and Tyler—I hope she didn't uncover those.

I laugh nervously. "No. Why?"

Her face turns beet red, and it's not from the physical exertion. She can do this workout in her sleep.

"I was just wondering because you've seemed

kind of sad all week, and I wondered if you got into a fight with your boyfriend," she mumbles, rushing to add, "I just wanted to see if you were okay, *butnevermind.*"

"Oh my god," I mutter, more to myself than to her.

The last thing I want to do is to make a scene, because then Ryan will come over and ask what we're laughing about.

"Hallie, no, that's very sweet of you," I say quietly, trying not to attract attention. "I appreciate you checking in on me. I'm fine, just a little tired, that's all."

"Got it, got it, got it," she says. "Uh, sorry for asking."

She dips backward into another crunch. "So, you're single, then? I know my aunt is always trying to set up my older cousin," she says, giggling.

"Hallie, focus!" I say, clamping down harder on her feet. "Ten more reps in this set. Let's go."

We make it through conditioning without any more forays into my personal life. When it's time for her to move on to bars, she skips off to the changing room to grab her grips. I'm relieved she didn't dig any deeper. I remember what it was like when I was her age. I knew that the girls I had grown up with had boyfriends, or at least dates to the winter semiformal. I opted for homeschooling instead of attending an actual high school, but even I heard rumors about my old classmates having sex, saying *I love you,* flirting at beer-soaked parties. I wondered if some people were born hardwired for it, the way I was primed for athletic excellence. I couldn't fathom having the guts to do any of that on my own. (But a death-defying stunt on a sliver of wood? Sure, no problem.) I'm impressed that Hallie was brave enough to ask me about my personal life— and I wonder how much of her curiosity stems from wondering what it's like to have a personal life at all.

My ponytail has loosened over the course of the morning, and it sags toward the nape of my neck. I take down my hair and am in the process of redoing my ponytail when my hair elastic snaps. I don't have another one on me, so I head to the supply closet, tucked in an alcove at the back of the gym. The door is slightly ajar. I push it open farther and nearly bump straight into Ryan, who's running his fingers over the shelves, like he's in search of something.

"Oh! Sorry," I say. "I didn't realize anyone was in here."

"No worries," he says, turning around to glance at me.

He *looks* worried, though, as if he's waiting for me to say or do something inappropriate again.

"Uh, hi," I say.

"Hi," he says, turning back around.

I rack my brain for some witty joke or easy banter to break the tension, but instead, I just freeze up. He tilts his head slightly, like he's waiting for me to say something, anything.

"I just came back here for another hair elastic," I explain, pointing to my awkwardly lumpy hair, still half-stuck in the shape of a ponytail. "Mine broke."

"I see that," he says, pulling the box of hair supplies off one shelf and offering it to me.

I find a fresh elastic, flip my head over, and smooth my hair back into a high, tight pony. I feel more like myself this way.

"Have you seen the blocks of chalk?" Ryan asks. "I know we're running low, but I thought there was at least one more case in here."

I scan the shelves, which are brimming with athletic tape, gauze, Advil, cans of hair spray and butt glue covered in chalky handprints, and water bottles branded with Summit's logo. A colorful pile of latex resistance bands spools in one corner of the closet.

"Uhhh, yeah, here you go."

I crouch down to the bottom shelf, where there's one remaining block of chalk half-hidden in a white plastic bag. Our hands bump when he takes it from me.

"Thanks," he says, turning to lean against the shelves.

Crammed into this narrow closet with him,

it hits me that I miss the easy way our conversations used to flow, before I kissed him and messed everything up. Aside from strictly necessary conversations about Hallie's training, we've barely exchanged a single word since then. We've stopped eating lunch together, too.

"How've you been?" I ask.

He exhales with the slightest hint of a laugh and looks down at the chalk in his hands.

"We're really doing this?" he asks, muttering it more to himself than to me.

"Doing what?" I ask, suddenly alarmed that I've crossed a line.

He gestures vaguely at the space between us and makes air quotes. "You know . . . 'How've you been?' Pretending things are all normal, when, in fact, the first time we've spoken about anything but Hallie all week is because we accidentally stumbled into the same closet."

I bite my lip, feeling the sensation of embarrassment flood my entire body. I always thought I had a decent poker face; it's something I picked up from years of competing in front of judges, hiding grimaces when I was in pain or pissed about a low score. It's mortifying that Ryan has seen right through me this whole time.

"Ryan," I say, sighing, doing my best attempt to sound supremely casual. "I am just asking how you are. This isn't some covert sneak attack attempt at rekindling anything. Not that things were, uh, kindled in the first place. Trust me, I got the message."

I cross my arms. I feel like a fool for trying to strike up a conversation with him in the first place.

But instead of looking upset or embarrassed, his expression is apologetic.

"Avery, I'm sorry, no, you're right. I know things have been kind of weird since that dinner, and I'm sorry about that. I'm trying to be a professional here—keep my distance, not make things awkward. This is new territory for me," he explains.

"Same."

He exhales heavily and gives me a hopeful look. "We're not doing too badly, right?"

"What, at keeping this quiet?" I ask.

"Yeah."

"Well . . . Hallie just asked me if I had a boyfriend," I say, not daring to mention that she only wondered because I seemed *sad* about potentially *fighting* with him. That's information Ryan simply never needs to know.

He laughs. "And what did you tell her?"

"The truth, obviously!"

He tilts his head, encouraging me to continue.

"I told her no, I wasn't seeing anybody," I clarify.

"Got it," he muses.

He shifts his weight, and my view of the

doorway behind him disappears completely. Nobody can see me in here with him, not even if they tried. I'm close enough to take just one step forward and kiss him, but I know I shouldn't. I inch backward, away from him, but my foot catches on the pile of resistance bands spilling out on the floor and I trip. The shelves are freestanding metal ones; I'm sure everything would topple down onto me if I grabbed them for support. I pitch off-kilter, and Ryan lunges forward to steady me.

I find my balance quickly, but Ryan doesn't let go. Not at first. His fingers are wrapped around my bicep and my waist, and I've braced myself against his chest. He looks down at me. I look up at him. He looks down at his hand wrapped around my torso, like he's just fully registered that it's there, and can't quite believe it. His lips, just inches away from me, curl up in an embarrassed sort of smile. I hate that I like his strong hands holding me up.

Then I hear Hallie's voice calling my name. The sound jolts me out of Ryan's arms. I squeeze past him, through the doorway, and into the main part of the gym so I can find Hallie.

"Avery? Avery?" she calls.

I find her near the bars, clutching her phone, frozen in place.

"Did you see the news?" she asks.

Her voice sounds timid.

"No, what news?" I ask.

She glances at Ryan, coming up behind me, then back to me. She holds her phone to her chest and motions for me to come closer. I get a bad feeling.

"Ryan, could you give us a sec?" I ask.

He looks confused, but ducks away.

Hallie flops belly-down on one of the plush crash mats by the bars. I sit cross-legged next to her. She sighs, hands me her phone, and then buries her face in her arms.

"Just read it," she says, voice muffled and dejected.

My heart sinks when I read the *New York Times* headline on her screen: "Olympian Delia Cruz Accuses Sports Medicine Dr. Ron Kaminsky of Sexual Assault." Of course Hallie isn't the only one he intimidated or abused. I feel so stupid for not realizing she isn't an isolated case. I know Delia, sort of. She's halfway between my age and Hallie's, so we briefly overlapped for a year at competitions, but we were never close. Back when I knew her, she was this bubbly, outgoing kid with a mane of springy, dark curls sprouting from her scrunchie. She used to sneak gummy bears into her gym bag and hand them out covertly in the locker room.

I skim the rest of the story, but after the endless wave of sexual assault allegations against politicians, CEOs, and Hollywood producers over the past few years, the details are sickeningly famil-iar. Delia says Dr. Kaminsky molested her while allegedly treating her for a hamstring injury. Her mom, like Hallie's mom, was in the room. The *Times* reports that a representative for Dr. Kaminsky vehemently denies the claims.

"I had no idea," Hallie says, voice shaking. "Delia never told me."

I'm at a loss for what to say. I try to imagine what I would want to hear if I were in her shoes, but I come up frustratingly short. It's not like I ever had heart-to-hearts with Dimitri.

"Hallie, this is awful. I'm so sorry you had to find out like this," I manage.

She stares glumly off into space for a long time.

"Maybe if I had said something . . . spoken up . . . this wouldn't have happened to Delia?" she asks.

She looks to me hopefully, as if I have the answers. It's too horrible to comprehend. But this time, I know what to say.

"No," I insist. "This isn't your fault. The only person who could've prevented this is him. This is not on you. Please remember that."

I realize that if Dr. Kaminsky did this to Delia, and nearly did it to Hallie, he must have done it to other girls, too. It's too awful to imagine how many others there are, how big this is.

Hallie is still flat on the mat, but now her chin digs into her hands and her lower lip curls inward, like she's trying to prevent it from trembling. I don't know what to do, but I know I have to try *something*. I stroke comforting circles on her upper back, and her eyes start to water.

"Hallie?" I ask tentatively.

"It's just . . . I don't . . ." she begins, hastily rubbing away her tears and sniffling. "This is not supposed to be happening right now."

"I know."

"I have to *focus* right now," she insists.

"Well—" I start, intending to remind her that taking care of herself is far more important than muscling through practice, but she's too incensed to let me speak.

"I hate him, I hate him, he makes me so mad, I hate him so much!" she says, voice curdling with anger.

She's close to shouting now. Other gymnasts and coaches have turned to stare. I want to snap at them. It's like a spotlight follows Hallie around the gym; she's the only one here worth gawking at. But right now, she's not performing. She just needs privacy.

"Why don't we take a break from this and head outside for a bit?" I ask.

I can practically see the first thought that flashes through her head: *No. I need to work.* But then she heaves a sigh, wipes under each eye, and nods silently in agreement. She strides across the floor and the vault runway—the other gymnasts defer to her right of way, letting her cross before they resume tumbling and sprinting—and pushes open the gym's side door. It opens out to the parking lot. There's a set of metal stairs there that we can sit on. It's cold outside, but she's been working hard; I bet the chill feels good on her bare arms and legs.

Hallie perches on the top step, hugging her knees to her chest, and kneads her chin into her kneecaps. She rocks back and forth silently, shaking her head. It looks like there's too much frantic energy to contain in one tiny body. She leaps to her feet and her arms fly out in rage. She lets out an anguished groan into the frigid air and stomps her bare foot against the pavement.

"It's just not fair!" she shouts.

And then she shrinks down into herself. She crosses her arms tight across her body and steers herself into me for a hug. I hold her close and stroke her hair. I guide us to sit down on the steps, and do the one thing I wish someone had done for me, back when I was in pain and enraged and swimming in sadness: I give her a plan. I suggest that if she feels comfortable, she should consider telling her parents the truth about her appointments with Dr. Kaminsky. She agrees to do it, and I offer to be there with her for that conversation, if she wants. And then, as a family, they can all figure out how to move forward— whether that means reporting what happened to her to the police, or simply letting it go. I remind Hallie that there's no pressure to come back to practice today, or tomorrow, or any day.

"The most important thing right now is to take care of yourself," I tell her. "Trust me, even if it doesn't feel like it right now, that matters even more than your training does."

She nods. I hope she believes me.

The next week is awful. Delia Cruz goes on *Good Morning America*, looking steely and powerful in a sleek white suit, and gives a searing retelling of the most horrific moments of her life. On Twitter, she releases a statement encouraging other survivors of sexual assault to get help. The replies to her tweet are mostly full of love and support, but there's a mountain of replies from hateful trolls, too. I can't even begin to fathom the mental gymnastics they have to employ to convince themselves that she's the one ruining Dr. Kaminsky's life, not the other way around.

Maggie Farber comes forward. So does her teammate Kiki McCloud. And then there's a wave of others who speak up, both household names who competed in the Olympics and athletes who never quite made it into the spotlight: Emily Jenkins, Bridget Sweeney, Liora Cohen. By the end of the week, there are six names splashed across most of the major TV shows and publications, and a sickening sense that more will come. I feel both shocked and relieved, like I dodged a bullet. It was only by sheer luck that I visited other doctors instead of him.

Tara Michaels, the prominent conservative pundit and self-professed lover of "family values" who wears enough pearly pink lip gloss to single-handedly keep Sephora in business, unleashes a tirade that goes viral. She says it's "disturbing" that America swallows up the stories of these six "unreliable" teenagers without giving a "respected" doctor a chance to tell his side of the story. "Facts are important," she urges, disregarding that most of her own facts happen to be wrong. Half the gymnasts who have come forward are in their twenties by now. Dr. Kaminsky's lawyer already issued a blanket statement denying any wrongdoing. Tara's speech is peppered with racist jabs toward Delia, Kiki, and Emily, whose photos flash on-screen. The producers could have chosen photos of the athletes with medals around their neck; instead, they picked crotch shots—straddle jumps and leaps, taken from below. By the third time I see the video clip circulating online, it has more than ten million views.

The internet churns with impassioned headlines about how America has failed its girls; how gymnastics is just a beauty pageant masquerading as a sport; how this is what happens when parents don't pay enough attention to their own kids.

There's a lot of outrage directed at the sport, the parents, the gymnasts themselves—but I don't see enough of it aimed at Dr. Kaminsky. You'd think, given how many powerful men have fallen into scandal over the past few years, that collectively, we'd know how to do this by now.

The gymternet—the blogs, podcasts, and Twitter accounts run by die-hard gymnastics fans with passionately engaged followers—lights up with commentary and analysis of the situation. I tried listening to one podcast episode, but turned it off halfway through. The hosts sounded defeated. There's no pleasure in dissecting this tragedy.

Hallie told her parents about how Dr. Kaminsky had made her feel, and they swiftly connected her to the best children's therapist in the Boston area. She insists on coming to practice each day, though there are dark circles under her eyes and her usual boundless energy sags. She used to keep her phone tucked away in the changing room while she trained, but now she keeps it nearby so she can stay updated in case any more gymnasts come forward. She doesn't seem to want to speak out publicly, and given what the other six gymnasts have gone through, I don't blame her.

What haunts me the most, though, is Ryan's reaction to the situation. Hallie had asked me to tell him the truth about her experience with Dr. Kaminsky.

"I'd feel awkward talking to him about it, you know?" she had explained. "I know he should probably know, but I just can't."

The day the Delia story broke, Hallie decided to leave practice early. She called her mom to come pick her up, and I waited with her in the locker room so people didn't keep staring at her. Once she left, I found Ryan in the gym and told him we needed to talk. We sat in a quiet, empty corner of the gym, and I relayed the entire dismal story. He looked shocked and sad when I summarized what happened to Delia, but downright grief-stricken when I shared how Kaminsky had made Hallie feel. His face crumpled.

"No," he said, shaking his head in disbelief. "Is she okay? How is she holding up?"

"I don't know," I said honestly. "She's angry. Upset. Sad. Who wouldn't be?"

He punched a stack of crash mats, and the solid *thump* of his fist echoed around the gym.

"I told her to go to that scumbag," he spat out. "This is my fault."

"It's not," I said gently.

And because nothing in the world was right, I stepped forward to give him a hug. I held him for a long time.

"I just had no idea," he repeated over and over, looking pained. "Everyone trusted him."

I was at a loss for words again.

"Maybe," I said finally, "that was the problem."

• *Chapter 14* •

It's been a hell of a week, so on Saturday morning, when Sara invites me to yoga for what must be the fifteenth time, I say yes. Anything is better than sitting around, reading infuriating tweets about the scandal. If yoga can help take my mind off that, I'm willing to try it.

"Yay, this is fab! I'm so excited to have you in class today," Sara says, giving me a quick squeeze of a hug. "You don't have a yoga mat, do you?"

"Nope. You know, I've never actually done yoga before."

"Not a problem. There are extra mats at the studio. You should bring a water bottle and wear something comfortable that you can move in— probably not a leotard, though, just FYI. Like, leggings, tank tops, that kind of thing."

"Trust me, it's not like any of my old leotards even fit anymore," I joke. "I wish."

"Don't do that," Sara says gently.

"What?"

"Make comments like that about your body," she explains. "There's no need to beat yourself up."

"I don't—" I start to protest.

But I do. Constantly. I can't remember a time

before I was acutely aware of every inch of my body: every muscle, curve, and soft spot. Dimitri taught us that our bodies were our tools, the same way an artist would use a paintbrush. That's why we had to be so strict and disciplined with the way we ate and worked out, he explained. And at the time, it all made sense: the intense diets, the weekly weigh-ins, the way he punished us with hours of conditioning if we overate or gained weight. Every week, he'd jot down our height, weight, and measurements in a little blue notebook. He wore a withering expression when we failed him, whether we gained a pound or confessed to eating a slice of pizza. That expression still flashes across my mind every time the waistband of my jeans digs into my stomach or I consider indulging in a dessert.

"I'm sorry, you're right," I say. It's awkward to realize that Sara can tell exactly how I feel about my body. "Old habits die hard, you know?"

Sara gives me a kind smile. "Yoga totally transforms the way your mind relates to your physical self. You'll see. I bet you'll like it."

An hour later, she leads me into Mind & Body Yoga. The studio has shiny wooden floors, a row of leafy green plants at the front of the room, and soothing music wafting from the speakers. The other participants in the class—mostly twenty- and thirty-something women, but a few teenagers and a handful of men, too—unroll colorful yoga mats facing the front of the room and begin to stretch. Sara hands me an extra mat, along with two foam blocks.

"In case you need to prop yourself up to get through some of the more challenging poses," she explains quietly.

I try not to scoff, but come on. I'm a former elite gymnast. I think I can survive an hour of yoga.

Sara sets up her own mat horizontally at the front of the room. When the studio is mostly full, she kicks off class by encouraging us to lie down in a comfortable position. I expected everyone to lie flat on their backs, but I'm surprised by the variations: legs splayed out, knees butterflied out to the sides, heads propped up by foam blocks. Sara leads the class through a breathing exercise in a melodic, trance-like voice.

"In through your nose," she intones with a kind but serious expression. "Out through your mouth. And then, when you're ready, another inhale."

After what feels like eons of breathing, Sara slowly leads the class into a sitting position, and encourages us to emit an *om* on the count of three.

"One, two, three, all together, now, *om* . . ." she says.

The class erupts into noise that stretches on for longer than I expected, and I run out of breath before the rest of the class. The second time we try it, I attempt to sustain the sound longer than anyone else—well, second longest, since being the very last person to keep it up would draw more attention than I really want. I'm surprised at the effort it takes.

By the time Sara leads us from a sitting position to a standing one, I'm antsy for the real work to begin. I know that yoga is about relaxation and meditation, but it's exercise, too, isn't it? Eventually, we settle into downward dog. People around me emit little sighs and groans as they sink into the position.

"Beautiful breath sounds," Sara compliments. "It's okay to let go and vocalize your efforts."

From downward dog, we move through a series of poses with names like warrior one, warrior two, half moon, and crescent moon. Sara encourages us to "flow" from one to the next and be "intentional" about our breath, whatever that means. The language of yoga feels funny to me, but I suppose gymnastics has its own language, too. The class moves slowly at first, but soon, we're breezing from one pose to the next in a way that makes me sweat. Sara winds her way through the maze of mats, correcting postures with a touch of her hand and whispering words of encouragement. I can't help but feel competitive about it: I want to perform so flawlessly that she won't have to correct me at all. It would be one thing if I were a couch potato who struggled to get the poses right—but I'm not. I'm a world-class athlete, or at least, *was* one. This should be a piece of cake. I crane my neck to glimpse the way my neighbor, a curvy woman in a pink workout tank that reads HUSTLE FOR THAT MUSCLE, sinks into warrior two, and try to angle my body to match hers.

That's when I feel Sara's hands on my hips. "Like this," she says, tilting my left side forward and my right side back. She trails a finger up the back of my neck, causing me to look ramrod straight ahead instead of at the people around me. And then, as if she's reading my mind, she whispers, "It's not a competition. Just listen to your body and do what you need to do."

"Okay, but is this right?" I whisper back.

She pauses and gives an infuriatingly serene wave of her hand. "There's no such thing as right or wrong, as long as you're focused on your breath and your flow."

"But—" I protest.

It's too late. Sara has already moved on to another student. *This,* I think, *is why I hate yoga.* There's always a right way to do everything.

Once the class has more or less all caught up to downward dog again, Sara takes her place at the front of the yoga studio and demonstrates another sequence of postures. Between the bent knees, angled hips, and outstretched arms, these are a little more complicated. I have to concentrate to get the series right. As I move from one pose to the next, I feel my muscles stretch and quiver; this class is more taxing than I expected. While my thighs quake through chair pose, Hustle for That Muscle Girl's quads look rock solid. I stare down at my legs, willing them to stay locked into place, but the only thing that happens is a fat droplet of sweat drips off my nose and splashes onto my kneecap. I inhale deeply, like Sara taught me to, and I'm surprised to find that maybe—just maybe—it actually does help. Thirteen trembling seconds later (but who's counting?), I breathe a sigh of relief when Sara tells the class to stretch upward into mountain pose, which is just standing up straight.

"You're stronger and softer than your mind knows. But your body knows," she says—whatever that means.

We cycle through the sequence again, and when I end up back in chair pose, I grit my teeth. This time around, I know what I'm up against. I'm determined to make it through the full duration without breaking perfect form.

"If at any point, you're not feeling what the class is doing, take a break," Sara intones in that oddly soothing yoga voice. "Sit in child's pose or *shavasana*. There's real power in tuning in to your body's truest needs."

Real power. *Real power.* Through the burning sensation in my thighs, I want to scream at Sara:

You know what real power looks like? Standing atop an Olympic podium with a gold medal draped around your neck, that's what. Or training hard for thousands of hours until you know you have ultimate control over your body's every movement. Not tapping out when it gets a little bit tough.

"Chair pose is challenging for a reason," she says, voice floating through the room. "The key is to listen to your body and make adjustments that honor your journey through the pose."

Before I can register what's happening, I'm dropping to the floor and stretching my torso and arms over my knees into child's pose. I'm "honoring my journey." It's embarrassing, but relief washes over me. My thighs relax, my breathing evens out, and the muscles around my shoulders loosen. I'm frustrated with myself for dropping out of the challenge, but when I roll my head to the side and peek out at my classmates from under my arm, it looks like nobody's even noticed me. Hustle for That Muscle Girl resolutely blows out a steady stream of air from pursed lips. The pair of teen girls on my other side don't seem to blink. Sara only comes my way to press her palms into my lower back.

I can't remember ever dropping out of a work-out like this before. When I was Hallie's age, if Jasmine or I were tired or in pain, we'd wait until Dimitri got wrapped up in a conversation with another coach or went to the bathroom before we dared take a break. A few moments of rest weren't worth the threat of his backlash. It was impossible to truly relax when you feared he'd deliver a physically taxing punishment or a cruel joke at your expense.

Back then, Dimitri's pressure-cooker coaching style made sense: winners work hard, and we wanted to win. Even if Sara's philosophy is a little new age for me, I hear what she's saying. *Listen to your body; connect to your body; honor your body.* Push yourself when you can, and rest when you need to. It goes against everything I was raised with, but in hindsight, maybe Dimitri should have been softer with us. More forgiving. Less intense. After all, I worked hard all the time, just like he wanted me to, and I still didn't win. I don't regret the way gymnastics shaped my life, but I do wonder if the few fleeting moments in the spotlight were worth the lifetime of pain I know I have ahead of me.

I take a deep breath. Sara's hands have drifted away from me; she's moved on to another student. I concentrate on doing a mental scan of my body. I feel the spongy surface of the yoga mat under my fingertips and the center of my forehead, and I can sense the thin sheen of sweat between my breasts. The soft curve of my belly rests against my thighs, and my hips hinge backward in a comfortable stretch. My feet are tucked under my bottom, and when I wriggle my toes against the mat, I feel the sensation flex all the way up my legs. More than anything, I feel present, and that makes a sob escape from my throat. It's mortifying to cry here, but somehow, I don't think anyone will mind.

For years, I ignored physical pain and warped my desires into discipline. I controlled my body with the sheer strength of my mind. Maybe now it's time to turn all that around—to let my mind dictate the way my body moves. On my next exhale, I transition into downward dog—my calves feel warm and loose this time around, even as a tear rolls down my cheek and mixes with my sweat. I kneel for a moment to wipe my tears with the hem of my tank top and drink in the cool water that's been waiting for me all practice. I do a sun salutation to catch up to the rest of the group. The simple way my breath and my movements sync up makes me feel airy, light, strong, and yes, powerful.

I make it through the next twenty minutes without taking a break, but I wouldn't mind if I needed to. It's strange—I didn't realize I'd come so far. I mimic Sara's movements as she leads the class from a one-legged balance to core-strengthening exercises to half-pigeon pose, which stretches out your hip flexors like taffy. In the final few minutes of the class, she asks us to lie down on our backs with our eyes closed in *shavasana*. She walks softly around the room with a bottle of lavender essential oil, dropping a dot of it on each of our shoulders.

"I'm going to close out the class with a few words of wisdom from the poet and activist Audre Lorde, and the song of the Tibetan singing bowl," Sara says softly. The little noises around the studio—coughs, sighs, slurps from water bottles—grow still in anticipation. " 'Caring for myself is not self-indulgence, it is self-preservation.' "

Then the melodic sound of the Tibetan singing bowl resonates and spirals throughout the room, growing and growing until Sara strikes the bowl and it clangs to a stop.

"You can stay in *shavasana* until you're ready to rise again," she says simply.

I let myself sink into the mat. Energy swirls through my body, but my limbs feel heavy with relaxation. I hadn't wanted to give into Sara's woo-woo, spiritual sort of stretching, but even I have to admit that it felt kind of, well, nice. The combination of exertion and mindfulness makes me drift off into thoughts about the ways in which gymnastics shaped my relationship to my body: my body image, my insistence of pushing through pain, the distant way I regarded my physical self first and foremost as a tool. Over the years, I've tried not to think about it too much. But here, it's impossible to avoid.

Suddenly, Sara is squatting next to me. "How'd you like the class?" she asks.

I crane my neck to look at the clock at the back of the room. Five minutes have passed, and the rest of the class has already rolled up their yoga mats and filed out of the studio.

"It was . . . wow." That's all I can manage.

"You think you'll come back again?" she asks.

Sunlight pours into the studio through the floor-to-ceiling windows, and I get a startlingly clear vision of myself returning to this spot again and again. I could do this, couldn't I? I feel peaceful here, similarly to the way I relax when I cook. The steady movement of the class meant my mind never wandered off to Ryan, Hallie, or even the terrible scandal in the news. Instead, I had no choice but to focus on the flow between poses, my breath, and the sound of Sara's voice. It's not a stretch to see how I could develop a craving for this, unwinding here at the studio after a long day at Summit. And if just one session already feels transformative for me, I can only imagine how it could help Hallie. Maybe this is exactly what she needs to rein in the anxiety she's felt lately.

"Yeah, I'll be back. And next time, there's someone else I'd like to bring, too."

• *Chapter 15* •

Hallie wrinkles her nose when I tell her about my idea at the end of practice on Monday.

"Yoga? I mean, I already do so much," she says, looking skeptical.

She's cross-legged on the floor of the changing room, stretching the white thigh-high socks she got at her friend's Sweet Sixteen, embroidered with the girl's initials, up her legs. The thick socks strain over her muscular calves, though, and barely graze her knees. She gives a final tug and gives up. I bet the party wasn't as fun as she expected it to be; she probably had to say no to the cake and head home early to stick to her sleep schedule.

"But what if you could have private yoga lessons here at the gym?" I counter. "Barely any extra work on your part, and I think it'll help reduce stress over the next few months."

"I'm not stressed," she snaps.

She looks wild, with a cloud of frizz escaping her ponytail at the temples. But then her expression softens. She must understand, on some level, how that's just not true.

"I'll try it once," she agrees. "*If* Ryan thinks it's a good idea, too."

"I'll talk to him," I promise.

Hallie shoves her feet into sneakers, stands up, and slings her gym bag over her shoulder.

When she turns to walk away, I catch a glimpse of what's on her screen. I recognize it because I saw it, too, earlier that day—Delia Cruz's Instagram encouraging her followers to donate to RAINN, a nonprofit that supports sexual assault survivors. Hallie's broad shoulders look small and slumped as she disappears around the corner and heads outside to her mom's waiting car.

I know Ryan's still inside, probably cleaning up alone. All the other classes and team practices have wrapped up for the night, and the rest of the coaches have headed home. The lobby is empty by now, too; the usual rows of Lululemon moms playing games on their phones have cleared out of the plastic folding chairs. I head back into the gym to find Ryan and talk to him about setting Hallie up with yoga lessons.

Sure enough, I find him in the back corner of the main part of the gym, cleaning chalk dust and sweat off crash mats with a spray bottle and a roll of paper towels. He's changed the music from its usual Top 40 radio station to what must be his own classic rock playlist.

"Hey, what are you doing back here?" he says, spritzing a mat with soapy water.

"I wanted to get your opinion on something, but while I'm here, can I help?" I ask.

He pauses and looks at the waist-high stack

of mats he's yet to clean. They're each eight or twelve inches thick, but still—that's a lot of mats.

"If you really don't mind, sure, take a mat," he says. "What's up?"

I drag the next mat off the stack and pull it parallel to the one he's cleaning. He hands me the spray bottle and I get to work.

"So, I finally went to yoga this weekend, and it was amazing," I explain. "Not just the workout part—though that actually wasn't half-bad—but the mental part of it."

"Nice."

"And it made me think that Hallie could actually really benefit from adding yoga to her routine, especially now and during the next few months."

"Yeah? Why?"

I consider how personal and vulnerable I actually want to get here. I want him to understand how yoga could clear Hallie's head in a way that gymnastics never could. But I don't know if I'm ready to share the rest of my thoughts with him. I don't doubt that Ryan had a hell of a time during his competition days, dieting and pushing through punishing workouts. But I also know that, as tough as it could've been for him, it wasn't the same as what I went through. While puberty signals the end of a girl's gymnastics career, it's the real beginning of a man's: gaining weight and developing muscle only makes him better at the sport.

And Ryan never trained under Dimitri. He probably never worked out on an empty stomach, worrying that his vision would go fuzzy and black around the edges as he sprinted down the vault runway. He probably never tried to convince himself the quaking pain in his stomach was from too many crunches instead of skipping a meal. He wouldn't understand how restorative it was to be in a place in which you simply had to listen and react to your body's needs.

Gymnastics has changed lightning-fast, even in the decade since I was Hallie's age. The top athletes in the sport these days aren't eighty-five-pound waifs like some of the ones I looked up to as a kid—they have real, solid muscle and power, like Hallie does. She's smarter than I ever was, and she knows she can't perform her best if she's starving. But she faces a new set of pressures I never could have imagined: a more difficult scoring system; watching her competitors' skills ratchet up every day on Instagram, just like their follower counts do; the disturbing sexual abuse scandal and its coverage on every news channel in America right now.

"I'm just saying, I think she's going through a tough time right now, and what I loved about the yoga class I went to was the emphasis on self-care," I say.

I cringe at how hokey that sounds, and I try again.

"I don't think it's a bad idea for her to have a place to chill and zone out, where she doesn't have to worry about being the best, or training for some goal," I explain. "She can just stretch, listen to my roommate's cheesy but weirdly effective mantras, and have an hour to herself, away from the news."

"She does seem pretty stressed," he admits, ripping off another square of paper towel.

"I think yoga would be a great way for her to relax," I say.

"Then sure, let's do it," he says. "You're thinking of having your roommate work with her?"

"Sara's awesome, yeah."

"Maybe an hour or two a week?"

"I'll set it up!"

I can't wait to tell Sara.

"Cool, thanks," he says. "You're the best."

He finishes cleaning one mat, drags it back to its regular spot under the bars, and takes off his sweatshirt before starting on another mat. Underneath, he has on a white tank top that reveals the full scope of the Olympic rings tattooed on his bicep. I've seen the bottom edges of it peek out from his T-shirts before, but I've never seen the whole thing. It's not quite as bright as I imagined it would be—instead, the colors are ever so slightly faded, as if it were simply a natural part of his skin.

"What?" he asks, a little self-consciously.

He must have caught me staring.

"Oh, nothing," I say, embarrassed. "I've just never seen your tattoo before, that's all."

I scrub furiously at the mat beneath me until my paper towel begins to shred.

"Oh! Here, look."

Ryan comes over to kneel next to me on the mat. I don't really like most tattoos—you only get one body, and I doubt most things in life are worth permanently etching into your skin. But this one makes my heart beat faster. I know the Olympic Games have their roots in ancient Greece, when men held footraces and threw javelins in a festival to honor the god Zeus. The athletic challenges were revived in Athens in 1896, when the first modern Olympic Games were held. When you remember the history, it's hard not to see Olympic athletes like modern-day Greek gods.

"Can I touch it?" I ask timidly.

He laughs. "Sure."

I run my finger over the outline of the rings. He earned this.

"If you wound up going to the Olympics, would you have gotten one?" he asks.

"Yeah, of course," I say, nodding. "I mean, I'd want a small one, somewhere easy to hide, but yeah."

"Why hide it?" he asks. He flexes his bicep, and

the rings jump. "It's an honor to join the club."

"I don't know, tattoos aren't really my thing," I say.

The expression on his face falters just a fraction of an inch.

"But yours, though . . . I like yours a lot," I rush to add. "That's probably the only one I'd ever consider getting for myself."

"If you were to get one, where would you put it?" he asks.

"I used to think about this all the time, you know?" I tell him. "I thought maybe my ankle."

"Huh." He wipes his finger over the bare skin of my ankle, like he's imagining ink there.

"Or the other place I was considering was the side of my ribs."

I brush my fingers along the spot over my tank top. Ryan's gaze follows my hand. He reaches out to gently slide his thumb over the same stretch of my torso. His knuckles accidentally graze the side of my breast, and I pretend like I don't notice, like my skin doesn't buzz with anticipation, like I haven't already imagined what his touch would feel like there.

But then Ryan leans closer, and his hand is on the nape of my neck, and his mouth is on mine. The kiss is slow and sweet, but that's all it is: one kiss. I savor the softness of his lips and the nuzzle of his stubble against my cheek for a long, lingering moment, and then he pulls away. As soon as I register the distance between us, a dull pang erupts in my chest.

"Why did you do that?" I ask in a hushed voice, even though I know there's nobody else around.

"I . . . I've wanted to do that for a long time," he admits.

"But we said we shouldn't," I remind him, hating myself for saying it out loud.

"We said we wouldn't," he says. "But the more I think about it, the more I wonder if we're making a mistake."

I can barely believe what I'm hearing. I go very still, almost too nervous to swallow, as if I could make the wrong move and ruin whatever is about to happen.

"So what are you saying?" I ask.

"I'm saying that I know what's at stake here. We're not wrong to be cautious," he says slowly, as if he's choosing every word with the utmost care. "But, god, Avery, I can't ignore how I feel about you anymore. If I don't tell you this now, I know I'll regret it for a long time. I need you to know that I like you—*really* like you."

There's more urgency in his voice now, and he shifts on the mat to sit up straighter. He takes my hand in his.

"I've had a crush on you from the day we met, you know that?" Ryan says, flushing pink at the memory. "At some competition years and years ago? I recognized you in some arena hallway, and you told me where to find the vending machines."

"I still can't believe you remember that," I say, grinning.

He nods. "Of course. You were hot and insanely talented and so entirely out of my league."

If this were any other moment, I'd brush off the compliment and make a self-deprecating joke, but I'm frozen in awe.

"Trust me, the crush is still there," he continues, squeezing my hand. "But it's more than that now. I want us to give this a shot for real."

Ryan's gaze is brimming with exhilaration and hope, and I know I'll remember the way he looks right now forever. Here's this Greek god of athletic prowess and ambition, made suddenly and startlingly human—full of emotion and desire. He's reached the pinnacle of human achievement, won one of the most coveted honors in the world, traveled the globe, and yet he's here. And he wants me.

"What do you think?" he asks.

There's a slight tremor in his voice—he's nervous. I have a million thoughts swimming through my head right now, and it's surprisingly difficult to pick just one to voice. Finally, I collect myself enough to speak.

"If anything real happens between us, I think we should keep it quiet, just so we don't distract Hallie," I say.

"Absolutely," he says, nodding.

"But if we agree about that, then my answer is yes," I say, scooting closer to kiss him lightly. "I want you. I want this. I want us. We'd be idiots not to give this a try."

"Yeah?" he says, like he can't quite believe I agree.

"Yeah," I say, feeling so happy my heart could burst.

This time, when he kisses me, I can feel him smiling. He cups my cheek with one tender hand, and I get lost in the hypnotic way his lips move against mine. It's like our bodies instinctually know that this is—finally—right. The kiss feels like a celebration.

He guides us down so we're lying on the mat, which is now, thankfully, clean. Somehow, the athletic equipment and fluorescent light overhead fade away, so all that matters is him in front of me. We're lying side by side, facing each other, with the rest of the world and all its distractions blocked out. As deliciously thrilling and tender as our kiss on New Year's Eve was, this is even better. His hands roam from my hair to my hips to the spot on my rib cage he grazed before everything changed. His fingers slip across the hem of my tank top, and I press into him, encouraging him to slide his hand underneath the fabric, against my bare skin.

After keeping a polite distance from him for so long, it's almost unfathomable to me that this is real. I don't care if this is the right place to do this—I don't want to think at all. I kiss the sharp edge of his jaw, then the soft curve of his earlobe, and then a trail down his throat. He groans softly and rolls on top of me, propping himself up on his elbows, with his legs intertwined with mine. I like the solid sensation of his weight on top of me. I let my hands wander across the taut, powerful muscles in his shoulders and down his back; they feel even better than I had dared to let myself imagine.

"Take this off," I say, tugging at his shirt.

Ryan obeys, revealing an exquisite set of abs. I can't help but reach out and touch them, just to make sure I'm not dreaming. They're perfectly solid—this *is* real.

I pull my own top over my head, not bothering to make a disclaimer about my lack of abs. He wouldn't have said all those things if he didn't think I was beautiful, if he didn't want me exactly how I am. And anyway, there's a glint of desire in his appreciative gaze that makes it clear he likes what he sees. It's intoxicating.

He lies back and pulls me on top of him so I'm straddling him. Now I can feel that there's no question of whether he's attracted to me. I lean forward and kiss him deeply; my hair falls like a curtain around us. He unhooks my bra and tosses it to the side. His touch is electrifying. It's been a long time since I've done this with anyone, but that's hardly the reason this feels so good. It's because this is Ryan, and that feels like a victory. I want more of this—I want all of him.

I trail one finger under the waistband of his green track pants, then another. He grinds his hips up into mine, like he wants more, too. I start to tug his pants down, but he stops me.

"Is that too much?" I ask.

He shakes his head and bites his lip. "No, but wait."

He stands up and extends his hand to me, pulling me up, too. He toys with the waistband of my black yoga pants.

"Can I take these off?" he asks softly.

"Yeah," I say.

He slides them off my hips and down my legs. I step out of them and kick them to the side. Before I realize what's happening, he's lifted me up so my legs wrap around his waist. If Ryan were anyone else in the world, I'd probably be self-conscious about my weight in his arms, but there's no reason to worry. I know he's strong enough to handle me. He carries me to a tall block by the metal high bar, usually used for training, though obviously not tonight, and sets me down so I'm sitting at the edge of it. He maneuvers smoothly so my legs are hooked over his shoulders. He looks at me, gauging my reaction, then plants a soft kiss on my inner thigh.

"Is this okay?" he asks.

"Mm-hmm." I nod.

More than okay, I think.

He kisses me again, farther up my thigh, and then again, right at the edge of my underwear. He skims his hands over me, landing with his fingers curled around the lacy fabric at my hips.

"And what about this?" he asks.

I lean back on my elbows and tilt my hips up so he can fully undress me. When his mouth is on me again, I could melt. At first, I want to watch him. But before long, I relax fully, flat on my back on the block. I'm not surprised when, minutes later, Ryan proves that his talents don't solely extend to athletics.

I slide off the block, not 100 percent sure that my legs won't turn to jelly when they hit the floor, and steady myself with a hand against his chest.

"You. Wow," I breathe.

I pull him toward me for a kiss, wrapping my arm around his neck.

"You're pretty 'wow' yourself," he says.

My instinct is to return the favor, but we wind up back on the mat. His pants and black boxer briefs are off now, and he kisses my hair. I reach for him, but then I realize we have a problem.

"Do you have a condom?" I ask.

His face goes slack. "No, I wasn't planning for this at all. There . . . *might?* be one in my backpack, and I'll check, but it's in the office."

He kisses me and gets up to put his underwear and pants back on. He looks like he's about to move toward the office, but thinks better of it. He grabs his shirt and tugs it on over his head.

"Just in case anyone's out there," he says, winking.

"There better not be!" I yelp.

I pull my knees up to my chest and watch him jog across the gym. He disappears around the corner, and once I hear the door swinging shut behind him, I can't help but let out a laugh. It's ridiculous that any of this is happening at all, much less at Summit. But, of course, it would happen here. This is where everything in my life has always taken place.

A minute later, Ryan's back, with a look of triumph on his face. "I found one," he says, shaking the foil packet.

Another minute later, and we're both naked again—sweaty, breathless, and happy. There's a certain stereotype about sex with gymnasts, and I heard enough jokes about it in my early twenties from gross guys at clubs to last a lifetime. The truth is that, yes, while we may be stronger and more flexible than the average person, we're still just regular human beings who like regular sex. Putting your feet behind your head isn't all that exciting when that's just your typical Tuesday morning. That said, there's nothing regular about sex with Ryan. He looks at me with awe, like he wants to memorize this moment. His fingers linger over the tender spots by my waist, the edge of my hip, the nape of my neck.

Later, once we're exhausted, he puts his arm around me and I lay my head on his chest. It's quiet, except for the low hum of the radio and us catching our breath. He kisses my temple and pulls me closer to him, so my thigh rolls over his legs. I kiss his collarbone and drift my fingers over the outline of his tattoo.

"Just in case I didn't make this clear earlier, I, um, like you," I say into his chest.

"I got that, yeah," he says. "I'm really glad this happened."

I grin. An easy silence passes between us. He strokes my hair absentmindedly.

"Sorry to derail cleaning the mats," I say.

He laughs and looks around. "Now we have a *lot* more cleaning to do."

"But we can do it together."

• *Chapter 16* •

I used to count time in days: thirty days till the start of football season; fourteen days till the rent is due; three days till I run out of clean underwear and have to do laundry. But now it drags out in minutes, ticking by slowly in my head: I know how many minutes it's been since Ryan's last sweet *good morning* text, or the last kiss we stole in the supply closet, or the last time he came home with me after practice and we stayed up until 2 a.m., trading stories over a bottle of red wine. I had forgotten how sweet it is to let yourself fall for someone. I can't help but replay our hookup when I'm washing my hair in the shower, and I snap to attention when I hear his name in the gym. I feel giddy whenever his texts pop up on my phone. On Tuesday night, I was so distracted that I forgot I had brussels sprouts in the oven until the smoke detector jarred me out of my daydreams.

It's nearly six thousand minutes later—four days—when Sara comes to Summit to give Hallie a private yoga lesson. Between Sara's work schedule and Hallie's training plans, Friday is the best day; it also happens to be Valentine's Day, although I don't dare fixate on that. It's too soon into whatever this thing with Ryan is to celebrate the holiday in any real way.

Sara was thrilled when I asked if she would work with Hallie. Without breaking Hallie's trust in me, I told Sara as much as I could—that Hallie is having a tough time in the months leading up to the Olympic Trials, and now more than ever, she needs to reduce her stress and build her confidence. Sara said it would be an honor to help her. And once I told her about what happened with me and Ryan on Monday night, she was doubly excited to come to the gym. I made her promise to play it cool in front of him, especially when Hallie is around.

"Since we're not telling her about us," I explained to Sara. "Because, you know, the whole point is to reduce stress, not add to it."

"Got it," Sara said. "I promise not to gawk."

Of course, the moment she saw Ryan at Summit on Friday afternoon, she gawked.

"He's so cute," she mouthed dramatically the first moment his back was turned.

I take Sara, Hallie, and Ryan upstairs, where there's a dance studio and a party room for children's birthdays. I flick on the lights, illuminating the wooden floors and ballet barres installed against a mirrored wall. Sara sets out the two yoga mats and a pile of foam blocks. Hallie stands with her back to the mirror and one hip jutting out, her arms crossed skeptically over her chest.

"Sara and I are roommates, and she's a great

221

teacher," I tell Hallie, trying to warm her up to the idea.

When I suggested yoga to Hallie, she had balked at the idea. Even after relenting to one private lesson, she still wasn't thrilled to try it.

"Have you ever done yoga before?" Sara asks Hallie.

Her voice has an extra drop of honey in it. It's clear that Sara recognizes this is not exactly Hallie's idea.

"Yeah, once, back in middle school gym class, before I got a tutor," Hallie says flatly.

I can practically read her mind: *This is* exercise?

"I didn't really like it," Hallie adds, as if she can make this lesson disappear just with the sheer force of her surliest teenage attitude.

"Well, this will be totally different," Sara says cheerfully. "Look, I'm not some weirdo old gym teacher who wears basketball shorts with tube socks."

It's a good point: Sara's wearing matching leggings and a cropped tank top in a pink, orange, and purple ombré that reminds me of the sunset. She looks visibly, recognizably strong, and this seems to soften Hallie to her slightly.

"I guess," Hallie says, tilting her head.

"Here, why don't you do the honors of picking today's playlist?" Sara offers, handing Hallie her phone.

"Cool," Hallie says swiftly, nodding.

She starts to scroll through Sara's Spotify.

Sara gives me a bemused glance, as if to say, *Look. We'll be fine.*

"Um, guys? This is a *private* lesson," Sara says to me and Ryan, pointing to the two mats on the floor. "I promise I'll return her in one piece once the hour's up."

"Right, right, we'll be going," Ryan says.

"Yeah, we'll go . . . somewhere," I say, scrambling to temper my voice so I don't sound too thrilled by the prospect of a free hour with Ryan in front of Hallie.

"See you soon . . . and have fun," Sara says.

I follow Ryan down the stairs to the first floor, but when we reach the lobby, neither of us has anywhere to be. He looks blankly toward the gym, then the office.

He steals a glance toward the parking lot. "We could get out of here."

"We can't!"

He shoves his hands into his pockets and gives me an irresistibly flirty grin. "Who'd notice?"

"What if Hallie needs us?" I point out.

The dimple in his cheek winks at me, which I find makes it somehow harder to focus on making good decisions. "I bet you've never broken the rules here in your life," he says.

He's right. The pressure of these four walls somehow makes me feel like a hardworking kid again, terrified to break a rule, lest Dimitri see me.

"Okay, let's get out of here," I agree, pushing open the building's front door, not bothering to even grab my coat.

I bounce down the steps to the parking lot. The gym is on a mostly isolated stretch of road, neighbored by a nondescript office building on one side and thickets of pine trees on all others. Even if we wanted to walk into the town center, it would take longer than the journey would be worth. Ryan catches up to me, jangling his car keys.

"I didn't think you'd actually say yes," he says.

"I can break a rule or two," I insist.

"Reliving your LA wild-child days?" he teases.

Ryan unlocks his car, and I get inside.

"Where to?" he asks, flipping on my seat heater, then turning the radio to his favorite classic rock station.

"Um . . ."

Greenwood is small and boring. Growing up here, if I wasn't at school or in the gym, my only real hobby was trawling CVS for Bonne Bell Lip Smackers and issues of *Seventeen*.

"Come on, you grew up here, you must know somewhere," he prods.

"Let's go to Lolly's," I decide.

"I don't know it," he says.

"You don't know Lolly's? Best chai latte in the world?"

He shakes his head. "In the *world?* I mean, that's

a pretty high bar. I don't know if you want to set my expectations there—"

"Oh, shut up."

I give him directions, and ten minutes later, we're inside the tiny café. I haven't been here in a decade, but the peeling floral wallpaper, chintzy armchairs by the brick fireplace, chalkboard menu, and gently piped-in soft rock songs from the easy-listening station are exactly how I remember them. Lolly herself is still behind the counter, though her once-dark hair is now mostly streaked with gray. She's wearing a floral apron and does a double take when she sees me.

"Avery, is that you?" she yelps, coming around the counter to give me a hug.

"Hi!" I greet her, suddenly feeling squeezed by the surprising strength of her embrace.

"I haven't seen you in, gosh, what, a million years? Where's Jasmine?" she asks.

Ryan cocks his head.

"This used to be my spot with Jasmine on cheat days," I explain. "We'd ask for extra whipped cream on the chai lattes and sit here for hours in front of the fireplace."

"The best kids hogged the best seats in the house," Lolly tells Ryan. "Not that I minded, of course."

"I didn't know you were that close with Jasmine," he says to me.

"Those two? My god. Matching orders,

matching outfits, all the way down to the matching scrunchies." She turns to me. "How is she these days? I don't see much of her, either."

"Oh, Jasmine?" I ask, stalling for time. Somehow, telling Lolly that I don't see much of her either feels like I'd be letting her down. I give her a big, plastered-on smile. "She's great. Has a big job. Married. The whole nine yards, all great."

"And you two?" Lolly says, gesturing between me and Ryan.

I try not to look too alarmed. "Oh, no, we're not married!" I say, maybe a hair too loudly. "We, uh, work together."

"I see," Lolly says coyly. "Well, you two look very nice together. What can I get you?"

Ryan follows my lead and orders a chai latte with extra whipped cream. While he pays Lolly for the drinks, I examine the framed newspaper clippings hung by the door. They're slightly yellowed with age, but I remember the thrill I got the day the first one was hung. Lolly saved the *Boston Globe* clippings announcing that two local girls were on their way to the Olympic Trials. Jasmine and I skipped the sugary drinks that day and asked for plain tea; Lolly, who had the round, soft body you'd expect from a woman who made baked goods for a living, had rolled her eyes and told us to live a little. "This *is* us living," I remember telling her, pointing to the newspaper clipping.

The story isn't long, but it features a black-and-white photo of me and Jasmine, frozen at nineteen years old, with our arms slung around each other's shoulders. The date on the framed article feels so far away—a lifetime ago. Next to it, there's a bigger framed article, the paper's front-page story from the day Jasmine returned home from London. There's a larger, color photo of her by herself with a pile of Olympic medals splayed out across her chest. I wonder what the younger version of myself would say if she saw me here now, lying to Lolly about Jasmine, Ryan trailing behind me, out on a furtive break from Summit. I don't think she'd understand how I got into this situation at all.

Ryan sets down the chai lattes on the table between the armchairs, then comes up behind me. He's quiet for a moment, reading the two framed clippings.

"Ah, I see," he says. "You took me here just so I don't forget you're a hometown hero."

"I brought you to a place I loved," I correct him. Sass floods my voice. "And, uh, *was* a hometown hero. Once upon a time. Not so much anymore."

Jasmine's photo floats in my peripheral vision, and I try to block it out.

"Your hometown must be the same way, no?" I ask.

He shakes his head. "Men's gymnastics isn't so

much of a big thing. People at home thought it was cool I made the Olympics, but they didn't . . . I don't know, 'crown' me, the way they crowned the women's gymnastics team."

He makes air quotes around the word, and I understand exactly what he means. I wonder if he felt bitter about it, too.

"So it's not just me?" I say, almost embarrassed that I want him to agree and confirm how I feel.

There are times I've wondered if Jasmine's success only looms so large for me because of how tight we were and how close I came to having it, too. I can't see her clearly because of who she is, who we were together. I'm fairly sure she's still a household name. But time makes fame evaporate; maybe her star has cooled long enough that now she's just a regular person again, the kind of former athlete who can make it through her hometown's grocery store without being stopped in aisles four and seven for autographs. But somehow I doubt that.

"Look," Ryan sighs, kissing my forehead. "Forget about Jasmine for now. Let's drink these lattes you love so much."

We sink into the armchairs by the fireplace. There's something different about the steaming beverages in the ceramic mugs, but it takes me a moment to figure it out. A heavy sprinkle of cinnamon forms a pristine heart on top of the whipped cream, and there's a heart-shaped chocolate bonbon on the side of my saucer. I spin around; Lolly is watching us.

"I may have whipped up a little something," she says.

"Happy Valentine's Day?" he says hopefully, like he's waiting for my approval.

I've felt like the most gooey, starry-eyed version of myself all week, but this pushes me even further over the edge. The gesture is just sweet enough without feeling too serious.

"Happy Valentine's Day!" I say, beaming.

He exhales, relieved, and leans across the table to give me a kiss. I feel warm and golden, and I know that has nothing to do with the glow of the fireplace.

"I know this is probably the tiniest Valentine's Day gesture ever, but I didn't want to go too overboard," he explains.

"No, no, anything else would've been too much," I agree. "This is perfect."

"Okay, cool. A lot of the guys I know complain about Valentine's Day, like it's such a hassle to do something nice for the person you're with, or like it's somehow less special to do flowers or dinner on a holiday. But that seems so backward to me."

"What do you mean?" I ask.

"If someone makes you happy, why *not* celebrate that?" he asks, blushing like he's just realized how vulnerable he sounds. He clears his throat and looks away from me. "Anyway, this is just a tiny way for me to say that this week has been amazing. That's all."

I try not to fixate on his words: Happy. Amazing. They make my stomach flutter in the best way.

"Just so you know, I didn't get you anything," I say apologetically. "And now I feel bad."

"Come on, don't feel bad," he says, taking my hand in his. "I came up with this on the spot, and it took two seconds. And anyway, your gift to me is introducing me to this place."

He sips slowly from his latte, considering it. I taste mine carefully, letting the beverage dribble out from under the cloud of whipped cream so as not to disturb the cinnamon heart. It's fragrant and flavorful.

"Yeah, it's official," he says. "You're right. This is delicious."

"I told you! I wouldn't steer you wrong."

"Now I finally trust you."

"What, like months of working together didn't earn that?"

"This sealed the deal."

Chatting in front of the crackling fireplace, nestled into the coziest spot in town, I feel at home in a way I never did in LA. It's not hard to imagine endless winter afternoons curled up in these armchairs with Ryan. It would be so easy, so satisfying, so comfortable. I've learned my lesson already: I know it's not smart to get lost in giddy feelings, daydreaming about a future with a man who might someday break my heart. I don't want to repeat that mistake. But for whatever reason, things with Ryan feel different. I don't worry about losing my spark around him.

Ryan glances at the clock hanging above the cash register. His face falls.

"We probably have to get going," he says.

We drain the last of the lattes, and I savor the sweet, spicy dregs at the bottom of the mug. I hug Lolly goodbye, and she makes us promise to come back before another ten years slip by.

"Because let's face it, honey, I'm not getting any younger," she says, sighing. "And anyway, I like him. Keep him around."

Ryan laughs lightly and reassures Lolly he'll come by for another latte soon.

On the ride back to Summit, I point out landmarks—not Greenwood's most notable spots, necessarily, but the places that marked my childhood here: my elementary school, the sushi spot my family likes to go for birthdays and anniversaries, the house where I attended my first and last boy-girl party growing up. The town looks extra sleepy in the winter. White and gray Colonial homes match the pale sky and dingy snowbanks; the trees are bare and skeletal. Inside the car, though, it feels like summer. Ryan drives one-handed with his fingers laced through mine in my lap as a Bruce Springsteen song blares from the radio.

We slip into the gym with three minutes to spare. Ryan heads into the office, while I sit at the bottom of the stairs, waiting for Sara to finish Hallie's lesson. I hear the Tibetan singing bowl, then silence, and finally, a few murmured words. I can't make out what Hallie and Sara are saying, but when they appear in the staircase a minute later, Hallie has a pleasantly dazed look on her face.

"How'd it go?" I ask.

She passes me on the staircase, and I notice that her typically excellent posture has a new ease to it, like she's gliding.

"That was actually pretty chill," she says.

"Huh, imagine that," I say, resisting the urge to gloat further.

"Thanks for having me in," Sara says, more to me than to Hallie.

"Maybe you'll come back again next week?" Hallie asks.

Sara and I exchange glances.

"I think that's a great idea," I say.

• *Chapter 17* •

I do dumb things when I'm falling in love. That's what I think for the entirety of the forty-five minutes I spend in the front seat of Ryan's car on Saturday night, nearly nauseous with nerves, as he drives us to Dimitri and Jasmine's house for a cocktail party in honor of my former coach's fiftieth birthday. When Ryan asked me earlier that week if I'd be his date for the night, he told me that if it was too awkward given my strained relationship with Jasmine, I could skip it. But oh, no. I told him it'd be fine. I think I might have even said it'd be *fun*. It was like my brain had entirely evacuated my body: I wanted to spend a night out with Ryan, so I said yes. It was that simple. Even though I haven't seen Jasmine since her twentieth birthday or Dimitri since the 2012 Olympic Trials.

Their house is in a tony suburb, tucked away from the street at the end of a long driveway that winds through looming clusters of pine trees. We park at the end of a row of cars adorned with bumper stickers of gymnasts performing handstands and splits. I smooth down the front of the dress I borrowed from Mom last night when I realized that nothing in my closet could magically make me look three sizes smaller and eight times more confident than I currently am. The dress is rich purple, with an off-the-shoulder neckline and a skirt that skims easily over my hips and thighs. If it were any other night, I'd feel pretty in it.

My heart races as we make our way to the front door. I wonder if Dimitri and Jasmine know that I'm Ryan's date. I wonder if they think about me at all anymore. I mentally review what I'm going to say to them, which boils down to polite but not overly enthusiastic compliments about their home and a few casual comments about how my life is amazing, my job is fantastic, I'm the happiest I've ever been, and everything is actually perfect, thank you very much. My palms are slick and clammy. I pull my hand away from Ryan's to wipe it on my dress.

Ryan heaves the golden knocker—of course it's gold—against the door. Jasmine opens the door and trills an eager "Hello!" She beams at Ryan first. When she registers who I am, her face freezes. For a terrifying moment, she falls silent. But then, just as she was trained to do, she snaps back into action.

"Avery?!" she squeals. "Come here, oh my god. It's been, what, how many years?"

She delivers an enthusiastic air-kiss and half a hug while balancing a precariously full cocktail.

"Hi," I manage. "It's so good to see you again."

She steps back, ushering us into her home. "I can't believe you're here," she says, and it sounds like the truth. "This is amazing."

The house reminds me of my parents' place. It's not decorated in the same style—Jasmine and Dimitri's tastes seem more modern and eclectic—but it's full of the kinds of odds and ends that older people accumulate over a lifetime. There's an expensive-looking credenza in the foyer that holds a single orchid in a hand-thrown pot and an unusual, abstract painting illuminated by a pair of matching silver sconces.

Jasmine shuts the door behind her. Clad in a figure-hugging black sheath, snakeskin stilettos, and the perfect hair and makeup she wears on TV, she looks foreign to me, like my old best friend is acting out a role in a play. She takes our coats and leads us into the kitchen, where a cluster of Dimitri's friends congregate around the marble island set up as a bar. I can hear Jasmine explaining the three custom cocktails they're serving that night, but I can't focus on listening to their ingredients at all, because the crowd of guests shifts, and that's when I see Dimitri.

It's unnerving to see him dressed up in a charcoal-gray sports jacket and tie. He looks older, too, with more pronounced lines settling into his forehead and a cleanly shaven head. His dark, beady eyes and bristling mustache are exactly the same as I remember. He's talking and laughing with a man about his own age while measuring a shot of vodka he pours into a shiny silver martini shaker. His voice booms above the chatter of the party, or maybe my ear is still tuned to listen for it, even all these years later.

"Dimitri," Jasmine calls across the kitchen.

He doesn't hear her.

She rises ever so slightly on her toes and lifts her chin, as if to repeat herself, but thinks better of it and settles back down. It's almost as if she's nervous—like he's still the coach and we're his athletes. She winds her way around the kitchen, stilettos clicking against the hardwood floor, and touches him softly on the arm.

"Look who's here, babe," she says, gesturing at us.

He looks up, and then I see it: a grimace, a glint of disgust. He presses his lips into a tight line, and that's almost scarier. I'm a split second away from grabbing Ryan's hand and whispering that this was all a mistake, that we should just go home, when Ryan waves enthusiastically.

"Hey, happy birthday!" he says, leaving my side to go shake Dimitri's hand. "Thanks for having us. I really appreciate the invitation."

Dimitri sets down the martini shaker, wipes his hands on a dish towel, and smoothly meets Ryan halfway. He shakes his hand slowly.

"This is your date?" he says.

His Russian accent has faded slightly.

Ryan nods and looks pleased, like he's proud to have brought me. "Yes, sir."

"I know her well," Dimitri says. He turns to me and holds out his hand. "Come."

My body's first response is to start moving, and I loathe how very deeply his training has been ingrained in me. I do my best to stand tall and not break eye contact. I don't want to look like a little girl that he can order around anymore. I lift my chin and give Dimitri my firmest handshake.

"Happy birthday. It's great to see you again," I say, straining to offer him a polite smile.

He steps back and lifts my hand, as if he expects me to twirl, and looks me up and down.

"Great to see you," he echoes. "There's so much more of you to see now."

He shoots Ryan a mocking wink, as if he expects Ryan to comment on my weight. I drop Dimitri's hand, but resist the urge to shrink from him. I don't dare glance back at Ryan for support. I can stand up for myself.

"I see you haven't lost your sense of humor," I say.

I pull myself up to my fullest height. In heeled leather boots, I'm an inch taller than he is, and I want him to remember it.

"And you haven't lost your sass," he retorts. He turns to Ryan and adds, "You must have your hands full with her, no?"

"Avery's an amazing coach," Ryan says.

"Wait, you *work* together?" Jasmine interjects, glancing from me to Ryan. "I thought Avery was your date?"

"Uh . . ." Ryan stalls and turns to me for guidance.

"We, um, yes," I fumble. "I'm Ryan's assistant coach at Summit, and I'm also here as his date."

Jasmine wraps her arm around Dimitri's midsection and leans her head on his shoulder. "Aw, another gymnastics power couple, just like me and my babe," she coos.

She looks at him adoringly and presses a kiss to his cheek. I look away; to me, that relationship will always seem wrong.

"Power? How many gold medals between the two of you?" Dimitri asks. He gestures to the living room, and when I turn, I see a wall studded with medals and trophies. "Let's count them up and compare, and then we can talk."

He's not joking. He's keeping score.

The doorbell rings, cutting through the tension in the room.

"I'll get it," Dimitri says quietly. "Jasmine, make sure our guests have drinks."

As he passes us, he ignores me and gives Ryan a respectful nod.

Jasmine takes a deep breath and puts her hands on her hips. "Drinks?" she asks.

"Please," I say.

I glance at the cocktail menu she must have printed up. The names could not be more painstakingly chosen: there's a whiskey-based drink named the Olympia, a wine spritzer garnished with a sprig of jasmine called the Jasmine Fizz, and a twist on the Moscow Mule dubbed the Moscow Man. I choose the Jasmine Fizz by process of elimination—it's the least humiliating option to order. Ryan opts for the Moscow Man, and I wonder if he chose it out of deference to our host. Jasmine steps back to the kitchen island to mix our drinks, leaving us alone.

"That was intense," Ryan mutters to me.

"That's Dimitri for you," I respond.

He raises his eyebrows and nods heavily. "I can't believe I'm actually here at his house."

"*Their* house," I correct, glancing at Jasmine.

I've known about their relationship for six years now, ever since they started dating, but that hasn't made seeing them together any less jarring.

"Are things . . . weird? Between you and Dimitri?" Ryan asks quietly.

I don't respond right away. I look carefully at Ryan, taking in his hopeful expression, his serious, dark eyes, and the tense way his shoulders are set. Despite Dimitri's behavior, I know Ryan idolizes him. I could spoil his impression of him in just a few words, but it seems cruel.

"He was disappointed in me," I say finally.

"He wanted me to be an Olympic champion, and when I didn't make it . . ."

The memory comes flooding back. I bite the inside of my cheek and shake my head, as if I can dislodge the reminder of that painful summer.

"He was done with me," I say. "He didn't check in on me. He took Jasmine to the Olympics and never turned back to see if I was okay."

I can't bring myself to tell Ryan about his abusive coaching style, or the way I still hear his taunts about my body every time I look in the mirror, or the fear I felt just now, trying not to flinch in front of this man who used to make me quiver. Not here. Not now.

But Ryan grimaces anyway. The way Dimitri dismissed me is enough to cause him to furrow his brow and sympathetically squeeze my shoulder. He knows how close a gymnast and coach can be; I'm sure he can imagine how awful that rejection felt.

Jasmine sidles up to us with the two drinks.

"Cheers!" she declares, clinking her own Jasmine Fizz to mine.

Ryan joins in the toast, and she peppers him with questions about his work, gushes about how much she misses Summit, and joyfully accepts his invitation to come by sometime. I linger by his side, feeling suddenly like the third wheel. I try to snap out of this tense, dark mood and match her level of enthusiasm, but it seems impossible. Jasmine wears her peppy persona like a second skin. I know she's not really like this. The megawatt smile, the relentlessly upbeat energy—back when we were close, she turned it on for the judges; now, she does it on TV. I'm curious if she lives fully like this now, hiding her sensitive soul, her nervous side, and her darkly funny jokes from Dimitri, smoothing out her quirks until she's a flat reflection of whatever he wants her to be. She always did know how to perform.

"I don't mean to keep you, Ryan," she says, touching him lightly on the arm. "I know you're here to socialize with the other coaches. Why don't you go off and enjoy? Avery and I can catch up."

My stomach drops. Ryan glances at me inquisitively, and I have no choice but to grin back at him.

"Go," I say.

He looks uncertain, but leaves my side to join in on a nearby conversation with three stocky men. Jasmine and I each take a long sip of our drinks. I don't think either one of us knows what to say.

"So," she says.

"So," I respond, searching for the right words.

I have seven years of burning questions for Jasmine, and none of them are appropriate cocktail party fodder. *Do you realize that you got everything I ever wanted? How did you end up married to that monster? Are you even happy?*

"I don't mean to stare, I'm sorry," she says, blinking, embarrassed. "It's just, wow. It's still so surreal that you're here."

"I only moved back a few months ago," I explain.

"From LA, right?" she asks.

"Yeah, LA," I confirm. "I came back for this coaching opportunity. It was just too good to pass up."

She never has to know the truth.

"So, are you two, like, a thing now?" Her eyes dart in his direction.

I wish I had thought to hammer out a joint answer to this question with Ryan before we walked in the door. I don't want to say yes, only to have him find out and think I'm overestimating his feelings for me. It's not like we've had the *What are we?* talk yet. But downplaying my situation with Ryan doesn't feel right, either. I settle for a purposefully coy sip of my drink.

"Oh my god," she says, dropping her voice down to a whispered squeal and clutching my arm. "This is nuts, isn't it? After all these years? We always thought he was so cute."

For a split second, I forget everything, and we're just teenagers again, best friends, team-mates. We were so close, we were each other's designated Butt Glue Girl—we'd take turns

242

applying the roll-on adhesive just under the edges of our leotards before competitions so we wouldn't get uncomfortably distracting wedgies in the middle of routines. I've never really understood flashbacks before, but this one comes roaring back with full clarity. And then the moment is over, and I get the ice-cold sensation that Dimitri is watching me, and I duck my head down. I remember to speak quietly and control myself.

"It's very sweet how this has all come full circle," I manage to say. "And you? You and Dimitri? I still can't believe it."

The enthusiasm on her face flickers before she catches herself. "I know. Isn't it funny how life works out?"

"I had no idea you were even into him back then," I admit.

I feel bold saying it, daring her to acknowledge how bizarre her relationship appears to be.

"Oh," she says, blushing. "Well, nothing happened until I was a little bit older, obviously. You had already moved by then. And it just . . ."

Her gaze drifts over my shoulder toward her husband, and she loses focus.

"Made sense," she says finally.

There's another flicker of emotion on her face, but then it disappears without a trace. I think about the way we used to play Fuck, Marry, Kill while stretching at practice, and how Dimitri was too old and weird to be put on the list, even as a joke. We seriously weighed the pros and cons of Kevin Federline, and Tom, the gym's janitor, and even Alexei, a gymnast with a gross rattail we saw at competitions. But Dimitri? Not even once. I cannot fathom one single thing about Dimitri and Jasmine that makes sense.

She looks at me brightly again. "Do you want a tour of the house?"

As she leads me through the home she shares with a man old enough to register for an AARP card, the man who once—when she was twelve years old—poked the side of her bottom left exposed by her leotard, observed it jiggling, and told her to "watch it with the cookies," I feel increasingly disturbed. She shows off the new velvet throw pillows meticulously arranged on the white bed in the master bedroom, and the monogrammed towels hanging in the en suite bathroom. She chirps about the gorgeous natural sunlight in the home office, though I realize neither of them works from home, and tosses a wink when we enter the guest room, or as she calls it, "someday, a baby's room." She does this all while traipsing three or four steps in front of me, far enough away that we never have to face each other. The tour is so tightly packed with minuscule details about where she purchased this rug, or why she deliberated over that paint color, that there is simply no room for me to interject and ask what the fuck is going on.

When the tour concludes on the first floor, Jasmine offers to refresh my drink, which I accept. The minute the glass is full, I find Ryan on the couch in the living room. He lights up when he sees me, scooting to the left and patting the space next to him so that I'll take a seat. He drops away from the conversation with the other two men in the living room.

"You'll never guess what Dimitri said to me while you were with Jasmine," he says, excitement straining through his hushed tone.

I rack my brain and feel a slow sinking feeling in my gut; nothing good could come of this conversation.

"He offered me a job," he says, beaming.

"At Powerhouse?" I ask.

"It would start this fall, after the Olympics. I could bring Hallie—she's young enough that she could train for 2024, and Dimitri and I could train her together," he explains. "I mean, think about it: more resources, better facilities, working with *Dimitri Federov*."

"Yeah, I got that part," I say.

Ryan's face falls slightly.

"I mean, wow. That's a lot," I continue, rushing to switch to a more congratulatory tone.

"I'm really excited," he says. "I can't believe he wants to work with *me*."

"What would Hallie's parents think?" I ask, trying to find a hole to poke in this plan.

"I don't know exactly, I'd have to talk to them," he says. The lilt in his voice makes me realize he hasn't thought through this part yet at all. "I can't see why they'd turn down Dimitri. True, Powerhouse is slightly more expensive than Summit, but not by much, and it's literally the best training center in the world. So."

He smiles as if to say, *That's that.*

"If you leave Summit, who else would train her?" I wonder out loud.

He shrugs. "Well, you'd still be at Summit, wouldn't you?"

Training her on floor is already intense—I'm not sure if I'd be confident enough to tack on beam, bars, and vault, too. And anyway, the Conways probably wouldn't trust me to pull that off. So if Ryan leaves and Hallie really does want to train for 2024, the Conways would probably follow him. And that means I'd be left behind.

Ryan sips from his drink and stares off into the distance. It's clear that mentally, he's no longer here at this party—he's in Tokyo, watching Hallie climb the podium; he's at Powerhouse, working as his idol's right-hand man; he's fast-forwarding decades ahead to when *he's* the most respected coach in the entire sport, just like Dimitri is now.

I have to tell him the truth.

"I just . . ." I say, lowering my voice to a notch

above a whisper. "I think you should really consider this before you say yes. I don't think working with Dimitri is the right move—not for you, and definitely not for Hallie."

I wish he would understand without making me say it.

"Let's head out?" I suggest.

He kisses my temple and rises to stand. "We've barely been here an hour. Let's stay for a little while longer, cool?"

I hesitate. I don't know what else to say. "Cool."

We mill around. An older couple asks if I "used to be Dimitri's girl," and I have no choice but to nod—*Yep, that's me. Dimitri's girl.* I get a third drink, just to have something to do instead of watch Ryan laugh at Dimitri's jokes. Finally, he comes to find me in the kitchen.

"You wanna get going?" he asks, touching my arm.

"Yeah," I say, tamping down the instinct to add, *Let's get out of here.*

I rustle up fake warmth to say goodbye to Jasmine and Dimitri. Jasmine insists that we must get together for drinks soon. Dimitri nods silently and stoically at me, then shakes Ryan's hand.

"We'll talk," Dimitri says smoothly.

Ryan looks beatific.

In the car ride back to Greenwood, Ryan invites

me to stay over at his place, but I ask him to drop me off at my apartment instead. I turn on the radio, but he turns it off a few seconds later. It's quiet, with just the hum of the engine to keep us company.

"You don't seem all that happy about Dimitri's job offer," he observes.

"It's flattering that he asked you," I say evenly.

"But you don't think I should take it," he counters.

"I . . ." I stare out the window as houses and trees whiz by us in the darkness. "I am incredibly grateful for Dimitri. He changed my life. He could've made me an Olympic champion, if things had gone differently. But he's not a nice person, or a good person, or a person who would treat Hallie fairly."

"He's tough and old-school," Ryan says, shrugging. "That's what makes him legendary. Coaches aren't made like that anymore."

"He's tough, yeah, but he's . . ."

I trail off and bite my lip. I want to say *abusive,* but that's not a word you throw around lightly.

"Did you hear what he said about me? Basically calling me fat?" I ask, changing tactics.

"What?" he asks, sounding disgusted. "I didn't notice."

"Yeah. 'There's so much more of you to see now,'" I recite.

Ryan sighs heavily. "That's not cool."

"Exactly, it's not. Imagine hearing that, but worse, all day, every day, when you're thirteen years old," I say.

Ryan flicks on his blinker and makes a turn, so it takes a while for him to respond. I get the sense that he's grateful for the extra time to formulate a response.

"I'm sure he's not a saint, but this is the opportunity of a lifetime," he says finally. "I get one shot at a job like this, and there's no better coach in the entire sport. Every boss has their shortcomings—there's no 'perfect' job."

I hate that he makes air quotes around the word. It makes me feel as if he thinks I'm overreacting. I study his profile in the moonlight. I wonder what would happen if I described to him in unflinching detail what it was really like to spend the most impressionable years of my childhood with Dimitri. I can't muster up the energy to explain what he's really like if Ryan will only defend him.

I sigh and slump back in my seat.

"It's late," I say. "We don't have to talk about this now. If you're happy, I'm happy for you."

He reaches across the gearshift to hold my hand. His warm fingers weave through mine and rest in my lap.

"Thanks for coming with me tonight," he says, squeezing my hand.

I don't squeeze his back.

MARCH
2020

• *Chapter 18* •

Nationals are a week away, and Hallie is still struggling. She can't control her power on her forward tumbling pass—the front handspring, front full-twisting layout, front double-twisting layout—so I suggested she add a stag jump on the end. That way, any energy that comes bounding off the tumbling goes directly into a real, choreographed *move*. She'll get points for a jump, rather than a deduction for not sticking the landing. A stag jump should be pretty: one knee bent at a ninety-degree angle in front of your body, with your other leg trailing out long and straight behind you, and your arms thrown triumphantly in the air. But Hallie's is tense and tight, and it throws off her timing going into the next segment of her routine. Once she loses her cool, it's hard to recover. The rest of the routine gets rushed.

"Okay, let's move to the tramp," I suggest. "We can work on your form there."

We've been finessing this one second of her routine for fifteen minutes now, and I can tell that Hallie is running low on both energy and patience. It's true that the trampoline is a less physically taxing place to jump repeatedly than the floor is—the elastic power mesh bounces you right back up, obviously—but also, no matter how old or sophisticated a gymnast gets, there's still nothing quite as joy-inducing as playing around on a trampoline. And more than perfect form, more than excellent technique, what Hallie *really* needs right now is to feel good. Going into a competition, an athlete's mental headspace is just as important as her physical well-being, if not more so.

She trudges over to the trampoline, and after a few lazy bounces, she gets serious.

"Stag jumps?" she asks, confirming her task.

"On every bounce," I say. "Focus on getting that back leg nice and straight."

She swings her arms to get some momentum, then bounces into shape. With each jump, she thrusts her right leg a little harder behind her.

"That leg needs to come up faster," I observe. "That'll keep the jump short and sweet, which is what we want."

She nods like a little soldier and jumps again.

"Faster," I insist. "The leg comes up quick and high, then snaps back."

"Snaps back," she repeats, continuing to bounce.

At the height of each jump, her chin tilts up and her fingers flick out with style. She looks like a star up there. It's gratifying to see her improve after months of working together.

And after seeing Dimitri last week, that's what

I need: I have to know that I'm helping Hallie, not hurting her. If I pass down what he did, I would never forgive myself. Hallie screws up her mouth in concentration as she tracks the distance between her and the trampoline. Her full body weight plunges down on the black mesh and she rebounds brightly into the air once more. Her limbs soar jubilantly into shape; at the peak of her jump, she beams. She knows she nailed it.

I haven't seen Ryan outside of practice since Dimitri and Jasmine's cocktail party. I've gone to yoga after work twice, and on the nights I've been free, he's had plans with friends. All week, I've felt starved for attention; I had forgotten what it's like to crave somebody like this. I could physically feel the way I yearned for quality time with him—sometimes, low in my gut; other times, like an actual pang in my chest. When he texted me yesterday evening to ask if I'd be free for a date night tonight, I replied *yes* practically while my phone still buzzed with the incoming message.

He texted confusing instructions: *I have a secret plan for us. Wear something warm, and make sure you have socks.*

Socks? *What's the plan?* I wrote back.

He replied, *Like I said—it's a secret ;)*

I knew I wasn't going to weasel the truth out of him, so instead, I tried to puzzle out what we could possibly be doing—hiking? skiing?—and took great care to find a matching pair of socks without any holes. Tonight, after drilling stag jumps with Hallie on the trampoline, Ryan and I waited until Hallie had left the gym's premises in her dad's car before we both climbed into his car. We decided earlier that I'd stay over at his place and he'd drive me back to the gym the next morning. The plan made me feel as if we were serious and committed, or at least on the way toward it.

"So, now you can tell me where we're going," I say once he's pulled out of the parking lot.

"Nope," he says.

"Not even a hint?" I ask.

He's resolute. "You'll just have to wait and see."

He talks about how much fun he had dreaming this up, and how it'll be the perfect way to chill out in the midst of Nationals prep, but I just can't focus. My mind ping-pongs from sleuthing out where he's taking me to our last in-person conversation about Dimitri's job offer. We haven't had a chance to discuss it. There's so much I could say to him—and as much as I want to ask how he's feeling about what Dimitri said, I don't want to ruin the romantic mood.

He drives through the town center and pulls into Osaka Sushi. The familiar wooden sign gives me a burst of nostalgia, but it takes me a moment to piece together why he's so excited.

"I told you about this place, didn't I?" I say, suddenly recalling. "When we were driving through Greenwood after Lolly's."

"Your family likes to come here for special occasions," he says.

"Ryan! You remembered." I take off my seat belt so I can properly lean across the car to give him a hug and a kiss. "But wait, the socks? Warm clothes? Was that just to throw me off?"

I'm overheating in a thick turtleneck and knit scarf. There are gloves stashed away in the pockets of my parka.

"That's for after dinner," he says, winking as he gets out of the car.

Ninety minutes later, when we're happily filled up on a sashimi platter and a sake flight, I still don't know where we're going next. But Ryan did insist on heading out of the restaurant as soon as the bill was paid, rather than lingering at the table. I get the sense we're on a deadline. In the car once again, I feel warmed by the sake from the inside out, touched by the romantic gesture of bringing me back to Osaka Sushi, and high on the anticipation of discovering where this adventure all leads. Whatever desire I had earlier tonight to ask Ryan about Dimitri has faded away. It's not that I don't care—it's that moments like this don't come around often. It's not every day that a gorgeous man throws together a surprise date packed with personal touches at a series of secret locations. I slide my hand into Ryan's and squeeze a silent thanks.

Finally, the jig is up: he pulls off a main road down a narrow street that winds into the town forest. He drives slowly through the heavy thicket of pine trees until we reach a clearing. There's a cul-de-sac full of cars streaked with winter grime parked near an outdoor ice-skating rink. Although it's a dark night, the rink itself is bright, thanks to white floodlights and golden Christmas lights wrapped around aluminum poles. I've been to this rink a few times for my elementary school classmates' birthday parties, but it's only now, as an adult, that I see how charming this spot really is.

"This is so *sweet!*" I exclaim, getting out of the car.

"Do you skate?" he asks.

He looks hopeful but hesitant, the way people do when they hand you presents with the tags still attached in case you want to return them.

"I haven't skated in years, but I always liked it as a kid," I say.

"Me, too," he says.

A rink attendant in a red clapboard shed asks for our shoe sizes and hands us clunky skates. We lace them up and totter to the edge of the rink. He steps over the threshold first, then extends his hand so I can steady myself as I step onto the ice. I take a few tentative glides with my hand hovering over the railing in case I lose my balance.

We make a slow first lap side by side, getting used to being on the ice. There aren't many other people here—three couples in casual clothes and a single skater in athletic gear who makes sharp turns and elegant spins—so it's calm enough to go at our own pace.

"So far, so good, but I bet I'll fall flat on my ass at least once tonight," I say.

"I'll catch you," he says.

"Don't you dare. I'll probably pull you down with me," I warn.

"You're not gonna fall," he predicts. "I remember you on beam back in the day—your balance is absurd."

"Don't jinx it," I say.

He's right, though; by our second lap, I feel sturdier, and by our third, I've regained my confidence. I slip my hand into his and trust my balance enough to plant a kiss on his cheek as we glide. I can't help but see flashes of the future—maybe we'll hike this spring, canoe this summer, train for a half marathon together this fall. We're both used to solitary sports, but there's something appealing about tackling new adventures as a pair.

As we continue to skate circles around the rink, we whisper theories about the other couples—

which ones seem happily in love, which seem more like old roommates who couldn't give a damn about each other—and resolve to never fall into the latter category. We trade stories about ice-skating experiences as kids, and the Olympic skaters we've met over the years. On some laps, we don't talk at all, content to enjoy the twinkling lights nestled into the forest and the blur of our hazy reflections gleaming on the slick ice. With Ryan, silence doesn't feel like pressure.

But there's one question I can't get out of my head.

"What's all this for?" I ask finally.

"A guy can't take a girl out?" he replies.

"Of course, of course. But, I mean, this is spectacular."

His cheeks go pink, and I don't think it's just from the thirty-five-degree weather.

"Don't get me wrong, I love seeing you in the gym," he says slowly. "And at your place, and at mine. But I've never really treated you to a real date night, and you deserve that."

"Oh!" I say, touched.

"In case you haven't noticed, I'm not, uh, the fanciest guy," he says sheepishly.

"You?" I joke back. "Huh, never would've guessed."

He smirks. "And I thought about a gourmet dinner somewhere, but I know you love to cook. I know you'd rather cook than be waited on."

"True," I admit.

"So I thought your old favorite sushi place would be a treat, and this would cap the night off perfectly. I hope you like it?" he finishes.

"I love it," I say. "Thank you for planning such a fabulous date."

I don't mean to, but I flash back to a "date night" with Tyler. Or, rather, it was supposed to be a date night. Instead, we watched *Fast & Furious 6* in silence while we ate Easy Mac. He had told me not to bother with cooking a special meal for date night. He didn't get that cooking for him felt like another way to show my love. He fell asleep before the movie was over. But this feels entirely different—it's thoughtful and personal. He put care into choosing something I'd like.

"So you'll keep me?" he says.

I can hear a note of restrained laughter in his voice.

"Eh," I joke, pretending like I'm attempting to make up my mind. "I'll keep you."

I skate to a stop and pull him gently toward the railing. I steady myself against it and kiss him deeply, slipping my fingers under his scarf to hold him close. It's true that there's a certain thrill about kissing someone for the first time, when you can only guess what it'll feel like, how your bodies will respond to each other's, and if there will be sparks. But this is thrilling in a different way: comfortable, familiar, easy. I can anticipate the way his lips will move against mine. I *know* there will be sparks. I can't believe how lucky I am.

The rink is quieter now; we're among the last people left. It's a picturesque moment, but I know there's a bigger reason tonight makes me so happy. Being here in his arms feels exactly right.

"What an incredible night," I say.

I have to stop myself from uttering the three little words that almost roll off my tongue next.

"*You* are incredible," I say, swallowing the too-soon words and choosing the safer ones instead.

He nuzzles closer and kisses me again. When he pulls back, he hesitates, like he's trying to determine exactly what to say next. I wonder if the same words are running through his head, too.

"I . . ." he says.

My stomach does a backflip.

He gazes at me for a moment that feels like an eternity.

"I'm really glad you're here with me," he says, pulling me closer for a kiss.

Everything about it—the steady pressure of his hand on the curve of my hip; the scent of pine; the slippery surface of the ice beneath our feet—I commit to memory. I want to remember every detail, because this is the night I know for sure that I am falling in love with Ryan Nicholson, and there's nothing I can do about it.

• *Chapter 19* •

A chill runs up my spine when I enter the National Championships arena in Miami. The nervous energy hanging in the air feels just as real as the mingled scent of chalk dust and sweat. I follow Hallie and Ryan around the perimeter to find a spot to settle down, and I can't help but drink it all in: the crunch of errant bobby pins underfoot; the spare cans of hair spray and bottles of butt glue rolling out from unzipped gym bags; the ritual gestures of gymnasts warming up; the satisfying *scrchhh* of grips being Velcroed on and off wrists; the anxious parents snapping gum in the bleachers. I savor every bit of it. I feel as if I've come home again. The moment I walked through the door, I straightened up, lifted my chin one notch higher, and tightened my ponytail. This time around, though, nobody's watching me. This isn't about me.

We're here for Hallie. It's her day. She finds a bench on the far side of the arena, closest to the beam, that has yet to be claimed by anyone else and drops her duffel on it.

We're all clad in matching navy tracksuits embroidered with Summit's logo over our hearts. Hallie removes her jacket, revealing a gleaming, emerald-green, long-sleeved leotard.

It's spangled with Swarovski crystals across her collarbone and down the center of her chest, like a glittering necklace or a piece of armor. If she goes to the Olympics, her competition leotards will be chosen by the American Gymnastics Federation, and she'll probably be clad in red, white, blue, or all three. But for now, she can wear whatever she likes. I know this leotard is one of her favorites because it brings out the green flecks in her hazel eyes.

There are armies of gymnast-coach teams just like us scattered across the venue. I spot Delia Cruz rolling her wrists in supple circles to warm up for bars. Maggie Farber and Kiki McCloud sit with hands over their faces while their coach tames down their ponytails with hair spray. Across the arena, Dimitri reclines on a bench while his group of Powerhouse gymnasts stretch silently. I recognize their faces and names, though I don't know them personally. His star student is Emma Perry, a fiercely talented competitor who's probably the front-runner of the entire sport. He has Skylar Hayashi and Brit Almeda, too—the former is a vault specialist who began performing flawless Amanars at fourteen years old and has only gotten more intimidating since then; the latter is a decent if less memorable athlete who brings in reliably fine scores but doesn't quite have that X factor. I don't think Ryan has broached the subject of Dimitri or Powerhouse with Hallie or her parents yet. In the frenzied lead-up to Nationals, there hasn't been time.

Each gymnast's competition roster is assigned randomly. When the schedule flashes on the big screen that looms above the arena, Hallie's face hardens. She's up first on bars, which means she'll spend the rest of the day rotating through vault, beam, and then floor. She doesn't complain, though; she knows NBC's cameras have likely already begun swirling, and she's smart enough to understand that her reaction to the news shouldn't be a dismal one.

"I just want to get floor over with," she whispers to me.

"I know. I'm sorry. Let's stretch," I suggest, stepping forward to place myself protectively between her and any cameramen who might be approaching with a long lens.

She dutifully nods, slips off her track pants, and stands to begin her warm-up. She runs through the same basic set of moves she's completed daily since childhood—bending over her knees in a pike, rolling out her wrists, straddling her legs wide—but this time, every movement is packed with intention: pointed toes, straight spine, sucked-in core. She waves at a pair of little girls in the bleachers holding up a sign with her name printed on it in colorful marker.

An announcement cuts through the noise of the stadium: fifteen minutes until the competition begins, which means it's time for Hallie to warm up on bars. She's on the same rotation as Delia and Brit, and the three gymnasts take turns chalking up and practicing elements of their routines. There's an unintentional hierarchy: Brit defers to Hallie because she's the stronger athlete, and both girls defer to Delia, because she's become something of a legend, a mother hen, a spokesperson for the horrors of the sport ever since the accusations broke. Today, Delia's leotard is teal. I heard Jasmine discussing it during her TV segment; teal is the color of sexual assault awareness.

At the one-minute mark, Hallie signals to us that she's all set.

"Last-minute pep talk," Ryan says. "Huddle up."

Ryan wraps a protective arm around Hallie's shoulders and slides a nonchalant arm around my waist. Hallie's breath is shallow. This isn't her first rodeo; it's clear that she knows as nervous as she is, she has to fake it till she makes it. Otherwise, she'll psych herself out.

"I just want to tell you one more time how proud I am of you," Ryan says, locking eyes with Hallie. "You're strong, you're tough, and you have trained so hard for this for so long."

She blushes. "Thanks."

"And don't let the prospect of floor rattle you all day," he says. "You have nothing to worry about."

"I don't?" she asks, surprised.

"The new choreography? Fantastic. The updated tumbling passes? Genius. I've known you a long time, and I've never seen you as poised or as elegant as you've been performing lately."

Hallie exhales. Her shoulders visibly relax.

"Oh," she says, almost laughing to herself. "Right."

"Avery?" Ryan prompts.

I didn't prepare anything to say. When I was competing, it's not like Dimitri ever gave any sort of warm, touchy-feely pep talk like this one. A gruff request to stop whining and keep my chin up, maybe, but nothing like this. I swallow.

"You have no idea how good you have it," I say. "How easy this will be. How prepared you are. You are a natural superstar, and you have Ryan, who's amazing, and you have an incredibly supportive family cheering you on."

The words come easily because they're the truth.

"Every single day, I am so proud to work with you, because you never give up and you never lose what makes you *you*," I continue, ignoring the lump forming in my throat. "I'm lucky to be on your team. And I can't wait to see you rock this competition."

I squeeze my hand around her shoulder. I didn't expect to be so emotional, but seeing Hallie here, just inches away from a competition that could make her a front-runner at Olympic Trials, I'm overwhelmed. I break the huddle to give her a tight hug.

"Thank you, guys," Hallie says, her words muffled into my hair. "Seriously. Thank you."

An event coordinator taps Hallie on the shoulder. "It's time," she says.

Hallie glances at each of us. "Bye."

"You got this!" I call out.

Ryan goes with her. He's there to hover by the high bar throughout the duration of her routine, ready to lunge forward during her riskiest release moves when she's most likely to fall, in case he needs to catch her. I don't want to be a distraction, so I'll watch from the sidelines.

Hallie reaches into the chalk bowl to add one more layer of dust to her grips, and nods to Ryan that she's ready. Moments later, an announcer's voice booms over the loud speaker. A hush falls over the crowd in the bleachers.

"First up on bars is Hallie Conway," the voice booms.

The audience roars a cheer. "Let's go, Hallie, let's go!" I call out, clapping.

Hallie strides to the center of the low bar, totally transformed. She stands tall, suddenly looking five years older and twice as serene as she really is. She raises both arms to the table of judges and beams, performing the customary salute of respect that every gymnast does at the beginning and end of each routine. I see a judge flick to a new sheet in her notebook and peer over the tops of her thick-rimmed glasses.

Hallie takes a deep breath, then jumps on the low bar and swings up into a perfect handstand with such easy grace that I forget to be nervous for her. She transitions smoothly to the high bar, then pirouettes in a handstand, and executes a clean Tkatchev–Pak Salto combo, flinging herself backward and soaring smoothly down to the low bar. Everything is tight, as it should be: vertical handstands, straight knees, pointed toes, rock-hard core. The routine concludes with a mesmerizing series of giants—swinging, 360-degree circles around the high bar—and then she's slicing through the air into a double-twisting double back tuck. The moment she hits the mat, she's sturdy and sure of herself—she sticks the landing. The audience erupts into a cheer as she arches backward.

Hallie waves to the crowd, turning to face each corner of the arena to blow grateful kisses.

Giddy, she crashes sideways into Ryan for a one-armed hug.

"Amazing job," I say, high-fiving her in a burst of chalk dust when she makes it back to the bench. "You nailed it."

"That felt great," she says.

"Because it *was* great," Ryan says.

Thirty seconds later, the judges confirm what

everyone knows: It was a beautiful performance. They award her a 15.025—and anything in the fourteen range or above is incredible. By the end of the first rotation, she's in fourth place—Emma, Delia, and Kiki have just barely edged her out for the top spots. Hallie's face falls slightly.

"Don't worry, you have three more rotations to go," Ryan points out. "The rankings will change."

"Yeah, but I just finished bars," she protests.

Nobody has to say out loud what she really means: her best event is now over, so it could all go downhill from here.

"Vault's next," I say brightly. "Just focus on nice, solid landings, and you'll be just fine."

Per the rules of the competition, she competes twice on vault. Judges score both efforts, then take the average as her final score. Her first run, an Amanar, is impressive. But any success there is canceled out by the deductions she receives for the two extra steps she takes upon landing her second vault, a Mustafina.

I know the rules of the sport well enough to know better, but it still seems incredibly unfair that Hallie gets points docked for her dynamite energy. She's like a high jumper in a ballerina's body—if she were a track-and-field star instead of a gymnast, her explosive power would make her an Olympic champion. But not here. My nerves feel frayed as I watch the judges grimly turn over the final score: 13.250. Hallie slips to fifth place. The mood on the bench is tense.

Her third rotation is beam, and if there's one event that demands confidence and precision above all else, it's this one. When I was a gymnast, beam was always intimidating, but at least I felt in control of the experience. If I shook or bobbled or fell, it was my own fault. But now, as Hallie competes, that sense of control crumbles. My muscles spasm as I watch her move. When she pirouettes, I crane my neck, as if I can manipulate the speed of her spin. As she wobbles on the landing of a front aerial, my stomach and glutes and thighs clench hard, as if I can keep her centered on the beam through sheer force of will. Her tumbling pass—a back handspring, whip back, back layout that's usually just pure fun to watch—tilts slightly off center. One foot curls desperately around the beam, while the other leg ricochets sideways in a last-ditch attempt to regain balance. She stays on, but just barely. After her dismount, she salutes limply to the panel of judges and trudges into Ryan's arms.

Hallie makes it back to the bench just as the stony-faced judges reveal her score: a flat 12.850. That means she's officially slipped down to ninth place. I feel sick. As long as she doesn't completely bomb floor, she should qualify to compete at Olympic Trials. (The top fourteen competitors will go to Trials.) But there's no guarantee of that—anything could happen at a competition, especially with her confidence at an all-time low right now—and ninth place is a brutal, embarrassing spot to be in, even out of seventeen total spots. Ideally, she'd be in the top five or six, if not fully in the top three for medal contention. I hate to imagine Jasmine's commentary right now. It can't be good.

Ryan spots Hallie's empty water bottle and goes to refill it.

"I'll be back in a minute," he promises.

Hallie scowls and slumps down further in her seat. There's a beat of silence between us.

"I'm completely failing," she says morosely. "I'm messing up over and over again on live TV, looking like a total idiot."

"Hey, scoot," I say, moving to sit next to her. "You're not an idiot. At all. I promise."

She slides over a few inches but doesn't look at me. She's staring at the big screen, transfixed as Emma sticks a powerful double-double on floor and makes it look easy.

"I'm in ninth place," she spits out. "*Ninth* place. That's for idiots."

"You have to stop calling yourself an idiot," I say.

She gives me a look full of skeptical contempt that reminds me she is still a surly teenager. She might have traded in the typical trappings of a teen girl's life for the discipline, demands, and

272

pressures of a fully grown adult athlete's, but this is one thing she can't change. She's a sixteen-year-old girl, behaving the way any sixteen-year-old would.

She scrunches up her face. "I didn't work this hard to be all the way down the scoreboard."

"I know," I say carefully. I try to figure out what to say to lift her spirits. "But maybe there's more to it than that. What if you can just appreciate the fact that you've worked so hard to be here? I know you get so much joy out of performing. Just go out there and have fun showing off what you can do, you know?"

She tilts her head and stares at me.

"You're nuts," she says. "You've lost it."

"I'm just trying to show you the silver lining," I insist. "Because there is one."

"If you kind of squint," she adds.

"Squint really carefully, yeah," I say. "You're here. You deserve to be here."

She takes a long sip of her water and shakes her head slowly.

"You sound extremely yoga right now," she says.

"I'm just jealous that you get to go out there and deliver the hell out of your next routine," I say. "You're living my dream."

She sighs dramatically.

"I'll go slay on floor if you promise to stop talking like a corny Oprah knockoff," she says.

"Deal," I say, extending my hand.

She shakes it. "Deal."

An event coordinator waves Hallie over to start warming up for floor. I shout ridiculously supportive comments as she walks away. But once she's gone, the pit in my stomach returns.

Floor warm-ups fly by. Brit delivers a surprisingly lovely performance to a delicate piece of classical music, and Hallie whispers to me that she must have gotten new choreography. Up next, Delia strides calmly onto the floor to perform a knockout routine that inspires the audience to give her a standing ovation. On the big screen, you can see tears glittering in her eyes as she waves to her fans and hugs her coach. The moment is powerful and heartbreaking. When the judges award her the breathtakingly high mark of 15.275, it's clear she's earned every bit of it.

Meanwhile, Hallie is trembling. She rises from the bench and shakes out each leg so her knees don't buckle beneath her. More than any other moment in her life, the pressure is on.

"Let's go, Hallie!" I call out.

"Come on, Hal, you got this," Ryan says loudly.

"We had a good talk while you were gone," I say. "I think she'll be okay."

"If she's not, I think her parents will skin us alive," Ryan mutters.

Hallie's name rings out over the loudspeaker, and the judges flick to new sheets of paper in their notebooks. She salutes at the edge of the blue mat, then struts into position. There's a high, clear *beep* to signal that she should prepare herself, and then the opening notes of her new floor music. This is her first time performing the routine I crafted in competition, and I'm anxious to see how it's received.

Hallie throws herself into the first few fierce steps of her choreography, just like we practiced, and I am so proud. She's a swirl of limbs and piercing gazes as she pivots, backs up into the corner, and lunges into her first tumbling pass. She whips across the floor with enough energy to power a fleet of Maseratis, rocketing skyward at the end into the stag jump we drilled on the trampoline. Her leg levers up elegantly behind her, and she lands on beat.

She beams and surges onward through a frenzied attempt at her leap series. She'll get a small deduction for failing to hit the full 180-degree split, but it's a marked improvement from the first time she tried that combination. When she slides down to set up her wolf turn, I cringe and grab Ryan's hand. His palm glistens with sweat. Hallie's brows knit together as she steels herself to spin. I can't breathe as I watch her rotate cleanly. It's the best wolf turn I've ever seen her do.

On her second tumbling pass, she flies high above the floor and sticks the landing. As she prances through her choreography, I whisper a prayer. *Please keep this up. Please let this be okay.* Hallie attacks her third and fourth tumbling passes with pure grit. She spirals through the air and digs in her heels when she lands. As the music hits its final note, she throws her head back into the dramatic pose we practiced so many times in the Summit mirror. Her chest heaves as she tries to catch her breath. There's a second of silence, and then Hallie climbs to her feet, saluting the judges with all the energy she has left. The crowd claps as the judges continue to scribble down notes.

Ryan and I intercept her along the side of the floor for high fives and hugs, and we walk back to our spot together. Her breathing is ragged.

"Hallie, that was unbelievable," I tell her excitedly. "The best I've ever seen you perform."

"You were awesome," Ryan confirms.

She pants and gives a half-hearted thumbs-up. "Don't congratulate me until the score is ready," she warns.

"Don't worry about the score; that was phenomenal," I insist.

I hope, of course, that the judges reward her for one of the best floor routines she's probably ever done in her entire life. But I'm also nervous—they don't award medals for personal improvement. Her score will be compared to the other gymnasts'.

The judges deliver their score: 13.475. It moves Hallie up to seventh place.

Hallie lets out a low moan. "That's not good enough," she wails.

"That's a full point higher than you got at Worlds!" Ryan crows. "That's a real improvement, Hal. You should be very proud of yourself."

A full point! Selfishly, I glow with excitement.

"If this were Olympic Trials, seventh place wouldn't be enough to make the Olympic Team," Hallie says, sounding panicked.

Ryan kneels down in front of her and takes her hands. "But this isn't Trials," he points out. "You have months to go. So much can change between now and then."

Hallie looks suspiciously around the arena. "Yeah, but everyone else will be training to improve, too."

I want to say something reassuring or encouraging, but everything I come up with sounds hollow or worthless. Seventh place is a complicated place to be: she's not knocked out of Olympic contention by any means, but she's not a shoo-in, either. It would be exciting to land here if this were Hallie's first elite competition, but it's not. She didn't come this far to only make seventh place. It's an uncomfortable middle ground, achingly mediocre when gymnasts are used to flashy wins or spectacular failures. Hallie could go either way from here . . . or she could float into obscurity, never quite making a name for herself in this sport.

"I know today wasn't what we hoped for, but I'm still proud of you," I say finally.

Hallie zips up her tracksuit and pulls the hoodie down low.

"Bars was beautiful," Ryan adds. "Vault was pretty solid, too. Next time, we'll work on—"

"I can't think about that now, all right?" Hallie snaps.

She shoves her feet into her Uggs and slings her gym bag over her shoulder.

"I can't stay here anymore. Bye."

She makes a beeline for the nearest exit.

"Wait!" Ryan calls out to her.

"I'll catch up with you later, okay?" he tells me, darting after Hallie.

My first instinct is to follow them, but I know Hallie doesn't want a full audience right now. If she wanted me with her, she would've told me. Instead, she wants to grieve today's results alone. I don't blame her. So I sink down onto the bench and watch glumly as other gymnasts gleefully celebrate their wins. My heart hurts.

• *Chapter 20* •

I'm still alone an hour later. I don't want to be. Ryan and Hallie never returned to the arena, and my text to him went unanswered. I head back to the hotel. I had originally assumed that Ryan and I would share a room—we spend two or three nights a week at each other's places, anyway, and I was even looking forward to our first trip together as a couple. But Ryan had pointed out that it'd look suspicious for us to share, especially since Summit had already paid for us to sleep separately. Our rooms are at opposite ends of the seventh floor; Hallie and her parents have a larger suite on the eighth.

When the elevator doors slide open on the seventh floor, I step out in the cool, blandly carpeted lobby. There's an array of kitschy beach-inspired decor hanging on the wall—shiny pink seashells, dried-out coral and starfish—alongside black-and-white photos of the Miami skyline. I should turn left and head down the hall to my room, but instead, I turn toward Ryan's. I knock, but he doesn't come to the door.

I walk the long stretch of hallway back to my own hotel room. The maid has been here: the bed is freshly made and my jumble of clothes and extra shoes and phone charger are stacked neatly on top of my luggage. I kick off my shoes, flop diagonally across the bed, and try to resist the urge to check my phone. Instead, I stare at the white stucco ceiling for a few moments, ruminating on Hallie's disastrous performance today and wondering if she simply had an off day or if I had failed to properly prepare her. Too depressing.

I miss Ryan. I feel silly admitting it to myself, because I just spent the entire day with him, but I do. When we're working, it doesn't really feel like we're spending time together—I can't fully relax around him when I know other people are watching us. If I had to guess, he's probably still with her, comforting her, and that makes me feel even worse: heartbroken for Hallie, ashamed over how I failed as a coach, depressed by what this means for my career, and self-indulgent for wishing Ryan could be here with me instead. I don't want him to come over and analyze what went wrong today. I just want him here as my boyfriend.

I get up to shower off the day, if only because there's nothing else I really want to do (and everyone could benefit from bathing after spending time in an arena that smells like feet). The hotel room's bathroom is outfitted in cream-colored tile with vanity lights over the mirror that feel like the height of glamour compared to my apartment in Greenwood. I linger longer than I need to in the shower. When I get out, wrapped in a fluffy white hotel bathrobe that feels wonderfully thick and heavy over my shoulders, I'm relieved to see a text from Ryan—until I read it.

Hey, sorry, I'm actually not free to hang out right now, he wrote. *Let's talk later?*

His words make me feel lonelier. I spent countless hours in LA waiting for Tyler to text me back, to come home, to want to see me. Eagerly waiting for scraps of attention is the most pathetic feeling in the world.

Sure, I type.

I consider delaying my response by several minutes to give him a taste of his own medicine, but that's too juvenile to feel rewarding. I should know better than to behave like a child. I press send.

I'm too restless to sit around this room, so I get dressed and head downstairs to the hotel's restaurant. Vending machine snacks aside, I've barely eaten all day, and it'd be good for me to get some real food. I didn't realize it until now, but I'm hungry. The restaurant's vibe mimics the beachy decor from upstairs: the upholstery on the chairs looks speckled like sand, and nautical bits and bobs like buoys and fishing net hang from the driftwood bar.

"Just one?" the hostess asks.

"Just me," I say, pretending to be cheery and fine about that.

She scans the crowded room.

"So, it'll be about fifteen or twenty minutes for a table for one, but I could seat you now at the bar, if you'd like," she offers.

"The bar's fine," I say.

There aren't many free bar stools, either, though I see one crammed between two larger men, and another . . . Oh. Next to Jasmine. I move toward the seat between the two men, but she sees me before I can sit down. For a split second, neither of us says anything.

"Hey!" she says, waving me over.

"Will that seat work?" the hostess asks.

Jasmine is watching expectantly.

"It's fine, thank you," I tell the hostess.

I wedge myself into the seat on Jasmine's right. She's dressed for TV: gleaming lipstick, sleek blowout, lemon-yellow shift dress. There's a glass of white wine and a leafy green salad in front of her.

"I wondered if I'd bump into you," she says, giving me an air-kiss by my cheek.

"Good to see you," I say, even though the prospect of a conversation with her makes me anxious.

The bartender slides a menu my way, and I order a glass of wine as quickly as I can.

"Plus, uh, whatever salad she's having," I add.

"It's delicious," Jasmine gushes.

She *would* grow up to be the kind of woman who raves about lettuce.

"It was so interesting to watch Hallie compete

today," she says. "You know, knowing you coach her now."

" 'Interesting'?" I echo.

That sounds like a euphemism for *bad*.

"I loved her new floor routine," Jasmine insists. "I made a note of it on-air, even—I was talking about how you choreographed it yourself, and how excited I was to see Hallie compete it for the first time today."

"Oh," I say, surprised. "That's actually very nice of you. Thank you."

"I'm sure she would've liked to do a little bit better in the rankings today," Jasmine says. "But, hey, you know I always love to root for the underdog."

She winks, as if there's a camera waiting somewhere to catch her reaction. There's not.

"She's a good, hard worker. I think she'll bounce back just fine," I say.

"She's not tough to discipline?" Jasmine asks.

The question catches me off guard. "We don't really need to discipline her."

"Sure," she says skeptically.

"No, really. It's actually been really interesting, figuring out a coaching style that's different from the one we grew up with," I continue. "You remember, Dimitri always said he was hard on us because that would be best for us. But with Hallie, I don't know, she just works hard."

Jasmine doesn't respond right away. Instead,

she sips quietly from her wineglass. I regret speaking so candidly about Dimitri in front of her.

"I'm sorry, I don't mean to imply anything about the way he coached. I know, obviously, things are different now that he's your . . . husband."

The word still leaves a bad taste in my mouth.

"No, it's all right, you don't need to apologize," she says, twisting her diamond engagement ring and staring down at her salad, like she's trying to find the right words. "I know he . . . I mean, he was . . ." She trails off and sighs heavily.

"Is he still like that? I mean, when it's just you two?" I ask tentatively.

I know I'm prying, but it occurs to me that Jasmine might not have anyone else she can talk to like this. We used to confide in each other all the time—more often than not about the man who's now her husband—but I wouldn't be surprised if she stays tight-lipped about what he's really like among her new set of friends.

My salad arrives. Jasmine pauses, politely watching the busboy set it down in front of me. She looks grateful for the opportunity to collect her thoughts before she speaks.

"He's a good man," she finally says in an even voice. "He provides a beautiful life for us, and he is so respected in the community, and he makes me happy."

I know what Jasmine looks like when she's not being totally honest. I've seen it before, back when we were kids. It was easy to lie about doing two sets of reps of crunches instead of three, or to pretend we didn't eat the extra whipped cream on our chai lattes at Lolly's. I'm not married, so I can't judge firsthand what's normal and what's not in her relationship. But she doesn't sound like a woman in love. She sounds like a defense attorney.

"Right," I say.

Discomfort clings to me like an itchy, too-small sweater. There's more I want to know.

"But what's it . . . *like?* Being married to him? I mean, I can't imagine," I say.

It sounds like I'm openly gawking, and I guess I am. I've spent years wondering what their relationship could possibly be like, and after getting a glimpse of it at their party, my curiosity has only intensified.

She gestures to the bartender for another glass of wine.

"I mean, you know him," she says, shrugging. "Sometimes, he has his . . . moods," she admits. "You remember those."

"Yeah, I do."

"And he . . . he's particular, you know? He likes things to be a certain way. Sometimes, he gets upset when things aren't right."

"He used to take it out on us," I say bitterly.

285

Maybe that's a step too far, but Jasmine doesn't disagree with me.

"He meant well, but it wasn't right," she says.

"It took me a long time to clearly see how that affected me, because at the time, it all felt so normal," I say. The words come more easily now, since I know Jasmine will agree with me on this point. "Or, at least, if not normal, like everything was in service of a greater goal."

"Glory," we intone at the same time, like we've heard thousands of times before.

In the back of my head, I hear the word in a guttural Russian accent, and I bet she does, too. For a moment, the past seven years collapse, and I feel like we're just kids again—giggling friends who finish each other's sentences. It makes me miss how we used to be. Nobody has ever replaced her.

"But I think that's changing, no?" she says. "Dimitri's old-school, but he's pretty much the only one left."

"I mean, Ryan and I do our best," I concede. "Hallie's mostly pretty easy, but even so, we don't push her any harder than she'd push herself. I mean, god, the world is not a good place for gymnasts right now. You know what I mean."

"I do," she says heavily.

We don't even need to say it out loud.

"But as horrible as that is, this isn't the first time there's been a scandal like that—awful things like that have happened before," I point out.

"In dark, shady fucking corners, yeah," she says grimly.

"The rest of the sport, though? I think it's getting a little better," I say.

"I think I see that, too," she says. "At competitions, it's like . . . *whoa*. The girls all have muscles and thighs and don't hide the fact that they eat."

We both look limply down at the remaining salad on our plates.

"I don't know about the girls Dimitri works with, but Hallie has personality. Sass. Or, as he might call it, attitude," I say.

"Nothing we were allowed to have," Jasmine adds, shaking her head.

"Ha. No. But Hallie's good. Happy."

"She's okay with food?" Jasmine asks.

"She eats, she does yoga, she's confident . . ." I say.

Jasmine lets out a low whistle, understanding the implication: Hallie's not like we were. "Good for her."

"She has a tutor, but she has a whole plan: Olympics first, then college. She talks about going to law school someday. For her, there's a whole world out there," I explain.

I don't have to spell it out for Jasmine. For us, there was no other world. We're here, after all, aren't we? I stab a piece of lettuce with my fork.

"I wanted to be a fashion designer," Jasmine says suddenly. Her eyes are spacey, vacant, like she's dreaming about some far-off memory. She turns sharply toward me. "Did you know that?"

"Maybe?"

I vaguely recall her sketching evening gowns and spindly high heels on a long car ride to a competition. We must have been twelve. She erased and redrew and erased and redrew each line on a model's body until it matched the vision she held in her mind.

"But then, you know, everything just happened. London and then the post-Olympics tour and then all these motivational speeches at gyms and then Dimitri and NBC, and here we are," she says, shrugging like she blinked and it all just fell into place, like one domino after another. She gives a short laugh. "What was I supposed to do, duck out and learn to sew?"

My question comes tumbling out before I have time to realize that it's a rude one. "Are you happy?" I blurt.

The words hang in the air. Jasmine uncrosses and crosses her legs, catching one stiletto along the rung of the bar stool and taking a long sip of wine.

"Of course I'm *happy*," she says finally. "I just wonder, sometimes, what else could've happened—would've happened—if we'd grown up differently."

"Without Dimitri, you mean," I clarify.

"With a different coach, more options, another life," she says, gesturing vaguely around the restaurant.

The wine is getting to her now; there's a looseness to her energy, so unlike the sensitive, tightly wound girl I used to know.

"Which is why," she continues, "you can't let Ryan take the job."

"What job?" I ask.

"The one they're talking about right now," she says, pointing above us, like it's obvious. "Upstairs. In our suite. No matter who they'll coach together for 2024—Hallie or someone else—that girl deserves better."

"Ryan's with Dimitri?" I ask blankly.

I have the sickening sensation of being the last person to know what's going on, and I hate it. I don't want to have to play catch-up with my own boyfriend's whereabouts and career.

"Where'd you think they were?" she asks, alarmed, as if she suddenly realizes that I've been in the dark. "Oh, honey."

I groan.

"You can't let Ryan take the job," Jasmine says, her tone growing urgent now. She clutches my arm. "I shouldn't say this, and if you tell anyone I did, I'll deny it, but keep Hallie away from Dimitri. Let her be good and safe and healthy. Let her have a future outside of this world."

"What's your room number?" I ask.

"Room two twenty," she says, rolling her eyes. "Like 2020—for good luck."

"Of course he would request that."

"I'll cover your meal if you cover for me," she says, holding a finger to her lips. "Go."

I race to the elevators.

• *Chapter 21* •

The moment before I knock on Dimitri's door, my stomach tightens and my mind spirals into tight focus. It's the same sensation I used to get right before I saluted the judges and strode forward to perform a routine. I knock.

Dimitri opens the door. Surprise flits across his face.

"Hi," I say.

He doesn't greet me.

"Your girlfriend's here," he calls over his shoulder.

He cocks his head and clicks his tongue, signaling for me to enter. Somehow, that's more humiliating than him shutting the door in my face. There was a time I spent more of my day with him than with my own parents. Now he won't even use my name.

The suite is far larger and nicer than the room I'm staying in. The bedroom is identical to mine, but there's also a lounge with a pair of upholstered armchairs and a love seat arranged around a coffee table. There's a crystal decanter of whiskey with two matching, half-filled glasses. Ryan rises from one of the armchairs, confused.

"Avery? What are you doing here?" he asks.

"I'd like to talk to you," I say, hoping my voice comes out steady and strong.

"I'm in the middle of something," he says helplessly. "I texted you earlier, remember? I said we'd catch up later?"

"I know," I say.

"Is everything okay?" he asks.

There's real concern in his voice.

"Well, yeah, I'm fine, but . . ." I wish I had prepared something more convincing to say ahead of time. "I just . . . I really would like to speak with you. Now."

"Where are your manners, girl?" Dimitri says, looking amused. "We're working out business here."

The way he calls me *girl,* it's like he's hurled me more than a decade into the past. He has a knack for making me feel so small. It makes me burn with rage, especially because I know he's right—I barged in here without an invitation—but I can't apologize. I can't bow down in front of him and pretend to be sorry. I'm not.

Ryan looks from me to Dimitri and back again.

"Go," Dimitri says, waving his hand to dismiss us both. "Ryan, we'll talk again tomorrow."

"No, Dimitri, it's fine . . ." Ryan starts to protest.

But Dimitri's already halfway to the bedroom. We've been dismissed.

"All right, bye, thank you for everything," Ryan rushes to say.

I hate how furious and flustered and thrown off course I feel, just from spending one single minute in Dimitri's presence. But maybe it's for the best—maybe this is exactly the raw, hateful energy I need to fully convince Ryan he can never work with that man.

Ryan follows me out of the suite. I turn to face him the minute the door closes behind us, but he shakes his head, pressing a finger to his lips, and ushers us farther down the narrow hall, toward the elevator. I jab the up button.

"What was that?" he says finally. "Are you really okay? Is Hallie okay?"

"I'm fine, she's fine," I insist.

We enter the empty elevator, and the tight quarters make it feel impossible to keep my thoughts to myself. We're so close, he can probably hear what I'm thinking.

"What were you talking about?" I demand.

The edge of my voice sounds hard. Angry. Ugly.

"I've made up my mind. I want to work with Dimitri at Powerhouse," he admits.

For a moment, I feel too bitter to speak.

"But you know he's not a good guy," I say.

The elevator doors *ding* open on the seventh floor, and I follow him to his room.

"I know *you've* said that," he says carefully.

I grab his arm and stop walking. "That's not fair."

He sighs and pulls his arm away. "Okay. It's not, you're right. I'm sorry."

Now, in his hotel room, I stare at him expectantly, waiting for him to produce any explanation that makes sense. He sits on the edge of the bed, and I join him reluctantly. My heart pounds. I just want this conversation to be over with.

"I think this is a mistake," I tell him plainly. "Dimitri would crush Hallie. You see how rudely he treats me, don't you? He'll be ten times worse to her, day in, day out. He'll yell at her if she doesn't perform up to his insanely high standards of perfection, and then he'll scream at her if she dares to cry or fight back. He'll call her cruel names. He'll make her keep a diary of everything she eats and he'll review it once a week while she stands on a scale in a leotard. He'll punish her for gaining half a pound. He'll isolate her from her friends. Ryan, I know you think he's a legend, but he's a nightmare."

Ryan bites his lip and shakes his head. I can't tell if it's in disbelief or disagreement.

"I'm sorry that you grew up like that," he says in a strained voice. "I really, really am. Please don't get me wrong. He must have changed— he's not like that anymore."

"I don't believe that," I say firmly. "And anyway, it's not worth the risk. Girls who train with him don't grow up to have healthy, normal lives."

"Well, look at you," Ryan says, shrugging. "You turned out fine."

"Exactly! Look at me," I say. "It's been a long road to feeling remotely okay."

It's increasingly impossible not to shout. It feels like a match just caught fire in my chest. I ignite with anger. I've seethed silently about this in the past, but I've never let it all out before.

"Since I moved back to Greenwood, I've finally, slowly, just barely started to cobble together a real, adult life that I'm proud of," I explain. "A lot of that has to do with working with you. But I am twenty-seven years old. *Twenty-seven!* It took me the better part of a decade to get here. I was reeling. I had no education, no ambition, no goals, no full-time job. That's not me. That's not who I was supposed to be. For years, my life just . . . stalled. And I couldn't get back on track."

"You can't blame that all on Dimitri," Ryan says softly.

"He's certainly not innocent. He pushes people down so they can't get up," I fire back. "And look at Jasmine. He broke her down so hard, she never left. He's despicable."

"Kaminsky's despicable. Dimitri's just tough," Ryan says.

"I'm telling you, what you're doing is just plain wrong," I argue. "No decent person would do this."

"I'm not feeding Hallie to the wolves, Avery,"

Ryan says. "I'll be there with her. I'll protect her."

"Does Hallie know you're doing this? Do her *parents?*" I ask.

He sighs. His face contorts, but I can't tell if it's with guilt or exasperation.

"We've been talking about it for weeks," he admits. "I didn't include you in the discussions because I knew you would never work with Dimitri."

My anger blooms into rage, then betrayal.

"And when did you think you'd tell me?" I ask. My voice breaks. "I'm not just your coworker. This isn't about you ditching your job. I'm your *girlfriend,* Ryan. You're supposed to tell me things, not go behind my back."

He sighs. "I'm sorry for not telling you about my plans sooner."

I shake my head. I'm too overwhelmed to speak. What is there to say? I don't recognize the person I'm arguing with.

"I feel so stupid," I say finally.

"Why?" he asks.

I shudder and the words slip out before I can register what I'm saying.

"Because this whole time that I've been falling in love with you, you've been keeping secrets from me."

Ryan bites his lip. His eyes search mine for a long time.

"I . . . I didn't know," he says. "That you felt that way," he clarifies.

I look away, cheeks burning hot. There's a painful, stretched-out silence. I wait for him to say those words back to me. If he loves me back, he won't take the job. He'll make things right. But he doesn't say a word. I feel tears threatening to well up and a painful lump building in my throat, but I know I won't cry. It's a skill I learned long ago, honed so Dimitri would never see me more vulnerable than I could handle. The irony of it all feels bitter. I clear my throat.

"Please don't take the job," I say. "That's all I can say. That's the only thing left to say."

I rise from the bed. I can't stand being close to him right now.

"Avery, I'm sorry," he says. "I wouldn't do this if I didn't really believe Dimitri's changed. He's a legend. He's going to make Hallie a star."

"Do you want her to be star? Or do you want him to make *you* a star coach? You'll leave me and Summit behind in the dust."

"I'd take you with me, if you wanted to come," he offers.

"Right, sure, because that's ideal: working alongside an emotionally abusive asshole and the guy who doesn't love me," I snap. "Sounds great."

He leaps up from the bed. "I didn't say I didn't love you," he says.

I take a deep breath. "Do you?" I ask. "Do you love me?"

He wavers for a moment, like he's going to say something. But he doesn't.

"We're done," I say, walking quickly to the door so he can't see the tears springing to my eyes for real this time. "We're over."

I turn the door handle hard and storm out, hurrying toward my room at the opposite end. I wait for the sound of him chasing after me, begging me to change my mind. But there's nothing except the cool hiss of Ryan's door as it eases shut behind me.

• *Chapter 22* •

The day after I get home from the National Championships, needing a distraction, I text Sara and entice her to be home at seven for one of the most exquisite meals I have under my belt: seared scallops on a bed of fresh corn and roasted hazelnuts, swirled in a creamy, paprika-infused brown butter sauce. Scallops cost a breathtaking twenty-four dollars per pound at the grocery store, and their soft, delicate white bellies make them tricky to cook without charring the skin and leaving the insides raw. In other words, don't bother attempting to make them unless you know what you're doing and have a reason to splurge. I'm making a pound and a half of them tonight because I want to feel talented and productive and like myself again as I recount the story of my breakup to Sara. I lost sight of who I am over the course of my relationship with Tyler; I need to prove to myself that I haven't forgotten that again while dating Ryan.

I've unloaded the groceries and preheated the oven when Sara walks in and drops her yoga mat by the door. She taught a class tonight, so wisps of blond hair frizz up from her topknot, and her cheeks glow pink. It's true that teaching yoga isn't as physically taxing as doing it, or so she tells me, but she's still one of those girls who never sweats. As a person who spent a good chunk of her teenage years sweating on national television, I'm jealous.

"You're officially my favorite person, do you know that?" she says, taking in the paper-wrapped scallops and the ears of corn. "This looks amazing."

"Thanks, but save your compliments for when you taste it," I say. "Hey, do me a favor? Will you shuck the corn?"

"Sure thing. Looks fancy. What's the occasion?" she asks.

I look up carefully from the paprika I'm measuring. "Ryan and I broke up," I say.

Sara gasps and gives me a sympathetic look. "I'm so sorry," she says, hugging me.

"Well, technically, I broke up with him," I add. "We had a fight, and . . ."

I press my lips together into a tight smile so they don't tremble. I can't let myself cry again—not now, not after I've spent the better part of the last two nights crying myself to sleep. It feels important to add the technicality that I was the one to break off the relationship. I can't stomach being the girl who gets dumped twice in six months.

Sara sinks into the kitchen chair next to mine, and while I slide the chopped hazelnuts into the oven and pat each scallop dry with a paper towel, I recount what happened. I don't have to litigate Dimitri's wrongdoings for her; I say he was emotionally and verbally abusive, and she understands.

"The most embarrassing part is that when we were arguing, I accidentally told Ryan I was falling in love with him," I say.

As mortifying as that was in the moment, I discover the humiliation feels just as fresh recounting it the next day. Sara visibly cringes.

"Did he say it back?" she asks.

"Nope," I reply. "If he had, maybe things would've gone pretty differently."

"Do you really love him?" she asks.

I sigh. The question sounds deceptively simple—yes or no. But there are too many other emotions swirling through my head right now to make sense of the situation: sadness, anger, embarrassment, shame, regret.

"I guess I'm just confused," I say, puzzling through the thoughts out loud. "I thought I loved him. But the way he's acting? Going behind my back, taking that job, not listening to what I'm saying about it? That makes me question who he really is."

The realization stings.

"I'm really sorry he let you down," Sara says softly. "He should've believed you."

"That's what's so weird about it, though! He was devastated over what Hallie went through.

He believes all the other gymnasts who have come forward about Kaminsky—it's not that he's one of those men's rights activists who's all about guys being innocent until proven guilty. He's always cared. Just not now."

"Maybe because now, this issue is personal for him? It's about his career, which means he's not thinking as clearly as he should?" Sara guesses.

I groan at how infuriating the situation is and drizzle olive oil into a hot skillet. I gently place the scallops one by one, listening to the sizzle as they bathe in oil. Cooking scallops looks intimidating, but it really all comes down to precise timing and skill—just like gymnastics. Not that I ever really want to think about gymnastics ever again, especially not right now.

"And then, ugh, the next day, we had to fly back from Miami together," I say. "Me, Ryan, and Hallie, all in one row."

"That really blows."

"Yeah, sitting between my secret ex and a kid who's mourning the potential end of her athletic career for three hours was a real treat."

"How's Hallie doing?" Sara asks.

I shrug and flip the scallops. "Not great," I say. "Her confidence is shot, she's stressed beyond belief, she's frantic that she'll fail at Trials."

"Yikes," Sara says.

I finish the recipe, mixing bright yellow kernels of corn with the rich, slippery sauce, and plating it carefully all together so it looks like a real gourmet treat. I turn around and I'm just about to set Sara's plate in front of her, when she makes a sour face.

"What?" I ask.

She bites her lip and slides her phone across the table toward me.

"I hate to show you this, but this just popped up on my feed, and I think you should see it," she says, wincing.

The screen is filled with Ryan's most recent Instagram, a photo of him I must have missed. His arms are slung around Dimitri and Jasmine's shoulders, and his satisfied smile gives me goose bumps. Dimitri looks the same as always—gruff, like he's only posing to humor them. I search Jasmine's face for clues, but she's wearing that blankly beautiful newscaster look again. It's impossible to tell what thoughts are running through her head. The background of the photo looks familiar, but I can't quite place it until I spot the glint of medals against the wall behind them—it's Dimitri and Jasmine's house. They're cozy enough to do dinner at home together now, I guess.

"I can't believe I have to work with him for months," I say, groaning.

It's late March; Trials are at the tail end of June, with the Olympics stretching from late July through early August.

"You gotta focus on Hallie? Forget about him?" Sara says. I think she means it like a statement, but the absurdity of working on a three-person team with your ex for months is too much, even for her. "Channel your energy into the right places, block out the distractions, all that kind of stuff."

I try not to grimace, but right now, I need something a little stronger than yoga. There's half a bottle of red wine left corked on the counter, although it feels like a bad omen to pour a glass from it: Ryan and I opened it together last week. But the only other drink with a buzz to it is Sara's home-brewed kombucha, so wine it is. Fittingly, the flavor has turned bitter. I drink it anyway.

"It's just not fair," I say, pushing away my plate of scallops.

Tears prick at my eyes. I inhale deeply to calm myself down, but it doesn't really work.

"I want to be strong about this," I say. "I don't want to let this drama with Ryan get to me. I h-h-hate that I'm the kind of person who gets so thrown off course by stupid, dumb *feelings*."

My shoulders start to shake with gentle sobs, and I wish I could disappear into a black hole. I don't want Sara to see me like this. It's embarrassing to lose your shit over a guy you've only dated for a handful of months, especially when Sara met me shortly after a breakup with a *different* guy. If it walks like a duck and talks like a duck, it's a duck, right? And if I look like a boy-crazy mess, well . . .

"Avery, you've got to give yourself a break," Sara says, interrupting my spiraling thoughts. "It's okay to feel sad. Breakups are sad! That doesn't make you weak."

"Ryan's not sad. He's 'networking,' " I say, making vicious air quotes.

"He posted one picture," Sara says gently. "That doesn't tell you what he's really feeling on the inside."

I nudge a scallop with my fork. I wish I could know what he was thinking: if he believes what I said about Dimitri; if he regrets not chasing after me; if he's wondering how I'm doing right now, the same way I'm wondering about him. I miss him, even though I know I shouldn't. He crossed a line, and he was wrong—I feel this on a cellular level—but the only comfort I crave is a hug in his sturdy arms. It strikes me as heartbreakingly unfair that the one person who would lift my spirits best is also the person who crushed them.

I want Ryan to stroke my hair and whisper apologies into my ear and promise me he'll take my word more seriously next time. I need him to tell me he cares as deeply for Hallie as I do, and that he wants to protect her and girls like her, no matter what the cost, even if it means his career doesn't zoom up the ladder as quickly as he'd hope. I took it for granted that I could trust him. Now I realize I shouldn't have.

"Sweetie, it's going to be okay," Sara promises.

She tries to catch my gaze, and because I don't want to ruin her night, too, I let her.

I muster up enough energy to pretend like her advice is helpful. "Right," I say.

"Let's eat," she suggests. "Dinner looks incredible."

But I've lost my appetite.

APRIL
2020

• *Chapter 23* •

I'm in a terrible mood. I'm fifteen minutes late to practice because I couldn't overcome the overwhelming dread of getting out of bed. The sight of Ryan's spare blue toothbrush in my bathroom made me crumple. I don't want to face him, but calling in sick would be worse.

I stride across the lobby, past the life-sized cutout of Hallie, beyond the poster with my face hanging dustily from a forgotten spot on the rafters, onto the floor. Ryan is chatting with another coach. His shoulders are hunched, and he leans his chin onto his fist as he talks; from the awkwardly self-conscious way he speaks, I'd bet anything that he's discussing Nationals, even though I'm out of earshot. Once he notices me approaching, he shifts ever so subtly. He straightens up and clears his throat. He gives a small nod of recognition in my direction but doesn't pause to say hello. The way he brushes me off looks so subtle to an outsider, but it stings because it's light-years away from his attitude toward me even just a few days ago. I can't believe I said that I was falling in love with him and was met with silence.

Hallie's not here yet. I cruise to the water fountain just to have something to do. I lean against a low practice bar and look at my phone to kill time, but I can't fully relax. The energy in the gym is all wrong. I can feel Ryan not even halfway across the room. Most of the kid gymnasts are too young or too casual about the sport to have understood the full ramifications of Hallie's performance at Nationals—if they're even aware a competition took place, they probably think it's cool that she went at all—but the older, elite-track girls understand. So do their parents. *Especially* their parents, the ones who watch Hallie as if she's a weather vane that can evaluate the gym's worthiness and predict their own daughters' success.

Hallie slinks into the gym ten minutes later with her tracksuit hood shielding half her face and quietly settles down in an empty corner of the floor to warm up. I head over to greet her, but she barely looks at me. Ryan joins us, squatting down to Hallie's level on the floor and giving me a respectable amount of space. Luckily, Hallie is so caught up in her own morose world that I doubt she'll even notice the tension between me and him.

"Actually, I'm just gonna warm up by myself, if you don't mind," Hallie says, slipping her AirPods into her ears and shutting us out.

This isn't like her. She hasn't been her typically energetic, goofy, fun-loving self since before Nationals. This isn't good.

"Okay," I say uncertainly.

"Just let me know when you're ready for conditioning, okay?" Ryan asks.

She gives a curt nod, slides into a wide straddle, and slumps forward so her cheek rests against the floor. Sometimes, coaches will sit behind a gymnast in a straddle and press her down flatter into the floor for a better stretch; all *I* want to do is give her a hug. I hate seeing her so sad like this.

Normally, if Hallie were working on her own, Ryan and I would hang out. But I have nothing to say to him—not anything appropriate that I could say here, anyway. From the way he avoids me, I don't get the sense he's interested in speaking to me, either. So, instead, I do a little ab work until I panic that it makes me look like I'm peacocking for him. I get up and straighten up the supply closet, even though nothing is really out of place. I bounce lazily on the trampoline, turning back tuck after back tuck just because they're simple and fun. I go to the bathroom and run my hands under the faucet for three times as long as I need to, just because I feel lonely and out of place in the one spot that's always felt like home. I loathe everything about today. Nothing about this entire disastrous situation feels right—nothing.

Eventually, I wander back into the gym and perch on one of the beams to watch Hallie condition with Ryan from a safe distance. After her shaky performance at Worlds last fall, Hallie returned to the gym with a powerful vengeance. She threw herself into her practice with dynamite energy, ready to shape herself into a better athlete. But this time, returning from Nationals, her spirit couldn't be any different. Across the gym, she's supposed to be drilling sets of reps on bars: chin-ups, pull-ups, and leg lifts. She dangles loosely from the high bar and works with sloppy form. If she cared about the outcome, she'd work better. Work harder. She's throwing today's practice away.

I don't know the specifics of the ups and downs of Hallie's athletic career as well as, say, Ryan would, but I know enough: she was a super-naturally talented kid, and when her coaches said she had a real shot at an elite gymnastics career if she took training seriously, her parents made sure she had every advantage: a private coach at Summit, summers at training camps, a tutor so school would be more flexible. She always performed well enough in competitions to nab medals and level up. For Hallie, the Olympics probably never felt like a long shot. And now, to come so close and still worry you're not quite good enough? That can't be easy.

I feel for her. I wish circumstances were different—it's only human to need some time to rebound, recharge, and return with a better attitude. But time isn't on her side, and if she wastes the next few weeks or months by sulking, she's letting a lifetime of hard work and sacrifice wither and die. It sounds dramatic and unfair, but so is this sport.

Hallie trudges my way, clutching her side and breathing hard from the workout Ryan just gave her.

"Ryan says we should start with floor today," she says.

So, apparently, he won't even speak to me unless it's through her.

"Sure, let's go," I say brightly, trying to lift her mood.

"You want me to warm up tumbling first?" she asks.

That's our usual routine, but today, I want to try something different.

"Actually, let's hold off on that for now," I say. "I want to go over the video of your Nationals routine together."

She groans. "Do we have to?"

"Yes, we do, because that's how we'll know what to target over the next few weeks," I insist, using my most authoritative voice.

It's often all too easy to feel transported back in time at Summit, and to lose sight of the fact that I'm actually a decade older than Hallie, but it serves me well to remember I'm in charge sometimes.

"Let's go, I have it on my phone," I say.

"I hate this," she mutters. "You're the worst."

"You'll thank me when you win a medal on floor at the Olympics, okay?" I say.

She rolls her eyes. "Yeah, right."

We sit with our backs to the cool concrete wall and watch the routine on my phone screen. If it's cringeworthy for me to watch her stumbles and mistakes again, this time with Jasmine and Barry's sharp commentary playing in the background, I can only imagine how she feels.

"Ignore the commentary," I say, turning my phone on silent.

To a casual viewer, Hallie's routine gleams. She looks like a superstar dream. But to me, the mistakes are obvious: her leap series doesn't hit the requisite 180-degree splits; there's just a hair too much power on one tumbling pass; her poise drops as she loses energy toward the end of her routine. The second the video is over, Hallie pushes away the screen.

"I get it," she says darkly. "I suck."

"You don't suck," I retort.

She pulls her knees up to her chest and rests her chin on top, looking very, very small.

"I'm not going to sugarcoat this for you," I warn her. "You gave an amazing performance at Nationals, but you need to deliver an even stronger performance at Trials if you want your athletic career to continue. If you don't use this moment to learn from your mistakes and grow, you might as well just quit now."

That catches her attention. She stares at me, dumbstruck and horrified.

"Quit now?" Hallie repeats.

"I get that you're sad, I get that you're jealous of girls like Delia and Emma, I get that none of this went the way you hoped. But you're still here, in fighting shape, and you have the opportunity of a lifetime coming up in just a few short weeks," I remind her.

She sighs and doesn't look at me for a long time. "I'm just afraid that it won't matter what I do to prep," she admits. "Like, what if I'm not good enough? What if that's just it? Some people have what it takes, and some people don't."

"You can't think like that," I say.

"But what if it's true?" she asks. "I mean, how many millions of little kids take gymnastics classes? And then, what, only four people actually make the Olympic team every four years? Come on."

She's right, but I don't want her to think that way. A failed Olympic hopeful probably isn't the most convincing person to deliver a pep talk right now, but I'm the person she's got. I fumble for the right words; I think back to the girl I was moments before competing on floor at Olympic Trials in 2012, and what I've so desperately wished I could have said to her. What I wished I had known.

"There are no guarantees at all," I say finally.

"Not in gymnastics. Not in life. But you have to give this the best goddamn shot you have, I swear to you, because it's the one chance you have."

Her lower lip trembles, and she buries her face in her knees.

"Now get up," I command.

I stand, hands on my hips. For a moment, I worry that I've gone too far. She doesn't move. But then she pushes herself off the ground to stand up. Her cheeks glisten with tears, and her chest rises and falls with emotion, but she's here. Standing. Ready to work.

MAY
2020

• *Chapter 24* •

The calendar slips into May before I know it. Each day at Summit is tightly packed: Hallie's schedule is dominated by heavy-duty practice and punctuated by appointments with a revolving door of professionals: yoga and meditation sessions led by Sara, acupuncture and massage by a team of sports medicine doctors I found at Children's Hospital in Boston, visits from a nutritionist to map out her pre-Olympic meals. I give so many pep talks, I spend my lunch breaks Googling inspirational quotes. My nights are busy, too: I hang out at home with Sara, go out for drinks with Jasmine more regularly now, and visit Mom and Dad for dinner when they complain it's been too long since they've seen me.

I'm glad I'm mostly busy, because even with the little free time I have, it's too easy to dwell on what happened with Ryan. The sadness creeps in during idle moments when I least expect it: I'll be washing my hair in the shower when I realize how badly I miss kissing him. Or I'll be waiting by the stove for water to boil when I get the urge to text him—and I can't anymore. When I'm lying in *shavasana* at the end of yoga class, I should be relaxed. But instead, I rake over every memory I have of Ryan from February and March, trying to spot the moment I missed him betraying me. The last thing I want to do is let the weight of the breakup crush me. I have to keep moving in order to eventually move on.

When practice wraps up on Monday night, I'm heading out of the lobby when I see a missed call and a text from Jasmine. I pause in the doorway of the building to read the message.

Do you happen to be free tonight? Would love to talk to you. It's important.

I'm about to text her back when I hear a noise behind me—someone clearing his throat.

"Oh, sorry," I say, stepping outside into the warm spring night. It's finally nice enough that you can get away without a jacket, and blips of music float by as cars drive past with their windows down. "Didn't mean to block the door."

I turn and flinch. There's Ryan, awkwardly ruffling a hand through his hair.

"I didn't mean to scare you," he says.

We've worked alongside each other just fine, but that's the key word: "alongside." Not *with* each other. Outside of communicating the essential logistics of Hallie's training schedule, we've barely spoken two words to each other since returning from Nationals. I'm afraid that if I start, I won't be able to stop, and I'll blurt something embarrassing and emotional.

"It's okay," I say.

That much, at least, I can manage.

He moves past me toward the parking lot, then stops and turns.

"Everything all right?" he asks.

"Yeah, I just got a weird text, that's all," I say.

I don't tell him it's from Jasmine. From what she's told me, he and Dimitri are spending more and more time together. I don't want whatever I say to Ryan to get back to Dimitri.

"I hope she's okay," he says.

He looks concerned, but he doesn't move from his spot on the pavement. If our relationship had unfolded differently, I'd be able to tell him everything. He'd reassure me things would be okay. But now, ten feet sits between us, and it feels like ten miles. I know that neither one of us will close the distance.

"Yeah, it'll all be fine," I say.

I cross my arms and lean back against the door frame. He seems to get the message—I have nothing more to say to him. He waves good night and gets into his car. I wait until he drives away to text Jasmine back.

I'll come over now, I tell her.

I'm nervous pulling into Jasmine's driveway. We've seen each other plenty of times since Nationals, but always in public—never at home. Together, we've split oysters and sauvignon blanc at a French bistro, shared a big veggie pizza at

Stonehearth in the town center, and even met up on a Saturday afternoon to get manicures together (I rarely indulge in them, but she promised it would be fun, and I have to admit, it was pretty nice). There's an unspoken agreement: we don't hang out around Dimitri. I don't know if he'll be home tonight.

I heave the gold knocker against the door and hear the pitter-patter of bare feet inside. Jasmine opens the door looking unlike I've seen her in years. Her face is free of makeup, so completely so that I can see the dark circles beneath her eyes and a blemish forming on her cheek. Her hair is unceremoniously pulled back into a low ponytail, and she's wearing saggy gray sweatpants and an oversized T-shirt. She looks both embarrassed and relieved to see me.

"I'm so glad you came," she says, pulling me into a hug. "Thank you so much."

I step cautiously inside. The house is quiet. "Of course."

"He's not home," she says, as if she can read my thoughts. "It's poker night. He'll be out for hours."

"Oh, okay."

I mean *Oh, good,* but I didn't want to sound too enthusiastic.

She leads us through the kitchen, where she pours me a glass of rosé to match the one she's already drinking, and then into the living room, where we settle onto the ivory-colored sectional beneath the wall of medals. She pulls her feet up under her. On the glass coffee table beside us, a fragrant candle burns brightly.

"I know we don't really do this," she says, gesturing at the couch between us. "Or at least, not for a long time."

A decade ago, there was nothing unusual about us spending hours in each other's bedrooms, sneaking snacks and talking about the movie stars we thought were cute. But that was before London, before she got married, before we grew apart and grew up.

"We can do this," I say. "We're friends."

She gives a small smile at the word "friends" and sips her wine. "Yeah."

"So . . ." I say, trying to prompt her.

I don't want to push her, but I know she didn't call me over here just to chitchat.

"I have news," she announces.

"Okay," I say gently.

I can't help but race through the options: she's not pregnant—she's drinking wine—but maybe it's something about Dimitri and Ryan, or her career, or worse, a health scare of some kind, or something terrible with her family.

She gives me a nervous look and takes a deep breath, as if she's psyching herself up to say whatever it is out loud.

"I'm going to leave Dimitri," she says.

Her voice is low and quiet, as if she can't quite trust that we're really alone.

"Oh my god, Jasmine," I breathe. "Wow."

She nods. "I know. I haven't told him yet. I need to get my life in order first. But . . . I've decided."

"How long have you been thinking about this?" I ask.

"Part of me has known for a long time that marrying him was the wrong decision," she explains. "It felt right at the time, but I was swept up by him, and I was so young, and I wasn't thinking straight. He had a way of intimidating me—more so back then—and when he said we should get married, I wasn't brave enough to say no. But . . ." She hesitates, then admits, "Part of the decision came from talking to you."

"Me?"

I clap a hand to my mouth. I never hid my contempt for him, but I never outright told her to leave him, either. Meddling in a marriage, encouraging a wife to leave her husband—it all feels too adult for me. I'm way in over my head.

"It started at Nationals," she recalls. "At the bar, remember? Nobody has ever dared to tell me to my face that Dimitri is . . ." She stops short and scowls. "An emotionally abusive asshole. But you did. You know what he's like, better than anybody."

"Not as a husband, though," I say.

"Even still," she says. "Once you said it, I couldn't ignore it. It gnawed at me for days afterward. Everything he had said and done over the years, I brushed it aside. But you didn't, and it made me think that I shouldn't, either."

"Of course," I say.

"Our relationship wasn't balanced, you know?" she continues. "There was never a time when it felt like I had the upper hand, ever. It was always him. We were gymnast and coach and then husband and wife, but the dynamic between us never shifted. We were never equal partners, the way you're supposed to be."

"I wondered about that," I admit. "When I first heard you were together, I just . . . I couldn't make any sense of it."

"I didn't know how strange the relationship was," she says. "I didn't see how unhealthy it was."

"You deserve so much better than him," I say. "I mean, nobody deserves him at all, but especially not you."

I'm relieved for her, but I'm afraid for what I've set into motion. I know that, on average, it takes women seven attempts to finally leave their abusive husbands for good. I wonder where Jasmine will go; I'd let her stay with me and Sara, if she wanted to, even though the prospect of Dimitri banging on our door late at night makes me feel sick with nerves.

"I think I know that?" she says tentatively, like she isn't ready to fully commit to the idea just yet. "I mean, I look at my life, and the only common thread throughout all the different parts—gymnastics, TV, marriage—is that Dimitri has always been right there behind me, making me feel small. Everyone else cheers me on. But with him, it's always . . ."

Jasmine falters, and her expression crumples.

"Nothing is ever good enough for him. *I'm* not good enough for him," she says. Her voice gets high and tight. "He says I'm too anxious, too sensitive, too mediocre."

"Maybe you'd be less anxious if he didn't *make* you so anxious," I point out.

I don't know if she even hears me—now that she's started to spill how she really feels, she barrels on, spitting out the insults Dimitri has hurled her way over the years.

"The dinner is late," she recites. "And my cellulite is bad. I supposedly interfere with his schedule. I really don't think all that is true, but no matter what I do, the comments keep coming . . . I thought marriage was about being on each other's team, you know? But not mine."

She gingerly places her wineglass on a coaster on the coffee table and sinks back into the cushions with a hand pressed over her mouth to muffle her sobs. For a moment, her shoulders shake, and I reach across the couch to hug her.

She leans into the embrace, and we stay like that for a long time. I rub her back and wonder, with a sickening feeling in my gut, what it must be like for her to prepare to leave the man she has been with for most of her childhood and the entirety of her adult life. I can't fathom it. She is so incredibly brave—she always has been. I hold her until she steadies herself, returning to the normal rise and fall of her breathing.

"I'm sorry for getting emotional," she says quietly, wiping away her tears.

"Please, there's nothing to apologize for," I insist.

She shrugs.

"You know, I'm here if you need anything—any help at all," I tell her.

"There's a lot I need to figure out," she says, sighing. "All my money is in a joint account, and I'll need a place to live, and I need to find a good divorce lawyer. That stuff, I can do on my own. But maybe, when it's time, you'll help me pack up and move out?"

"Of course," I promise.

She suddenly looks shy. "Or even if you just continue to be my friend, that's more than enough, you know. I can't tell you how grateful I am that we came back into each other's lives. Really and truly just blown-away grateful."

She gives me the most tender smile, and I feel so touched that she sees me as a person who will have her back again. It's heartbreaking to watch her reckon with the broken pieces of her relationship, but I'm proud that she trusts me to help her heal and move on. Before Nationals, I never would have guessed in a million years that Jasmine and I would be friends again—could be *best* friends again, the kind of presence in your life where it doesn't matter if you cry in your sweatpants or your voice cracks when you reveal the gnarled insecurities and fears that keep you up at night, because that person loves you for you and loves you for good, forever. I didn't think a friendship of that magnitude could abruptly drop dead and be revived nearly a decade later. But this time, I'm glad to be proven wrong.

• *Chapter 25* •

A few days later, as I'm jamming my feet into sneakers and getting ready to head out of my apartment for practice, Jasmine sends me a text.

Another one, she writes, copying a link to a news story.

The text shows a preview of the NBC story, with the headline "A Seventh Gymnast Accuses Dr. Ron Kaminsky of Sexual Abuse" and a photo of Skylar Hayashi taken at a competition. I feel disgusted as I click on the story and wait for it to load. I don't know much about Skylar other than that she's one of Dimitri's gymnasts, she only competes on vault, and as far as I've seen, she can stick perfect landings in her sleep.

I sink down on the couch to read more. NBC reports that Skylar came forward on Twitter early this morning, writing, "I have some difficult news to share. Like many of my fellow athletes, I survived sexual abuse by Dr. Ron Kaminsky. For those of you who may be suffering in silence, I encourage you to seek the help you deserve. #MeToo." NBC notes that Skylar accused Kaminsky of abuse following similar allegations from Delia Cruz, Maggie Farber, Kiki McCloud, Emily Jenkins, Bridget Sweeney, and Liora Cohen, and that Kaminsky's criminal trial is set for this winter. The American Gymnastics Federation, the sport's governing body, issued a statement this morning in support of its gymnasts' bravery, but that doesn't feel like enough to me. They must have known what was going on. Didn't they?

Reluctantly, I head outside and drive to Summit. I know Hallie is going to be shaken up today, and I wish I had a way to shield her from all of this pain. What Skylar and Hallie and all the other girls are doing is already painful enough. They've already sacrificed enough of their childhood, their freedom, their health, and their families' peace of mind in order to be where they are. It's unbelievably unfair that grown men, monsters, can step in and make everything even worse.

When I spot Hallie glumly sprawled across a crash mat, I don't have to ask if she's seen the news. I can tell.

"Skylar," she says heavily. "You saw?"

"I did," I say.

"Out of everyone, I didn't think it would be Skylar," she says, shaking her head. "I mean, out of all of us, she's, like, the normal one."

"What do you mean?" I ask.

Hallie sighs. "She has school friends. She has a boyfriend. She's really pretty and goes to Aruba with her family every winter, and she went to a Post Malone concert last month."

"This can happen to anyone," I say gently.

"Yeah, but you'd just think . . . ugh, god . . ." Hallie says, trailing off. "You'd hope that not everybody's life would be ruined, you know?"

I nod, because what else is there to say?

Ryan approaches us gingerly, squatting down so he's on Hallie's eye level. He glances at me and gives a nervous half smile as a greeting.

"Hi. How are you doing?" he asks Hallie.

She shrugs at him and looks at me. "Bummed, I guess."

"Because of Skylar's news?" he asks.

She nods. "Yeah."

"I don't want to push you too hard today," he says. "I'm sorry you're having a tough morning."

I'm surprised by how gentle he is with her. Trials are six weeks away—there isn't time to take it easy, especially not when Hallie's less of a shoo-in for the Olympic team than we all had hoped.

"Thanks," she says. "I mean, I'm okay. It's just . . . unfair."

"It is. It really is," he says. "Is there anything I can do to make things easier for you right now?"

She gives him a skeptical look.

"I'm here if you want to chat," he says warmly, sounding like a coach and a protective big brother all rolled into one. "Or if you want to smash things, I can bring in my old printer and a hammer. Or we can skip practice today and pick up tomorrow."

She laughs. "No, I'll be good. I appreciate all that, really, but no smashing necessary."

"Okay. Just let me know," he says.

"Will do."

He starts to rise, but appears to think better of it. "If it's any comfort, I have a tiny piece of news that might cheer you up," he says.

"Trials are canceled, and I can go straight to the Olympics?" Hallie guesses.

I think I know where Ryan is going with this, and I don't like it.

"Don't get your hopes up," I mutter.

"Well, I've been talking with Dimitri, and he seems really excited about training you for 2024, if you still want that," he says, offering a small smile.

There's no way Dimitri would have ever used the word "excited." Ryan's exaggerating.

Hallie beams. "Well, that's nice!"

"Just passing along a compliment," Ryan says.

"I mean, I guess a lot depends on what happens this summer, but . . . without making promises, I think I do still want to keep 2024 open as an option."

"Cool," Ryan says, high-fiving her.

"Dimitri's intense, isn't he?" Hallie says, turning to me. "I mean, he's the best, but he's intense. Right, Avery?"

"Yeah, he's intense," I say darkly.

"Avery," Ryan says quietly, as if he's warning me.

He shoots me a meaningful glare, and I hesitate.

"I'm sure whatever happens, you'll be amazing," I tell her diplomatically.

It's the truth. Not the whole truth, but there's only so much I can say without crossing an inappropriate professional line.

She squeals and drums her hands against the mat. "Eep, thanks."

Ryan smirks. "Glad I could cheer you up. Let's get to work."

• *Chapter 26* •

I shouldn't have been surprised that Jasmine got her shit together to leave Dimitri pretty quickly. Within two weeks of her telling me she wanted to divorce him, she had already contacted a good divorce lawyer, funneled away enough money into a separate bank account in order to put down a deposit and the first month of rent on an apartment in Cambridge, and officially broke the news to Dimitri. She told me she was going to do it on a Friday night; I spent all evening holding my breath, waiting for the frantic phone call that she needed help. I stayed in and watched a movie on Netflix with my phone resting in my hand, just in case. But the call never came—just a text at nearly midnight, asking me to come by the next morning to help her pack up her things. I was relieved.

So, on Saturday morning, for the final time, I drive to see Jasmine at her house. It's a gorgeous seventy-five degrees outside, but I get a chill waiting on the front step for her to open the door. It's hard to imagine that after nearly a lifetime with Dimitri, she'll be leaving him behind for good. She opens the door in white jeans and a pink tank top and throws her arms around me into a hug.

"Thank you for coming!" she says.

She seems relieved to see me, which is, I guess, better than the alternative—miserable.

"I'm happy to," I say. "Is Dimitri home?"

She wrinkles her nose. "No. He was at least nice enough to leave me alone while I packed today."

"So, then, last night went okay?" I ask.

She heaves a sigh and starts to trudge up the stairs to her bedroom. "Yes and no. At first, he was furious. He screamed at me. He wanted to know if I was cheating, and he accused me of sabotaging Tokyo by throwing this distraction his way at a 'crucial time,'" she says, rolling her eyes and making air quotes with her fingers. "He was mad at me, but ultimately, he didn't argue with me. I mean, he can't pretend like our marriage is happy. I think we'd *both* be happier with a divorce."

"Wow."

It's a tiny, meager thing to say, but words just aren't forming for me. I can't imagine standing up to Dimitri like that. I'm impressed by her bravery.

We enter her bedroom, and I try not to think about the would-be baby's room down the hall. The crisp white bed is covered with folded piles of clothes, and there's a stack of cardboard boxes piled in one corner of the room. On the night-stand, there's a roll of packing tape and a black

Sharpie alongside Jasmine's engagement ring and wedding ring, and a silver photo frame turned facedown.

"He told me that he would ruin me, that I'd never work in the sport again, that I was an 'ungrateful bitch' who was giving up the best life with the 'greatest man' I'd ever know," she recalls, spitting out each brutal word. "But, I mean, fine. Nothing worse than anything he's said before. And, most important, he let me go."

"He let you go," I repeat dumbly, trying to absorb how casually Jasmine tosses off his cruel remarks.

I remember how horrible he was to us years ago, but it's different to hear of him hurling insults like that at his wife. It's depressing.

"He said he was angry with me, but he wouldn't stop me," she says. "His exact words, I think, were that I'm now 'an adult woman who can make her own choices.' "

"As if you weren't when you got married," I say, filling in the implication.

"Barely," she admits. "I was twenty-one. I had been on a few dates with guys my own age, but he was the first person I dated. He was the only man I'd ever really known."

Someday, when a little more time has passed, Jasmine will eventually dip one toe in the dating pool, and she's going to discover an entire world out there: electrifying first dates;

butterfly-inducing texts; real, equal love. Maybe heartbreak, too. But at least this time around, she'll be standing on her own two feet, away from Dimitri's shadow.

"So. Help me put everything into boxes?" she asks.

"Of course."

We work side by side, stacking her jewel-toned shift dresses, workout clothes, and thick winter sweaters into cardboard boxes, securing them shut with strips of tape, and labeling each box with thick, definitive black lines of Sharpie. I don't want to dwell on the reason she's moving out, but there's still so much I'm dying to understand. Once she leaves here, that will all be in her past—today feels like the last chance I have.

"Do you ever think you would've had a real relationship with Dimitri if he weren't our coach first?" I ask.

She looks up from the box she's taping shut with a sour, stunned expression. "No. We wouldn't have known each other."

"How did it happen? We weren't really . . . talking then," I say awkwardly.

Even after all these years, I still can't picture it.

She returns to taping the box, maybe so she doesn't have to look at me as she explains this part.

"I did a TV segment at a news station in Boston

after the Olympics," she recalls. "He came with me—he was on-air, too. Instead of driving me straight back home afterward, he said he was in the mood for a drink, and so we went out to this Irish pub."

He probably didn't invite her out; he probably just told her they were going, and that was that.

"He ordered beer after beer after beer," she says. "I didn't order anything; I was just twenty, not old enough to drink legally yet, and I was too afraid of being recognized to even try. He gave me sips of his beer when he thought the bartender wouldn't notice. And then, right there at the bar, he kissed me. I didn't know what to do—it's not like I was going to say no to him."

"Were you okay with that?" I ask.

"Not at first! I was terrified," she says.

"But as time went on, it wasn't so bad?" I ask.

"You have to remember, Avery, I didn't have anything to compare it to," she says sadly. "No other boyfriends. My mom had been single practically my entire life. It's not like I had other friends my age with regular relationships, either. So . . . in time, it felt normal. That's all I knew. Plus, he was established, respected, he had money . . . When he wanted to get married, it didn't even cross my mind to say no. I thought this is just what people did."

She pushes the box to the side and starts on another one.

"We were so sheltered," I say.

"Mm-hmm," Jasmine agrees. "It's nice that Hallie has you, someone she can talk to, someone she can trust. We didn't have anyone like that at the gym growing up."

She absentmindedly fidgets with her necklace, surveying the spread of clothes still laid out on the bed.

"I guess," I say. I still find it hard to take a compliment.

An idea comes to me, half-formed and fuzzy.

"We could do something," I say, trying to pin down the exact thought. "I mean, we could help these girls. We've been through enough to know what they need."

"You mean like a support group?" Jasmine asks.

"Yeah," I say. "I mean, gymnasts know to take care of their bodies . . . but I don't know if most of them take care of their minds, too. I didn't. What if we help connect girls to mental health resources? That way, they can get the support they need, no matter what they're dealing with."

"That would be so cool!" Jasmine says.

"If anyone could do it, it would be us," I point out. "I mean, mostly you—you still have a real name in gymnastics. You could get people to care."

Jasmine leans onto the bed, too, and tilts her head.

"We could do that, couldn't we?" she says, awestruck. "We could really help."

"This could change girls' lives," I say.

Jasmine gives me a knowing look. I don't have to spell it out for her. The fact is if you train and compete as an elite gymnast, you get hit one way or another, if not multiple ways: maybe you get molested by a doctor or maybe you fail out of college because you're too depressed and disoriented to give a shit anymore. Your body breaks down: your spine aches if you stand for too long, or your ankle is held together with metal screws, or you never fully shake off the habits you picked up to starve yourself.

"I like this a lot. And god only knows I'll need something to keep my mind off . . ." She waves her hand vaguely around the bedroom. "All of this."

We finish packing up Jasmine's bedroom and bathroom quickly. The entire time, we work through ideas: what the group needs to do, how to make it happen, and even a name. We settle on the Elite Gymnastics Foundation, which would provide mental health services and support to top gymnasts.

I feel the same flood of adrenaline and desperate sense of longing I felt when I first fought for the coaching job at Summit. It's not a new feeling, either; I remember the tangled rush of emotions from my own gymnastics career.

Wanting things—wanting things so badly, my heart races and the hair on my arms stands on end—makes me feel alive and full of energy. Right now, I feel like I could stick a double-twisting layout flyaway off the high bar.

I'm not naïve—I don't expect two former athletes to change the sport overnight. But if gymnastics taught me anything, it's that if you work long and hard at something, astronomical, unfathomable success can be yours.

When Jasmine tapes up the final box, we carry everything downstairs to the foyer so the movers can pick them up later this afternoon. (All those years of conditioning really did come in handy.) We sit on the cool tile floor in the front hallway, leaning against the cardboard boxes with our feet splayed out in front of us.

"Girl, thank you," Jasmine says, exhausted.

"This? This was nothing," I say truthfully.

I'm happy to help her with whatever she needs. She should know that by now.

"I don't mean just the boxes," she says. "That was clutch, but I mean everything—the boxes, your friendship, this idea. It's a *big* idea."

"It is," I admit. "And there's nobody better in the world to do it with. It has to be you and me."

Suddenly, her eyes sparkle, and she bolts upright.

"Huddle up?" she asks mischievously.

The old memories of our competition ritual, our good-luck charm, come flooding back.

"Let's huddle up," I say, beaming.

We loop our arms around each other's shoulders. I'm not sure what to say.

"We can do this," she declares.

I squeeze her tighter and join in.

"We can do this, we can do this, we can do this," we chant.

It feels like coming home.

• *Chapter 27* •

It's tough to focus at practice on Monday. When I'm working one-on-one with Hallie—warming up, drilling tumbling, fine-tuning her techniques on floor—I feel present. But otherwise, my head is adrift. I clean crash mats and wonder about Jasmine's move out of Dimitri's house; I organize the supply closet and daydream about the Elite Gymnastics Foundation. The idea felt fresh and exciting when I first came up with it, but here, at Summit, it feels even crisper. I watch Hallie sprint down the vault runway and catapult herself through the air, and my heart surges with the desire to protect her. Brainstorming with Jasmine felt more abstract, but here, it's impossible to ignore the very real person at risk right in front of me.

That's why I have to talk to Ryan. I can't sit by and watch as he takes Hallie into a dangerous situation. Arguing with him didn't work the first time, but maybe then, I didn't give it all the effort I had—maybe I held back out of fear of damaging our relationship. That's not a concern I have anymore, obviously. If he ignores one last-ditch effort to deter him from joining Dimitri, then at least I can say I've truly tried my best. But I have to try now, before it's too late.

After Hallie has left for the night, I wait for Ryan. I sit on the stairs in the lobby that lead up to the second floor, which positions me with the best view: from here, I can see half the lobby, the door to the gym, the door to the office, the door to the bathrooms, and the exit. No matter where Ryan is, I'll be able to catch him. Sure enough, two minutes later, he rounds the corner from the office.

"Wait!" I call, springing up from my seat on the stairs.

"Hey," he says. "What's up?"

"I need to talk to you," I say.

He looks surprised. "Oh! Believe it or not, I was actually coming to find you."

"Why?" I ask.

He tilts his head. "There's something I'm hoping to get your opinion on. If you're open to talking to me about it."

This is practically the most communication we've had all day.

"What's going on?" I ask.

He's piqued my curiosity.

"You first," he says. "Let's sit in the office?"

We sit down. I gear up to tell him what's on my mind, but my thoughts get tangled—I don't know where to start. So much has changed since our breakup: my renewed friendship with Jasmine, her separation from Dimitri, what I can only imagine is Ryan drawing further into Dimitri's inner circle.

"So, you might know that Jasmine and I are close again?" I start.

"I've heard," he says, nodding.

"We've been talking a lot about how the culture of gymnastics at this level is just totally messed up, particularly for girls," I explain. "I mean, even injuries aside, there are the issues with food and body image, mental health, sexual assault . . . and we want to do something about it."

"That's great," he says.

"We're launching a support network," I continue. "We're calling it the Elite Gymnastics Foundation. We'll connect gymnasts to mental health professionals."

"Impressive," he says. "You're the perfect people to make that happen."

His compliment warms me, but I can't let it soften me toward him.

"Well, you might want to wait before you start saying nice things to me," I warn. This is my last-ditch attempt to get him to listen to me: "I need you to turn down the Powerhouse job."

He looks surprised.

"So, that's actually what I wanted to talk to you about. I went to Powerhouse on my lunch break today. It was . . . intense."

I purse my lips. "I'm sure it was."

"I've heard your stories about what it was like

to have him as your coach, but seeing it firsthand felt different," he explains. "I didn't like the way he treated his gymnasts. He made fun of them for getting winded during conditioning; he called them 'sloppy,' 'lazy,' 'useless.' He came up with these absurd punishments, like running laps for falling off beam during just a regular practice."

"I don't want to say *I told you so,* but . . . Ryan, come on, what did you expect?" I ask.

"It made me have serious doubts about taking the job," he admits.

I'm shocked but hopeful.

"Well, obviously, you know what I think," I say.

"I guess I just wanted to confirm with you— do you think what I saw today was a one-off, bad day? Or is that who he really is?" he asks, squinting like he already knows the answer.

"That's just him," I say.

Ryan leans his elbows onto the desk and presses his fingers to his temples. He exhales a ragged sigh.

"Okay, then," he says, more to himself than to me, with a small shake of his head. He looks up at me with a resigned expression. "Then that's that."

There's too much at stake for me to jump to conclusions.

"That's . . . what?" I clarify.

"I can't take the job," he says.

I'm reeling at how quickly he changed his

mind. I can't wait to tell Jasmine. I almost can't quite believe that I'm hearing him correctly. Despite how much I hoped Ryan would come around, deep down, I don't know if I ever really believed he would.

"It's not the dream job I thought it was—not if he's like this," he explains.

My heart races as I tell him emphatically, "It's not. You're right."

"I'll talk to the Conways and tell Dimitri I won't be working for him," he says.

That's the next step that will make all of this feel real.

"I can't promise the Conways will accept my decision, though," he warns. "If they got excited about Powerhouse, they might choose to transfer there, anyway."

That makes my stomach flip—not only would Hallie still work with Dimitri, but if she leaves, Summit may not have much use for me anymore.

"If they still want Dimitri, they can go see his gym for themselves," I suggest.

"Right," he says. He pauses and bites his lip, then continues in a soft, serious tone. "I'm sorry it took me so long to listen to you. I should have trusted your opinion of him from the start. This isn't an excuse at all, but I had a hard time wrapping my head around exactly how abusive he really was. I knew he wasn't an easy coach, but everything you've told me is so different from the way I was trained—I just didn't get it at first. And maybe I was starstruck by him. But I understand now, and I apologize for taking so long to get here. I understand if this isn't possible, but I hope you can forgive me."

He looks somber but heartfelt. When he offers up a hopeful smile, his dimple flashes beneath his tender, dark eyes.

"Thank you for saying that," I manage. "It means a lot—it really does. Apology accepted."

He ruffles a hand through his hair in relief and shoots me a grateful look. "I'm really glad to hear that."

If Ryan and I broke up because he wouldn't listen to the truth about Dimitri's abuse, and now he's come around and apologized, where does that leave us? I can't help but wonder if the same question is on his mind. But even if we are on the same page, I'm not ready for us to move forward together again. All those months of hurt and distrust can't dissolve in an instant. A single apology doesn't reverse the pain I felt because of him.

And yet . . . I can't lie to myself: my feelings for Ryan never went away. I shoved them down so I could stomach working with him day in and day out, and I tried to distract myself with Jasmine, with Sara, with cooking elaborate meals. Even still, I crave the easy way we used to joke around; I miss his secretly romantic side;

I can't forget how everything else melted away when he touched me. When we were together, he made me feel seen and understood—and I've spent enough time in the wrong relationship to grasp how special and rare that is.

I stand up to give him a hug. He holds me close to his chest. We fit together like we always did, with his chin resting on top of my head and my cheek nuzzled against his shoulder. It strikes me as unfair that love isn't like a switch you can flip on and off at will; despite the storm of conflicted emotions I have over Ryan right now, he's the one person in the world whose hug will make me feel better.

I pull back just enough to look up at him. He meets my gaze, and there's a heaviness to his expression that I can't quite read. Is it regret? Or longing? Either way, it makes my heart ache. For a split second, I feel his body tense beneath my arms, like he's about to steel himself to kiss me. But then, just as quickly as it arrived, the moment disappears.

Ryan backs away, digging in his pockets for his car keys, furtively looking over my shoulder to the door.

"I should get going," he says stiffly. "I'm glad we had this conversation."

I nod. "Same—me, too."

We exit through the lobby. He holds the door open for me.

In the parking lot, we walk in opposite directions to our cars, but I hear him call my name before I get inside.

"Yeah?" I say.

"Thank you. I mean it."

He drives away, and I watch his headlights vanish around the corner. I shouldn't miss him already, but I do.

Chapter 28

Ryan invites me and the Conways in for a meeting before practice the next morning. Kim, Todd, and Hallie look anxious when they arrive. I'm secretly glad Ryan included me in negotiations about Hallie's career this time around.

"Thanks for coming in on such short notice," he says as we take seats in Summit's office.

"It sounded important," Todd says.

Kim frowns. "And vague."

"Is everything okay?" Hallie asks.

Her parents dart confused glances from me to Ryan. I bet they're surprised to see me here.

"Things are fine, but there's something I wanted to discuss with you," Ryan says.

He comes around the desk to lean against it, hesitating like he's trying to find the right words to explain his mistake. This can't be easy for him, even if he understands now how crucial it is to turn down Dimitri's job offer. Thick tension fills the room.

"Avery and I have been debating the pros and cons of moving to Powerhouse for months," he begins. "She knows Dimitri better than any of us. And from what she's told me about her experiences with him and having seen him interact with his gymnasts, I can't recommend that Hallie trains at his gym."

Kim and Todd look surprised; Hallie looks deflated.

"What does that mean?" Kim asks.

"You told us he was the best," Todd says, narrowing his eyes. "I mean, his track record speaks for itself."

"It does," Ryan hedges.

He looks at me for backup. I appreciate that he doesn't take the liberty of revealing uncomfortably personal details to the Conways without my permission.

"He's emotionally abusive," I confirm. "Bullying, name-calling, fits of rage . . . He lashes out when girls get sick or don't perform up to his standards. He might be responsible for a lot of gold medals, but he's not a good coach. He's toxic."

Hallie's jaw drops. "Whoa."

"You're sure about this?" Todd asks.

"Believe me, I trained with him for five years," I say. "I know what he's really like. And I didn't even get the worst of it."

"Oh my god," Kim says, appalled.

"Well, Hallie's not going there," Todd says flatly.

"Yeah, no, he sounds horrible," Hallie says. She gives me a sympathetic look.

"I'm glad you understand," I say. "Thank you for listening."

For so many months now, I've felt powerless to

stop Hallie from getting hurt. To see how quickly and effectively I could change her fate is mind-blowing. I'm so grateful that the Conway family came around to my side immediately.

"It was my mistake to recommend a move to Powerhouse earlier," Ryan says. "I really do apologize for that, and I hope you can trust my judgment going forward."

Hallie nods in approval, but Kim and Todd exchange worried glances.

"You have to understand—we've put Hallie's career, our family's lives, in your hands," Kim says. "We've always trusted that you know what's in her best interests."

"I . . . I understand that," Ryan says, faltering.

Todd piles on. "I don't mean to be rude, but I have to ask: can we trust you?"

"Dad," Hallie says, slinking down in her seat and covering her face with her hands. "Don't be so dramatic."

"This is important, Hallie," Kim says.

Ryan straightens up. "You can trust me. You can trust both of us," he says, nodding at me. "I couldn't do this without Avery."

I watch Kim and Todd chew that over for a few moments. She sighs heavily.

"All right," she says. "All right."

Todd gives me a small smile. "Thanks for everything you do," he says.

"Of course, you're welcome," I say.

"So I'm going to tell Dimitri we're both staying put—you and me," Ryan says to Hallie, who appears to be recovering from the humiliation of her parents having an opinion about her well-being. "That is, if you still want to keep training."

"Yeah," she says. "The more I think about it, the more I really do want to train for 2024. No matter what happens this summer, I've worked too hard to retire at sixteen, you know?"

Ryan grins. "That's what I like to hear."

JUNE
2020

• *Chapter 29* •

Then, bam, it's June. While the rest of the country starts to slow down for summer vacation, time speeds up for us. The Olympic Trials take place on Saturday, June 27, and the Olympics begin less than a month after that, on Friday, July 24—soon enough that I have a running countdown in my head that tracks how many days we have left. I don't need to check a calendar; the days tick down automatically for me. It's twenty-five, then twenty-two, and now we're in the teens. This is what I've been preparing for since last October, and what Hallie has been looking forward to for quite literally her entire life.

The Olympics are just close enough now that regular people are getting excited. On one lunch break, Hallie squeezes in a phone interview with Kiss 108, the local Top 40 radio station; on another, she takes a call from a *People* reporter. A whole crew from the *Boston Globe* arrived during practice one afternoon to take pictures and interview her for a front-page story. Ryan shooed the journalist and photographer away after forty-five minutes, insisting that Hallie's energy was best spent on training at the moment. As the reporters packed up their camera equipment, her face fell just a little bit. I don't blame her.

Competitive gymnastics isn't like football or baseball in the sense that the general public will tune in for a big game or even be aware when the sport is in season—it gets one blip of fandom every four years. So, even though throwing a new responsibility on top of preparing Hallie for the Olympics seems like pure lunacy right now, Jasmine insists that we have to capitalize on this moment in order to gain media attention. She wants to launch the Elite Gymnastics Foundation publicly *now,* before the Olympics kick off, while elite gymnastics is having its moment in the sun. If we wait until after Tokyo, the public's interest in whatever we have to say may be lost. People will only see Hallie and her Olympic cohort as buff Miss America stand-ins—shiny, patriotic trophies—not flesh-and-blood young women battling real systemic issues. And then, well before the first crisp day of fall, gymnastics will have fallen off most people's radars.

So, while Hallie has been slipping out of the gym for interviews and heading home early to rest up as much as possible, I've been working alongside Jasmine to transform the foundation from a hazy idea into a solid reality. I text and email as much as I can during the day, and on nights and weekends we hole up in my living room to get work done. Maybe it's because we trained alongside each other for years, but we're a strong team now, too. Within a week, we've contacted a slew of former gymnasts to get them on board with publicly supporting this initiative and to collect donations. We've used that money to hire a web designer to create a site. And most important, we've started to assemble a team of mental health professionals, including therapists who have worked with athletes and sexual assault support group leaders. They'll provide services either in person or remotely, depending on where the gymnasts live. We've gotten them to agree to working pro bono up front, and our goal is to fund-raise to pay for their services so there will never be any question if a gymnast can afford to access help.

Jasmine hooked us up with a five-minute spot on NBC's morning news show for Monday, June 8, so we'll be the first story breaking after the weekend. The goal is to announce the launch of the Elite Gymnastics Foundation, spread aware-ness for the sport's desperate need for reform, and, of course, raise money. NBC is the obvious choice, given Jasmine's connections; she's a familiar face, so their viewers will be primed to hear what she has to say.

My alarm blares at five thirty on Monday morning. As I shower, I try not to dwell on how nervous I am. It's been eight years since I've spoken to a reporter or been on TV. Doing press used to feel exciting—I liked when my competitions were broadcast live for viewers at home, and any questions thrown my way were easy to answer: How hard had I been training lately? Was I happy about my big win? Were the London Olympics on my radar? This is entirely different. I'm publicly calling out the failures of the sport that gave me everything.

Jasmine dictated specific instructions on everything from what to wear to how to speak. She says I need to wear a simple, professional, solid-colored top or dress—no prints, because they look distracting on camera, and no green, because the green screen will turn me into a floating head. I own nothing remotely right, so I've borrowed a coral-red shift dress from her closet that I can just barely squeeze into. Jasmine promises the camera will only film me from the waist up. I've never mastered the ability to blow-dry my hair, but I do my best attempt at it while running through the sound bites I've practiced. Jasmine will do most of the talking on-air, but I can't be entirely mute. It's funny, I was never afraid to hurtle myself into the air and perform impossible-looking stunts, but saying a few lines to a camera crew strikes me as terribly intimidating.

I step into my most professional-looking pumps to give myself a confidence boost, pour coffee into a thermos, and drive to NBC's studio. Jasmine meets me in the lobby. She's in a bright blue wrap dress with fluttery cap sleeves that show off her toned arms, reminding viewers of her athletic past. She chose these outfits on purpose: red and blue to remind everyone that even if we criticize the American Gymnastics Federation, we're still wholly in support of Team USA.

"You ready?" she asks as the security guard at the front desk scans my driver's license and double-checks my name against his computer.

"I barely slept last night," I admit.

She looks closely at me and scrunches her nose. "The makeup artist can cover up your dark circles—no worries."

Jasmine leads us to the fourth floor, where the receptionist greets her by name, and then through a maze of hallways until we're in the greenroom.

"Every guest on the show waits here to go on," she explains.

The room isn't actually green—it's white with gray carpeting, brown furniture, and multiple TVs tuned in to the show. A handful of people sit around in suits and dresses like ours; they have faces that seem vaguely familiar, or maybe it's just that everyone on TV looks more or less the same: conventionally attractive but airbrushed in an eerily bland way.

A twenty-something producer in a headset comes flying toward us.

"Hiiii, you're in hair first," she says to Jasmine, then glances down at her clipboard. "And you, Avery? You're in makeup."

"Oh, I actually did both at home," I say.

Jasmine shakes her head. "Everyone gets touch-ups," she insists.

The producer drops me off in a room just big enough to contain a single chair in front of a mirror decked out in lights and a table full of beauty products. A makeup artist dabs concealer under my eyes, as Jasmine promised, and slicks on hot pink lip gloss before I can protest that I don't really feel like myself in so much makeup. Next, the producer brings me to the room next door, where a hairstylist finishes the transformation with a curling iron and an intense blast of hair spray. When she's done, I look like . . . well, I look just as polished and professional as Jasmine always does. With a pang, I realize that if my life had turned out differently, none of this would faze me. I wouldn't be bare-skinned in a ponytail at Summit; I would be contoured and curled at NBC. This would be my reality.

I find Jasmine back in the greenroom. On TV, the meteorologist talks about the seventy-five-degree days coming this week. Jasmine stares vacantly in the direction of the TV, but she's not focused on the screen. Her knee bounces up and down. I understand why she's nervous—my heart is pounding, too—but I'm surprised the pressure is getting to her, of all people.

"You okay?" I ask gently.

She turns toward me, and her jittery knee slows

to a stop. "Yeah," she says. "Yeah, I will be."

"You sure?" I ask.

"I'll be fine once I'm out there, trust me," she says. "It's just . . . this is bigger than anything I've ever done before."

"You've been on this same channel, what, a hundred times? A thousand times," I remind her.

"Commenting on *other* people," she says. "This time, the spotlight's on us."

I grab her hand, and she gives mine a squeeze.

Soon, the producer breezes back into the green-room. "Come with me," she says to us, jerking her head. "Commercial break just hit."

We follow her down a hallway and around a corner into a dark studio space jumbled with lighting equipment, rubber cables, and, further back, a glossy, L-shaped desk with two open seats for us diagonal from Cynthia King, the news anchor. Another producer clips tiny microphones to the necklines of our dresses. If I hadn't watched Jasmine do it first, I would have been bewildered: Jasmine expertly threads the thin cable over her shoulder, hiding it under her hair, and turns to let the producer clip the mic's battery pack to her bra underneath her dress. I follow her lead, flinching at the feel of his hands. He zips my dress up again and gives the first producer a thumbs-up. We're ready.

"Thirty seconds," she barks. "Go."

I follow Jasmine onstage, letting her take the

seat closest to Cynthia, who greets her warmly. In contrast to the dimly lit backstage, the lighting here is bright and white and blinding. Cynthia, clad in a pearly pink dress with a neat bob and gravity-defying eyelashes, looks like a *Real Housewives* star in the sense that she could just as easily be thirty-five or fifty. She says hello and asks how I am, but I'm too nervous to squeak out anything more than a hello. She and Jasmine make pleasant small talk, which seems frankly insane to me with just seconds to go before we're on live television, but Jasmine looks unfussed. I'm relieved that she's settling into her element.

"The producer says it's Jasmine Floyd, not Floyd-Federov now, right?" Cynthia confirms.

"Floyd's perfect, thanks," Jasmine says.

Cynthia cocks her head like she's connecting the dots. "You're leaving your husband the coach, and speaking out about abuse in the sport?" she asks slowly.

Jasmine freezes next to me. "Well, um . . ."

"Five, four," the cameraman calls out.

Cynthia raises an eyebrow, shuffles her papers, and clears her throat.

The cameraman falls silent, flashing three fingers, then two fingers, then pointing straight at us.

"Welcome back. The Olympics are just around the corner, but before you get too excited about watching the gymnastics, you might want to hear what two former athletes are saying about the sport," Cynthia begins. Her voice is strong and smooth like honey. "Olympic gymnast Jasmine Floyd and her former teammate Avery Abrams claim that the culture of competitive gymnastics puts young athletes at risk, and they're launching a new organization called the Elite Gymnastics Foundation to offer these gymnasts what they believe is much-needed support. Ladies, tell us more."

"Thanks for having us, Cynthia. It's always great to be here," Jasmine says weakly.

We've practiced that Jasmine will deliver the announcement of the foundation, but now she seems shaken. I glance at her, unsure if I should take over her lines. On live television, every second feels like it stretches out for ten minutes. But finally, thankfully, she collects herself and launches into the speech we wrote together.

"As many people unfortunately saw with the recent sexual abuse claims against Dr. Ron Kaminsky, gymnasts aren't always safe. And as two former elite gymnasts ourselves, we know there are other issues out there that threaten the athletes' well-being. Not every gymnast out there is struggling, but there are real challenges in this sport. I'm talking about eating disorders, depression, anxiety, emotionally abusive coaches, and yes, sexual abuse. There's a serious lack of regulation from the sport's governing body—the

American Gymnastics Federation—and given our personal experiences, we know how challenging it can be to advocate for yourself to get the help and resources you need in order to thrive. That's why we're launching the Elite Gymnastics Foundation, an organization that offers mental health support for elite gymnasts."

"That's very admirable," Cynthia says. "We've heard a lot about the allegations against Dr. Kaminsky—who, by the way, is set to face trial early next year."

A chill runs through me. Delia, Skylar, and the other girls should have justice.

"While I'm saddened to hear of the mental health issues that plague top gymnasts, I'm also not exactly surprised," Cynthia continues. "It seems like a particularly high-pressure sport—and who is looking out for these girls?"

"The sport's toxic culture is a real problem," I agree. "That's why our first step was to create what we're calling a wellness network for elite gymnasts. We've assembled an excellent team of professionals, including therapists and sexual assault educators, to provide top-notch care for these athletes. Gymnastics is a mind-body sport—gymnasts, mostly adolescents, train hours a day to keep their bodies strong, but it's equally important for them to take care of their mental health, too."

I pivot to the sales pitch. "This is important

work, but it's not easy, so we are raising money on EliteGymnasticsFoundation.com to fund these initiatives."

I'm surprised at the steady way my words flow. It feels as if the lights and cameras and unnatural stage makeup fade away, and all I need to do is explain why I'm here.

"Avery, for you, this is personal, isn't it?" Cynthia asks.

I knew this question was coming. It was part of our pitch to the network—a good sob story will catch people's attention more than anything else we could say. Neither of us is ready to talk publicly about Dimitri yet, but there's still plenty I can say.

"It is," I confirm. "I suffered a knee injury during the Olympic Trials in 2012. Physically, I was able to bounce back after a few months, but I was depressed. I didn't seek out help, but I should have. This organization would ensure that nobody feels alone. Gymnastics is a solo sport, but that doesn't mean you're on your own."

Jasmine and I wrote five different versions of that line before we hit on the right one, and maybe the familiarity of it stirs something in her.

"Nobody has to be alone," she adds. Under the desk, she grips my hand. "I'm grateful to be partnering with my friend Avery here."

"That's a great message. Now, Avery, you're hopefully heading to the Olympics in Tokyo later this summer, isn't that right?" Cynthia asks.

"I'm coaching a young gymnast named Hallie Conway, and I have to tell you, she is such a superstar," I say. "I can't wait for you to see her compete at the Olympic Trials."

"I wouldn't miss it," Cynthia says. She turns away from us to face a different camera, and wraps up the segment. "This has been Jasmine Floyd and Avery Abrams, cofounders of the Elite Gymnastics Foundation. Back to you, Michael."

The network cuts to a commercial break, and the producer shuffles us quickly offstage, unclipping our mics and sending us back to the greenroom.

"I'm shaking," Jasmine whispers.

"You were great," I reassure her.

"I lost it," she says. "Her comment before we went on threw me off. *You* were amazing."

"I don't think we sounded so bad," I admit.

"Next time, I'll be better," she insists.

"Next time?" I ask.

She beams. "Girl, this is just the beginning."

In the greenroom, I dig my phone out of my purse. I'm caught off guard by a text from Ryan. After the breakup, our endless stream of texts came to a sudden halt; now we rarely text, and only about work.

I caught you on TV, he wrote. *Very impressive. Just wanted to say congrats—what you and Jasmine are doing is so cool.*

I had mentioned the segment to him, but I didn't think he'd bother watching it. It's one thing for him to pay lip service to our cause, but this shows he actually cares. I'm happy to hear from him. I slip my phone back into my purse without mentioning it to Jasmine.

I drive directly from NBC to the gym, where I change out of Jasmine's dress into an old pair of Soffe shorts and a faded T-shirt with Summit's logo splashed across the chest. I pull my hair back into a ponytail but don't bother scrubbing the gloss off my lips.

"Whoa," Hallie says when she sees me on the floor. "Why do you look so fancy?"

I hesitate to explain where I was earlier that morning. I haven't told her anything at all about the Elite Gymnastics Foundation because it felt too embarrassingly personal. But now that she's asking, I don't have a choice.

"You probably haven't heard about what I'm up to," I confirm.

I doubt she watches cable news—and anyway, she's been in the gym all day. But I also wouldn't be surprised if this was lighting up her Twitter feed.

"Jasmine—Jasmine Floyd—and I went on NBC this morning to announce the launch of our new organization that helps out top gymnasts," I explain. "You know how I connected you to

369

Sara and got you into yoga? Think of that, plus connecting people to therapists and other experts who can help gymnasts stay healthy."

She squeals a little. "Avery!"

"What?" I laugh nervously.

"I'm so proud of you," she says.

It's a funny thing for her to say—if anything, *I'm* proud of *her*. That's how this relationship dynamic is supposed to go. But, hey, Jasmine and I created the foundation for the sole purpose of making life healthier and happier for girls like Hallie. If she's on board with the idea, I'm elated.

Hallie sashays across the gym and finds Ryan filling up his water bottle.

"Ryan, Ryan, Ryan!" she calls.

He turns to look over his shoulder.

"Hallie, Hallie, Hallie, what's up?" he mimics.

She leaps—and I mean literally executes a perfect, 180-degree split leap—in front of him. I wish I was her age and had that much energy on a Monday morning, or ever at all.

"Did you hear what Avery's up to? It's super cool! And very fancy. See how fancy she looks?" she says.

He laughs. "I heard. Pretty amazing, huh?"

"Guys, stop it," I say bashfully. "Don't we have work to do today? There are just—"

"Eighteen days left," Hallie groans. "I know, I know."

• • •

Maybe it's because the Olympics are drawing closer, or maybe it's because of Jasmine's near celebrity status, but either way, the response to the NBC segment is thrilling. The story gets picked up by other outlets, including ESPN, *Sports Illustrated*, the *Boston Globe*, *Cosmo*, and BuzzFeed. Jasmine and I are invited on GymCastic, the gymternet's most revered gymnastics-themed podcast, and a wave of current and former elite gymnasts urge their Instagram followers to donate to the foundation. Within three days, we raise nearly ten thousand dollars. It's far more money than I could have hoped for.

We were disappointed that AGF never reached out to us directly, though when prodded by *Cosmo*, the organization apparently "declined to comment." Predictably, the worst reaction came from Dimitri. He called Jasmine five times, and when she refused to pick up, he left a voicemail threatening that we better not say a word about him. She saved the voicemail—just in case we ever need it.

It's nerve-wracking but exciting to have the foundation getting this much attention so early on. It feels like yet another good omen: now that I've encouraged Ryan to turn down Dimitri's offer and work alongside Jasmine to make a real difference in this sport, I feel more capable and confident than I have in a long time. People say good things come in threes. And this summer, there's only one goal left to tackle. It's a big one. But I'm ready.

• *Chapter 30* •

By Friday, of course, the countdown has dropped to just fifteen days. In two weeks' time, Hallie will be about to compete at Trials; in six weeks, she could potentially be marching with the rest of the United States Olympic fleet at the opening ceremony in Tokyo. This afternoon, though, the only place Hallie is going is back and forth across the length of the beam. Ryan and I watch patiently as she drills her tumbling pass—a back handspring, whip back, back layout step-out—over and over. The goal is for her to smoothly connect each move into the next and finish the series with a satisfying *thwack* of a clean landing, no wobbles whatsoever.

As a rap song blares from the speaker, Hallie stands with her toes a millimeter from the edge of the beam and stretches her arms out in front of her, centering herself. Her chest rises and falls as she takes a deep breath. Then, in one sleek, catlike motion, she swings her arms behind her and lunges backward into the tumbling pass. The back handspring is solid, but she's probably been doing that since she was nine years old. What's trickier is the whip back, a fast-moving, arched flip in which her hands float a foot above the beam, and safely transitioning from that to a soaring back layout, which requires rotating high in the air with her body and legs extended to their fullest length. She lands with one heel just inches from the opposite end of the beam, and teeters ever so slightly to catch her balance. It's not good enough, and she knows it.

"Again," Ryan calls.

She looks a little frustrated with herself, but she nods and scurries back to the other end of the beam to start over.

Ryan turns to me.

"So, uh, I've been thinking about ways to support the foundation you and Jasmine are launching," Ryan says, looking down at his feet.

"What?" I ask, surprised.

"Yeah. It's an amazing cause and I want to do my part," he says, shrugging.

"Oh, uh, wow. Thank you," I say.

"I hope this isn't overstepping anything, but I called a few places around town to see who might be willing to host a fund-raiser," he says.

"You did *what?*" I blurt.

He speeds up nervously. "Jade Castle agreed that if we wanted to partner with them for a fund-raiser, one hundred percent of the proceeds for drinks ordered there would go directly to the Elite Gymnastics Foundation, as long as we tip the bartenders."

He looks directly at me now, and I'm almost too stunned to speak.

"Ryan, oh my god," I say.

He winces. "Or if you hate the idea, I don't have to do anything at all. I haven't agreed to anything with Jade Castle yet—I just called to ask."

"No, are you kidding me? That's so ridiculously nice of you, really," I say.

I can't believe he really did this. It's not out of character, exactly—I know he's a thoughtful person, and I'm sure his friends would have no problem drinking enough to raise a sizable chunk of money—but I'm blown away that he would do all this for me.

Hallie flips across the beam and sticks the landing. She leans dramatically into a bow.

"Good one," Ryan calls. "Again."

He drops his voice and turns to me. "I wanted to find a way to show you how sorry I am for almost taking the Powerhouse job. I made a huge mistake by not listening to you from the moment you told me what Dimitri's really like, and I hate that I upset you by taking so long to come around. I know this isn't enough, but I hope it's a step toward showing you that I really do care about keeping Hallie and the other girls safe and happy."

His apology that night at Summit was one thing, but this is on another level entirely. This shows me that he's listening and learning, and isn't that all anyone can ask for? He made a mistake and isn't just owning it—he's fixing it. I wish we were somewhere else so I could give him a hug.

"Thank you," I say, squeezing his arm. "I really appreciate that. This fund-raiser sounds really helpful."

He exhales, relieved. "Jade Castle had a big birthday party reservation cancel, so they actually have space for us at seven o'clock tomorrow night," he offers. "Unless that's too soon, in which case, we can figure something else out."

My stomach drops, and it's not just because Jade Castle was the scene of my disastrous first Tinder date after moving back to Greenwood.

"Oh! I would, but I actually have dinner plans tomorrow," I lie.

I'm not ready to spend time with Ryan outside of work. If I'm honest with myself, I know I'm not fully over him yet. That's why we've barely spoken about anything except for Hallie since our breakup, and that's why I can't bring myself to open Tinder again, even though the app sends plenty of reminders that people nearby have swiped right on me.

"Oh, no worries, we can schedule this for another time," he says, scratching his ear and blushing.

"Uh, no, go for it. I don't have to be there— what matters is that people are raising money," I say awkwardly. "And maybe I could swing by later."

"Are you sure?" Ryan asks.

I hesitate. "Have an amazing time."

Hallie finishes beam and heads to vault next. I'm not her coach for either event, so even though I watch from the sidelines and offer encouragement, there's unfortunately enough space for my mind to wander.

I'm touched that Ryan would organize a fund-raiser. I'd worried that I'd trusted him too easily, and felt duped that I'd fallen for a guy who would shove the worst moments of my life under the rug so that he could climb the career ladder. In the aftermath of the breakup, it was easy to boil everything down to simple black and white: he was wrong, he was a bad guy, and so we were over.

But life isn't so black and white. People are complicated, and they can grow. I certainly have. I can't deny that between Ryan turning down Dimitri's job offer and him organizing this fund-raiser, I'm starting to see him in a better light. He wants to learn and make amends. He's open to changing his mind, even when it comes at a personal cost. Despite the frost between us ever since Nationals, it wouldn't be fair to ignore that he's taken significant strides to earn my approval again. The next step might be forgiveness.

I sit on the edge of the blue floor and pick at a piece of fuzz coming loose from the fabric.

Sixty feet away, Ryan leans over the vault table, explaining something I can't quite hear to Hallie. He talks with his hands, and she nods along. Hallie's attention is tightly fixated on what he's saying; I can tell from the serious way she stands with her hands on her hips, biting her lip. She trusts him, doesn't she? Maybe I should trust him, too.

SOS, what are you doing tomorrow night? I text Sara on my lunch break.

I'm eating last night's leftover tilapia and zucchini straight from the Tupperware in my car. Ryan's invitation, however casual, made me too jittery to eat within the same building as him.

I have a friend's housewarming party at 8, wanna come? she texts back.

Ryan invited me to drink with his friends tomorrow night at Jade Castle, I write. *It's a fund-raiser for EGF.*

Her response pops up before I can continue typing: *???*

I lied and said I had plans with you. I don't wanna go alone. But I do think I might want to go. Please come with me? I text.

It sounds so pitiful laid out like that, but I know Sara won't judge me.

How's this: I'll come with you for a bit, then head out to the party once you find your footing? she asks. *Slash you have two drinks and feel fine.*

That second one sounds about right, I write. *Thank you. Love you.*

I finish the fish and text Jasmine to join us. She knows, of course, that Ryan turned down Dimitri's job offer, but I think she's still skeptical of him—or anyone who would willingly associate with her ex, to be honest. I can't blame her. I care about her opinion, and I'd feel less guilty over my storm of conflicting emotions toward Ryan if I had her approval of him. I want her take on this situation. I'm strangely relieved when she texts back that Ryan's fund-raiser sounds amazing. She says she wants to go.

On Saturday night, I arrive at Jade Castle a little after eight with Sara and Jasmine by my side. The restaurant's lounge is dimly lit and crowded, filled with vaguely familiar faces I've seen around town. I spot Ryan standing with a cluster of people by the window, holding a beer and in the midst of conversation with some guys. He's in a pair of dark jeans and a light blue button-down shirt with the sleeves rolled up. I don't recognize most of the people he's with, but I spot his friend Goose with his girlfriend, Melissa.

I catch Ryan's eye.

"Hey! You made it!" he says, choking down beer, looking surprised to see me here.

He winds his way through the crowd and tentatively gives me a one-armed hug.

"We finished dinner and figured why not come by?" I say.

It's close enough to the truth. Jasmine brought over a bottle of wine for the three of us to share while Sara and I dabbed on makeup and put on sundresses. I felt more comfortable coming here tonight with a little liquid courage in my system.

"Oh, wow, nice," he says. "Can I get you a drink?"

"We can get our own," Jasmine says, cutting in.

"All for a good cause anyway, right?" Sara says.

Ryan gestures to the bar. "Of course."

Sara orders a vodka soda, and I ask for the same. Jasmine squints at the array of spirits lining the back shelf of the bar and sighs at the row of draft beers.

"I'll have a prosecco," she says.

The bartender gives her a weary look.

"We don't have that here," he says, without bothering to check.

"Jasmine, this isn't the fanciest place," I say quietly, nudging her.

She grimaces. "Another vodka soda, sure." Under her breath, she mutters, "Great bar."

We take the drinks over to the edge of Ryan's crew.

"These are Ryan's friends?" Jasmine asks, looking curiously at the group.

"Yeah, anyone you recognize?" I ask.

The gymnastics world is tiny—I wouldn't be surprised if she had crossed paths with anyone here.

"No, I'm just . . . interested, I guess. These are guys our own age," she comments.

"Don't get too excited," Sara warns.

I feel uneasy—not sure what to say to Ryan, too awkward to say hi to Goose or Melissa, and too nervous to strike up a conversation with any of his other friends. Maybe I shouldn't have come. But then, the high-pitched *ding* of a knife against glass cuts through the noise of the bar.

"Can I have everybody's attention for a minute, please?" Ryan asks.

He steps on a chair so he's high above the crowd. Conversations fade out, and people turn to face him.

"I wanted to thank you all for coming out tonight. As I've mentioned, all proceeds from the drinks go to a really great organization called the Elite Gymnastics Foundation, which supports elite gymnasts like the very talented athlete I'm hopefully taking to Tokyo this summer," he says.

"Whoop, whoop!" Goose calls out.

Ryan raises his glass. "So please, drink up, and don't worry about how you'll feel tomorrow morning. Okay? And while I have your attention, the *founders* of the foundation are here—let's give a round of applause to Avery Abrams and Jasmine Floyd."

He raises his drink in a toast, and everyone else follows suit.

It's a strange sensation, having people clap for me. It's happened before, of course, at plenty of competitions, but that was different. Back then, crowds cheered me on because of what I had been trained to do. Tonight, they're cheering me on for what I'm doing for others. This is new for me, but I like it.

Ryan hops down off of the chair and joins us.

"Hey there. Not a bad turnout, right?" he says.

"Pretty good," I say. "I really appreciate the effort."

"It's pretty cool that you did this," Jasmine says. She purses her lips. "Especially now that you've chosen to hang around better company."

He raises his hands in defense. "I know, I'm glad I turned down the job," he says. "You're going to Tokyo, right?"

"Yep. You haven't booked your flight yet?" she asks.

"Nah. It doesn't really make sense to book it until we know for sure if Hallie is going or not," he explains.

I'm in the same boat.

"Well, I'll be watching from home," Sara says.

"As long as you're watching NBC, that's fine by me," Jasmine says. "Gotta keep those ratings up."

"I'm jealous. Visiting Japan sounds amazing," Sara says.

"Are you planning to stick around after the Games?" I ask Ryan.

Ryan runs a hand through his hair. "Yeah, my plan is to travel around Asia."

"Ooh, fun," Sara says. "Where? I've always wanted to visit Thailand. Amazing food, gorgeous water, not crazy expensive compared to other destinations, you know?"

"Well, since I'll be starting off in Tokyo, it makes sense to explore more of Japan first," he says. "But it all really depends on what happens with Trials."

"Fingers crossed," Sara says.

Later, after Ryan moves on to chat with other people, we get another round of drinks. When they're finished, Sara says she has to get going to her friend's housewarming party. She invites Jasmine and me along. Jasmine, sorely in need of a real girls' night out, gladly accepts, and so I do, too. I don't want to put a damper on her night. We all say goodbye and thank Ryan for throwing the fund-raiser. Sara and Jasmine move ahead while I hang back.

"One sec, guys, I'll meet you outside," I tell Jasmine and Sara. Then, to Ryan, I add, "I just wanted to say thank you again for doing all of this. It really means so much to me that you care enough to bring your friends out for our cause."

"It's the least I could do, really," he says sheepishly.

"How much money do you think you've raised so far?" I ask.

He scans the room. "Let's say twenty people, an average of two drinks each, maybe . . ." He pauses to do the mental math. "Three hundred and fifty–ish?"

That pays for two therapy sessions, maybe three, tops. But I'm still grateful.

"That's awesome," I say—and I mean it.

"I'm really glad you came," he says. "I'd completely understand if you didn't want to, but it's cool that you got a chance to see this."

The emotions I've been feeling all day crest. All at once, I'm grateful and bittersweet and nostalgic for what we had together. I have to leave; I know if I stay any longer, I'll only be keeping myself in a situation primed to make me miss him.

"I think the Uber's coming," I say. "Gotta go—have a great night."

Before I can overthink it, I throw my arms around him in a quick hug. The wave of comfort I get from my body flush against his feels like a shock. It's overwhelming.

"Good night!" he calls as I hurry toward the door.

I join Sara and Jasmine outside, and soon we're on our way to the housewarming party. It's a get-together at a condo in Coolidge Corner in Brookline with a sliding glass door that opens the terrace up to a pretty, starry night. Sara introduces me proudly to her friends, and they all go slack-jawed when they hear I'm possibly on my way to the Olympics. A lanky guy in a chambray button-down brings me plastic cups of beer—apparently, the real glasses haven't even been unpacked yet—and shyly asks for my phone number at the end of the night. He's so not my type that the request catches me off guard, and even though the prospect of dating someone new still feels too strange right now, I give it to him. Maybe what I need is a distraction that will take my mind off Ryan for good.

It's only hours later, when I wake in the middle of the night to get a glass of water to soothe my parched mouth, that I see the text from Ryan. I must have missed it while I was sleeping. I rub at my eyes, not sure if I'm awake enough to read the message properly. But I read it three times in a row, and it seems solid. I can't believe it's real.

It was really great to see you tonight! The fund-raiser was a huge success. We raised $410. But I know that's not enough to make the kind of difference this cause deserves, and so I'm also donating the money I would've spent on my travels after the Olympics. Total, it'll be nearly $3,000. I know you're probably going *to protest, but I've been thinking about this for days. I saved up the money for something important, and there's nothing more important than this.*

• Chapter 31 •

Team Hallie Conway flies to the Olympic Trials in St. Louis on separate flights: Hallie and her parents in the morning, Ryan in the afternoon, and me and Sara on an evening flight so she didn't have to call out of work. Hallie insisted that Sara fly halfway across the country with us because she wanted a private yoga session before the big day. Paying for Sara's roundtrip flight, hotel room, and meals probably costs the Conway family nearly two thousand bucks, but they don't seem to flinch. They've already sunk hundreds of thousands of dollars into this dream so far—it's not worth risking everything and winging it the morning of Olympic Trials by insisting that Hallie practice yoga on her own.

Sara and I are sharing a hotel room, so at seven thirty in the morning we walk together from our room to Hallie's, where we pick her up and continue on to the hotel's fitness center. Sara called ahead and confirmed that the fitness center's yoga studio would be available for them to use. She has a yoga mat strapped to her back and totes a bag full of supplies: a foam block, a speaker, a bottle of lavender essential oil. Hallie emerges from her hotel room in leggings and a stretchy tank top; she'll get ready and put on an actual leotard for Trials after yoga and a light breakfast.

"Morning," I say. "Ready for the big day?"

"Ha, no, but it's here," she says honestly.

Sara nudges her down the hall toward the elevator. "*Oh*-kay, let's go chill out for an hour and find a more positive attitude."

The yoga studio is located at the back of the fitness center, through a door along the far wall of the gym. As we walk past a row of treadmills and ellipticals, through a crew of sweaty dudes working out on weight machines, we cross paths with Ryan, who's bench-pressing weights. He grunts, sets the bar back on the holder, and removes one headphone.

"Hey," he breathes. "Morning."

"Morning," we chime.

"We won't distract you from your workout," Sara says.

Sara leads Hallie into the yoga studio and closes the door. I've never joined one of their sessions, and I wouldn't dare interrupt now. It's good for Hallie to have some solo time with Sara to focus on relaxing for the day ahead.

"So, I, uh, I'm not sure I ever properly thanked you for your text," I say to Ryan.

He removes his other headphone and sits up, grinning. "Yeah?"

"It's an absurdly extravagant donation," I point out. "Just, like, way above and beyond. You know that, right?"

He shrugs. "Eh."

"I just want to make sure you're really sure you want to do this," I say.

"Of course I'm sure," he says seriously.

I can't help it—I cover my face with my hands. "Okay!" I say brightly. "I'm gonna take your money and run, I guess, before you change your mind."

He laughs. "I'm not going to change my mind."

"When I told Jasmine, you know what she said?" I ask.

"What?" he asks.

"That the donation is enough for her to forgive you for almost working with Dimitri," I say.

His mouth twitches nervously. "Well, that's good. And . . . you?"

"It's one thing to apologize, but it's another thing to make a situation right again. And you did both," I explain. "So, yeah, I forgive you."

"Really?" he asks, almost like he can't believe what he's hearing.

"Yeah, we're cool," I say. "Obviously, I know things have been kind of . . . weird? Between us? For a while now. But I miss how easily we used to get along, and I'd like to go back to that."

I can feel my heart pounding as I tell him how I really feel; vulnerability is fucking scary. But then, a smile spreads across his face, and I'm flooded with relief. It's the exact same exhilarating sensation you get when you're flying upside down above the high bar on a release move and catch it solidly. It's a dangerous thrill, but then you know you're safe.

"Avery, you have no idea how much I feel the same way," he says. He looks down apologetically at his sweat-drenched T-shirt. "I'd want to hug you right now, but . . ."

"Yeah, no, I'm good without it," I tease.

"Your loss. I smell . . ." He sniffs his shirt and makes a sour face. ". . . *amazing* right now."

"Please just promise to shower before I have to spend the rest of the day with you today, okay?" I ask.

"I promise," he says earnestly.

"Now, back to work. Don't slack on those biceps, okay?" I joke.

He flexes one arm, and the muscle swells. I resist my instinct to look impressed, and instead say goodbye and walk out of the gym with my head held high.

I get some coffee, fruit, and yogurt at a café near the hotel, and then return to my hotel room to make myself look a little more presentable for the day. I know the cameras will catch at least a few glimpses of me, and some concealer and mascara will go a long way. I'm blending the makeup under my eyes when I see my phone light up with an incoming text. My stomach drops when I catch the name on the screen—it's

Tyler. We haven't spoken once since I left LA.

Hey. I just wanted to say that I heard you're doing really well now, coaching and launching that organization. It all sounds really impressive. Congratulations!

I laugh, dumbfounded. I can't believe he reached out at all, especially to praise my accomplishments. He never expected me to make anything of myself again; he didn't think I had the drive to dream, achieve, or succeed anymore. It's deliciously satisfying to see him recognize how wrong he was. I wish I could travel back in time to that fight, the one a few months before our breakup, when he found me sitting on the kitchen floor with my wineglass in the middle of the afternoon and criticized what looked like a lack of ambition. If only that version of myself could see my life now.

I dash off the briefest, politest text I can muster. It's funny: for years, I cared more about him than anyone or anything—where he was, how he was doing, what he was up to. But now I don't even care to know what his life looks like.

Thanks! Hope everything's going well.

I've got more important things to do.

At nine, I meet Hallie in her suite. She invited me to sit with her as she gets ready, and when she opens the door, she looks visibly more relaxed than she did just ninety minutes earlier.

"I sent my parents out for breakfast," she explains, welcoming me inside. "They get even more nervous than I do on days like this. Stressful vibes."

"Mine were like that, too," I say. "Actually, they still are."

"Maybe they could all learn to meditate," she suggests. "Sit with me while I do my hair and makeup?"

We head into the bathroom, where I flip down the toilet seat and sit, and she plugs in a hair straightener. When it's hot, she irons each section of hair until it's perfectly smooth, then brushes it all into a high, tight ponytail and blasts the crown of her head with extra-strength hair spray. I never wore much makeup when I was her age—not even to competitions—but this generation of gymnasts grew up watching beauty tutorials on YouTube and spending their allowances on Urban Decay Naked palettes and Kylie Jenner lip kits. They're so much savvier and sophisticated than I ever was; during competitions, they look like Hollywood starlets on the red carpet.

"I'm going to skip foundation because it'll just sweat off," she explains, digging through her makeup bag.

"Not that you need it anyway," I point out.

She shrugs. "But I'll do concealer, highlighter, and a little blush and bronzer."

She expertly applies those, then moves on to eye shadow primer, three different shades of sparkly eye shadow, black eyeliner, and several swipes of mascara. I feel like I could learn a thing or two from her.

"Good?" she asks, seeking approval.

"Let's just say that if you ever get bored of gymnastics, you could have a backup career as a makeup artist," I say.

"So, I have two leotard options for today, and I wanted to get your opinion," she says.

She opens the closet door and pulls out two hangers.

"I didn't hang them—that's nuts—but my mom spent, like, a half hour steaming them so they wouldn't wrinkle," she explains. "Like I said, she's stressed."

Hallie holds up one leotard in front of her, then the other. The first is bright purple, with an ombré effect on the bodice, mesh cutouts on the sleeves, and a spray of rhinestones over the chest. It's like the sporty version of a beauty pageant gown—what Miss America might wear for her talent portion. The second one is much simpler: entirely red and flecked with silver shimmer.

"You'd look great in both," I say.

"But if you *had* to pick one," she implores.

It truly doesn't matter what she wears; the most important thing is that she feels confident. I don't want to accidentally pick the one she's leaning against and trigger her to second-guess her instincts.

"I really like both," I insist.

She purses her lips. "You know why I like the red one?" she says shyly.

"It's more comfortable?" I guess.

"This doesn't look familiar?" she asks.

I try to remember if she's worn it before, but I can't recall.

"You wore one just like this," she says, blushing a little. "I saw you on TV when I was little, and I was so starstruck."

Suddenly, I know exactly what she's talking about.

"Olympic Trials, 2012," I say.

She nods. "I wanted to be just like you. I still do."

"That was my very last competition, you know," I say carefully.

"But this won't be mine, because you've coached me so well," she says. "I wouldn't even be here at Trials without you."

A hard lump forms in the back of my throat. For so many years now, I've felt like a failure: I failed to make the Olympics; I literally failed out of college; I floundered through a failing relationship. I squandered my fresh start in California, and I neglected to take care of myself the way I deserved. But none of that matters to Hallie. In her eyes, it seems as if

I'm an inspiration. I'm a role model. And most important, I'm a coach who has helped to give her a fair shot at achieving her lifelong dream.

"Oh, Hallie," I say, wrapping her in a hug. "Being your coach is truly the best thing I've ever done. I mean it. I don't know what I would've done without this job."

"Thank you for everything," she says, squeezing me back.

I blink hard twice and shake my head to keep the tears at bay. Now is not the time. Hallie puts the purple leotard back in the closet, then takes the red one into the bathroom to change. When she opens the door again a minute later, she twirls in a circle to show off the look.

Now that she's pointed out the connection, it's impossible to ignore. Clad in red, she looks an awful lot like I did eight years ago. Except now, Hallie looks confident. Self-assured. Happy. I desperately hope she has better luck today than I did.

• *Chapter 32* •

The competition arena looks the same. It always does. No matter where you are in the country or the world, regardless of who's winning or what the year is. The familiar, standard-issue apparatus and mats and chalk bowls are arranged on a basketball floor under fluorescent lighting, surrounded by bleachers, with frenzied energy pulsing through the air. Ryan and I flank Hallie as we arrive, looking like a real team in our matching Summit tracksuits. For the first time in months, I truly *feel* like the three of us are in sync again. I'm glad Ryan and I got the chance to talk this morning.

Hallie takes in the view of the arena with a curious expression.

"This is it," she says, sounding stunned.

"Nothing you haven't seen before," I remind her.

"That's kind of chill," she says.

"Good," Ryan says. "I like that attitude. Go warm up."

She nods, slips out of her tracksuit, and jogs to the floor to run a few laps. Ryan slides closer to me on the bench, bridging the empty space Hallie left behind.

"You know, no matter what happens today,

whether she makes it or not, I'm proud of us," he says. "I think we did a killer job."

"We made a pretty good team," I say.

"We did, didn't we?" He lets out a short laugh. "It's crazy to think of how much has happened this year. You moving back to Greenwood, joining me at Summit, the Kaminsky scandal, the Powerhouse offer, your foundation . . ."

He trails off. He doesn't need to say the rest. I know what he's thinking: we got together, broke up . . . and yet, we're still here. So is Dimitri, across the arena. He won't even look at me.

"Hey, the schedule's up," I say, nudging him, glad to have a safe talking point emerge.

It's a crowded roster: fifteen gymnasts competing for just four real spots on the Olympic team. Technically speaking, two other gymnasts are named as alternates, just in case anyone gets seriously injured during the Olympic Games—they can swap in and compete as backups. But obviously, nobody aspires to be an alternate. That means that after barely missing the chance of a lifetime, probably by a fraction of a point, you have to sit on the sidelines and cheer for your teammates to achieve your dream. It sounds like torture. As terrible as my experience was, at least I could choose not to watch the competition from the comfort of my own home.

Hallie is up against several gymnasts I know—Emma Perry, Delia Cruz, Maggie Farber, Kiki

McCloud, Skylar Hayashi, and Brit Almeda—and also several that I don't: Olivia Walsh, Madison Salazar, Riley Robinson, Jocelyn Snyder, Ayanna Clayton, Taylor O'Connor, Charlotte Chan, Lucy Shapiro. It's dizzying and heartbreaking to consider that the majority of these girls will have their careers end today. The next few hours will change all of their lives.

Once again, Hallie has been assigned to start on bars, which means she'll cycle through vault, beam, and then floor. Apparently having finished her cardio warm-up, she trots back to where Ryan and I are sitting to stretch. She rolls her wrists, bends over her feet, and occasionally waves at cameras passing by.

Before the first rotation starts, Ryan squats down next to her and waves me over to join.

"Look, I'm not going to make a big speech to psych you up, because I know you've got this," he says simply. "All I want you to do is go out there and perform just as beautifully as you've been doing every day. Don't worry about anything beyond the actual work. Because that's all you can control."

She nods heavily, then hugs each of us.

"Got it. Thank you for everything. Let's do this," she declares.

I'm secretly glad that she's up first on bars, because that will get her started on the right foot. She puts on her grips and warms up for the allotted few minutes, and then waits for her turn. When the announcer booms her name over the loudspeaker, she waves to a girl in the stands holding a poster with her name on it as she strides toward the bars. This is her moment to shine, and she knows it.

"Let's go, Hallie, let's go!" I cheer.

She centers herself in front of the low bar, lifts her chin, and with just a hint of a smug smirk, jumps forward into her mount. Across the arena, another gymnast's floor music begins to play, but it's clear that Hallie has tuned out everything except the bar under her hands. Her body rockets cleanly to the high bar, where she swings up into a handstand, pirouettes, and flings herself into the series she's been drilling all year with Ryan: a Tkatchev into a Pak Salto. It's gorgeous. She finishes strong with two giants and her breathtaking dismount, a double-twisting double back tuck. Hallie sticks the landing solidly with her fingers splayed out in an elegant flourish. The audience cheers as she straightens up into a proud salute for the judges, then waves to the crowd. That was a goddamn perfect routine.

Ryan, who was spotting her release moves, high-fives her with both hands. They look triumphant as they make their way back to where I'm sitting.

"That was epic!" I say.

"Let's see what the judges have to say," she says modestly.

The judges barely need to deliberate. They award her routine with a well-deserved 15.150.

Hallie squeals, smooshing a hand over her mouth to muffle her excitement.

"See? Nothing to worry about. You're doing an amazing job," Ryan tells her.

By the end of the first rotation, she reigns in second place. The only person who scored even a sliver higher than her for the first round was Dimitri's gymnast Emma, with a 15.250 on beam. That doesn't faze me. Emma is freakishly, super-naturally, horrifyingly talented. Hallie's second-place showing is still fantastic. With a strong start like that, she could be a real contender for one of the four Olympic-bound spots.

Thanks to her excellent bars routine, Hallie's sure-footed confidence carries over to vault. The event goes by in such a flash, I don't even have time to get nervous. She sticks clean landings on both her first run, an Amanar, and her second, a Mustafina. After her final salute, she glides back to the bench serenely. The judges reveal her score as she settles down: 14.975.

Vault is the shortest event, which means there's a bit of wait before the second rotation ends and we can see where Hallie will fall in the rankings. As she sucks down the contents of her water bottle, I watch the competition. Delia polishes off a glorious floor routine. Ayanna completes an impressive series of release moves on bars. On beam, Charlotte sways off balance when trying to land a front aerial and loses her footing. The crowd lets out a somber "Ooooh" when she falls to the ground. I cringe; I feel so terrible for her. She climbs back up on beam and finishes her routine with a disappointed grimace.

When the second rotation ends, Hallie has dropped into fourth place. That's still a very good spot to be in—if the competition were over right this second, she'd make the Olympic team—but it also means there's no more room for error or bad luck. If she doesn't perform the hell out of her next two routines, or if anyone *else* happens to have a startlingly successful showing, it's game over.

I've always known, of course, that making the Olympic team is a long shot. I knew there were no guarantees of Hallie's success when I signed on to coach her. But somehow, I've never thought through exactly what to say or do to console her if it turns out that she doesn't make the team, despite our best efforts. There's no good way to comfort a person whose sole dream has just slipped away. I hope it doesn't come to that.

Hallie heads off to warm up for beam.

"You okay, Avery?" Ryan asks, once she's gone.

"Ha. Hanging in there," I say.

"You look stressed," he says.

He knows me well enough to see through the calm act I'm putting on for Hallie.

"I didn't realize this would bother me until I got here, but being at Trials again? It's just kind of a lot," I confess.

"Because of what happened to you?" he asks.

"I know *I'm* fine, and it's not that I expect Hallie to have a freak accident the way I did, but today's major, even if we're pretending it's not. No matter what happens today, a few people's lives change for the better, and everyone else's lives will really suck," I explain. "I know that sounds really stupid and obvious, but I just . . . I feel for these girls."

"It's high stakes," he says, nodding.

He reaches for my hand and runs his thumb soothingly across my palm. The gesture is comforting.

"I hope Hallie makes it," I say glumly.

He heaves a giant sigh. "Me, too."

I barely breathe when it's Hallie's turn on beam. The problem with this apparatus is that you can't get cocky: it doesn't matter how talented you are or how hard you've worked to prepare—you can still fall, and then you're screwed. "Come on, come on, come on," I whisper, watching her execute the back handspring, whip back, back layout step-out combo we've drilled so many times. It's solid, but I still can't relax. Every muscle in my body tightens as she winds up to perform the wolf turn. I'm relieved when she stays on the beam without a wobble. There's a brief glint of surprise on her face, too. Her dismount goes smoothly, too, and it's only when she salutes the judges that I can finally exhale. The routine was good, but not great: I can imagine one tiny deduction for not seamlessly connecting two jumps, and another one for a leg that could've been a little bit straighter. But overall, it was a fine showing.

She barrels back to the bench, where I wrap her in a hug and stroke her hair.

"You're amazing," I say. "You're doing a really beautiful job."

She shudders. "At least beam is over."

The judges give her a 13.500, and by the time the rotation ends, that lands her in sixth place—barely in Olympic contention, but only as an alternate. She's fallen behind Emma, Kiki, Delia, Taylor, and Ayanna. From what I can tell, the problem wasn't that her beam routine was terrible, but rather that everyone else had an unusually great rotation. I wish I could calculate what score she'll need in order to guarantee a full spot on the Olympic team, but I don't know how to even begin figuring that out. My stomach cramps with nerves.

Hallie presses her lips together like she's trying not to wince or groan. I kneel down in front of her, gripping both of her hands in mine. I have to go off script.

"Look, I know that we've been saying all day that you should just pretend like this is a normal day, and that you should just chill out and not sweat the competition, but that isn't going to work for floor," I tell her bluntly.

"What do you mean?" she asks.

"This is the most important performance you've ever had," I tell her honestly. "You need to pour every ounce of energy, every ounce of passion into this routine. Go out there and enjoy every single second of it, because this is what you've been training for your entire life."

The hairs on my arms stand up on end. Hallie locks her eyes with mine and nods seriously.

"This is it," she says.

"This is it," I repeat. "No matter what the outcome is, I'll always be so proud of you. But I want you to feel proud of yourself, too, and that means giving it your all."

"I can do that," she says.

She gives me a hug and heads to floor to warm up.

"That was a solid pep talk," Ryan says.

I groan. "I just hope it was enough."

I'm almost too antsy to watch Hallie practice her tumbling passes, but I know I have to pay attention in case there's any last-minute practical advice I should offer her. I wish we could just fast-forward through the fourth rotation.

Finally, enough time creaks by and it's Hallie's

turn to compete on floor. Ryan and I stand fifteen feet to the left of the judges' table, which is just about as close as we can get without causing a distraction. Adrenaline rushes through me as her name is announced over the loudspeaker one more time.

Hallie composes herself at the edge of the floor. She smiles warmly at the judges as she salutes, then gracefully walks to her starting spot. She settles into position and waits for her music to begin. For a moment, everything is still and quiet—or as quiet as a bustling arena like this can be. She's a vision in sparkling red. As the jazzy opening notes play, she blossoms into a swirl of motion. The flick of her wrist is precise and delicate; the swing of her hips is flashy and flirty. She's always been a gymnast, but here, after months of hard work, she's developed the grace of a dancer, too.

On her first tumbling pass, she bounds cleanly across the floor, rocketing skyward in an elegant stag jump to channel her extra energy. It works beautifully: she looks powerful, strong, and in control of every movement. She dances toward another corner of the floor, polishes off two precise leaps, then dives straight into a second excellent tumbling pass. As I watch her prance, pirouette, and flip, I get a chilling sense of excitement. This is one of the most gorgeous routines I've ever seen from her. Something genuinely special is unfolding here—this is a determined athlete at her peak.

After Hallie executes her third tumbling pass seamlessly, something in her posture shifts. By this point in a floor routine, even the fittest gymnasts can start to look a little sluggish or out of breath. But Hallie looks even lighter and more buoyant than ever. With fifteen seconds left in the routine, she bursts forward into a triumphant fourth tumbling pass, landing easily on her feet. As she sinks into her final dramatic pose, her face crumples with joy. She holds the position just long enough to give the end of her routine a real sense of gravitas, and then bounces to her feet to salute the judges. The minute she's done, I see her eyes glistening with tears of joy. She claps one hand over her mouth and waves to the crowd with the other. The audience roars in applause.

She lingers on the floor for a few seconds longer than necessary, soaking up this once-in-a-lifetime moment. The judges are still deliberating over her score, so for the next few precious seconds, *this* is all that matters—she delivered the hell out of a routine that challenged her, scared her, and forced her to grow into a better athlete. Soon, her fate will be sealed, but for now, I can tell that she's happy with herself. That's a rare feat in this sport.

She bounds off the floor into my waiting arms.

"I'm so damn proud of you," I repeat over and over.

Ryan joins us for a group hug. "You were phenomenal. Incredible. The best I've ever seen," he says.

"I can't believe I just did that," she says, breathing hard.

Suddenly, she freezes. Her score appears on the scoreboard: 15.100, pushing her into second place. Even though there's one more gymnast left to perform on floor, it doesn't matter what score she'll receive—she won't knock Hallie out of the top four slots.

"I made it, I made it, oh my god, I made it," Hallie sobs.

Ryan and I break away to look at the scoreboard, then turn back to her in awe.

"Oh my god, Hallie!" I say, voice breaking.

Watching her recognize that her lifelong dream is coming true is one of the most beautiful things I've ever had the privilege of seeing. I can't help the tears coming. I don't mind. We've all worked hard enough to justify them.

"I knew it," Ryan says. Even his voice is shaking. "You're going to be an Olympian."

"We did it," Hallie says, sounding stunned. "I can't believe we did it."

Not her. Not Hallie and Ryan. *Us.* All of us.

In my own time as a gymnast, there were so many ecstatic moments, like when a gold medal was draped around my neck or the day I qualified for Olympic Trials. But truthfully, nothing quite compared to this victory. I feel as if I could burst from bliss.

The medal ceremony is a happy blur. In the end, Emma takes the top spot, as everyone knew she would. Hallie is the surprise dark horse in second place, followed by Olympic veteran Delia, with Kiki rounding out the team in fourth. The girls confer for seconds before they announce their team name: the Fantastic Four, superhero reference very much intended. Madison Salazar and Taylor O'Connor are named alternates.

There's no avoiding it—I feel terribly sad for the girls who didn't make the cut. But if I can come back to this sport years later as a coach and make a real difference, they can, too. There's life for all of us after our gymnastics careers end. It just might take some time to figure out exactly what that means.

Hallie's parents have stumbled, dazed and overjoyed, from the bleachers into the main part of the arena, where they shower their daughter with hugs.

"Let's give them some space," I whisper to Ryan.

It's crowded in the center of the arena, anyway—gymnasts, families, judges, photographers, reporters.

"Good idea," he says. "Come with me to get something to drink? I'm thirsty."

"Sure," I say.

We walk by the bench with our bags so Ryan can grab his wallet, then wander down a maze of hallways until we find a vending machine, chattering the entire way about the highlights of Hallie's performances.

"I don't think I'll ever get over that floor routine," Ryan says with a note of awe in his voice. "I mean, it was *perfect* from start to finish. She's never been better."

"I can't believe we pulled that off," I say, feeling giddy.

"We? No, that was you," he insists. "I'll take full credit for hiring the best floor coach on the planet, but that whole routine was all you."

The vending machine is stocked with Gatorade bottles lined up in bright, color-coded rows. Ryan tilts his head.

"Berry or Fruit Punch?" he asks.

"Berry all the way," I say.

"I'll get two, then," he says.

He feeds dollar bills into the slot and presses the right buttons. I lean against the side of the machine as it whirs to life, retrieving the plastic bottles and dropping them down with two solid *thunks*. It's cool and quiet here. After today's whirlwind, there's nowhere else I'd rather be. Tonight, I'll sleep easily in the luxe hotel bed, and tomorrow we'll all book our flights to Tokyo. This doesn't feel real. It's unbelievable, somehow, that after all these years, I'm finally going to the Olympics. Everything is falling into place. Or, rather, almost everything.

Ryan bends down to pick up the drinks and hands me one, interrupting my train of thought.

"Thanks," I say.

He starts to open his bottle, but I stop him.

"Wait," I say, reaching for his hand.

"Yeah?" he asks.

I kiss him before I can lose my nerve, sliding my arms over his shoulders and pulling him toward me. I can feel the muscles in his shoulders tense for a split second, and I lean back, but then I see a dimpled smile spreading across his face.

"Come here," he says softly. "I like that."

We find our way back to each other tenderly. His hands brace my hips, and soon, our lips fall into rhythm together. I've spent so many months aching to be close to him, and from the way his mouth moves against mine, it's clear that he's felt the same way. He kisses me deeply, and it just feels so right.

"I didn't expect that," he mumbles into my hair.

"I didn't plan on that," I explain.

"I'm glad it happened, though," he says earnestly.

"Me, too," I say.

I didn't know it was humanly possible to feel

more relief and happiness than I've already felt today, but I'm so glad that my gut instinct was right—he wanted that kiss as much as I did. Ryan takes the Gatorade out of my hand and places both bottles on the linoleum floor by our feet so that he can kiss me again. It's perfect.

"Look, I know I messed up—" Ryan starts, but I shush him with another kiss.

"There's no need to keep apologizing," I say, wrapping my hands around his waist.

"No, hear me out," he insists. "I never stopped caring about you."

He speaks slowly and fiercely, giving each word the weight it deserves.

"I didn't say it before because I was an idiot, but the past few months have made me realize exactly how I feel," he continues.

I go very still, even as my heart races. His dark eyes search mine.

"Avery, I love you," he says.

I feel a rush of pure joy and a ballooning sense that everything is right in the world. This moment? It's better than a perfectly stuck landing. It's sweeter than the view from the top of the medal podium.

"I love you, too," I say.

I know I've never stopped. This time, I'm not self-conscious to voice how I really feel. Suddenly, the significance of where we happen to be standing hits me, and I can't help but laugh.

"What?" he asks.

"Do you remember our first conversation?" I ask.

"The night I called you about coaching at Summit?" he guesses.

"No, think—the very first time we ever spoke," I prompt.

His eyes light up. "It was Nationals. I asked if you knew where the vending machine was."

I smirk and lean back against this current vending machine, fingers dancing over his chest.

"Here we are," he marvels.

JULY
2020

• *Epilogue* •

It's competition day in Tokyo. I gasp when I enter the arena for the first time; the space is larger and flashier than anywhere I've ever competed, and handmade signs written in multiple languages wave in the crowd. Cameras capture every angle.

Hallie and the rest of the Fantastic Four warm up for the competition's first rotation. They're resplendent in matching royal blue leotards, and they work with an efficient, upbeat energy. Even though the stakes are higher today than ever before, everyone seems just so plain happy to be here. Hallie's on floor first.

While the gymnasts get ready to compete, I stand on the sidelines with Ryan. We flew to Tokyo a few days early so Hallie could prep for the competition while adjusting to the fourteen-hour time difference, and though we've been working a lot, there's also been just enough downtime to sneak out together on dates. The sushi dinner, sumo match, and Zen garden visit were amazing, but truthfully, we could've had just as much fun sitting in the supply closet at Summit. Since we got back together at Trials, I've felt so at peace. We've decided to keep our relationship private until after the Olympics.

A competition official signals to Hallie that she

415

has time for one more tumbling pass, and then the warm-up will be over. Hallie nods, and I watch as she launches into a high-powered, tight double Arabian with a cleanly stuck landing. I shake my head in awe.

"Today's going to be a good day," I predict. "I can feel it."

"Me, too," Ryan says. He watches me studying Hallie on floor, then asks quietly, "Do you wish it were you out there?"

The question catches me off guard. For so long, I so desperately wanted to be in Hallie's exact position. Losing out on the chance to compete in the Olympics was the single most devastating experience of my life—worse than surviving Dimitri's rage, worse than watching my relationship with Tyler fall apart, worse than the time I thought I lost Ryan for good.

But the funny thing about your dream coming true is that it never quite happens the way you think it will. There's always a twist. When I walked into the Olympic stadium for the first time, nobody cheered for me or waved signs with my name. My heart didn't race with anticipation for my upcoming routines. Sports reporters didn't hound me for interviews. And even stranger than all that? I didn't care. I'm overjoyed to be here as Hallie's coach. I've let go of my old dreams. My new life has replaced them.

Before I can tell him any of that, though, Hallie

joins us on the sidelines for a slurp from her water bottle.

"We were just talking about how strong your tumbling looks today," I tell her. "You're gonna kill it out there."

She grins and throws her arms around me. "Thank you so much for everything. I wouldn't have made it here without you."

She hugs Ryan, too, takes a deep breath, and walks proudly to the side of the floor with her head held high. An official booms out her name over a loudspeaker, and a hush falls over the arena. She waits patiently for the judges to indicate that she can begin. When it's time, she salutes them and arranges herself into the starting pose I choreographed for her all those months ago. From where I'm sitting, I can glimpse the confident expression on her face. There's a real poise to her today that she didn't quite have when we met.

My eyes well up with tears as the first notes of her music ring out through the arena.

"No, Ryan," I tell him. "I'm happy to be right here."

• *Acknowledgments* •

First, I'd like to thank you, reader, for picking up this novel. I'm honored that you chose to spend your time immersed in the world of this book. Thank you for reading!

I'm so grateful for the thoughtful, whip-smart guidance of my editor, Kaitlin Olson. This book is better in countless ways because of her creative instincts, attention to detail, and belief in these characters. From catching plot holes to sharpening dialogue, Kaitlin made this project shine.

I'm incredibly lucky to work with the same wonderful team at Atria Books yet again: many thanks to Megan Rudloff and Isabel DaSilva for ensuring this book falls into all the right hands, Tamara Arellano for her tireless copyedits, and Lindsay Sagnette, Suzanne Donahue, Jimmy Iacobelli, and Libby McGuire.

My agent, Allison Hunter, championed this idea from the moment my half-baked email landed in her inbox. Her vision for my career, faith in my abilities, and true friendship make her the best teammate an author could ask for. At Janklow & Nesbit, Clare Mao and Natalie Edwards made this process so seamless.

This book was born of my lifelong love of

gymnastics. I will forever be awestruck by athletes, including Shannon Miller, Carly Patterson, Nastia Liukin, Shawn Johnson, Alicia Sacramone, Gabby Douglas, McKayla Maroney, Simone Biles, and more. Most important, thank you to my own hometown hero Aly Raisman, whose work ethic, talent, and bravery has been a source of inspiration to me since childhood.

I'm thankful for the support of all my colleagues at *Elite Daily* and Bustle Digital Group, including Kylie McConville, Veronica Lopez, Iman Hariri-Kia, Emma Rosenblum, and Bryan Goldberg. I always feel fortunate that I don't have to choose between my work as an editor and as an author.

My friends were the ultimate cheerleading squad. They gave me plenty of positivity during tough writing days and celebrated with me every step of the way! Many thanks to Annie Kehoe, Morgan Boyer, Roshan Berentes, Kelsey Mulvey, Elyssa Goodman, Alexia LaFata, Dayna Troisi, Emily Raleigh, Emma Albert-Stone, and Devon Albert-Stone.

Thanks to Jerry and Eleanor Hart; Karen, Bob, and Jake Sykes; Bruce, Heather, Xander, Nathan, and Zoe Orenstein; and Jamie, Karin, Dani, and Rosie Orenstein for all their love.

To properly thank Mom, Dad, and Julia, I have to borrow my favorite word from Yiddish: when I think about how fully they've supported me with encouragement, enthusiasm, and so much love, I'm *verklempt* (that roughly translates to "overcome with emotion"). I can't imagine a better family in the world.

HANNAH ORENSTEIN is the author of *Playing with Matches* and *Love at First Like*, and is the senior dating editor at *Elite Daily*. Previously, she was a writer and editor at Seventeen.com. She lives in New York.

Center Point Large Print
600 Brooks Road / PO Box 1
Thorndike, ME 04986-0001 USA

(207) 568-3717

US & Canada:
1 800 929-9108
www.centerpointlargeprint.com